Michael Reynolds's debut n...  ...hauls you into an Irish family at the ...ginning of the potato famine. Sending their grown children to America might save them all. Clare lands in New York City to find another kind of famine, lack of morals, all encompassed by greed and corruption. Clare's dogged fight to keep her family alive amidst overwhelming odds makes her a standout heroine. I heartily recommend *Flight of the Earls* and look forward to the next. Michael Reynolds is an author to look out for.

—Lauraine Snelling, author of the continuing family saga of the Bjorklunds, the Blessing books, as readers call them, and the new Wild West Wind series with *Whispers on the Wind* and coming, *A Place to Belong*

Michael Reynolds has given us a stunning debut novel—a saga that will capture both your heart and your mind as you journey back in time to experience triumph in the midst of crushing—except for Christ—circumstances. A soaring chronicle of immigrant America and beleaguered Ireland that will keep you reading late into the night.

Stephanie Grace Whitson, Christy finalist and best-selling author of historical fiction

My ancestors on my grandfather's side immigrated from Ireland during the great potato famine. It's something I knew but didn't really understand until reading *Flight of the Earls* by Michael K. Reynolds. The questions, fears, and hopes of a generation come to life through this novel. I found my emotions wrapped up in the middle of it . . . a sign of good fiction!

Tricia Goyer, best-selling author of thirty-three books, including *Beside Still Waters*

From the Irish potato famine to the seedy streets of New York, Michael K. Reynolds takes the reader on a moving adventure. The writing sings, the story thrills, the characters are unapologetically realistic, and the message of hope and trust shines even in the grit. A novel not to be missed!

Sarah Sundin, award-winning author of *With Every Letter*

# FLIGHT of the EARLS

An Heirs of Ireland novel

# FLIGHT of the EARLS

*An Heirs of Ireland novel*

# MICHAEL K. REYNOLDS

Nashville, Tennessee

978-1-4336-7819-6

Published by B&H Publishing Group,
Nashville, Tennessee

Dewey Decimal Classification: F
Subject Heading: IRISH AMERICANS—FICTION \
IMMIGRANTS—FICTION \ FAITH—FICTION

1 2 3 4 5 6 7 8 • 17 16 15 14 13

*For my mother, Sheila, who gifted her love of writing*

*For my wife, Debbie, who inspired me to write of love*

# Prologue
# THE DEATH FOG

BRANLOW, COUNTY ROSCOMMON, IRELAND
*September 1846*

 Most days blended into the grayness of Liam Hanley's life, but this particular one haunted, a brooding prophetess tormenting the potato farmer with visions of his precious dream succumbing to the Irish downpour of misfortune, washing out his aspirations in familiar brown rivulets of defeat.

The shrouding twilight lingered and Liam, with rumpled and silvering brows, surveyed his ancestral field as if for the last time, his head throbbing with dark suspicions he had yet to share with anyone. A secret he wouldn't reveal until absolutely certain of his shame.

He was like a general on the eve of a hopeless battle, while his soldiers, not fully aware of their impending doom, played cards in tents, exchanged uneasy jokes, and wrote letters for back home that would never arrive.

Just two days earlier, something sinister arrived in the ashen mist. This fog, an encroaching apparition, arms engulfing mud homes, stony hovels, and lowing cattle of his pastoral village, brought with it a peculiar scent of decay.

Beneath the usual earthy smells of peat smoke rising from rock chimneys, hoe-churned soil, and tall moist grass, the odor was subtle to discern. But for Liam, whose heart pulsed in rhythm with his land, the growing presence of the stench overwhelmed his senses to the point of debilitation.

Still, there remained a chance his instincts were deceived, and Liam clenched on to this fraying possibility with all his being as if it were the final breath left in his pained soul. Perhaps the foulness was merely a drifting wind from the bog or a rotting corpse of some stillborn calf.

As it was, the full revelation stood beneath his ragged and soil-stained leather boots. All he needed to do was bend down and rake his fingers through the soil.

But Liam wasn't ready for the truth. Was it cowardice? Self-preservation? Or was he stalling in some bitter expectation the curse would be withdrawn?

These thoughts were interrupted by the unsuspecting laughter of his children echoing behind him. Their voices emanated from the one-room, thatched-roof mud hovel where many of the Hanley ancestry were birthed with groans, raised in squalor, and died without distinction.

Liam drifted down the short slope leading to the entranceway of his shanty. He paused before the bent oaken door and released a heavy sigh before entering.

The chattering halted, and the faces of his family looked at him with poorly concealed disappointment. And for this welcome each evening, he toiled without cease.

"Father." Clare, his unwed twenty-four-year-old daughter, managed a smile. "The meal's just now for serving." With her flowing black hair, fair complexion, long lashes, and sparkling sapphire eyes, his daughter was too beautiful to be alone, but she sought more than this town had to give and was unwilling to accept her standing.

Liam hung his patched jacket on the iron wall hook and took his place at the head of the sagging dinner table. Ronan, his ten-year-old boy, limped to a seat, all the while tracking his father with eyes of apprehension.

The freckled and curly-locked Davin, the youngest by a couple of years, slid into his chair as well. He lifted his tin cup, put his eye to it, and then turned it upside down. "Is the well dry?"

"You'll be last served now." Caitlin, with blonde hair adorned with a faded pink ribbon, poured water into Liam's cup from a wooden pitcher, her two jittery hands fearful of spilling.

Clare placed a large bowl of potato pottage in the center of the table and then, beginning with Liam, ladled portions for each of them.

"Seamus?" Liam started slurping his meal.

Caitlin glanced at Clare and then spoke. "Out." Having served the water, she settled into her chair.

"He said he had doings with Pierce." Clare shook her head and with her free hand pulled a wet rag from her dress pocket. She dabbed a splotch of dirt off of Davin's cheek and then patted him on the head.

Liam grunted and pointed a dripping spoon in the direction of the two boys. "You turn out half as shiftless as your elder brother and I'll trade you at the market for a new shovel. Might just do it otherwise."

"Da. Speak gently. They can't tell you're quipping." Clare positioned herself next to the rocking chair in the corner of the room where Liam's wife, Ida, idled throughout the day.

"Quipping? You keep those words in your fancy books, where they won't be frightening away working lads." Liam cringed at the sight of his daughter beginning to spoon-feed the old woman.

The cackle of an ember from the peat fire drew Liam's attention to the hearth, where the flames stretched for freedom. "Clare! Must you be so wasteful with the logs?"

"Ma had the shivers."

"Ah, she did? Is that so?" Liam paused, brimming with the urge to speak his thoughts. Would it be anything but merciful if his wife took ill? Two years was forever to be in this condition. He had grieved when his little boy drowned, just as much as Ida, but he didn't allow himself to go mad. Who would have provided? Who else but Liam?

"C'mon, Ma," Clare said. "You must eat."

"We can go to the bog and cut more peat," Ronan said, his face brightening. "We'll do that for you, Da. Clare will take us, will you?"

Davin didn't wait to swallow his food. "He just wants the frogs. For their legs."

"Not so." Ronan glared at his younger brother.

"What nonsense is this?" Clare stood and wiped her hands on her apron.

"True it 'tis," Caitlin said. "Seamus was 'splaining to Ronan if he chewed on ten legs, it would heal him up."

Davin nodded with sincerity. "And with twenty? With

twenty he could leap to the roof." He motioned with his dirty hand from the table into the air.

Ronan shrunk in his chair.

"Is that so?" Liam said abruptly. He pointed to his cup and Caitlin lifted the pitcher, leaned over, and tilted the handle. The snapping fire and the trickling of water was all that could be heard.

Liam was aware his emotions were poisoned by today's circumstances, but he lashed out nonetheless. "Not certain what's more foolish. You two boys believing Seamus for anything, or the very thought of Ronan hobbling . . ." He started to chortle and it felt good. "Or you, Ronan, limping after frogs in the bog."

He laughed for a few moments, then hacked a few coughs before drinking some water. His family gazed at him with numbness.

Clare walked over to Ronan and kissed the boy on the forehead. "He's a fine frog catcher, don't you know?"

Liam hated when his daughter intervened and played up her kindness, making him villainous. It spurred him to gouge deeper, and he was pondering a retort when he noticed something was askew. "Where's the chair?" A sudden pulse of anger swelled.

Clare appeared as if she was going to joust for a moment but then submitted to his temper. "I'll be right back with it." She scurried outside the house for a few moments and then returned with one of the table chairs cradled under her arm.

"What was it doing out there?"

"I was writing in my journal out back. I'm sorry, I forgot—"

Liam stood, placed his palms on the table, and jutted his jaw. "For the last time, and this goes for all of you, Margaret's chair is not to be moved. Have you any memory left of her?"

Clare's eyes glazed and she looked down. "More than you know."

He panned the forlorn faces, and regret came over Liam as once again he earned their disdain.

"All right." His countenance softened as did the tone of his voice. "I'll give you what you want. I will do you all a great favor."

Liam grabbed his jacket, put on his hat, opened the door, and escaped into the darkness.

Once outside, as was his nightly habit, Liam began the two-mile journey to O'Shannon's Public House, down the remote country road, walking over the faded footprints of many generations. Above, a nearly full moon glimmered, its brilliance restrained by a chilling mist.

Liam paused for a moment and took in the odd whispers of this uneasy evening. Then he lumbered forward, striving with each step to chase away his anxieties. Like a child's tattered doll, he cradled his evening forays as his most-dear possession.

After some time, the lights of approaching buildings rewarded his tired legs. Closing in on O'Shannon's, he yearned to hear the muted sounds of alcohol-induced joy, spontaneous song, and lively argument.

But tonight, the reverberations escaping the pores of the tavern were subdued, confirming the fears he fought to deny. His pulse began to beat its somber drum.

Liam entered through the creaking door, and the dimly lantern-lit establishment shared little of its usual liveliness. He slipped in unnoticed, save for a quick nod or two from those he joined at the bar, each perched like magpies on a dead tree branch.

He waved an arm at Casey O'Shannon behind the counter, who responded with an unimpressed roll of hairy-browed eyes and an unhurried approach.

Liam allowed the anticipation of drink to begin to replenish his spirits. "I'll have me mine."

The hulking proprietor shot a towel over his shoulder with an air befitting the second most important man behind Father Quinn Connor in this region. As he bent in, Liam could smell distilled grains on the barman's breath.

"Yours is yours, Liam Hanley, when your tab is current."

Liam heard this too often to be discouraged or even insulted. Besides, everyone knew Casey wouldn't have a coin to his name if not for his wife's side of the family.

"Mr. O'Shannon. Is this any way to treat one of your finest patrons? I'll remember you well enough when you come to me parched, begging for a wee sip."

Casey shook his head and turned. He returned shortly with a previously poured mug of stout, which had been sitting for many minutes to allow the head to settle. In Branlow, as in all of the Emerald Isle, no one paid for a glass of foam.

The brown liquid opiate, warm, frothy, rich to taste and bitter all of the way down, melted some of the pain of Liam's life. It helped feed the fragile illusion that in this humble sanctuary, he was among friends.

Liam took his wool cap off and laid it on the bar. Brushing his earth-brown hair back with his hand, his fingers felt the dampness of the foggy night. He looked over to old Lucas Furley to his right, who was wringing his hands nervously around an empty glass.

Liam liked Lucas because he was a man Liam could pity above himself, which gave him some comfort. The old man was late to marry and drew more than a few raised eyebrows years back when he took the hand of a teenage lass as his bride. Less than a year later, he lost both his young wife and the baby at birth, and now spent most of his time drinking sadness from a glass.

A glance around the room revealed many of the local farming congregation engaged in hushed conversations, their wearied faces a tapestry of frustration and concern.

Only Niall Tavers seemed untouched by the melancholy. He was slumped over in his chair, as he was every evening at O'Shannon's following a few pours. There was some debate as to how he had lasted seventy years in his condition, and wagers were placed almost daily on whether or not during the course of a particular evening, he would slump over for good.

With not many alternatives for conversation, Liam turned to Lucas. "It appears somebody dragged the clouds in here. 'Tis a sour mood, don't you think?"

Lucas seemed reluctant to take his eyes off the bottom of his glass. "We could benefit from the cheer of your Tomas on a day like this, I suppose."

The words pained Liam. It had been four years since his younger brother left Branlow, and still Tomas's charm overshadowed Liam. Since he was a wee lad, and despite a lifetime of effort, Liam's light always shone dimmer.

He took another slow draw of his stout and wiped the foam from his lip with the back of his hand. He tapped his fingers on the countertop, which drew Casey's glance from the other end of the bar. Liam waved him off with his hand.

He reached into his shirt pocket, pulled out a shilling, and placed it on the bar, spinning it several times with his thumb and forefinger. The sight of money drew his thoughts away from the characters in the bar to the dim reality of his own life. He stared at the silver coin, running his thumb over Queen Victoria's embossed profile. The shiny metal contrasted with his fingers, stained and cracked by the fields.

*What does the queen know about an honest day's labor?*

Suddenly, the door of the tavern rattled open, attracting the attention of most of the patrons. A few welcomes and waves came out as the broad-shouldered Riley Flanagan entered, but he just grunted past them and placed his belly against the dark, polished countertop of the bar.

In a moment, Casey arrived with a tall shot of Irish rye for his newly arrived guest. He eyeballed the man while he wiped the counter. "What troubles you, Riley? Did the old lady cast you out again?"

The unshaven Riley drew the whiskey to his lips and snapped his head back. He mumbled something.

"What's that you say?" Casey leaned in.

There was an uneasy pause and then Riley slammed the glass on the bar, which brought a lull across the entire room. In a loud and deliberate voice he said, "The roots gone bad."

Lucas stood up from his seat. "What's the man saying?"

Riley pressed himself away from the bar counter, his ruddy complexion growing even redder. A few more patrons sauntered over to eavesdrop on the conversation. "Why are you looking at me like fools? You know what the smell means. It's the rot."

The gathering crowd began to murmur, and soon most in the room were around Riley and nudging closer.

Casey pressed him. "Are you sure? Are you certain the roots are bad?"

"What? None of you looked for yourself?" Riley's gaze darted around seeking an answer. "I wouldn't have thought the whole room of you for cowards."

Lucas pushed through the gathering crowd and poked his finger in Riley's chest. "Liar. That's what you are. You're too full of the drink to know your toes from your ears."

The room silenced as Riley responded with a raised fist, but then his demeanor dissipated into something more akin to pity. "All of it." He buttoned up his wool jacket. "Black. Black. Every last tater in me field. The ground is nothing but a grave of corpses."

Riley's eyes moistened. He spoke in a defeated tone. "It's the death fog. The death fog brought it in. The full harvest will be ruined. It will be the ruin of us all, I'm afraid."

He pulled a coin out of his coat pocket and placed it on the counter with a snap. "Night lads. God be with you. May God be with you all." Then he hunched out the door.

Riley's dreary words draped the room and only a few cursory comments were exchanged. He had merely put a voice to the dread in their hearts.

Some put on their coats, hats, and scarves and sifted out of the pub. Others dwelled, choosing to mend sorrow with drink.

But the stout in Liam's mug was no longer sufficient to quell the writhing in his stomach. His plight would be worse than most as he had risked his entire crop on the potato this season, a decision he had thought would at last reap a season of prosperity.

All that remained was the faltering hope that the contagion had not spread to his fields. The death in the air could be from farms downwind.

*Riley must be wrong.*

He picked up his shilling from the counter and unfurled from the stool, his mind in a blur.

Liam drifted out of O'Shannon's and down the road. Gradually, he shifted into a limping gait, that of a broken mare, sometimes tripping over rocks and divots in the low light. When he did, he would curse, lift himself up, and move up the stream of adversity, as he always did.

Liam struggled to console himself with the belief his life was too full of misfortune for God to strike him yet another blow.

So he ran.

# Chapter 1

# THE HOVEL

"He's gone. I can't see him anymore." The boy flashed an expression of glee.

Clare thrust her arms on her waist. "Davin Hanley. Shut that door before your ma takes ill, and I've told you about disrespecting your father as such. For all he does for you? You must be ashamed."

Davin scowled. "I'm just happy for Da, that's all. Now we won't be such a bother."

"We're not a bother." Caitlin gathered the bowls and spoons from the table.

"Cait's right," Clare said. "There's much on his mind, what with raising the likes of us in these troubling days."

Ronan waddled to the doorway and put his arm around his younger brother. "Come. There's a cow that's been missing ya."

"That's it, off you go to milk her, boys." Clare put her hand on Cait's shoulder. "And you tend the chickens. Not too much as the feed is low. While you're at it, make sure those ladies know they're behind on the rent."

Caitlin giggled. "Their eggs?"

"Tell them I'm serious." Clare wagged her finger.

"That I will."

Clare waved at them with the backs of her hands. "Why are you all tarrying? Hup, hup. Much to do still."

When the three of them emptied out of the door, Clare sighed. "Much to do still." She actually embraced complete exhaustion. Throughout the difficulties of her labors, she anticipated it as the treasured visit by her evening angel. It meant the family would soon be asleep and she could finally pass her heavy torch to the maker of dreams.

Although one more day of her fading youth would escape her, those she loved would be safe. At least until the morning sun delivered new burdens.

She hurried to clean the dishes. It wouldn't take the boys long to milk the heifer, empty the tin pail into a jar, and lower it by twine to the bottom of the cool waters of the well to keep it fresh until morning. Caitlin returned eggless and helped her older sister finish the cleaning just as Ronan and Davin returned from their chores.

Clare provided evening lessons in reading and arithmetic, made certain they bathed well with careful inspections, and now it was time for her to lead evening prayers.

"All right now. Let's offer our thanks to the Lord."

"Thank Him for what?"

Clare glared at Davin, but before she could respond, Ronan rapped him on the side of his head.

"Why did you do that?" Davin rubbed the feral brown tufts of his hair.

Clare was disappointed to see the task of brushing his hair was yet undone.

Ronan pointed up above and glared at Davin. "Don't be making the Almighty angry when you're standing next to me."

The seriousness in his command made Clare smile. But how much longer would Ronan get to rule over his brother? With his lame leg, it was just a matter of time before Davin would be strong enough to assert himself.

Caitlin joined them, her wavy blonde hair draping over the front of her faded yellow dress. The dress was the one Uncle Tomas gave Clare as her sixteenth birthday present, and when it no longer fit, Caitlin adopted it as if it were brand new.

When her uncle was still alive, he always was kind to them, bringing gifts and sharing fanciful stories of fairies, ghosts, and faraway lands. For years, Clare didn't know why this would make her father angry, but as she grew older, she recognized it as envy.

In speaking about Clare's father and uncle, Grandma Ella had shared how the two fought since they were boys. "Jacob and Esau had nothing on these ones, I tell you." Her grandmother always saw life through a veil of Scripture.

Standing a few inches above Ronan and Davin, Caitlin reached out her arms in expectation and soon they all were clasping hands in a circle.

Clare glanced over her shoulder at her mother, who was in a chair knitting the same scarf she had been working on for nearly two years. "Ma. Are you going to join us?"

"Hmm?" Ida looked up with a weary, troubled face. "What? How's that?" Her expression darkened. "No. I have no desire for praying."

"As you wish." Clare bristled but tried not to show it. She heard the same sentiment almost every day since her youngest brother drowned as a toddler.

"All right, Davin. Since you're in need of much penance, we'll have you pray."

Looking up to Clare as if to protest, he let out a deep breath and bowed his head. There was something in his spirit that was so appealing to her, but she feared the day would come soon when the trials of life and her father's cruel disposition would dampen his flame.

Davin squeezed his eyes shut and spoke with sincerity. "Lord. We thank You for the taters." Then whispered, "Which we eat every night."

This was met with a sharp tug of his hand by Ronan, who stumbled before catching his balance.

Undeterred, Davin continued. "I pray for my ma. That she'll learn how to smile better. For my da." He glanced at the door behind him. "For my da. That he'll talk to me kindly. For Cait. That she'll get a new bonnet. The blue one with the ribbons that she likes."

Caitlin opened her eyes and grinned. "Thank you, Davin. That would be lovely."

"And I pray for . . . I pray for my big sister that someone will finally marry her. Amen."

"Oh, Davin." Caitlin looked up at Clare to see if she was offended.

Clare smiled, but the innocent barb resonated. At her age, a woman was close to being out of time, a bruise her father often poked. Perhaps love and adventure only did exist between the worn covers of her books.

"Sorry. I forgot Ro." Davin, with a sense of devotion, clasped his hands. "For Ronan. I pray I'll grow bigger than he. So I can give him the whipping he deserves."

Ronan grabbed a handful of his little brother's hair and tugged it, which drew an immediate yelp.

"That will do," Clare broke in with an intensity that captured their attention. She decided to complete the prayer on their behalf. Since her Grandma Ella passed, Clare struggled to believe there was anyone listening to her petitions. But prayer still had a role in the proper upbringing of children. The fear of God was a helpful tool of discipline, and one she wasn't willing to discard.

"Lord, please continue to hold my family in Your gentle arms." The words seemed inauthentic and Clare hoped it wasn't obvious. "We thank You for the daily food You provide, this beautiful home we share. We are so grateful for Your favor. Amen."

"A-men," they chorused. The boys headed toward the ladder to the loft to compete for their favored position in the straw bed they all shared, but Clare grabbed Davin by the arm. "Brush." She motioned to Caitlin.

With her brother wriggling in her grasp, Clare watched Ronan labor up the ladder as Caitlin retrieved the hairbrush from the drawer. Although the interior of the tiny home was confining, it was meticulously groomed, with food bins, dinnerware, and knickknacks all organized against the wall on evenly distributed wooden shelves.

Caitlin handed the brush to Clare, and after a few jabs through the hair on his impatient head, Davin climbed up to bed. But Caitlin just stood there.

"Well? Have you something on your mind?"

"You look tired," she said to Clare with some hesitation.

"Because you all are tiring. Now off to sleep, you."

But Caitlin didn't budge. She stood as if she had something else to say.

"What?"

"Well. Will I look tired as well soon?"

Clare let the words of the question sink in before she answered. She carried the challenges of the family on her shoulders, and although she resolved herself to an uneventful life, she yearned for Caitlin and the boys to have more.

"The face of a princess will never wrinkle." She put her lips to Cait's forehead.

Caitlin hugged her sister in return and then went up the ladder to join her brothers in the loft. Her legs vanished over the last rung, and Clare turned her attention to her mother, who had nodded off in her chair.

Kneeling beside Ma, Clare removed the knitting tools from the woman's brittle grip and picked the scarf up from the floor. It was tangled and knotted. It saddened Clare to recall how beautifully her mother's hands once clothed the entire family.

With a gentle touch, Clare tucked the stringy, gray hair behind her mother's ears. Oh, how grief had aged the woman. Even in the calming arms of slumber, Ma looked troubled.

Kevan's death was still hovering in her mother's fragile mind. Last Saturday would have been the boy's fifth birthday had he not fallen into the creek that fateful day. Although Ma could barely function in ordinary day-to-day duties, she had a remarkable awareness of that date.

The anniversary of his death was difficult for Clare as well. It brought back the haunting vision of her mother sitting in that chair, eyes vacant, while holding the limp toddler in her lap, his moist skin a pale blue.

In many ways, the tragedy extinguished the last flicker of Clare's youth. Following her mother's ensuing breakdown, she was next in line to assume the duties and responsibilities of the matriarch.

"Up we go, Ma. Let's get you to bed."

Clare helped the fragile woman to her feet and escorted her to the far corner of the room. There she pulled back an opening through the hand-embroidered canopy Grandma Ella made as a wedding gift. It didn't provide much privacy for the bed, but in Clare's mind it represented the last symbol of her mother and father's threadbare marriage. She obsessed to maintain the fabric to its original beauty, but the years of turf smoke in the room left the linen with a yellow tinge and a sooty smell.

She helped her mother curl into the bed and laid a worn wool blanket over her. Clare seated herself on the edge of the bed and watched the frail woman fall asleep.

"Nightie, Mam."

Clare rose and became aware of the aching in her back and the throbbing in her temple. It was only when she was no longer tending to others that the pains in her own life surfaced.

She stood still, allowing a silence to confirm her two brothers and sister had settled to rest above in the loft. The room was eerily still, save the crackling of the fire, as the red glow of its burning peat cast shifting shadows upon the walls.

Margaret's chair was angled at the table, and out of habit Clare straightened it. She ran her fingers over the time-smoothed oak chair and tried to imagine her older sister sitting there, her laughter winning the room. Clare didn't blame her father for favoring Maggie, because her sister had a natural radiance about her few could match.

What kind of life would Clare have had if Maggie never left for America with her Uncle Tomas four years ago? Certainly she wouldn't be carrying this burden alone.

She immediately felt shame for her self-pity and punished herself with guilt. Such a horrible tragedy her sister endured, and here Clare was feeling sorry about taking on some additional chores.

She went to the bookshelf above the mantel and ran her slender hands over the cracked leather bindings, as if there were something magical in the touch of her fingertips that would discern a proper choice. Clare had read these few books many times over; the adventuresome places and intrepid characters so well known to her they seemed as real as her life here on the farm.

Something compelled her to pull down the Holy Bible her grandmother had given her before she died. It was the very one Nanna read to her often when she was a wee girl. Clare's face burned at the dustiness of the cover. Her grandma would have been mortified and rightly so.

With the Bible in one hand, she lifted Maggie's chair and grabbed a heavy blue knit shawl from one of the hooks on the wall. After shifting a few things in her clutches, she placed her hand around the cold iron handle of the smoke-stained oak door, opened it, and winced when the hinges let out a moan.

Clare stepped into the coolness of the fog-enshrouded night and paused to allow her eyes to adjust to the darkness. Then she sank into the oak chair and experienced closeness to Maggie in some strange manner. Clare wrapped the shawl around her shoulders and absorbed the gentle chorus of the evening's sounds.

She had hoped the moon would provide enough light for her to read, but the murky clouds prevailed and the book lay unopened on her lap.

Somewhere in the uneven chants of the night winds, she sought out a healing voice above the din of her life. Her imagination drifted to sweeter places and she fought back the weariness, grasping on to what remained of the day.

Nevertheless, Clare faded as the aroma of death closed in around her.

# Chapter 2

# THE ROOTS OF CHANGE

Clare woke with a startle.

It frightened her to realize she was still outside and sitting in Maggie's chair with the Bible in her lap. Clare always tried to be in bed before her father got home from the pub each night. He was a difficult drunk, and Clare found it prudent to be at least feigning sleep in her bed when he would stumble back.

She stood and grabbed the book in one hand, the chair in the other. But before she turned, Clare glanced along the road leading away from home. Something was amiss.

She strained her eyes and sought out moving shadows through the fog. Nothing. But her nerves were on edge.

In a short moment, she discerned a figure approaching off in the distance, and even in the mist-obscured moonlight she could tell it was moving toward her at a hurried pace.

*Is it an animal?*

Instinct flooded and Clare scrambled to find a stick or a shovel, something she could use to fend off a predator. But then she could tell it was the shape of a person, and soon the pounding of feet could be heard. Clare's heart pressed against her chest until she realized it was her father, Liam, and the tension released from her body as quickly as it had arrived.

*But why is he running?*

His breathless voice shouted, "Clare. Clare. Get the lantern."

The urgency in his words sprung her to action. She flung open the door loud enough to wake them all, but there wasn't a stir in response. Clare tiptoed to the mantel and grabbed the oil lantern. She bent down, dipped a thin stick into the peat fire, lit the lantern's wick, and the glass chamber filled with light.

Clare hustled outside where she discovered her father crouched over, struggling to catch his wind. The lantern's glow highlighted the weathered lines of his face.

"Bring that to the field."

"What's wrong, Da?"

She didn't expect him to answer, and he didn't. He skittered in bent fashion toward the potatoes they planted in spring. Clare hesitated, not knowing if she should step ahead to light his path or if she should just stay out of his way.

When they arrived at the first row of planted roots, her da fell to his knees.

"Give me light, girl. This is why you're here."

Clare leaned down to hang the flickering lamp close to the ground before him. As she did, Clare could smell the foul odor of the night. She weighed her growing concern and curiosity against her wariness of her father's mood and chose to remain silent.

He dug trembling fingers into the cold, moist Irish soil of the farm where his family drew sustenance for generations. His hands emerged from the earth, and even with faint illumination it was clear to see the blackened root of a dying potato crop in his palms. Emptying the contents of his grasp slowly, Da's shoulders slumped and his browned fingers retreated to his face.

Clare could tell he was trying to hide his grief, and as her nose filled with the smell of rot, she listened helplessly to the dull sobbing of her proud father. Her life would never be the same.

"What's wrong with Da?" Caitlin massaged a soapy blue dress against the rusted iron ribs of a washing board.

Clare plopped a wicker basket of dirty clothing at her sister's feet and eyed her father who was slouched on a wooden fence rail off in the distance with his back to them. He hadn't moved much since sunrise.

"Your father has much weight he's carrying. It's not yours to be concerned."

"It's just, I've never seen him . . . you know . . . not work." Caitlin started scrubbing again.

Clare reached in the water. "It's getting cold. I set a kettle to boil inside."

On the way back to the house, she noticed the boys were pushing a cart full of manure from the barn toward the field. She wondered whether to assign them another chore, but let them be. There was no need to spread muck on a dead crop, but Clare wasn't prepared to tell them the family was angling toward ruin. Even though she was writhing inside with anxiety.

She entered the door and heard the hissing sound of water splattering on red peat coals. She grabbed a cloth for her hands, then reached in and pulled the large black kettle off its hook above the flames as steam rose in anger. The heaviness caused her to stumble, and Clare shrieked as the boiling water just missed splashing on her legs. After catching her balance, she set the kettle down on the floor.

The noise must have woke Ma from her slumber in her chair. "Clare? Is that tea you're making? Tea sounds lovely, dear."

Clare snatched up the kettle and stomped toward the door, but then paused and exhaled. She composed herself and then faced her mother with all the gaiety she could muster. "Yes, Mam. I'll make you a cup. Did you nap well?"

"Sleep? No. Not these days."

Clare lifted the lid to the clay teapot on the table. The tea leaves inside were pale and flavorless, but it was all the family had left. She poured some of the venting fluid into her mother's empty teacup on the small table by the rocking chair. When it was full, Clare looked up to see Ma had already fallen back to sleep.

Clare's shoulders slumped, but then she smiled and kissed her ma on her forehead. "Enjoy your tea."

With the cast-iron kettle in tote, she went back outside. "Stand aside, Cait." She spouted the boiling water into the cleaning tub. Laughter rang out in the distance and Clare looked to the field. The two boys were throwing dung at each other. Ronan limped after Davin, losing ground before throwing wildly at his younger brother.

"Mercy." Clare plopped the kettle down and let out a deep sigh.

Caitlin laughed but then covered her mouth when Clare glared.

"You think it's humorous, do ya?" Clare struggled to fight back a smile herself. "Well, then. After you finish up these garments there, you can put this water and soap to work on scrubbing your brothers."

"What? Why me? Just for laughing?" She looked at Clare with her choreographed sad eyes. "What crime is joy?"

Caitlin always had a way of disarming Clare, who had to restrain herself from surrendering her authoritative stance.

"Caitlin Mae. Neither you nor your brothers will set one toe into our home smelling like the wrong end of the cow. Are we clear?"

"We are."

Despite Cait's assurance, Clare figured she would probably end up washing the boys herself. But the sullen figure of her father ambushed her thoughts. A flush of compassion swept over Clare and she desired to console him.

"Shouldn't you leave Da be?" Caitlin's concerned voice trailed behind her, but Clare's determination grew with each step.

"Father."

He barely acknowledged her, continuing to seek wisdom from something far and unseen on the horizon. His body was knotted in tension and Clare wanted to embrace away the hurt. But he was not a man who cared to be touched.

"Da. We'll be all right." Clare approached as one would a wounded animal.

He made a grunting noise, as if laughing to himself. Without facing her, he spoke with an unusual tenderness. "My Clare. Always there to salve our bleeding wounds. Well, I'm afraid I've done too much damage and for the last time."

"No. We'll be fine, you'll see. We'll just plant again and next time will bring us a rich harvest." Clare sensed his discomfort rising.

"Wish that it be so." Da lowered his head. "Hope is for another family. The Hanley curse is your only dowry, I fear."

"Don't say this." On impulse, Clare wrapped her arm around her father and rested her head on his shoulder. She anticipated he would flinch, but he didn't, and she longed for him to return her embrace. It had been years since her father allowed her to be this close.

His smell returned memories of being in his arms when she was a little girl. Those sweet days when her da was still able to laugh and dream. She reveled in the intimacy of silence.

Then Da lifted her head from his shoulder and swung his legs down from the fence. The moment was gone, and with it the warmth of her feelings retreated to those lonely corners of her memory.

"I made a decision, I have." Da angled his chin. "I'll need you to prepare yourself."

"Prepare for what?" Clare's knees started to shake.

"I'll need you to go the way of Margaret," he said sternly.

"What?"

"Your sister Maggie."

"What are you saying? To America?"

"Yes. America. You need to finish what Margaret began. If she had only made it there, we wouldn't be facing such hardship."

"But you can't mean this?" She took a step backward. How could her father risk the life of another daughter? She was glaring into the eyes of a madman.

"You and Seamus. Both of you." He fumed, but then his disposition melted. "Clare. It's the only way. The field is dead. There's no life in her. We'll surely starve. You. Cait. The boys. Your mam. All of us." He raised his eyebrows as if to punctuate the point. "Hmm?" He patted her on the shoulder and started to walk away.

Her lips trembled, then her face drew taut. Clare chased after her father and yanked his arm. "I won't go."

He scowled at her hand clasping his arm and she loosened her grip. Clare's nerve was slipping. "You want me to leave for America? Haven't you lost . . . enough?"

His gray eyebrows hooded cold eyes and she could sense the venom growing. "I wanted you to go with Tomas instead of Maggie. I wanted her to stay back with us. But he wouldn't take you."

The words pierced through her anger like shards of glass, and Clare's stomach roiled. On the edge of defeat, all that remained was her concern for her siblings. She pointed toward the house. "I can't leave the little ones. Look at them. What would they do?"

"Caitlin will manage fine."

"Cait? She's just a wee girl."

Da reached out and cupped the balls of her shoulders, and the pain traveled through her arms. "You will go. And you will take that worthless brother with you across the sea. And if Seamus drowns on the way, then at least he'll be food for the fish."

He spun and tromped toward the house, halting only to dare Caitlin to speak. She cowered from his path and he disappeared into the house, slamming the door behind him.

Tears blurred Clare's vision, the vibrant green of the farm around her abstracting. When she saw the form of her younger sister running toward her, Clare dabbed away the moisture.

"What did he say?" Concern swallowed Cait's demeanor.

In her mind, Clare saw her sister as a child, never appearing as innocent and vulnerable as she did now. The idea of passing on this heavy burden to the little girl before her was cruelty.

She embraced Caitlin, who reached back with arms of desperation, somehow aware of the unspoken significance. Clare drew back her sister's hair and whispered into her ear.

"Remember how this feels. You will always be in my embrace, Cait. Though gone for a season, I will never leave you. Never."

She felt arms wrapping around her waist and saw her brothers had joined them, each with dread in his eyes. Clare tried not to let them hear her crying, and after a while she stepped back and knelt before them, summoning all reserves of confidence.

"Seamus and I are going to a faraway place where there is money enough to buy food for everyone. A place where people are never hungry. We're going to send all of our spare earnings back here. And while I'm away, I will think of you every day and I'll say a prayer for each of you."

"But we don't want you to go," Davin said. "We'd rather be hungry."

Clare caressed his cheek. "Nor do I want to leave you. But leave I must. And soon, you'll look up from your chores and off in the horizon, with the sun rising behind it, you'll see Clare and Seamus walking toward you, with smiles on their faces and gifts in their arms. And we'll be home forever. This I promise."

They clutched as one family and cried together without restraint. After a long while, Clare's gaze drifted toward the road leading away from their farm. She repeated the words again, this time for her own benefit.

"We'll be home forever."

# Chapter 3

# AMERICAN WAKE

Cormac Brodie, a tall, slender man dressed in a worn tweed vest, white shirt, brown frieze pants, and a faded, black stovepipe hat, wiped the sweat from his forehead. He turned his reddened face, framed by bushy, gray sideburns and nodded to the other two men in his band, who met his gaze with military seriousness. He lifted his fiddle to his shoulders and, with a sharp pull, began to dance his bow across the strings, and a song of unbridled merriment arose.

Soon his son, Aedan, a young, brown-haired lad, joined on the wooden flute and added beautifully high and clear syncopated notes. Then on cue, Cormac's cousin Bartley, who was renowned through many villages for his musical talents, pressed his elbow against a bag of air, and the pipes protruding chimed in with low, echoing tones.

As if unable to do anything else, puppets on the strings of their masters, dozens began to join in the hearty dance—boys, girls, young and old, without reservation and bearing a cheery disposition far removed from their underlying poverty.

Clare watched from a distance and marveled at the ability of her townspeople to dance in the face of gloom. With the green grass, unseasonably warm weather, and festive atmosphere abounding, she imagined a stray visitor would never know that here on her family's field, death's shadow was seeping through the soil.

The potato plague had not yet reached all, but plenty of farms were crippled with more succumbing weekly. As they would say amongst themselves, if the feet of darkness had not yet tread on their soil, the steps could be heard approaching.

Clare shared a large makeshift table with several women. In between town gossip and commentary about the dancers, they were cutting potatoes, onions, carrots, turnips, and parsnips. These vegetables, along with barley and an assortment of lamb neck bones and shanks, were being put into two large black cooking pots, hoisted above pits of fiery peat.

The warm smells of the lamb stew, lively music, children's laughter, and the vibrant chatter of the ladies near her were muted by Clare's disguised angst. She chopped away at a stack of vegetables and wrestled tomorrow's fears.

In the morning, she would be leaving Branlow, perhaps never to see it again. There was a reason why they called these traditional Irish farewells an "American Wake." Few ever returned.

A soft and nurturing voice fluttered above the chattering of celebration. "Are you okay, dear?"

"Pardon?" Clare turned to see Fiona MacBrennan beside her.

"Is everything all right with you, Clare?" The woman who had become her surrogate mother since Ma's illness peered at her with lively and caring brown eyes, framed in a deep wrinkled face.

"Oh yes, mam. It's a lovely day. A lovely day." Clare reached to grab another potato to cut.

"You lie poorly."

"Do I?" Clare laughed. Fiona had eight grown children and twenty-four grandchildren, yet she always made time for Clare.

"Aren't you going to miss us at all?"

"Of course, Mrs. MacBrennan. Certainly I will."

"Well, then, shouldn't we be getting a tad more attention than those taters?"

Clare looked down at the large pile of potatoes she had stacked and grinned. "I suppose."

"Liam spent dearly on all of this, you know."

The mention of her father's extravagance raised Clare's ire. There he was perched on a tree stump, blowing smoke rings from his pipe. He was soaking in the stories and laughter of the parish's men, who were taking a rare Sunday off from their heavy labors. As host and supplier of the music, food, and libation, her father found himself in an uncommon position of honor today, a role he was relishing.

"I was fond of that cow," Clare said. "There's a big risk in selling her to buy our passages . . . and for all of this . . . merriment . . . don't you think?"

"It doesn't matter how he paid for all of this, it's that he did."

"Well, it's troubling to think of how little we'll be leaving behind, what with the winter approaching." Clare enjoyed being able to confide with the woman.

Fiona clasped Clare's arm and pointed. "I see Seamus, at least, is making good on your father's investment." There, off a ways, was Clare's brother, entertaining three young girls.

Clare sighed. *Oh, to live a life so free of worry.*

"Why don't you leave this drudgery to old women." Fiona took a half-chopped potato and the knife from Clare's hand. "That way, we can gossip without fear of corrupting a young one."

A large cheer broke out from the dancers. There was Pierce Brady, grandstanding with a solo jig, his curly red hair bouncing, kicking up his legs and waving his arms with a lusty expression of youth. The crowd encircled Pierce, encouraging him with applause and whistles.

An elbow poked at Clare's arm.

"There's your boy, eh?" Fiona had a taunting smile.

Clare's face warmed. "Is that what you gossip about?"

"Oh, I know you don't fancy the lad. It's just you've been frustrating we meddlers for a while. Seems to be from a good family. The Bradys practically run this town, if it weren't for the landlords."

"Maybe it's not power I'm craving. Perhaps I don't want to be Queen of Branlow."

"Could be worse. You could have been a plain looker like myself." Fiona nudged Clare. "There. Right behind you, two lads deciding who'll have the courage to ask the town's most beautiful woman for a dance."

Clare couldn't resist her curiosity and glanced over her shoulder to see the Finley twins ogling her. The boys were handsome and hardworking, and a nuisance to Clare. She spun back to Fiona. "What's wrong with me?"

"Oh, child. God made you special, 'tis all, full of dreams and great expectations."

"Now you sound like my grandma."

Fiona chopped the last of the carrots. "If you see a hint of Ella in this withered tree, I'd consider it the greatest of compliments." She pointed the knife toward Clare. "I swear to you, I'd catch her speaking to the Almighty Himself all of the time. I can understand why she would, what with those two sons of hers battling all the time, your father and that wild uncle of yours."

She scooped up the vegetables in her apron, turned, and dumped them evenly into the two cauldrons. "Your grandma worried about you, Clare."

Clare shrugged. She wasn't sure she wanted to be reliving the pain of losing her nanna. She wished she hadn't mentioned her name.

"Ella was concerned how life was pressing on you, wearing you down. She told me this in her last days."

So many gentle moments sharing tea on the front porch with Grandma Ella and never could Clare remember seeing concern on the woman's face. "She never spoke of this to me."

"She wouldn't. That wasn't her way. But I knew she saw in you the hope of righting the wrongs of her two sons."

"Doesn't sound like she was worrying." Sometimes Fiona got too close to the hurt and this bothered Clare. She wanted to push back.

"I'm sorry, dear." The matronly woman tried to smile. "This is your special day, and here I am getting somber, tired old lady that I am."

Now Clare felt guilty. Fiona lived a hard life and it was written on her body and face. "Please, I truly want to know. What was it Grandma Ella told you?"

"Were you waving at me, Mrs. MacBrennan?" Pierce said, who had approached out of Clare's line of sight.

"I most certainly was." Fiona ignored Clare's shielded expression of disapproval. She put her arm around Clare's shoulder. "This young lady needs a dance in the worst of ways."

Pierce bowed. "Then dance the lady will." He held his arm out to Clare, who yielded and then gave Fiona an expression of protest.

"Your father outdid himself," Pierce said, guiding her to the dancing.

"It's a bit much, don't you think?"

Pierce's shirt was drenched with sweat and he was breathing heavily. "Ah, Clare. You should just enjoy yourself. Don't keep joy in a box all of the time."

She tugged on his arm. "If I heard clearly, I believe you just called me a prude."

"Well. A bit of warmth at times would well accompany your looks."

"Now I'm certain you've called me a prude."

Cormac finished another wordy introduction to the next song and the music started, this time with a slow tempo. Clare tried to hide her displeasure.

Pierce's face opened up with a toothy smile, and he held out his arms to her. "Come. We need to practice so we can show the Yanks how it's really done."

As the words of the song lamented about lost battles and wistful lovers, the two waltzed across the tufts of grass. Pierce was a good dancer, and as she followed his lead, she allowed herself to join in the revelry of her guests. While pirouetting and gliding to the music, she was pleased to see many of the people she had known all of her life.

Clare wrestled with the idea that Pierce would be accompanying her and Seamus on their voyage to America. It would be good to have another strong companion on the trip, and one she trusted, but it would be uncomfortable being in close quarters with someone who cared for her in ways she couldn't return.

Or could she? Maybe she was being too particular. Even arrogant. Who was she to believe herself worthy of something different? Was this how love was supposed to feel? Clare at least knew she didn't want to endure the pain of being alone all her life.

When the song ended Clare curtsied to the ground and swept her dress behind her.

"Just one dance?"

"Thank you kindly, Pierce. You are a gentleman and a fine hoofer. But I think my brother could use some attending."

Pierce followed her gaze to where Seamus was cavorting. "Oh . . . I'd say your brother is already well tended."

Clare gestured a farewell to him and breezed by the Finley boys before they could put in a request for her attention. She traversed the field past some children at play and on to Seamus, who had the rapt attention of three young ladies.

Tall and fit, with wavy, dark hair and the Hanley blue eyes, her brother garnished the favor of many women in the village.

With a step of authority and a lack of politeness, she interrupted her brother's conversation midsentence. "Why, Seamus. How kind of you to be entertaining our young guests."

Seamus gave his sister a captivating smile. "Just being hospitable, 'tis all."

He turned back to the girls, who appeared to be in their late teens. "I believe you already have the acquaintance of my sister, Miss Clare Hanley." Seamus always emphasized the *Miss* when he introduced Clare to give her a friendly poke.

Clare nodded politely to them and then whispered, "Perhaps you could pick from a tree where the fruit is a bit riper, old man."

"I'm a patient suitor," Seamus said loudly, ignoring her efforts to be discreet. He cupped his hands. "I'm willing to wait with me basket until they fall from the branch."

She put her arms on her hips. "Well, all I can say, Seamus Hanley, is that it's a good thing you're leaving town. It's just a matter of time before all of the women conspire to give you the send-off you deserve. That's without consideration of what the gentlemen think of you."

"The men think highly of me, dear sister," he said in mock indignation. "Certainly, many a lad will bawl when I leave to seek my riches. Why, what's there to fancy in this dismal, rain-soaked country without good Seamus to bring cheer?"

She failed to prove immune to his charm. "Well. You be certain to cheer with restraint. We leave at the top o' morn."

He let out an exaggerated sigh. "There you are, sister. Robbing the day of pleasure. Let me share some wisdom freely. Enjoy your blessed Ireland today, because it's one of the last times you'll gaze on the fair lady."

"Just be ready, Seamus." She glared at the pint of stout in his hand. "And a case of the head knockers won't be slowing us down neither. We'll leave without you."

Seamus gave her a toast with his mug, then turned his attention back to the girls.

As Clare headed back to join the women with the cooking, she caught a glance of her mother. Clare had neglected to check on her for some time.

*Who will carry this torch when I am gone?*

There propped in a chair, with her finest dress and a purple bonnet, was her ma, who looked uncomfortable in what she was wearing. Clare fetched a glass of water on her way over.

"Here you are, Ma. You must be dreadful thirsty."

Nonplussed, Ma looked at Clare. Her mother grabbed the glass with a trembling hand. "So many people out here today for Kevan's funeral." She paused to drink some of the water from the wooden cup, and a trickle spilled down her chin and onto her dress. "We'll give him a right burial, we will." Her expression pivoted to concern. "But why is everyone laughing?"

Clare reached out with a linen handkerchief and dabbed the

water droplets from her mother's chin. "They are not here for a funeral. They are here to celebrate our journey to America."

"America? Is Margaret back from America? Where is she? I want to see my Maggie."

"No, Ma. Maggie's not back. But Da is sending Seamus and me over there for a while. Just to help out until the land heals. I told you this all."

"You're leaving?" Ma brought the glass up to her lips with both hands.

"Yes, only for a season." Clare wondered how big of a lie she was telling.

Ma's expression brightened, but only for a moment. "When will you be back, Clare?"

"Well, I'm not certain. But I won't be any later than I need to be. Cait is old enough now. She's going to tend to you and the boys." The words felt hollow.

Feeling a tap on her shoulder, Clare spun around to see her father's sister-in-law. She was adorned in a feathered hat and a mauve dress, which was stylish years ago but now appeared threadbare. "Aunt Meara. I'm so pleased you came. Are you enjoying yourself?"

"I'd enjoy it much more if it wasn't you we were saying good-bye to." Her aunt's eyes were reddened and moist. "You know how I feel about these farewells."

Clare embraced her aunt. "I'm so sorry, Auntie. 'Tis calloused of us being so grand. It must bring back such hard reminders of Uncle Tomas."

"Tomas?" Ma broke in. "Has your Uncle Tomas returned? Where's my dear Maggie?"

"No, Ma," Clare responded gently. "Enjoy your drink. I'm going to speak with Auntie."

Clare put her arm around her aunt and went out of earshot of her mother. "I'm so terribly sorry for all of this."

It saddened Clare to see the woman in such emotional disrepair. As a young lady, Clare had aspired to the kind of love her aunt and uncle shared. Vibrant. Unpredictable. Meara was thought to be the only woman who could tame Tomas's capriciousness. She carried a grace and dignity that contrasted against his boorish allure. But when Tomas emigrated, she had aged quickly, her spirit fading.

People would try to console her by saying things like, "When Tomas's ship sank, you can be sure he was shouting from the mast, exhorting the crew to hold steady," or "You'll see him swimming to shore soon enough."

But Meara was not fond of the caricature of the wild man performing for the crowd. Meara was in love with the man she always hoped he would be. She saw him as unfinished, a canvas not fully painted. When he left, her life's work would always be incomplete.

"There's a part of me yearning to go with ye, Clare." Meara's glazed eyes looked out to a place beyond her vision. "There's not much left here for me, you know."

Clare grasped for words to console her.

Meara rubbed her nose with a linen handkerchief. She leaned in close to Clare. "You know, I've never told anyone this, but your uncle had no intention of coming back to Ireland. His plan all along was to get settled in New York and then send for me."

"I never knew—"

"Nor did anyone. If your grandmother had known, she would have never paid for his passage. He had Ella in his pocket, he did. Poor woman. Poor wonderfully kind woman. No. He hated it here. Wanted a bigger life. A higher standing. He had ambition."

"But Uncle Tomas always seemed . . . happy." Clare tried to align some of the memories she had of the man with what her aunt was sharing.

"Oh. He had skills, that one." Meara dabbed the corners of her eyes with the cloth. She laughed brusquely. "People here believed he'd sit on the throne of Ireland if he had his choice. And if he were here today, he'd be kissing the soil to feed the lie."

Meara looked up. "There wasn't enough to hold him here. Not even me. And, of course, the letter never came. He never made it halfway past the ocean. A miserable plan it was."

Clare's thoughts sunk and her aunt must have sensed her clumsiness.

"Oh, but Clare. This is just me rambling. Your uncle would have never brought Maggie if he thought it dangerous. He loved her as his own and would die for her." Her eyes widened. "What a mess I'm making! Am I just frightening you now? Oh, just tell me to stop."

Clare understood her aunt's loneliness and hugged her. "The ships are safer now. We'll be just fine."

At that moment, the dinner bell chimed and it was met with joyful shouts and the mad scurrying of children. The music stopped midsong and all migrated toward the cooking fires.

The families congregated around the two black kettles. Hushes were directed at the children and hats were removed.

Father Quinn Connor, the newly ordained parish priest, stood forward to give the blessing. He was still as green as a blade of grass, only a few months removed from the wake he performed for his predecessor, Father Bartley Higgins.

Father Bartley was found deceased in the confessional. It was determined that as many as four congregants had shared their sins with his lifeless body prior to discovering he had passed.

This seemed impossible by those who never met him. But for those who did, it was understandable, for he was a morose man of few words. The exception to this was in the pulpit, where he drew even more resentment due to the intolerable length of his droning homilies.

The young Father Quinn was welcomed with celebration and relief, as any change was thought to be an improvement. He also appeared to be malleable, and perhaps most important, he understood the wisdom of brevity when he stood before the lectern.

His short stature and slight body, combined with his boyish face, made him look much younger than his twenty-eight years. Clare still struggled to see him other than the milk boy, who for years would ride his father's weary wagon down the road, collecting full canisters left by the dairy farmers for transport to market.

The guests of the wake, who were eager to get on with the eating, watched as he fumbled through his pockets before finally pulling out and unfolding a piece of parchment. He cleared his throat and looked at the faces bearing down on him. Clare felt anxious for him and tried to meet his eyes to share encouragement.

He began to speak with a wavering voice. "Dear Father. We gather before You today with happiness and sorrow. In joy, because of this plentiful feast You have provided us in these times of difficulty. And for the gathering of family, friends, and . . . and a few willing to consider themselves thus in return for food and heavy drink."

After a few laughs from the assembly, he continued, now with more confidence. "But sorrow, Father, as our beloved young ones, Clare, Seamus, and Pierce, will journey far, far from home away from the safety of our embrace. We bid farewell to them with great sadness in our hearts and with this petition for Your sweet mercy."

He glanced at Clare and her eyes darted downward.

Father Quinn turned the paper on the other side and cleared his throat. "We appeal to You, Father, to always shed Your blessed light on the path ahead of them, especially when the roads grow dark and lonely and when hope comes scarcely. And if it be Your great pleasure, as it will assuredly be ours, bring them back safely into Ireland's loving arms. In all of this we pray to You with sincerity. Amen and let's feast."

## Chapter 4

# THE KEENER

 To her father's obvious displeasure, the gathering thinned considerably following dinner, and the fading of daylight was accompanied by a chilling wind. After the black kettles were removed, the turf fires were married together, and they were stoked to tall, spark-spewing flames. The remaining guests circled around, sitting on chairs, logs, and turned-over pots.

Clare escorted her mother to bed and was pleased when Ronan and Davin retired as well with few complaints. The day's activities had worn them into submission.

When she came back, she saw her da had broken out his stash of hand-distilled poteen, a particularly strong batch of liquor he made from last season's crop of potatoes. His guests took turns pouring themselves a glass, challenging each other to throat the burning liquid without flinching. Few passed the test.

Da then began to mete out tobacco to everyone who had a pipe, which was nearly all. Hands reached up eagerly to receive his offering, and several of the women, including Fiona, partook as well.

Clare sank into a chair she had brought from inside the house. It was painful to observe her father playing the merry host. She knew money would be life and death for her family, and she couldn't bear to see him squandering it so lavishly for his own amusement.

Suddenly, dogs barked and a carriage could be seen approaching down the road, barely visible in the fading light. Da put the leather tobacco bag in his vest and scurried out to greet the late arrivers.

It was rare to see such a proper carriage in these parts of town. Every once in a while, the English landlords would come to survey their properties, but few of them would drive this far into these rutted, country roads.

As the coach slowed to a halt, a well-attired driver pulled back on the reins of the two handsome black horses and engaged the brake. Da rocked on his heels with his arms behind his back as the crowd slowly gathered around and murmured with inquisitiveness. Even Clare was alive to the suspense of the moment.

When the driver opened the door, the burnished boots of a woman slid out, followed by the hem of an exquisitely laced black dress. As the teamster reached out his arm for support, the woman emerged from the shadowed interior of the cabin. Her dark plumed hat contrasted with her pale complexion, and her aquiline nose and graceful poise gave her the appearance of one of great means. There was an audible collective breath of admiration for the mysterious visitor.

"If I may beg your attention," announced her father with pomp. "Please allow me to introduce you to Madame O'Riley."

As the name rolled from his lips, there was a gasp from those who recognized it.

The woman nodded and the gathering quieted to listen. "My apologies for being late in arriving. The conditions of your roads required a . . . rather patient approach."

Clare spoke in a hush. "Mrs. MacBrennan. Do you know who this is?"

Fiona pulled a slender pipe out from the corner of her mouth and exhaled a billow of smoke away from Clare. "That's the keener. If I recall the name properly, she's well thought of, that one."

"My father invited a keener?"

"What's a keener?" Caitlin asked, who was standing close to them.

Clare leaned close to her younger sister. "It's someone who has a gift in mourning."

Caitlin was perplexed.

"They're paid to cry," Clare added.

"What kind of job is that?"

"One that pays well." Fiona conjured a bright orange glow from the bowl of her long-stemmed pipe. "Your father must truly love you."

Da escorted Madame O'Riley to the ring of seats around the fire, where he waved others out of the way and placed her in the best chair. Clare observed a hint of disdain in the woman's eyes in response to the crude environs. But she also noted something else about the guest. Her da treated her with a degree of familiarity. The alluring woman was more than an acquaintance.

Clare lurked outside of the light of the fire, disinterested in the collective fawning of the keener. She sifted through possible excuses allowing her to slip away to bed, knowing their morning departure was close at hand.

"Do you not approve of all of this?"

Clare recognized Father Quinn's voice before turning to see his all-knowing smirk. He had loosened his collar and for the first time tonight appeared relaxed. Was it the lateness of the evening, or the workings of the poteen in the glass he was holding?

"Of course," Clare responded. "Who wouldn't want such a send-off?" The light from the fire shone intermittingly on his unconvinced face.

"Yes," she said and surrendered the ruse. "You know how much I dread all of this. What a shameful waste."

He looked deeply into her eyes, the ones she allowed few men to gaze into without withdrawing. "That isn't what is really troubling you, is it?"

"And you expect true confessions to the milk boy?"

Father Quinn gave a muted laugh. "It's kind of you to disrespect me privately."

She smiled. "You know what I mean."

He paused. "You do know the . . . milk boy . . . always slowed his cart when he went by your house."

"Indeed. There were few times I didn't notice." Clare looked down and a surge of emotion came over her.

He placed his arm on her shoulder. "What is it, Clare? This isn't about your father's wake, is it?"

Clare feared she would start crying and draw attention. Glancing over toward the fire, she was pleased to see Madame O'Riley still commanding a rapt audience.

"Shouldn't I be telling my father I won't go?"

"You know Liam. Once he's formed his intentions, it wouldn't matter one scant. He's a thick one."

"Yes. I know you're probably right. But the thing is . . . I haven't much tried to dissuade him. The truth is . . ." Clare worried she had said too much.

"Go ahead."

She assured herself with his trusting eyes. "There's some of me at this moment . . . which reminds me of the little girl I thought I left behind." Clare looked at him expecting disapproval, but she saw none. "Not that I was ever brave like Maggie. I'll never have her courage. But inside, I've always imagined going to strange places. Meeting fascinating people."

"Adventure?"

"Yes. Adventure. In some ways I can't wait to leave. To discover what lies at the other side of the ocean. Can you imagine?" She smiled, her face burning. "Am I a terrible person?"

"Why would I ever think that?"

Was he serious? Hadn't he understood anything she had said? Clare was frustrated it even needed words. "Because. Me just abandoning them all. This farm. The boys. Cait. My mother, who can't hardly put on her own shoes."

The frustration of the day, the tiredness she was feeling, and the anxiety of what lay ahead built up to where she started to cry.

"Come, come now." He shook his head. "You are the most talented, thoughtful, young lady . . . woman . . . I've ever known. But do you really believe this beloved island of ours will be swallowed by the tides when you leave her shores?"

She was not expecting to get chided and it caught her unawares. "No. Of course I don't."

He wiped a tear off of her cheek and lifted her chin so he could peer into her eyes. "You can leave Ireland, but Ireland will never leave you. Listen to me. The parish will take care of your family. Your ma. Your brothers and sisters. And your crotchety old man. We'll tend to him as well. We need Clare to take care of Clare. For once in her life."

With those words, a great burden lifted from her shoulders and gave Clare a sense of freedom she hadn't experienced for some time. She looked at his face to determine if it was Father Quinn, the parish priest, or merely Quinn, the boy she admired from afar. Clare was drawn to him, and she embraced the young priest and felt comforted. She could sense the moisture of her tears drying on his opened collar.

"Will you being joining us, Clare, for your own celebration?"

She spun around at Seamus's voice, having almost forgotten they were not alone. To her distress she saw all the guests huddled around the fire gawking at her and Father Quinn.

"We don't want scandal to mar such a lovely day, dear sister," her brother said, which resulted in a few nervous twitters.

"Be forgiving of our dear Clare," chimed Fiona. "The good Father is still acquiring his spiritual disciplines."

This brought laughter, which cleared the discomfort of the moment, for which Clare was grateful. She and the priest joined the group alongside her brother. Sitting next to Seamus was Pierce, from whom Clare thought she caught a glare of disapproval in the flickering light.

"Mrs. MacBrennan," Clare said. "Will my last memory of you be as a blatherer?"

"Fine then, as I would prefer you to remember me in my true light." Fiona raised her glass to the group. "To America."

"To America," they all replied in a staggered chorus.

Pierce's father, Mac Brady, weighed in. "I've heard through way of reliable testimony that there are so many jobs over there for Irishmen, they'll meet you on the docks, begging you to take wages."

Fiona spoke up as well. "Well, I've heard it said you can earn more with a day's shovel with the Yanks than you can draggin' plow for a whole year in our fields."

"That's a dear shame seeing as my boy isn't fond of lifting shovels." Da tossed a twig into the fire.

Eyes shifted toward Seamus to see how he would respond, but Clare knew her brother wouldn't give Liam the satisfaction of validating the sting in his words.

"And I'd say, Da, this potato whiskey was worth every blister on your fingers." Seamus emptied the glass. "If there isn't any to be had in the Promised Land, you'll hear tales of how young Seamus swam back home." He turned to their father and raised his glass. "To the poteen."

"The poteen," was the echoed cry.

When the toast settled, Father Quinn waved a raised arm to draw attention. "Should we share a few kindly words about those who will be leaving us? What say you, Madame O'Riley?"

"Would be tradition." The keener turned to Clare and stared in a strange manner.

Mac put his arm around Pierce. "I will be first." He cleared his throat and held an air until all gave him attention. "I remember this lad, my son, when he was no higher than me boots. And through the years, he got to feel me boots on a few occasions."

Pierce nodded in agreement.

"But he's grown up to be a fine man, he has," Mac said, his voice growing in intensity. "This boy loves his country. This land. And it's only because of his deep concern for his family that he's willing to take leave from this place."

Mac's eyes glistened. "There won't be a day, son, when your mother and I won't wonder how you are, or where you be. This sacrifice of yours will ne'er be forgotten."

Pierce seemed to feed off of the sincerity of his father's voice and was moved by the sentiment. "Thank you, Father."

Seamus gave him a teasing elbow. There was an empty silence as they anticipated their da would speak, but the moment filled only with the crackling of the fire. Clare didn't look to her da. She didn't want anyone to realize how much she craved the slightest hint of his affection.

After a duration of unease, Father Quinn prodded further. "Does anyone else have something to share?" He tried to make eye contact with Liam, but Clare's father continued to gaze down into the fire.

"I have something." The deep, sensuous words of the keener were unexpected. The graceful woman rose to her feet, advancing with well-practiced elegance. She carefully took off her hat and handed it to Father Quinn.

The woman reached with both hands behind her neck and unclasped a necklace around her neck. The pendant glinted as it emerged from the keener's bosom.

In a ceremonious fashion, and with a wry smile on her lips, the keener bent down and, with each hand holding one of the ends of the necklace, asked, "May I?"

Clare nodded and her body shuddered in the cool air with anticipation. The woman's long fingers reached behind her neck and pushed back Clare's hair. The keener's face was only a few inches from hers, and up close the woman appeared much older, and her brown, probing eyes and long, slender nose gave her a crowed appearance. There also was the prevailing charisma that Clare imagined was the fragrance of wealth.

As Madame O'Riley hooked the clasp, she bent toward Clare's ear and whispered words in a firm and haunting tone. She pulled back and placed a finger before Clare's lips. What she spoke was not to be shared. In full control of the moment, the keener displayed a measured smile, one wrought of confidence and melancholy.

When Madame O'Riley returned to her seat, Clare's gaze slid to the pendant at the end of the chain. She cupped it in her hand and examined it in the dim light. It was braided silver in the shape of a clover with three leaves. In the center was a small translucent gem, but it was too dark to discern its hue.

When Clare looked up again, she realized her guests were grasping for an explanation. She froze, not knowing how she should respond.

"Do you like it, my dear?" Madame O'Riley said. "It was given to me years ago by a . . . close friend."

Clare noticed her father was glaring at the keener with disappointment.

"Yes." Clare caressed the pendant. "It's quite lovely. A most unexpected gift."

"How kind," Fiona said, breaking into the awkwardness. "I'm shamed to say it, but my gift is only words. I believe I can speak freely for all of us. Will be a sad day in the morn when the three of you young ones leave us behind. Will be a poorer place without you."

Fiona rose and gave hugs to the three of them, and a few other guests joined in the procession. As they each returned to where they were sitting, a solemn sense of imminent loss came upon them and several began to cry.

Then, as a cresting instrument in a symphony, a voice chorused in and raised the sound of mourning in a majestic way. The keener's mouth opened in sacrifice to the night sky, her face writhing in such profound emotion all spiraled into her expression of grief.

Soon, many of them wailed together as one, although each to their own sorrows—and for the first time today, Clare sensed they all were gripping with uncertainty of the future. Without words and beyond measure of time, they connected in their pain, reaching out in desperation for God to breathe mercy into their lives.

After a while, the coolness in the air subdued the strength of the dissipating fires, and Clare felt uncomfortably cold. It was late enough for her to be exhausted, but nervousness about what lay ahead kept her alert, her thoughts rising as a nearing storm.

Worries about the family she was leaving behind were blended with a creeping exhilaration for the unfolding unknown. It was years since Clare embraced the idea of tomorrow, and she greeted this both as an old friend and a guilty pleasure.

There were also the strange words the keener shared with her in confidence, which kept repeating in Clare's mind. What did they mean?

Father Quinn put his arm around Clare, and she rested her head on his shoulder. No one said a word.

# Chapter 5

# ON THE ROAD

Clare smiled in her sleep. There was a laughter to her dreams she rarely enjoyed while awake.

The warm body cuddled next to her gave her a sense of security. She had grown accustomed to sharing her bed in the loft with her siblings, which satisfied the practical need of surviving the frigid nights.

When she slowly opened her eyes, Clare experienced an odd sensation of motion just as her fingers felt the coarse hair of her sleep mate. She sat up with a start and heard the giddy cackles of Seamus and Pierce. Suddenly, the memory of hitching a ride on a swine wagon returned.

Seamus placed his face beside the snout of the pig lying beside her and puckered his lips. "Has the lady forgotten me morning kiss?"

Clare straightened her dress and brushed the straw from her hair, relieved to see the area she was sleeping in was relatively clean. "How long was I asleep? Where are we?"

Just then they hit a bump and the three of them, along with the six pigs who shared space in back of the cart, were hurled in the air.

The bounce was big enough to erase the smirk from Seamus's face. "I'd say you slept through about twenty of those."

"We're about a half day out from Cork at this pace." Pierce was sculpting a piece of wood with a pocketknife.

Clare replayed the last week in her mind. By the time all of the guests had left the wake that night, the three of them managed only a few hours of sleep before assembling at dawn in front of the Hanley farm, their bulging knapsacks in tote.

Many of the town's families arose to escort them out with a farewell parade. Sleepy-headed children held the hands of their elder siblings, while mothers toted babies on their arms and hips as even the grayed citizenry hobbled along with the aid of walking sticks.

After a long and teary embrace, Caitlin stayed behind with Ma, who watched listlessly from a chair in front of the house as the clattering throng moved as one down the dirt road.

As they passed by rain-worn hovels along the way, more of Branlow's residents joined the procession, and by the time they all arrived at Turner's Crossing, there were nearly four score gathered to pay their respects. The final gifts of sweet cakes, seed loafs, soda crackers, potato bread, white scones, and sacks of potatoes were gratefully received, despite needing to be forced into their sacks.

After the last embraces and kisses on cheeks were shared, the three ventured away to the encouragement of shouts and prayers from those they were leaving behind. Clare only had the courage to look back once, and her eyes sought out Father Quinn, who raised a hand in farewell. They churned with a good pace and in near silence for the first few miles.

Now days later, thumping in the back of the cart, their emotional separation from their family and friends seemed distant. Since leaving, they sloshed in tumultuous rainfall, poached slumber in the fields of farmers, slunk by dark strangers, struggled to find warmth in chilling winds, and after several days of arduous travel, welcome indeed was the sight of the hog cart pulling up beside them.

Despite the unpleasant smell and the jolting ride, there was luxury in the knowledge they had a ride all the way to Cork.

Their ride on the wagon, though it paced slowly, was still much swifter than fellow migrants who lumbered on foot by the hundreds. There were the young and strong who had vibrancy to their steps. But many were entire families, whose progress was curtailed by the weakest among them: the sick or crippled, small children and aging grandparents. Many carried their life's possessions on their shoulders or in handcarts so overfilled they were on the brink of toppling.

The nation was on the move.

"You'll be happy to know, dear sister, we lightened your pack while you were sleeping."

Clare didn't know whether to feel grateful or violated. "You didn't throw anything away, did you?"

"No, your precious books are split between your two mules here, although I'm sure we'll assess some type of fee for our services."

"So Clare," Pierce grinned, "are you ready to share your little secret?"

Her hand went to her pendant and she stroked it. "I told you already, the keener asked me not to share."

"But you never promised her you wouldn't," Pierce said. "It's just the two of us."

"The hogs can be trusted," Seamus said. "They told me themselves."

"There's not much to entertain you, I'm afraid." Clare decided the boys were as justified as she was to hear Madame O'Riley's words. "She told me once in New York I was to give this pendant to some man named Patrick Feagles."

They both looked at her as if to say: *Is that all?*

"I told you both there wasn't much to it. Other than she said this Patrick Feagles would be most generous once it was returned."

"Generous?" Seamus raised a brow. "Now that makes it more tempting. How big a town is New York, do we know?"

Just then, there was a neighing of horses, and the wagon slowed, and then angled to the side of the road before coming to a complete stop. In a few moments, a gray-stubbled face peered over the edge of the wagon at them.

Finn, the pig farmer, cleared his throat and spat before speaking, and when he did, Clare could see there wasn't a tooth visible in his whole mouth.

"We're losing our light soon," the old man said. "Are you hungry at all?"

They exchanged looks of agreement.

He cleaned out his ear with his finger. "Me cousin and her husband. Friendly folks they are and she's handy with a kettle. They live just a way off the main road."

Without a genuine protest, they rolled again and passed through peasant farmland, speckled with houses more like rock shanties.

Clare leaned back and rested her arms on the walls of the wagon and observed Seamus's exchanges with his boyhood friend. Her brother seemed relaxed and happy, something he usually only feigned within the shadows of his father.

The clopping of the horses brought Clare back to the day Ronan, who was just beginning to walk at the time, had his leg crushed by the family's milk cow. The damage caused the bone to protrude from the skin above his ankle. When Breandan Collins arrived, he promptly assessed the injury to be beyond his talents.

"But sir," Clare's father said, as Ronan screamed in the background, "you're the only healer in Branlow."

"Aye, with horses and chickens, this is true." Breandan stroked his beard as sweat beaded on his forehead. "But your child needs a doctor. I'll take care of the boy's pain, but you need to head to Roscommon proper and fetch someone properly trained."

Her father blanched. The city was thirty miles outside of town, and it was raining in windy sheets.

"You can take my mare," Breandan said. "She's out front. Go on. Get going. The sooner we can get his leg set, the better chance your son will have of ever walking again."

"Shall I go with you, Da?" Seamus looked up to his father with an expression of deep pleading. "I want to help Ronan."

Clare would never forget the silent exchange. Her father had dismissed Seamus with a poisoned look of disgust, and then her brother's confidence drained, his shoulders slumped, and his head went down.

Da jacketed himself and headed out into the tempestuous night and Ma hollered at him to hasten.

Less than thirty minutes later, their da returned sporting a bloody gash on his forehead and with his clothing soaked and covered in mud. He was too proud to admit that he had never ridden a horse before, and it was no night for learning.

With no other choice, the animal doctor labored through the crude surgery, managing to save the leg but leaving Ronan with a permanent hitch.

That night, when the downpour relented, Seamus had been taken out by his father and given the reed in the field. When her brother climbed into the straw mattress next to Clare, the pains on his back caused him to whimper in muffled groans.

"What did you do?" Clare whispered in his ear.

"Da said I looked at him with blame." Then Seamus sobbed until he fell asleep.

A whistle from the pig farmer snapped Clare out of her musings, and up ahead she could see two figures approaching. She squinted and as the wagon drew them nearer, she made out a short, squat man escorting a woman who was taller than him by a good half foot. Suddenly the woman let out a shriek and hurried toward them in waddling fashion, waving as she came closer.

"Finn!"

"Whoa." The old driver stopped the cart to a creaking halt and was only halfway out of his seat when the woman reached up and embraced him hard enough to cause Finn to stumble out of the wagon.

The woman spotted his passengers, all three of whom were now standing in the back of the wagon. "And what have you here?"

"These are me new companions," Finn said, who was now standing beside her and brushing some of the dust from his clothing.

She looked up at them with an odd smile. Despite the leathery appearance of her skin and the large wart jutting out of her cheek, her face bore a gentle spirit.

"Welcome. Come down and greet us, won't you? Not every day a lonely woman gets the pleasure of young visitors. Brings joy to me eyes, it does." Then her face shifted to concern. "I've got some tidying to do."

By this time, the short man accompanying her arrived. He wore faded black pants peppered with patches and a well-stained white shirt mostly hidden beneath an olive green vest. He had an unlit pipe in one hand and a brown hen struggling to free itself tucked under his other arm.

"Jack," she barked as she limped over to him. "Hand her to me."

He objected with a sharp gaze, but then released it to her with some reluctance. The woman grabbed the chicken and scurried down the road in a gait that looked as if it pained her.

Jack shrugged. "My wife fancies visitors," he said in a way that indicated he did not.

Wanting to walk the aches out of their legs, Clare and the two boys followed behind Finn's rattling wagon the remainder of the way to Jack's house, which was as forlorn as its owner.

Clare was the last to enter the doorway of the weathered shanty, and before doing so, she paused to glance far down the road behind them. In the tapering of light, and amidst the humming of crickets and the flaps of the wind, Clare thought she discerned a voice.

It was whispering for her to return home.

# Chapter 6

# THE TINKERS

 Finn was perched on the driver's seat, and he tapped the handle of the horsewhip in his hand. Impatient swine grunted in the back of the wagon. "Supposin' it's time. And the boys. Know where they might be?"

Clare stood at the side of the cart and yearned for the shapes of Seamus and Pierce to appear in the horizon. Last night they had enjoyed a chicken stew with their hosts, and she ended up sharing a straw mattress with Colleen in the dingy confines of the hovel. But the men were sent outside to the barn for the evening, and as they were departing Clare overheard her brother asking the whereabouts of the closest pub.

"'Fraid I do."

The pig farmer spat. "The market closes at sundown in Cork. Gonna need to press on."

Clare's mind sped through the different possible outcomes of her options. If she stayed, she would be giving up Finn's generous ride, not only for herself but for the boys as well, as they wouldn't climb aboard without her. But if she went with the old man now, she risked being separated from Seamus and Pierce, and for how long she couldn't know. After several anxious and conflicted moments, she made her decision.

"We'll pass the tavern on the way out, won't we? Yes. I'm sure we'll find them there, or on the way." She climbed up onto the splintered wood bench she would share with Finn, still uneasy about her choice. The mere thought of her brother's careless laughter caused her to clench her fists.

The old man gave a shout at the two mares, and they responded with a lurch, their warm breath clouding from their nostrils as it blended with the cool air.

The clamor of wagon wheels grinding over the rough road made discussion difficult, and Finn didn't offer much conversation anyway so they remained quiet. Occasionally he would look over to her and blush, obviously pleased with her companionship.

Clare surveyed the road closely in both directions for any sign of the boys, in the chance they were napping in a rain trench. As they went by a sprawling manor, the two were nowhere to be seen, but the fields were replete with laborers feeding the livestock and attending to the garden and hedges.

After a while of passing through the familiar sights leading back to town, she shouted above the wagon's rattle over to Finn. "Your cousin is a fine woman. Very charitable."

He nodded. "'Tis."

The crunching sounds of the wood on dirt filled the silence before she braved her next question. "Do you think Jack was displeased with our visit?"

He didn't answer her straight away, and Clare wasn't sure

whether he hadn't heard her or if he chose not to respond. After a lengthy minute Finn spoke up. "It was the fowl."

"The fowl?"

"He was on his way to pay the lease."

"The lease? I don't understand."

"My cousin and her husband were on the way to the land-lord. Last night in the road when we met them. They were hoping the chicken would give them some time . . . keep them from being evicted."

"Oh. I see." Clare's heart dropped with guilt. She didn't inquire further.

After a couple of miles, they entered a small complex of buildings that were just shy of the intersection with the main roadway to Cork. They passed a woman leading a goat by a rope, with two small children struggling to keep pace.

Finn slowed the cart to a halt in front of the tavern, which looked more like a large house. Only the wooden Public House sign creaking in the wind on a post revealed its purpose.

He came down from the wagon, and as he was encircling it, she leaned over the slats of the wagon behind her and buried her pack in straw. She had to shoo away one of the pigs to do so, straining her back in the process. When she turned, Finn had a hand extended to her and she gratefully used it as leverage as she stepped down to the road.

When they arrived at the large oak door of the tavern, they discovered it locked. He rapped several times at the iron knocker, but there was no response. Clare shook the handle of the door in frustration as Finn walked over and stepped on a boulder so he could peer into a small window at the front of the building. She watched him with hope, but his body language spoke before he did.

"No one inside. Only empty tables."

He stepped down, and as he looked at Clare, she could tell his angst over being delayed had dissipated and was now replaced with compassion for her predicament. "I'm awful sorry." Finn headed back toward the wagon.

Clare turned around, leaned her back against the door, and put her hands to her face. She was beginning to panic. What would she do now? Where could they possibly be? Trying not to cry, she began to question why she ever left Branlow. She should have stood up to her father and never left the farm. If he was so intent on a trip across the sea, he should have gone himself and left Clare and her siblings to fend for themselves.

"We're closed if it's not obvious."

Clare removed her hands from her eyes, and a stern-faced woman approached carrying an armful of produce.

"Is this your establishment?" Clare asked.

"If you need to ask, it means you're not from around here."

Clare brushed off the comment. "Have you seen two young men? One who is tall and the other with red hair?"

The woman put a key into the door and turned it with a click. "Oh, we've seen those two more than we wished. They were here to the wee hours, full of drink and full of themselves. My husband finally sent them off barely fit to walk."

"Do you know where they headed?" Clare asked.

With her free hand, the woman tucked some of her stringy blonde hair behind her ear. "Away. Which was all I cared about." Without tarrying for a response, she went into the building and closed the door behind her.

Clare headed back to the wagon in defeat and confusion. It would take her several hours to walk back to Jack and Colleen's farm, and with what she knew about the sacrifice they had already made, she couldn't bear to burden them further.

She also couldn't hinder Finn, even though he wasn't pressing her anymore. He was seated in the driver's seat, with the reins limp in his hands, patiently awaiting her decision.

Clare put her hand above her eyes to shield against the morning sun and scanned the road in both directions one last time, desperate to spot approaching silhouettes. Nothing.

Perhaps she should just go home and beg for her father's mercy and forgiveness. This all seemed too much for her to bear. But this thought lasted only for a moment, and she grasped on to the last strand of her faltering courage. No. She would not go back. She would not quit.

Seamus and Pierce must have decided to head on the road to Cork ahead of them. She climbed up on the seat. "Let's go."

Finn flashed a smile of relief and didn't allow Clare an opportunity to change her mind. The wagon's joints and wooden planks groaned in protest, and arriving shortly at the main fork in the road, they headed south in the direction of the great port city before them. Behind, the buildings of the small town diminished from her view. Were her chances of meeting up with Seamus and Pierce fading as well?

She closed her eyes as she cried softly. "Lord. Please bring the boys to me."

They covered the miles, each alone to their thoughts, passing vast acreage of field and farm of rich verdure. Clare was surprised by how many were sewn with potatoes. Her father spoke of how the tuber was being touted as the crop that would bring the tiny nation out of the clutches of poverty, and she could see firsthand the land was lined with believers. If the contagion spread throughout the country, this faith would be repaid with tragedy.

Clare continued to keep a heedful eye in all directions for signs of the boys. If they were on foot, even the plodding wagon would eventually catch them. With each group of sojourners they approached in the road, she would look them over with expectation, but each stranger's face only added to her growing disillusionment.

As they were more than halfway to their destination, and with her resolve well tempered, the road began to lead through a forested area. Clouds gathered ominously above and Clare began to rue her choice. She would be in Cork before too long and then what would she do?

She heard a noise and spun to see two figures running up from behind them.

"Wait! I see them." Clare's heart lifted as the prodigal sons approached.

"Whoa." Finn pulled on the reins and the wagon slowed. But when he glanced behind him, his eyes widened and he snapped the reins, clamoring at the reluctant beasts to regain their momentum.

"Why aren't you stopping?" Clare shouted above the sudden frenzy.

"Tinkers!" Finn's complete focus was on the road before him.

Clare turned and saw indeed there were two men gaining ground on them rapidly, and neither of them was her brother or Pierce. Her elation morphed to fear. She heard many stories about gypsies terrorizing the roads of Ireland, but they were rarely seen or heard of in Branlow.

The tinkers drew closer to where she could hear them panting from the chase, and the horses were too encumbered by the load to offer much of a contest. Within a few moments, the men were on both sides of the cart. They pulled back on the bridles and coaxed the horses to a standstill.

Clare's eyes were now wide with dread. She sought strength from Finn, but he appeared defeated.

"What's the hurry, old man?" The tinker gawked at him with dark, penetrating eyes, and flowing from his chin was a scraggly beard. "It appears you've forgotten the toll."

He brandished a long knife in one hand and stroked his facial hair with the other. "These are hard times. All of these fine animals in your possession and there are children without a clean bone to pick. What justice is in that?"

"Just leave us be." Finn's lower lip quivered.

The tinker sneered, his blackened teeth showing. "No. No sir. We won't be leaving anyone be. We all deserve to eat." His voice raised in anger. "Would you have us all starve?"

The hair on Clare's arm lifted as she realized the second man was creeping beside her. His ears sprouted wide from the sides of his head and there was a large gap in his teeth. He gaped at her with hunger.

A chortle came from the bearded tinker. "It seems me brother Orin has taken a fancy to your daughter, old man. Or would she be your grandchild? Don't worry, young miss. Ol' Orin is not much of a talker, but they say he's quite a fine kisser."

Clare felt her arm being touched, and she drew it back from Orin and glared at him in disgust. His fingers reached up to feel her hair. She heard a crack and he stumbled back with a squeal. A thin line of blood appeared on the side of his cheek. He put his hand to the wetness and red liquid flowed over his fingers.

A shout was heard and Clare turned to see the bearded tinker dragging Finn off the wagon. In a moment, the old man was tossed to the ground, his whip tumbling out of his hand.

Orin came around and both men pounced on Finn, kicking him as he tried in vain to block their blows with his arms.

Clare leapt from the seat, screaming as she desperately attempted to pull them off of Finn, who had ceased fighting back. "Please stop. You'll kill him."

She was flung and rolled painfully on the dirt. When she managed to get back up again, the tinkers departed to the rear of the wagon. The sound of the back latch opening, and the gate's hinges creaking was followed by the heavy steps and snorting protests of the pigs. Clare crawled over to Finn and held him close.

Relieved to feel his chest rising and falling, she took her handkerchief out from her dress pocket and wiped the blood and dirt from his face. His eyes opened slowly and he was disoriented.

"Keep down," Clare said quietly.

From her position on the ground, Clare could see the legs of pigs moving away and toward the foliage. "Please, God. Make them go."

Suddenly, Orin appeared from around the wagon. Smudges of blood stained his cheek, contrasting eerily with his smile.

Clare's pulse throbbed and she gasped.

The bearded tinker shouted from the trees, "Orin. Let's go. We've got to get going."

Disappointment came over Orin's face. He turned, looking over his shoulder once before disappearing behind the wagon. In a few minutes, the sounds of the pigs and the chatter of the tinkers could no longer be heard.

Finn struggled to get to his feet and Clare gave him her hand in support. "Shouldn't you lie down for a while?"

"They'll be back for the mares," he said. "And you."

Clare didn't need any further motivation. She helped Finn climb back in the seat and wrapped her arm around him to make sure he wouldn't topple. The old horses seemed anxious to leave, and without the heavy load behind them, they galloped ahead.

A sudden concern came over Clare. Her pack! She leaned over into the back of the wagon and was relieved to see the bulge in the straw where it had been covered. In their haste, the thieves hadn't noticed. At least one of her prayers was answered.

They raced forward toward Cork, as if wolves were clipping at their heels. Soon, an increasing density of homes and busy fields appeared on either side of the road. They passed more and more travelers on foot, some alone, and others in small groups or large caravans, pushing handcarts and guiding pigs and goats before them as they approached the outer boroughs of the city.

As Finn and Clare continued to get closer, buildings large and plentiful began to rise around them. The pavement shifted abruptly from divot-filled dirt to smooth cobblestone, polished by hundreds of years of transport.

Although the sun was setting on the city, it was still bursting with commerce, with street vendors selling fruit and vegetables, skinned pigs hanging from hooks, live poultry in wire cages, clothing and fabrics from afar, parasols and cookware.

Barkers competed for the attention of the streams of visitors, advertising their wares with booming voices rising and falling depending upon the class, or apparent gullibility, of the prospects walking by them.

The bustling activity was so captivating and invigorating, Clare nearly forgot her misadventure on the road. Yet when the sky cracked with waves of thunder, the darkening clouds spoke to her of the difficulties of the day and of those looming yet ahead.

As they entered a particularly spacious and active plaza, Finn slowed the cart and locked the brake. His face was already swelling and bruises were beginning to show. "This is the marketplace."

She looked at him blankly, not understanding the significance of what he was saying.

"You'll find a place to rest here."

Panning her gaze around, she saw heavy horse-drawn traffic in both directions, a flush of merchant activity, and old rock-hewn buildings, green in hue from moss and blackened with time. But she didn't notice anything that would indicate lodging was available.

Finn read through her confusion. "You won't need to find an inn. Here, the inns find you."

She didn't understand, but when he winced in pain as he raised his arm, Clare's concern shifted back on Finn. "What about you?"

"I'll be fine." He put his hand to his chin and rubbed it. "But I think they kicked out all me teeth." He paused for a moment and then opened his mouth wide in full, unbridled laughter.

She was flabbergasted that the battered old man was laughing at his own calamity. But laugh he did, intermittently slapping his legs and then holding his ribs as if in pain. Had the blows to his head caused some kind of madness? But soon she couldn't resist the draw of his mirth, and she joined him in laughing.

The fear and angst eased from the core of her being. Yes. They'd both be fine.

She gave the wiry, old man a hug and got down from the wagon, and he handed Clare her canvas bag. After brushing off the straw, she tossed the pack over her shoulder. The weight of it reminded her how grateful she was when Finn's wagon first slowed to give them a ride. It seemed like months ago.

Abruptly, as it was accustomed to do in Branlow, and apparently in Cork as well, rain started to fall in sheets of frigid water. People in the streets shrieked as they scattered for cover.

"Take good care of yourself, Mr. Finn."

"That I will. Good luck to you, young lady. May there be better roads ahead."

With that, he snapped his wrists and the cart tugged forward and wheeled its way down the city corridor, passing through frantic people retreating from the rain, some with umbrellas and others simply covering their heads with their hands.

Sadness swept over Clare as Finn and the wagon disappeared from her vision, leaving her wet, cold, and entirely alone in this crowded square.

But tugging at her as well was another emotion that began to rise from the depths of her being. Although frightened and feeling abandoned, Clare also experienced a strange flash of exhilaration.

# Chapter 7

# THE WAYFARER'S INN

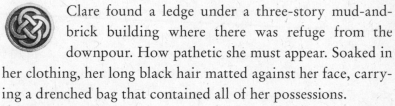 Clare found a ledge under a three-story mud-and-brick building where there was refuge from the downpour. How pathetic she must appear. Soaked in her clothing, her long black hair matted against her face, carrying a drenched bag that contained all of her possessions.

What had she done? Clare had never seen so many people gathered in one place, yet she knew none of them. How obvious was it that she was alone and vulnerable with no place to go?

People passed by, shapeless, faceless, bumping into her, voices shouting, running to get out of the rain. Yet what made her most uncomfortable was how many souls went by without acknowledging her existence. Clare was used to greeting everyone she locked gazes with in her small town, but doing so here seemed both discouraged and dangerous.

Across the street, somewhat obscured by the pounding of the rain, two men leaned against a brick wall, feasting on her with their glares.

She felt a tug on her arm and Clare swung around. A boy of about twelve years stood dry beneath an umbrella. His face was ruddy and he was adorned in a tattered dress suit and top hat, which in its glory days might have been worn by a governor's son.

"Lodging, miss?"

She nodded mutely.

His face brightened. "Knew so. Always spot 'em miles away. He has a nose on him they say. Master Redmond is me name. But you can call me Pence. All my friends do. You know why it 'tis? They say he'll do anything for a pence. Well. Look at me being ungentlemanly."

The boy handed Clare the umbrella and grabbed the pack from her arms. First stumbling when the burden transferred to him, he gave it a lunge, and though bent over, he steadied it firmly.

"Follow me, miss. Keep your eyes on Pence as he wouldn't want to lose you in the crowd and the rain." He started to walk and waved her to follow. "Come now. Finest lodging for guests you'll find. Did you come from far?"

Clare started to answer but didn't get a chance.

"First time to Cork? That's certain. The farmies like your-self, miss. You all stand out like flies swimming in a pitcher of milk, you do. Not meaning any offense. Just pointing it out to you. The farmies only used to come for market, they did. But now it's off to the harbor to the big ships and far places. Best harbor in the world in Cork right here. At least they tell me so. Someday Pence will go. Who knows where?"

Surprised at how difficult it was to keep up with him, despite the fact he was carrying the bag, Clare focused on the task. Ever more amazing was his ability to turn his head and hold a conversation while leading them at a swift pace.

They weaved through streets and alleys that grew darker and more run-down as they pressed forward. As he took her deeper into the bowels of the city, she grew worried, especially as faces peering through doorways and windows seemed more sinister and discontent.

When she would ask him how close they were, his response was always the same. "Just around the corner, miss. Keep lively."

And then he would burrow farther through alleyways, rattling on at a shout about the history of the city, favorite places to eat, marketplaces to negotiate the best bargains, and he even described the architecture of certain buildings, explaining in some cases how he would have designed them much differently. Neither the burden of the bag he was carrying or the pounding of the rain dampened his step or mood.

Just when she was about to dig in her heels and insist she wouldn't go a step farther, Clare's young guide turned to her. "Here we are, miss. Told you it's a beauty."

Down the alleyway where it curved to darkness, a sign that read Wayfarer's Inn flapped in the wind and rain. They arrived at the entranceway to the building, its outside walls blackened in sections by what once appeared to be flames.

Sitting on a stool in the archway, just deep enough to be out of the reach of the rain, was a man with a pockmarked face and a bulbous nose.

Pence removed the bag from his shoulder and placed it gingerly on one of the few dry spots on the floor. Rattling tin buckets lined the hallway ahead as they caught the heavy dripping from the ceiling. "Here you are, Mr. Evans. The lady has come to enjoy your hospitality."

The man was cleaning his fingernails with a knife, and he barely acknowledged his guest. "Are you staying for just the night?"

"Yes." Clare thought she smelled urine coming from inside. "Most certainly."

"Then it's five pence. In full. Up front."

Clare grimaced. The hallway was damp and dark, and she didn't know how much worse it would get once she got inside. But she was deathly tired, it was pouring outside, and she had no fight left in her.

"Very well." She opened the canvas bag and probed her hand blindly past clothes, books, and food until she came to the leather purse her mother had given her many years ago. She pulled it out, and after fumbling through the change, she pulled out five pennies.

Pence reached out to receive them from her, but the proprietor slapped his hand away and scowled at him. "Where's your manners, lad?"

His coarse fingers snatched the coins from Clare's palm and he inspected them closely, even biting one with his teeth. Apparently satisfied with his inspection, he put them in his vest pocket and reached behind for a ring of keys hanging off of a rusted nail on the wall. He unfastened one from the metal loop and handed it to Pence. "Number 12."

The boy reached down and lifted Clare's sack again. "Follow me, miss." They headed down the lantern-lit hallway, being careful not to trip over any of the buckets. They passed by numbered doors on each side, and Clare could tell by how closely they were nestled to one another that the room would be tiny.

When they got to the end of hallway, Pence was careful again to set Clare's sack on a dry spot on the floor, which was not an easy task. He grabbed a lantern from a hook on the wall and used it to illuminate the keyhole. He turned the key, and the door opened reluctantly with a squeak.

As she followed behind Pence through the door, Clare was pleased to see that although it was barely furnished with only a bed and a table, its floors seemed to be free of moisture and the chamber pot appeared to be mostly empty.

"Is there anything else I can do for you?" Pence stood almost at attention.

"No. That should be all. Oh yes, of course." She opened her purse and withdrew a copper coin and handed it to the boy.

"Obliged." He tipped his hat, bowed, and turned to go.

Clare thought of something, which seemed futile but perhaps worth trying in light of the boy's knowledge of the city. "Pence. There is something else. I'm hoping to rejoin my brother and his friend here in town. My brother's name is Seamus Hanley. He is tall with black hair. His friend Pierce is a stocky redhead. How would one go about finding them?"

Pence brightened. "You just did, miss. Seamus and Pierce, you say? If they are travelers like you, they are as good as found. Pence knows all of the places and the people to ask. They say Pence has a nose, you know."

Clare wasn't hopeful, but she found his confidence charming nonetheless. She reached back into her purse. "Here is another penny for your troubles. And if you find them for me, I'll have four more for you."

His mouth opened in surprise but then straightened, as if he didn't want her to think she was overpaying. He flipped the coin she gave him in the air and caught it deftly. "Five pence. Consider it done." With that, he put his hat back on his head and spun, the tails of his coat lifting up.

The door closed behind him and the lantern went with him, leaving her in darkness. She probed her way to the door, and by the time she found the handle and opened it, he was gone from the hallway as well. Too tired to protest, she retreated back inside and lay down on the bed, fearful to know the condition of the linen.

For Clare, who had shared a bed with her siblings her entire life, this lonely room offered a touch of luxury. And before she could enjoy her independence, her eyes closed and she was gone. Her dreams replayed the past week's events to her, albeit in raw and distorted fashion. Rather than the pictures of tranquil retreat she usually enjoyed in her sleep, these were fraught with worry and hopelessness.

She woke sometime later with a start, her face flushed and her body sweaty.

Clare was not alone.

# Chapter 8

# A Tale of the Woods

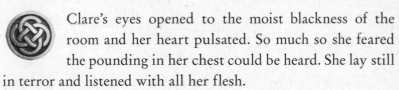 Clare's eyes opened to the moist blackness of the room and her heart pulsated. So much so she feared the pounding in her chest could be heard. She lay still in terror and listened with all her flesh.

There was the sound of snoring and labored breathing near her bed. She strained her eyes, hoping they would adapt in the darkness.

Should she risk moving? What could she use as a weapon?

Raising her head inch by inch, Clare pressed up from the bed with her arms. A creak and then a groan sounded from the old mattress.

She froze again. Waited. Listened. If only the room wasn't so dark.

Sliding from under the blanket, she pivoted until her feet touched the ground. Pause. Then she rose as silently as possible, but the bed betrayed her with a squeak ripping at her tattered nerves.

The snoring stopped. A shadow moved and Clare let out a yelp as her body propelled toward the direction of the door. But her legs got caught in a mass on the floor and she tumbled to the ground. Arms reached out to grab her. She began to scream and a hand covered her mouth.

"Clare. Clare. It's me."

She recognized the voice instantly and the terror waned.

Suddenly, light filled the room and Clare saw she was in her brother's arms. Pierce held a lantern in his outstretched arm, his tired eyes filled with concern.

Clare's panic shifted toward rage. "What? How did you—?"

"The little man in the suit," Seamus said. "He brought us here."

"Pence?"

"Who?"

"Pence. The boy. That's his name. He actually found you?"

"Found us, he did," Seamus said. "And he tried to shake us for five pence. Says you told him it was fair bounty. I paid him well with a twist of his ear."

"You didn't?"

"I did. And I would have done the other ear if the boy hadn't turned and run."

Clare sighed as she climbed to her feet and embraced Seamus. "Well, I suppose it's good to see your faces. I thought them for lost."

A pounding noise interrupted them.

They exchanged perplexed looks. "Who is it?" Clare asked.

No answer. A key turned in the lock and the handle of the door turned. The door cracked open to the splashing light of a lantern. Soon the bulbous nose of the innkeeper emerged, followed by the man himself.

"What's the racket in here all about?"

Pierce stepped forward between the man and Clare. "What manners are there in barging into a lady's room without permission?"

The innkeeper raised his lantern toward Clare and then glared toward the boys.

Clare was grateful she had slept in her clothes. "This, sir, is my brother and his friend."

"Yes. Certainly they are. But regardless, it will cost you another two pence each for your . . . relations."

Before her brother could protest, Clare grabbed her purse, pulled out four coins, and handed it to the man. "Very well. Now would you be kind enough to let us be?"

Stubby fingers reached out to grab the coins. "Unless yer planning on staying another night, it's time for you all to leave. It's well past morn."

Surprised to hear day was already upon them, they offered no opposition and the innkeeper retreated out the door.

It took the three of them only a few minutes to gather their belongings. Clare noticed the filthy pillow she had been sleeping on all night. The light filtering into the room revealed more dirt, cobwebs, and strange fluids spilled on the floor, and she couldn't bear staying for another moment.

They went down the dark hallway and returned the rusted key to the keeper, and in the bright sunlight and midday street activity, they winnowed their way toward the center of the city.

They passed children playing in the streets, mothers hanging bedding and clothing from second- and third-story windows, pigs wandering on cobblestone roads, and vendors proclaiming their wares.

Clare reveled in the rediscovered security of being with Seamus and Pierce, but she wasn't ready to forgive them for the torture they put her through yesterday. "So what happened to the two of you? And how did Pence find you?"

"Pence?" Seamus took off his hat and brushed back his hair. "Oh, your little man."

"He found us at a pub," Pierce said. "Not much to it. The story is in how we found the pub."

"'Tis." Seamus nodded. "It was a favorite of your dear friend Mr. Finn, the pig farmer. He took us there himself."

"The old man?" Clare shifted her pack to relieve some of the pressure from her shoulders. "Tell me you didn't trouble him to bear you all the way back to Cork?"

"Trouble him we did," Seamus said. "But not before we got his pigs returned to him. The ones you lost."

Clare stepped out of the alleyway to stand clear of an old woman pushing a cart of potatoes. "How did you go about doing this?"

Seamus went to grab a tater from the cart as it went by, but the woman stopped and stared him down. "Sorry, miss." He lifted his hat before turning back to Clare. "The pigs? That's a story there, I'll tell ya."

"Seeing as you left with our ride, we were on foot when we came upon the old man," Pierce said.

"Ah, he was a sad sight to see." Her brother readjusted his pack on his shoulders. "Almost to tears, he was, the horses too, believe it. Of course, after proper greetings we had inquiries about your whereabouts, and that's when he told us of the tinkers."

"We were near abouts where it happened," Pierce said.

"Aye. And we jumped in and Finn rode us there, and sure enough if we didn't see one of them tinkers, sitting at the side of the road, as innocent as the day."

"Finn was aiming to stroke him with his whip." The redhead motioned with his arm. "But your brother had a better plan."

"That I did. Finn told us about this tinker being a bit slow-ish and taking a liking to you. Orin remembered you well, and I asked him if he was looking to marry soon."

"You did not do anything of the sort." Clare folded her arms across her chest.

"And I told the poor fella that as your kin, I'd agree to it if he would only return the pigs as part of a fair trade. A dowry of sorts."

"A fair trade, indeed." Pierce smirked.

Seamus put his arm around Clare. "Overpriced if you ask me, but a trade offered nonetheless. So, sure enough, the fellow walks us right through the woods to a pen with all of Finn's lovelies, putting their noses in the air like they were seeing their mammy. Your man even helped us herd them and load 'em up."

"What about the nasty tinker?" Clare asked. "The hard-spirited one."

"Didn't see 'em," Pierce said. "Which was disappointing as I had words to share with him."

"As it is," Seamus said, "your man is probably still waiting on the road with flowers in his hand, wondering when his bride will be coming around the bend."

"As if I can believe any of that tale." Clare withheld a smile, which would only encourage them further. But she did hope at least parts of their story were true, especially when it came to Finn reclaiming his pigs.

They turned a corner on the pathway, and it spilled out into the main vein of the city—a bustle of horse-drawn carriages, fruit wagons, peddlers, ladies wearing imported fashion sharing steps with the shadiest of street urchins and thieves.

"What now?" Pierce said.

They all froze, Clare feeling small against the frame of grandeur. None of them answered for a few minutes, and they took off their heavy packs, propping them against the wall of a three-story, brightly painted yellow building.

"We should probably split up in two." Seamus took off his hat and ran his fingers through his black curls. "I'll go to the port to get the passages and you two can provision up."

Clare didn't like the idea of being separated from her brother again. "Do you think this wise?"

"Seamus is right." Pierce's eyes widened as he gazed at the activity of the bustling street, noisy with the trots of horse buggies and the shouts of vendors. "The longer we stay in the city, the more we'll spend what little we don't have."

Pierce reached into his pack and pulled out a wallet. After fumbling through it, he pulled out several bills and extended them to Seamus. "My father said it should cost about ten quid per passage. Here's ten for me and a few more."

"Well?" Seamus held out his hand to Clare.

She hesitated for a moment and then reached into her pack as well. Liam had given her the full treasury and made her promise not to leave it with her brother. But her father was not here and Seamus would need to be trusted at some point on the journey. It might as well start now.

She carefully counted out twenty-five pounds and handed it to Seamus, feeling as if she had just given him the air they would need to breathe. She looked back into her purse. There would be little for supplies, let alone something to hold them over when they landed in America.

"We'll need to be prudent," she said to Pierce.

"We won't starve. My father gave me enough for there and back."

"What's yours is yours," Clare said.

"And what's mine is mine to do what I want with it," Pierce said sternly.

"All right you two." Seamus folded the bills in his leather pouch, which he tucked away in his tunic. "Pierce, you have my blessing to spend all of your pa's money on me. My sister's portion of your generosity as well. Now, where to meet?" He panned the marketplace. "There. Let's gather at the tavern across the way before sunset. Perhaps your dear father will pay for a pint while he's in the mood of generosity."

With that, Seamus tipped his cap to them and then scurried into the crowd.

"Hey, you left your pack," Pierce shouted after him. He turned to Clare. "Can you believe your brother?"

Clare smiled. "Ah. It's well he's traveling light."

Pierce stumbled as he tried to hoist the two packs over his shoulder. "It's a fine thing for him, I'll say."

Clare looked back in the direction where Seamus had disappeared, and her eyes sought out one last glimpse of her brother among the throbbing of disquieted humanity.

But he was gone and Clare's brows bent.

Chapter 9

# SHAMROCK'S LAIR

In her entire life, Clare had never stepped into a tavern. An unusual feat considering how her father considered the pub an extension of home. But Grandma Ella always told her a lady shouldn't enter a place where drink eroded the character and restraint of men.

For Clare, it reminded her of all she detested in her father: his anger, his drowning in bitterness, and his cruelty to her mother and siblings. She found nothing amusing nor admirable in Seamus's antics, even though he wore his patronage of stout as a badge.

Yet upon entering the Shamrock's Lair, Clair was surprised to experience a surging spirit of adventure. There was something about being away from home in an establishment full of lost souls, villainous characters, and treasure-eyed travelers that gave her an odd sense of merry fellowship.

This brief euphoria was stunted as a wave of warm, moist air met her nostrils, the musty smells of spilled beer, spoiled seafood, and body odor.

Clare felt as if every gnarled face was ogling her as she entered, and she clung to Pierce's arm for protection. He escorted her to the back of the room, close to a fire that vibrated with voluptuous dances.

Pierce flopped his two packs against the brick wall. "Ah. I'll never feel me shoulders again." They sat on two tall, knotty oak stools. "Your brother done me good this time."

Clare was preoccupied. "Did we spend foolishly? We're nearly drained." Clare rubbed the muscles on her back where the straps of her bag had pressed.

The redhead pulled up another stool and used it to prop his feet to tie his muddy boots. "The passage requires two months of supplies. We may be short, in fact."

"Isn't that part of our passage? Don't they feed us properly?" Clare's scalp burned and she dug at it with her nails.

Pierce waved at the matron, who seemed too pleased to ignore him. "Some moldy bread and perhaps a taste of briny, old cod. My father said to bring our own or starve."

"With the cost of those tickets, you'd expect meals served on silver."

"Expectations. Hah! You better shake those." Pierce shot up his hand. "Miss, do you think we could get some attending?"

The haggard woman approached with a rising fury and a bosom bursting from the seams of her apron. "Well, aren't you a chappy, young fellow? And supposing you mend your manners, or you can get your attending elsewhere."

"There's no hurry," Clare said.

"We'll have two of the house stews, a couple of dark pints, and a cup of tea for the lady." Pierce canted his head. "Could you bring some crackers as well?"

"Oh. You'll get your crackers." The woman spun and weaved away through the crowd.

Placing her arms on the table, Clare felt stickiness and retreated. In a spill of some prior patron's beer, a flying insect flailed in an effort to free itself. She used her finger to slide the pool and its unfortunate swimmer off the side of the table.

There was a holler from the other end of the bar, and two rogues began to shove one another as a half-clad woman, the evident target of their dispute, pleaded for peace with drunken shrills.

Clare shuddered, silently thanking Grandma Ella for her counsel. "Is this how they all are?"

"What?"

"You know?" She waved her eyes across the room.

Pierce laughed. "These taverns? Oh. The night's early. Just coming to life. It gets much better."

"Lovely. Something to look forward to."

The stout and tea arrived shortly, and between sips they entertained themselves by observing the theater of the room. Soon, their waitress slammed down two overflowing bowls of mackerel stew, which was rich and flavorful.

All the while Clare sensed Pierce had serious conversation to broach, and she parried it with light commentary as long as possible, hoping her brother would arrive to claim his stool and drink.

"What about you?" he finally said, his voice cracking.

"What about me?"

"What we're doing. This voyage. What are you hoping for?"

This was a question Clare hadn't thought much of until now. She knew there was an answer more complex and truthful but instead replied, "I hope my journey brings me home soon. Back to family. Isn't that your desire as well?"

Pierce gazed at her deeply, then laughed quietly, looking into his mug for strength.

"It's dusk," Clare spurted. "Where's my brother?"

"You remember the day. You know. Little Kevan."

A flush spread across her body, the one she experienced every time she thought of her brother's drowning.

"Seamus—"

She broke in. "That's not kind remembering."

"Wait," Pierce said, with eyes watering. "It's been years for me to mention. To tell you this."

Clare nodded.

Pierce ran his finger around the lid of his glass. "The way you covered for Seamus. I'll never forget that day."

"I wish you would. It was no favor to Seamus. My father would have killed him had he known Seamus was supposed to be minding Kevan for me." Clare felt the turgid emotions of her past surfacing. "I knew my father would merely hate me for it."

Pierce handed her a handkerchief, and she snatched it and wiped her tears away.

"Only you know this, Pierce Brady, and if you care for me, for Seamus, you won't mention this again."

"Yes," Pierce breathed. "I was there." He took a drink of his stout, then wiped his mouth with the back of his hand, which was shaking. "I saw courage in you that day. A kindness. Far beyond your beauty. That's when I knew."

A sinking came over Clare's stomach and she felt trapped at the table. What was it about Pierce that made her feel so uncomfortable? He was strong and kind enough in spirit and wasn't the only one who fancied her. Was she destined to be a spinster due to her own obstinacy?

"I have strong feelings for you, Clare, that I can't deny. I don't wish to deny any longer."

Some commotion and a braying of laughter emanated from

the front of the tavern and Clare was grateful for the distraction. She strained her neck to see above the thickening crowd.

Above the tangled fray of arms heavy in conversations, a man leapt onto the bar and waved and clamored for attention. He was short enough to stand erect without hitting his graying head on the ceiling, but when he spoke, his voice bellowed through the cacophony.

"Here ye, ladies and kind sirs." When few minded him, he raised the sound a level and slapped his palm on the ceiling. "Your attention for a wee moment. May we converse? I'll keep it ever so brief."

A shout came from the back of the room. "Sit down, you old beggar."

Unmoved, the man continued. "A few tender words and I'll be gone. I am here to present to you the great Captain James Starkey . . ."

Feral laughter splattered the room as fingers pointed at the captain, an ancient man who stood beside his presenter, dressed sharply in all of Her Majesty's full naval regalia.

"Skipper. Has the sea given you back your wits?"

Eruptions of heckling ensued.

Clare's heart sank for the old man, who looked like a character pulled from the pages of so many perilous books she devoured. In his stoicism, with the medals on his jacket preening, he appeared undamaged by the insults. Either he was shielded by the kindness of senility or perhaps had fought too many greater battles against tempests, whales, and pirates.

The barker pounded on the ceiling again. The crowd silenced itself, possibly seeking more fodder for their cruel mockery. "We are most pleased to announce the fortuitous availability of nearly a dozen places on the *Sea Mist*, leaving dock for open waters in the morning. She's a sound brigantine, this one, with a proud history as a once-esteemed member of the royal fleet."

"It should be called the *Sea Bottom*," someone shouted.

"Make sure you go down with 'er, old man."

The patrons grumbled and waved arms at them in disinterest, returning to their own conversations.

Fighting obscurity in the clatter, the barker shouted, "We break at dawn, to a land of opportunity. Wealth, jobs, and a better life awaits you!"

"Get down, you old blowhard!" was heard as a few wrestled the man down from the counter to the floor.

Clare felt for the man and his captain, but something shifting toward her in the crowd stole her attention. Straining to see around the mass of bodies, she saw a familiar green jacket, tall hat, and unmistakably bouncy gait. Pence. And after meeting her gaze, he burrowed his way through with even more determination.

"Well. Look who's here to collect his due," Clare said, and turned to see Pierce shifting from doleful contemplations.

"I'll square up with the boy for you," Pierce said in a defeated tone.

"Miss Clare, Miss Clare," Pence burst out as he approached.

She reached into her purse and started to sift through her coins. "I know, Pence. My brother treated you shamefully . . ."

"No, Miss Clare." He took off his hat, pulled a dirty handkerchief from his coat pocket, and wiped the sweat off his brow. His breathing was heavy. "I'm not here to settle. It's the other man. Your brother, right?"

Clare's pulse soared. "What about my brother?"

He lofted her pack on his shoulder. "Come, Miss Clare. We shan't tarry. He's in the thickets, he is."

*Chapter* 10

# GAME OF CHANCE

Out of the dank warmth of the Shamrock's Lair, they splashed into the coolness of a moonless night. As Pence sped through the dimly lit roads like a jackrabbit through a country field, Clare labored behind under the burden of Seamus's pack, which was much heavier than hers.

Racing through the city toward the harbor, Clare worried for a moment that Pence might be misleading them toward a retaliatory ambush. She saw justice in this possibility but didn't believe it to be in the boy's character.

"Where are you taking us?" Pierce appeared less convinced of the purity of their guide's motives.

"Come," Pence pleaded. "There is no time for gabbery. Miss Clare, tell your friend. We may be too late as it 'tis."

The seriousness of his tone convicted Clare and apparently Pierce as well as they trailed without further protest the remainder of the way. They dodged horse carriages, late-night romancers, and a scattered army of miscreants who swaggered, peered from alleyways, and ogled them conspiratorially as the three scurried by them.

As they went deeper in their journey, Clare smelled the fishy odors of the approaching shores, and the lonely echoes of night gulls increased in intensity. Pence banked off the main road, sifting through darker, decrepit alleyways, prompting her suspicions to return.

At last, as they neared a corner, Pence halted, motioned them to a stop, and signaled for silence.

"Pence saw your brother in that building," whispered the boy. "Don't be seen or they'll skin us all."

Clare processed the severity of his words as she peered around the corner, gasping to recover her breath. Filtering through walls, into the streets, was the cruel waggery of drunken rogues. The two-story building was a brooding residence, with ragged fabric flapping from the windows. It leaned like a hunchback in pain, needing only a strong gust to topple it to ruins. A flickering light shone mutely through filthy glass, causing the figures inside to appear as distorted apparitions.

"Where is Seamus?" Clare asked.

"Not certain. Been following your brother. Yes. Sorry, Miss Clare. Looking for the chance to take what he owed Pence."

"That's not to blame," she said.

"Not long when he came to port, Pence saw 'em being met by the O'Donnell brothers."

"Who are they?"

"Thieves of the worst sort," Pence said. "Swindling the farmies is sport to 'em. Cruel as you can imagine."

"What was Seamus doing here?" Pierce said.

"Cards. Bones. Games of chance. Doesn't matter. Just a cat

toying with the mouse. Not sure why they don't rob 'em and be done with it."

Pierce put his hand on his forehead. "He had all of our passage fare."

"Don't even whisper that," Clare said. "The trip will be ruined."

"We'll be finished. We got to take it back."

The boy grabbed him by the arm. "You didn't hear Pence. He might be dead, and you'll be too. As well as Miss Clare."

Just then the wooden door of the building creaked open, and two men with lanterns argued as they headed toward them.

"Hide!" Pence whispered urgently. "They're coming."

Pierce ushered Clare toward a crevice in the alleyway, which offered barely enough space for them to tuck in with their packs. Once settled, Clare was horrified to see Pence reclining against the wall with his arms folded, the pack he was carrying for her beside him.

The rancor approached.

"You're a liar and you always have been. There was no less than twenty quid on the table the other day, and if Billy knew you pinched him, he'd run you through and pull out your guts. I'm inclining to tell 'em meself."

The two figures rounded the corner into view, illuminated by the lantern held by the man who was speaking; who was stocky, bald, and raven faced.

"Who goes there?" he said, startled by Pence. "Why are you lurking about?"

"It's just the orphan boy," said the other man, whose face was scarred from eye to lip.

"It's just Pence, Mr. O'Donnell," the boy said to the bald man while stepping into their light.

Mr. O'Donnell grasped Pence by the collar and put a knife to his neck. "Wanna join your mam and pa?"

Clare could feel Pierce's muscles tensing, and she held him back with all her strength while fighting her own instinct to leap to the boy's defense.

"I'm just here to collect what's due," the boy said with surprising calm.

Mr. O'Donnell spat out a hacking laugh at Pence's gravitas. "Due to you? We owe you something, laddie?"

"No sir." Pence edged his neck away from the blade. "It's the farmie. The man named Seamus. He owes five pence, he does."

"Is that so?" Mr. O'Donnell grinned as he put his knife in his pocket. "What's in the pack?"

"It belongs to the farmie. Pence is keeping it 'til he pays."

Mr. O'Donnell snickered and with a wave the scarred man grabbed the pack. "We'll help you keep him honest, laddie."

Clare sighed deeply. Her entire life was in that bag. But it was the least of her worries.

"Would you mind tellin' me where Pence can find him then?"

The scarred man knocked Pence's hat off. "We'll ask the questions."

"Ah. We'll give you that, orphan," Mr. O'Donnell said. "For a few pence, 'tis all."

"That's what he owes me." Pence seemed conflicted but relented, pulling out a leather pouch and beginning to count out some coins before it was yanked from his grasp.

"The fee went up a wee bit, if you don't mind." The bald man nodded to his companion, who flung Clare's pack over his shoulder. They departed, passing the nook where Clare and Pierce cowered breathlessly.

After a few steps Mr. O'Connell shouted back to Pence, his

voice echoing through the alleyway. "My brothers took your boy for a swim. Good luck getting paid."

The two of them cackled and returned to their bantering, which trailed as they faded from sight.

Clare leapt from the shadows and went over and smothered Pence with her arms and tears.

"I'm so sorry, Miss Clare. That was foolish for me to lose your pack."

"You're sorry?" Clare realized her body was quivering.

"I should have given them a good comeuppance," Pierce said.

"What did they mean about Seamus?" Clare asked.

"It's not good," the boy said. "Follow Pence." He grabbed Seamus's pack from Clare and flung it on his shoulders. "Don't worry, Miss Clare. Won't lose this one. Promise you. But if your brother is where I think, we must hurry."

They were on the run again, and without a pack, Clare had less difficulty keeping pace. She soon discovered they were only a few streets removed from the water's edge, and they gulped the viscous sea air as their labored breathing and heavy steps accompanied the screeching of gulls and the creaking of the great, shadowy skeletons of ships moored in the harbor.

Pence came to the entranceway of a long, wooden pier, and after shedding the pack on the ground, he hurtled down the rattling timbers with the tail of his coat flapping in the wind. Pierce dropped his pack as well, with Clare scampering right behind them.

When Pence arrived at the cap of the pier, he collapsed to his knees. And after peering over the edge, he turned toward them and waved frantically.

In a moment, all three were there to see a body hanging upside down, tethered to the pier by a frayed cord.

"Seamus!" Clare screamed.

The rope had been measured in such a way that his head was under the water. His only means of survival would have been to pull up with his legs to keep from drowning, but it appeared the fight was gone.

Her anger at Seamus for his foolishness vanished with the thought of his suffering. "Please, dear God. Let him be alive."

Pence and Pierce grunted under the strain of pulling up Seamus's lifeless body and Clare tried to as well, but there was no room for her until the hem of his pant legs were in reach. And with her assistance, they had his cold form on the splintered planks of the dock.

Clare wrapped her arms around him, desiring to give him every last breath of her warmth as they untied the rope from his ankles. "God. I beg You. Don't forsake me."

She stroked Seamus's cheeks and kissed him on the forehead. Even with her uncontrollable sobbing, she could smell the reek of whiskey, which gave her hope he was breathing.

A noise came from his chest and then Seamus gurgled before water and then vomit spewed from his mouth. It was a joyous sight to Clare, and she tilted his head to the side. His pale flesh was frigid to the touch.

"Get me a blanket," she shouted.

"There's a bonfire over there." Pence pointed behind them.

Clare followed the trace of his finger and saw the lapping tongue of a distant fire lighting the darkness. With a clumsy start, and having to readjust their grip several times, they lumbered down the pier and onto the shoreline in the direction of the flames, nearly dropping Seamus several times.

As they approached, she saw a rudimentary camp had been erected on a grassy hill just above the woodworks of the harbor. Peppered around were several dozen slumbering on the ground, but a few remained awake and huddled around a diminishing fire. The startled faces, their eyes glistening as gems in the light of flames, soon arose to assist them, and in a few moments, Seamus was close to the heat and wrapped in wool, with many caretakers looking down at him with concern.

Several attended to stoking the flames with pieces of flotsam gathered from the waters. Clare leaned over Seamus and caressed his face with her hand and fallen tears. He was groggy but color appeared to be returning, and he struggled to open his eyes.

"Here is some hot tea," said a woman with broad shoulders and a bent to her hip. Clare received the mug, which was warm to the touch.

"Help me sit him up," Clare said without pause for manners.

The woman chided her companions. "Shame on all of us. We should have aided the boy."

"Muriel, dear. Your words are true." A man with ever-smiling puffy cheeks had eyes of remorse. "We thought it proper to keep out of it."

"And because of our cowardice?" Muriel said. "The poor boy's nearly gone."

"It was far away," the man said, this time for Clare's ears. "We heard shouts, but it was hard to see. Still, we knew someone was in trouble. If we were in our own town, I suppose."

"It's a grievous excuse." Muriel shook her head. "You're welcome here now."

A young man came with a stack of blankets and laid them beside Clare.

"I understand." Clare looked at Muriel. "We would have behaved the same." She put the mug to Seamus's lips. "Drink," she urged him and he did.

Muriel pulled some cheese curds from her pocket and handed them to Clare. "I'll stay up with our visitors," Muriel said to the others. "Off to bed, you all. Long day tomorrow and maybe the Lord will forgive us."

They were tired enough to acquiesce, and with Pence and Pierce returning to the pier to retrieve their packs, Clare and Muriel were alone to tend to Seamus.

"Clare."

"Seamus!"

"Clare. I lost it all, didn't I?"

"Rest now. It doesn't matter."

"Clare. Why didn't you let me drown?"

"Shhh." She ached for her brother. "Not another word."

"It's what I deserved, isn't it?" He spoke with hollowness in his voice. "Perfect that way, don't you think? You should have left me."

Seamus closed his eyes and soon he was sobbing, and Clare cried with him. Muriel wrapped an arm around her.

Oh, why did she ever leave home?

## Chapter 11

# THE SHORES OF CORK

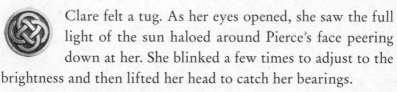 Clare felt a tug. As her eyes opened, she saw the full light of the sun haloed around Pierce's face peering down at her. She blinked a few times to adjust to the brightness and then lifted her head to catch her bearings.

Seeing Seamus beside her revived the horror of the prior evening, and she leaned over to see how he was faring. He was sleeping deeply with his usual snore. But despite a swollen eye and a cut on his nose, there was little evidence of last night's tragedy. Although plagued with misfortune, often wrought from his own hands, Seamus was always resilient.

Clare peered around her and discovered the entire camp had vacated without much of a trace.

"You two slept through it all," Pierce replied to her unspoken question. "Dozens of them, whole families all but trudging on your head."

"Is that so?" She sat up and stretched her arms.

"Yes. And I think we should go with them."

"Go with them where?"

"They're taking passage on a ship leaving this morning and they told me there was room left, but not much to spare."

"Pierce. We have nothing left. No money. It's lost."

"I told you already." Pierce helped Clare to her feet. "My father gave me plenty for provisions. We're down a good bit, it's true, but I have enough to get us on that ship, I believe. We've already got supplies."

"I have no bag. Nothing left. We're too much of a burden, my brother and me. But you go. For all of us."

"No," Pierce said sternly. "I want to do this for you, Clare. For you and your family. More than anything I've ever wanted. You can't refuse me. Not this time."

Clare felt itching in the back of her scalp. She scratched deeply as her mind spun through her options. What good would it be to limp back to Liam without a penny? The Hanleys would be ruined. She was the family's hope, as bleak and onerous as that sounded.

"Are you certain?"

"I've never been more sure." Joy filled Pierce's face and he picked up both his and Seamus's bags. "We gotta go. We can't miss that ship."

"What about him?" She pointed to her brother.

"He'll have two months to sleep. We just need to get him aboard. That's all."

"I don't think he's fit."

"Listen, Clare. You know your brother well enough. As soon as he gathers himself, he's going to go back to those men to try to get his money back. And he'll be dead for his efforts."

There was no denying this logic. Pierce was right. They

needed to get Seamus out of Cork and right away wasn't soon enough.

Pierce bent down and shook Seamus gently. "Hey, old boy. Up with you. There's a ship full of young ladies calling your name."

Clare reached down and together they lifted Seamus to his feet, and as he rose, he pushed them away.

"I can carry meself just fine." He rubbed his temples.

"With haste," Clare said, surprising herself how quickly she had been persuaded to Pierce's reasoning.

"Where to?" Seamus yawned.

"We've got passage for a ship that may have left," Pierce said.

"But it's all gone . . ."

"We'll explain it all later but we must go."

Seamus reached to get his bag from Pierce, but Clare interceded. "Let me haul it just until your strength finds you."

"Where's your pack?" he asked gruffly, but she chose not to answer.

They trotted and soon turned around a bend of the shore into a burst of activity along the harbor lined with massive piers and hulking timbered vessels. The sun had only newly risen, but the roads spilling up to the docks were already overflowing with droves of people emptying from horse-drawn carriages and pushing hand wagons. They meshed with the longshoremen and sailors unloading and lifting in bulging cargo of barrels and wooden crates and vegetables. Pigs and children engaged in a tapestry of dance on land as did sailors on the rigging and the seagulls, terns, and herons in the sky.

The three stopped and stood in awe of the majestic ships that stood before them. Beautifully crafted wood giants, with masts reaching heavenward and sails prepared to unfurl with full glory. Ropes as thick as a man's thigh threaded with a seamstress's touch. Crews pranced from crow's nest to boom with urgent artistry.

"Come on," Pierce said, pulling them out of their trance.

"Which one is it?" Clare just stepped out of the way of a woman shoving a cart so full of strange objects it appeared she stacked the full contents of her home.

"The woman from last night . . ." Pierce began.

"Muriel."

"Yes. Muriel said to go to where the dock ends, and there we'd find them."

The energy of the shores and the sudden fear they would be left behind hastened their step, and they proceeded through the congestion in full pursuit. Finally, just as Clare thought they had run out of dock, they rounded a corner and a sight sprung up that caused her to slow in dread.

Before them was a creaking, retched mass of ancient wood, held together by moss, barnacles, and frazzled ropes. The hull of the vessel was weathered, waterlogged, and blackened by the battering of salt water, and there were scars where cannonballs had once breached. The sails were yellowed and quilted with patches, and the masts had a bow to them that made them almost smile with sadness. It was a once-proud warrior, tyrannized in its submission to commerce.

On the side of the ship were faded painted letters that read *Sea Mist*, and Clare quickly spotted Captain James Starkey himself overseeing the clamoring of crew and passengers, in full uniform with his arms folded tightly behind his back.

"Well," Pierce said. "Should we wait for another ship?"

"I'm afraid if we don't get on now, we'll never go," Clare said.

A woman's voice railed from the deck, and Muriel waved a red handkerchief. "Hurry," she shouted, and others beside her were beckoning them as well. Some of the crew were beginning to untie the mooring. They were out of time.

"Let's go," Pierce said.

Suddenly, Clare's apprehension gave way to concern of whether they could force their way through the horde of well-wishers before the ship launched.

Pierce led the way and took the brunt of disgruntled looks and cursing as he shoved people out of the way. Clare tried to apologize to each of them as she followed but soon abandoned it in futility. Finally they arrived at the walkway leading to the ship just as the gate was being closed.

"Wait for us!" Pierce shouted.

The porter at the gate wore a ragged blue shipmate's uniform that was inadequate in containing his belly. His face looked as if it had been crammed into a glass jar. "All right. Three of you? Thirty pounds."

"Thirty?" Pierce said with exasperation, and Clare could tell he was calculating what he had. "Fine." He threw down his bag and fished out his money, fumbled through his bills, and handed it somewhat reluctantly to the outstretched hand.

They lifted their bags, and with both relief and defeat, they started forward when the porter raised his hand.

"The lass. Why is she scratching?"

Clare glanced around in expectation he was speaking to someone else.

"Yes. You. Come here."

Reluctantly, Clare moved forward and the man with cracked, stubby fingers lifted the back of her hair and leaned in with bulbous eyes to examine her. Clare's body writhed inside in embarrassment and with a sense of violation.

"Hmmm." The porter's brow wrinkled and he pursed his lips.

"What is it?" Pierce asked.

"She needs to shave her head," the porter said.

"What?" Clare took a step back.

"You're teeming with head bugs, my dear. Captain's orders. No one comes on board with lice. The health and safety of our passengers, you know."

"She's not shaving a single hair on her head," Pierce spat out.

The porter handed the money back. "Do you want it all back, or just for the lady's passage?"

Why this? Why me? Clare resisted the temptation to scratch her hair, but now with the knowledge of her affliction, her scalped burned brighter. Her mind flashed back to her stay at the Wayfarer's Inn and that mold-specked filthy pillow.

There was a part of Clare that wanted to shave it all off and be rid of the parasites. But the idea of losing her hair? How long would it take to grow back? She fought back a sob. Would this ruin any chance she had of meeting the man she dreamed would share her life?

The tension of the moment gave Clare little time to think, and she began to panic. It was clear the ship would leave without her—and soon if she didn't make a decision.

She took a deep breath and slowly released it. "Where do I go?" she asked the porter in a wavering voice.

He pointed to a short distance down the dock where a man was sweeping up hair. She left without delay.

"Clare, no!" Pierce shouted behind her.

"You don't need to do this," Seamus said. Clare wasn't expecting to hear from her brother.

She worked her way along the edge of the pier, and the barber greeted her with a nod as she slunk into his chair, streams of tears coursing down her face.

Without a word he came around behind her and started with scissors, grinding as close to her scalp as possible, presumably to preserve the length of her hair to sell at its highest value. Then he lathered up her stubble and skillfully drew a blade from one end to the other.

Clare closed her eyes and tried to imagine the faces of Caitlin, Ronan, and Davin to keep her mind off of the agony and shame of the moment. Not only was she pained by the idea of being stripped of her dignity in such a public fashion, but with each cut, Clare felt the barber was taking away much of who she was. How could she feel that way? She had always believed herself to be above the shackles of vanity.

Then she felt warm water, the patting of a towel, and it was done.

"Did you want to see, child?" the barber asked gently, with a looking glass in his hand.

"No," she whispered. She reached her hand to the top of her head and felt the smoothness of flesh, still warm from the washing. Wiping away her tears, she saw a familiar face peering at her.

"How much did they pay for your hair, Miss Clare?"

"Pence." She laughed and cried at the same time, glad to see the boy.

He tilted his head. "Pence preferred you with less skin."

He made her smile, which she was in desperate need of. "I'm afraid we owe you money we haven't to pay."

"No matter, Miss Clare."

"I wish you were coming with us."

"Maybe Pence will go next time."

She gave him a hug as if he were her own Davin, her own Ronan. "Be well, Pence. You are a fine, young gentleman."

Clare felt an arm on her shoulder. She turned to see Seamus with an expression of gratitude and compassion she had never seen from him before. He took off his hat and placed it on her head.

"Are you ready for a new journey?" His eyes were beginning to show life again. "I know I am."

In a matter of moments they were on board. The ship was lurching away from the slip, and with seeming complaints from every plank of wood, the old vessel pressed away from shore as passengers and those they were leaving behind waved tearfully and exchanged hearty cheers and whistles.

As the ship drifted beyond the vision of their loved ones and the island they called home began to diminish against the horizon, somberness came over the passengers. A remnant of elation remained about the idea of seeking out a place unknown, a better life, and world of opportunity. But also sinking in was the permanence of a decision to surrender to the arms of the ocean and the fates before them, and that their lives would never be the same.

A man with a fiddle began to play tunes of Ireland, tunes of joy and the unshakable resolution of its people. They sang and some danced, lifting their skirts, locking arms, and spinning as the crew trimmed the sails and looked down from above.

A small girl dragged her grandmother by the hand and began to dance with the others. The girl spun and hopped with a face so full of bliss, she charmed all of those around her, who smiled and clapped as much for the gray-haired woman who labored to keep up with her grandchild's mirth.

Not comprehending why, Clare felt a sense of relief in the expression of joyful anticipation of the journey ahead. There was power in the idea there would be no turning back, and it helped erase the pain she faced in getting here today.

But before long, the only music being requested were the sad songs of a broken people with a history of shattered dreams in a world of cruelty and disappointment, and the melancholy returned.

In earshot of the music but out of sight of the others, Clare leaned up against the rails and peered into the infinite sea before her, as the wind lapped against her face, drying the tears of remorse from her eyes.

She mourned the fleeting Emerald Isle that was now but a thin, black strip barely above the water's edge. Clare blinked, and the ocean swallowed up what remained of the land and life behind her.

They were off to America.

## Chapter 12

# THE WHALE'S BELLY

Merely two weeks into the transatlantic voyage aboard the *Sea Mist*, Clare discovered the iniquities of the life she hoped she left behind had followed her aboard the ship.

There were those who lived above and those who dwelled below.

When they weren't sequestered in their tiny cabins, the few privileged passengers hovered in the restricted forecastle area at the front of the ship, clinging to the modicum of pretension and entitlement available. In a ship originally designed for open sea battles, there were few luxuries retrofitted in the vessel, with perhaps the most treasured being the boundary between the general citizenry and the impoverished ones in the bowels of the steerage section.

Down below in the stench-filled cargo hull, a rumor was spreading there was sunshine above, something distributed as scarcely during this winter journey as food and water.

As fleeting as this chance for fresh air and needed chores could be, a scramble was afoot. In the dim light of rationed candles, the cramped passengers pushed their way to the ladder leading above, with curses and raised fists. They gathered soiled clothing, overflowing chamber pots, and food to cook on the few stoves available above deck.

They funneled through the narrow aisle, with three rows of wooden shelves protruding from the walls on either side, serving as crude bed frames. Filthy straw mattresses lay on them, as well as scattered clothing and moth-eaten blankets. In the knotting of scurrying legs, Clare tripped and bumped into the back of an older gentleman. "Beg your pardon."

"Mind your step!" There was anger in his gray-browed eyes, but down below, in such tight and miserable quarters, they were all ill-tempered, rats in a cage baring their teeth.

"Watch your tone with the lady." Clare turned to see Pierce pressing behind her.

Seamus was farther back in the crowd. He held up a few potatoes and shouted to them. "Get us in line for a boil."

"You'll wait for hours," grumbled a woman next to Clare. She held up a bag. "Might as well eat these oats raw. We could chew on the biscuits they give us, if we had no intentions for keeping our teeth."

Up front there was a shout and a clearing in the crowd.

As the line stopped, Pierce was now being shoved into Clare. "What happened?"

The woman turned and pinched her nose. "Oh, dear me. Someone spilled a stench pot. Ah, curse the life in the belly of the whale. That mad captain of ours deserves to be hung for this."

Pierce shouted up to those crawling up the ladder through the hatch to daylight. "Get up with you. Let us out."

A voice hollered back, "That's good on you, boy. I'll have one of these boots greet you when you come up."

Clare rubbed her temples, her head now aching from the anxiety and foulness in the air. Her only hope for comfort was for the days to pass quickly.

Several mornings later, well before dawn, Clare suffered such discomfort from the hardness of her cot, her back throbbed with pain. After turning dozens of times through the hours of the night and unable to find relief, she decided to go above deck.

She crept past the snores of the masses below and guided herself only by memory and the feel of her feet along the creaking floorboards. Clare finally reached out to the ladder and climbed up through the hatch, which moaned as it lifted. Above, in a moonless night, with a scattering of brilliant stars, she felt invigorated by this rare moment of aloneness.

The creaks of the masts, the flaps of the sails and the bending of the rigging in the wind, and the lapping of the waves added to an ambience that sent chills through her body. The cold of the night caused her to wrap her arms tightly around her chest. So silly. She should have brought a blanket.

In the background, as figures moving in the shadows, a small crew labored above and around her in silence, spiders moving among the web. At times, she would catch a face or see arms trimming a sail, and they would pass each other and converse. Clare reveled in the fact she had eluded their notice.

Looking over the port side, her thoughts meandered with the rise and fall of the ship in the massive emptiness of the dark waters. When had she ever felt so alive with freedom?

The smell of the ocean transported Clare back to a time in her youth. In happier days, she enjoyed a rare family excursion to the sea cliffs of Galway. Although she was only four at the time, the memory remained rich. Cool and crisp salted air, the craggy, moss-covered boulders, and endless views beyond a deep tapestry of churning blue.

Down on the shoreline, Clare and her older sister, Margaret, pranced in the waves among the swooping ballet of gulls, herons, and swans, as moist sand pressed between their bare toes.

Maggie, who was eight at the time, shone her familiar grin of mischief. "C'mon, will ya, Clare? Let's see how far the ocean goes."

"Ma says no." At age four, the waves raged tall and mighty and Clare would brave only as high as her ankles.

"Fine then, I'll go without you."

Maggie waved and then danced and yelped in the frigid chest-high waves and she pressed farther and farther. Above the chattering birds and the ocean's thunderous percussion, her rebellious laughter soared.

"Maggie!" With baby Seamus cradled in her arms, Ma screamed from the shoreline, waving her free arm, begging her oldest to shallower waters.

But Maggie merely leapt and spun in the deeper waters. She must have known her mother wouldn't brave the chilly waters to retrieve her. And Da was far down the shoreline, untangling his fishing line and presumably cursing at ocean spirits.

Years later, Maggie recaptured this adventure through one her many ink drawings, a particular favorite of Clare's, a sketch so precious she stored it in the pages of the Bible Grandma Ella gave her.

And now, peering into the emptiness, Clare reflected with some horror at the thought of Maggie's last moments as her ship sank to the bottom of the sea, her brilliant torch of life extinguished by the salt water amidst screams of anguish. The tragedy compounded in Clare's mind as she imagined her Uncle Tomas's desperate efforts to rescue Maggie, prior to succumbing himself to the ocean's cruel, cold arms.

Clare was angry with herself for drifting toward these forbidden thoughts as she had been enjoying the euphoria of solitude as master of the ship. In an effort to recapture the moment, she slipped toward the forbidden area of the forecastle, and the giddiness returned as she climbed the steps in purloined pleasure.

As her feet touched the floorboards, she felt elevated to the level of her elite shipmates. Imagining herself cloaked in a dress fashioned in Paris, she was about to mock a curtsy when she caught something askance. She froze.

Someone else was at the bow of the ship, gaping toward the distant lands ahead. The darkness obscured her view to where she could vaguely make out a shadow.

She saw a movement and realized it was someone drawing a cup of tea to his lips. As her eyes adjusted, she was horrified to realize she was looking at the backside of the captain, who other than a pair of boots was as naked as the day he was born.

He appeared to be unaware of her presence, enraptured by the endless horizon.

Clare stepped backward, ever so gingerly, crept down the stairs, and slid down the hatch.

*Chapter 13*

# THE TEMPEST

It took Clare three weeks before she mustered the courage to peer into a looking glass.

The silver-handled mirror was among the few supplies Pierce and Seamus had scavenged on her behalf from the other passengers. These included another dress, which nearly fit and only sported two patches, a brush with stubby bristles, and a yellowed handkerchief, which she used for all of her cleaning.

She was delighted the boys had taken her books out of her pack on the pig farmer's wagon—they were spared the thievery. They were a delight to have on the ship to whittle away the dreary hours below, even though it strained her eyes to read in the scarcity of light in the hull.

Most cherished was the journal and pen Seamus had bought off another passenger for her. She wrote of her experiences aboard the ship, described in lengthy detail passengers she found interesting, and crafted love letters to an imaginary man she hoped someday to meet.

But the possession she focused on now was the mirror gripped in her hand. Clare chastised herself for being as worried as she was about her appearance. *It's just hair.*

At the other end of the hull, the steerage congregants prattled about the impending storm. Hours ago, the tawdry decks had been cleared of all but crew, and the weary passengers were told to prepare for an extended period below hatch. Several were retching from the growing lurches of the *Sea Mist* and sprawled themselves in their straw mattresses, trying to take refuge in sleep.

A few, including Seamus and Pierce and some of their new-found kindred spirits, distracted themselves by playing cards or casting lots.

Some of the children challenged each other to remain standing on one leg as the great hull heaved in the waters, their resulting merriment grating against the overriding gloom.

Closing her eyes, Clare removed Seamus's wool cap, which had rarely left her head even as she slept. She positioned the mirror before her face and, after a moment, was resolved to brave what she would see. There in the flickering of candlelight, crystalline blue eyes, timid and weary, peered out of her soiled face. Extending the mirror farther away, she rubbed her hand over her short black hair, soft like that of a baby chick, covering her scalp.

Clare shifted to view her profile. "Not bad for a boy," she whispered.

When Clare pulled down the mirror, she was startled to see a small girl, no more than four years of age, gazing at her with fascination. This was the tiny dancer who along with her grandmother danced so merrily on the day the ship left dock. Since then, observing her from a distance, Clare had grown concerned as the trip was wearing on the little one. Her joy seemed to be fading, and in some ways Clare saw this as a troubling harbinger.

Reflexively, Clare hid the mirror and hastily put on Seamus's hat. "What's your name, little flower?"

The girl only clung tighter to a small, worn doll. Her scraggly, blonde hair reminded her of Caitlin at this age.

The *Sea Mist* jarred forward and Clare reached for the girl to keep her from falling. The ship steadied and Clare released the uneasy child.

"If you won't tell me your name, what about your mate's?"

The girl looked to the cloth doll in counsel and after some consideration spoke in a barely audible, breathy voice. "Mae."

"Mae. Why that's a lovely name. Which is befitting such a beautiful friend. I'm Clare. What do they call you, sweet one?"

She ran her tiny, dirty fingers through the yarn of Mae's head. "Lala."

"How pretty that is. Is Mae enjoying her voyage?"

Lala sized up Clare, as if to determine whether she was trustworthy. "She's sad."

"Mae is sad? That makes me want to cry. Why so sad?"

The girl gazed down at her doll with compassion. "She's hungry, and I don't have food for her."

"Oh my." Clare set a hand on her chest. "Well, it just so happens I have some to spare. And I'd be happy to share it with my new friend."

Lala's eyes lit up and Clare had to restrain herself from embracing her. She reached up for Seamus's bag, pulled out a cloth package, and unwrapped the thread that bound it. Pulling back the ends of the fabric, Clare was pleased to see the crackers were mostly intact. She held it out to Lala.

"I think it prudent if you were to taste some yourself, Lala. Just to make sure it will please Mae."

The girl nodded and smiled, and she received one with her slender, scabbed fingers. Lala put it to her mouth, eating it while eyeing Clare all the while.

"And you know what else I think? You should take all of these crackers because little Mae looks famished."

"Yes. She's very hungry," the girl whispered.

"Where's your ma?"

"Grandmama? She just sleeps."

"Oh. I see. Well. I hope you visit me again. I get lonely and could use a friend."

Lala nodded and turned, glancing back a couple of times as she navigated the lunges before folding into the gathering.

Clare couldn't help but think of her sister and brothers, and she felt deep longing. The thought of the *Sea Mist* taking her farther away from Ireland was too much to fathom. What wisdom was there in taking her so far from her family? Maybe her father just wanted her to leave.

Through the walls of the ship came a great clamor, raising gasps from the passengers until they realized it was the clatter of thunder. Within a few moments, a heavy pounding of rain against the deck ensued, and Clare lay on her cot, curling, as she tried to paint the faces of Davin, Ronan, and Caitlin in her mind.

But it was Lala's sad eyes Clare last imagined as she drifted to sleep.

It was another clap of thunder that awoke her sometime later and she sat up just as someone near her was igniting a lantern. Many still slept, but the sound had stirred enough of them so there was anxious movement emanating throughout the hull. The ship bucked as an angry horse, and another clatter arose causing a baby to cry. And then another.

Clare heard many praying and she did as well. These sounds

of petitions coalesced into more of a desperate chant as souls clung to one another as the dreary vessel surged through wave and wind, arms raised hopelessly in fending itself from the violent rage of the skies.

Above the heavenly angst came a malevolent noise that could only be the splintering of wood itself. *Phwacck!*

Several screamed and children cried and through the splashes of dim light below Clare could see nothing but faces of horror.

Something was terribly wrong. The ship was now tilting, and the frenzied shouting of men echoed from above deck.

In a fit of panic, a woman climbed up the ladder and pressed up against the door of the hatch screaming, "Let us out!" She pounded her fists with fury until a couple of men pulled her down with her arms flailing.

One man did climb to the hatch to test it, but he descended in defeat.

They were locked down.

# Chapter 14

# SEA COFFINS

The news was unkind. Part of the foremast had shattered and although the ship was not crippled, it would travel at a slower pace. The vessel was too far across waters to turn around, they were told, which meant rations would be halved in order to last the remainder of the journey.

But there was a greater tragedy. Ship fever had struck and nearly a third of the steerage passengers had already perished.

"Come now. Give her to me, will you?" Seamus looked at Clare with a somberness rarely seen on his face. He drew the tiny, limp body from Clare's arms and handed it to Pierce, whose eyes were crimson and moist.

Seamus put his arms around her trembling body and rested his head on her shoulder. "There was nothing you could do, Clare."

His words barely saturated her consciousness as her mind blurred over the past two weeks. The time Clare first noticed the gurgle in the girl's lungs was as she consoled her shortly after her grandmother's coffin plummeted into the sea. The two had become quickly bonded, as Lala represented those Clare had left behind.

Since then, the ship had long exhausted its supply of coffins, and instead bodies were merely wrapped in blankets. The long-winded ceremonies were shorter, blunted, and fewer had the strength to come above deck to even honor the deceased.

Death had become just another passenger.

The spread of typhus caused a further quarantine of the steerage passengers. Yet it also sapped the mind and spirit from foments of rebellion. They had grown dependent entirely upon the miserly mercies of their caretakers.

As she sobbed against Seamus's chest, Clare felt a tiredness deep within her soul. Her hands gripped onto her brother as if he was all that was keeping her from slipping into the depths of hades.

"We've got to take care of you now, Clare." His words reverberated through her pulsations of nausea.

When Clare opened her eyes, she felt the cool sea air against her body, and chills streamed through the core of her bones. Seamus's arms propped her, and the first mate's voice drifted in and out, ". . . ashes to ashes, dust to dust."

He signaled and then the tiny body was dropped over the side of the ship.

Lala was gone.

The imagery repeated over and over again and Clare couldn't escape it.

"She looks weak," she heard Pierce say, and then she awoke again in her cot as Seamus wiped a cool towel across her forehead.

"Shhh . . ." He brushed his hands across her cheeks.

Clare felt the toes of her feet curling into the moist grass of the fields at home and she was but a child and her ma chased behind laughing, gaining on her with every step. Clare turned and saw Ma's legs churning, her face spilling with joy.

"Don't leave us," she heard Pierce say and saw him holding a candle as he leaned in and kissed her on the cheek. She felt his lips, soft and tender, and Clare blacked out.

This time she relived the banished sounds of hysteria and instinctively she knew what had happened. She dropped the basket of elderberries and the tiny black orbs tumbled to the ground as she ran, pulse pounding as she summited the hill. Then stopped. She found Seamus bent over Kevan's lifeless body and Pierce's shouts frozen in horror.

"I took my eyes from the boy, no more than a blink," Seamus's shoulders shook as sobs ripped through him.

In a purity of thought beyond reason, in that moment of tragedy Clare could see the spirit sapping from her brother, and she knew with certainty what must be done.

She brought Kevan's cold, blue-lipped corpse to the house and watched as Ma glanced first with a smile, which transposed to terror as she sprinted toward Clare, screaming and clasping her hands to her ears.

When Clare looked down again, this time Lala, still and limp, was in her arms.

Clare choked on the pungent liquid in her mouth and opened her eyes. Muriel pulled a spoon from her mouth as her husband, Mack, leaned over her shoulder.

"Is she going to make it?" he asked.

"What if she hears you, you old fool?" Muriel replied.

The spinning and nausea returned, and it gyrated faster and faster and she fell deeper into the chasm.

And then it stopped.

Clare lay in the grass and, lifting her head, saw Caitlin, Ronan, and Davin just turning to leave.

Davin spun and looked back, his face red with anger.

"Come on." Caitlin put her arm around her brother's shoulders. "She's never coming back. She's never coming back."

Clare could only watch as they drifted away.

# Chapter 15

# WAVES OF LIBERTY

 "You know about sea justice. They'll kill for this, you fools." In near darkness, only a few flames flickered below, in the musty, putrid hull of the steerage. Muriel's face flashed in and out of the dim lighting as if oil flesh tones painted on a black canvas. Her anger and frustration contrasted with the gentleness of her hands as she tended to Clare, thin and frail, who lay beside her curled in a cot.

"Ah, Muriel, we've been through it with you several times." Mack held the rusted bucket of salt water out for his wife, and she dipped in a cloth, squeezed out the drippings, and placed it on Clare's forehead.

"The plan will work just fine." Seamus knelt beside Clare and placed the back of his hand on her cheek, which was warm to the touch.

"Where's the Tailor? Why isn't he here?" Pierce's expression was draped with concern.

Seamus couldn't remember ever seeing his sister in such a position of helplessness. She was always the one who bore the weight of the family, and the idea of her leaving him alone to fend off the cruelty of the world gripped him to the core. Clare was the only one who ever believed in him, even though he wasn't worthy of her belief.

"Can he be trusted?" Pierce's voice wavered. "He's an odd one."

"The Tailor? Bah! Having a shady fellow like that to be part of your scheming." Muriel stroked Clare's hand, which seemed ghostly even in the dimness.

"What you say may be true, but without him, the lock won't be picked." Mack placed the bucket on the floor and put on his jacket.

"If we don't get Clare more fresh water and better rations, she'll surely die," Seamus said. "And there's many lying here below suffering while they're up on deck fattening their bellies." He rose, tucked on his hat, picked up an iron bar, and started to tap it in his open palm. Seamus was growing irritated with Pierce. "Are you coming or not?"

"I'm just asking questions, 'tis all."

Muriel stood and embraced each of them, finishing up with Mack, whom she kissed on his broad lips. "You bring these lads back safe."

Seamus glanced back to Clare. Would he ever see her again?

Muriel must have construed his thoughts. "She'll be well tended. I won't leave from her side."

With a nod, Seamus turned and the two men trailed behind as he trudged his way past the sick, the discouraged, and the dying, and they extinguished any candles or lanterns upon passing. The Tailor was waiting for them at the ladder leading to the hatch, and even with a lack of illumination, his eagerness for their impending mischief was discernable.

His name was Brennan, but they all called him the Tailor because of the leather awl he carried with him wherever he went. As to his true profession, no one knew nor dared ask. Most conjectures were influenced by his shiftiness and the deep, black brows that roofed his darting eyes. Despite his ill nature, he managed to gain friends around the card table as his passion for gambling was far superior to his skill. Yet those who won often worried if the Tailor would recoup his losses one way or the other before the trip ended.

They crept up the ladder rungs and Seamus, who was in the lead, raised the hatch with care. With the lanterns and candles of the cabin silenced below, there was no escaping light to betray their assent. Instead, Seamus was surprised by the surge of cool air and a tuft of snow that fluttered by him to the floor.

This wasn't anticipated. As they stood on the deck and looked to their worn boots, which had sunk in at least six inches of powder, Seamus realized the flaw in their tactics.

"It's over," Pierce whispered, sounding almost relieved. "We've got to go back down."

The sky was filled with falling giant flakes that drifted down like chicken feathers. Seamus held out his hand to something he rarely witnessed in Ireland. "This will surely cover our tracks. We just need to be quick about it."

This made little sense, but Seamus moved forward, hoping they would follow and they did. The windless nature of the storm created an eerie calm, and only the crunching of their steps in the snow could be heard above the lapping of waves and creaking of brittle masts.

It was almost too quiet.

The clouds sealed out the moonlight and stars, and they were fully cloaked in the blackness of the evening. To this point, they had committed no crime or conspiracy. They were merely passengers seeking fresh air.

But with each step closer toward the front of the ship, they were angling toward incrimination, walking into the arms of a death sentence. Seamus feared turning back, to show any weakness or doubt in his intentions. Yet his ears were perked for the sounds of footprints trailing, and he was comforted to know he was not abandoned.

Finally, as if they had traveled a hundred miles, they arrived at the trapdoor to the bulkhead and strained to peer through the heavy snow and darkness in search of interlopers among the sails.

"Have they spotted us?" Mack rubbed his hands together and scanned the ship with straining eyes.

The Tailor hadn't waited for confirmation. He sunk to his knees into the snow and wiped away the white powder from the hatch. Then he pulled a couple of tools from a leather pouch dangling from his belt and began to work the padlock. His experience in these kinds of pursuits was confirmed when after only a few seconds, the lock snapped open, which sounded as if it were artillery shot from a cannon.

The plotters froze to absolute stillness, and they heard shouts in the distance. They stood, unwilling to move, for almost a full minute until they were certain the voices faded.

"They're just adjusting the sheets." The Tailor opened the hatch, and for the first time Seamus felt the noose tightening around his own neck. The deed was done and they would have no excuse other than the truth of their actions.

Apparently comfortable with such chicanery, the Tailor assumed the lead and stepped down below with Seamus now content to follow.

Seamus probed each rung of the ladder with his foot, the task made more difficult by the quivering of his knees and the hurriedness of his breath. He felt safer when Pierce, the last to descend, sealed the hatch above them.

There was the sound of a match being struck, followed by a burst of flame ripping through the darkness, and Mack's face peered from behind a freshly lit lantern. The cramped space around them seemed barren, although there was a scattering of stacked barrels, burlap sacks of food, and a few other provisions perched on cobwebbed shelves.

"They'll see the light through the cracks of the floorboards." Pierce jabbed at the ceiling.

"The snow should shield it well enough, I suppose," Mack said. "It won't serve us at all to be blind."

"Then let's be done with it," Pierce said, the panic rising in his voice.

"Settle yourself, boy." Mack's voice was terse. "Let's finish what we came for, calmly."

"Just grab something." Pierce reached down and hoisted a sack of oats over his shoulder.

The Tailor was fumbling his way to the back of the storage area.

"What's he doing?" Seamus asked of Mack.

"Oh. The Tailor's seeking the captain's prize."

"He's here for whiskey?"

"I believe he's joined us for amusement, if you ask me." Mack picked up a bag with his free hand.

"I think I heard something." Pierce's face in the lantern light splashed fear.

Mack blew out the lantern, and they stood motionless to hear any creaks from above. That was, everyone except the

Tailor, who continued to stumble in the dark, obviously refusing to give up his search.

There was a clatter, and with his eyes adjusted to the dimness, Seamus saw Pierce scurrying up the ladder.

"Wait!" Seamus tried to reach for Pierce's ankle, but with a kick Seamus was eluded and the redhead burst through the hatch, abandoning all efforts at stealth. With only one way out, there was nothing left to do but chase behind in haste.

Seamus knew something was amiss when the hatch lifted to reveal a glow from above. Just as his head cleared the opening, he saw many of the ship's crew forming a circle around the opening, bearing lanterns, pistols, swords, and saps.

He recoiled, but arms reached down and yanked him through the hatch. His lip ruptured as it collided with a hinge, and with everything spinning around him, he was tossed facedown on the frigid deck and a cold, wet boot pressed on the back of his neck, suffocating him in the snow.

In a frenzy, Seamus struggled to lift his head to free his airway, and then pain seared through his skull, and it all turned black.

## Chapter 16

# THE PLANK

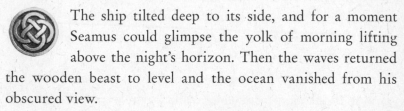The ship tilted deep to its side, and for a moment Seamus could glimpse the yolk of morning lifting above the night's horizon. Then the waves returned the wooden beast to level and the ocean vanished from his obscured view.

But the morning air was warming and he was alive, which considering the evening he survived, was no small miracle.

Seamus tried to determine how many hours he had been in this outdoor prison, shackled against the side walls of the *Sea Mist*. Only now as dawn began to saturate the sky did he realize his snowy tomb was brightly splattered with crimson, as if before him lay a freshly slaughtered lamb. Was it his blood? He tried to raise his hand to touch his throbbing head, but the clanking of his rusted irons reminded him of his fettering.

It pained him to do so, but he turned to his side and saw Pierce bent over, his red hair crusted with snow. Billows of steam rose with each exhale from his blue lips. Pierce stared vacantly at the ground while rocking back and forth in sways of madness.

Seamus craned his neck to his other side to see Mack appearing lifeless, leaning forward while manacles held his arms behind him in grotesque fashion.

Beyond Mack's twisted body, off a fair distance to himself, Brennan sat with aloofness to their circumstances as one sitting beside a creek on a summer day.

Soft flakes fluttered in the wind and Seamus was struck by the irony of his current situation. It brought him back to a day he so often tried to purge from his memory.

From that day when he was a child of seven, he still experienced the searing pain of his father dragging him to the shed by his ear, while his arms flapped to keep his balance.

"You say you milked her, did you? Well, let's just see for ourselves."

There was nothing Seamus could say at this moment. His mind spun through every imaginable way to escape his predicament, but none found its mark.

Inside the shed, his father flung Seamus down to the hoofs of the cow, and shortly thereafter a metal bucket bounced to him. "Go ahead, boy. Give her a pull. Show me she's dry as you say, and you'll be back warm inside cuddling with your sisters."

Seamus looked up at his father with a pitiful expression blending guilt and a desperate call for mercy. But there was none coming. "I suppose I didn't milk her too much."

His father smacked the side of Seamus's head and the blow provoked sobs, which would only make things worse. He was snapped up by the collar and dragged across straw and excrement to the water trough.

His da's face flashed anger. "We'll learn you about telling the truth."

The back of Seamus's neck was thrust downward, and then he was underwater for what seemed a long time, gagging and gasping before being pulled back up by his hair.

"There, drink up, boy. Lap it like the lying dog you are. Do it before I drown you."

His throat swelled and he cringed. Seamus believed his da good to his threat. There was no use adding to the flames of his father's fury. Seamus licked at the water and fought back the tears.

His father bent down close to his ear. "Now, boy. What happens to a heifer when she misses her milking and gets the swell? Keep drinking! Remember what I told you? You can break her, you know. 'Cause of your idleness? Starve us all? Your ma. Your brothers. Your sisters. Why we feed you, I wouldn't know."

His father now held a tin cup to Seamus's mouth and poured the muggy water down his gullet until he gagged.

"Drink!"

"I'm trying, Da."

"Drink!"

After the third cup of water, the contents of Seamus's stomach rose to his throat. Gripping the back of Seamus's neck, his father stood him up, guided him out the door, and took him through the flurry of whiteness to the side of the barn where he was pushed down into a sitting position in a bank of snow.

"Now, let's give you some time on your own so you can see how it feels." His father started to stomp away and then turned. "And don't move an inch, or I'll come back and give you the rod. You hear me, boy?"

Seamus was terrified of his father's eyes so he stared down and listened as the steps crunching in the snow faded and the front door slammed.

He drew in a jagged breath. Now he could cry.

Why would he do such a thing when his mother was out of town? Must he be so lazy? Why didn't he just milk the cow?

The cold bristled his face and moved from his hands to his arms, feet to legs, and then to the core of his quivering body. Even worse, as minutes seemed to be hours and an hour to be a day, the water traveled through his body, and the agony swelling in his bladder brought unbearable pain.

The fear of his father returned when the door of the house opened again, but Clare approached with a red plaid blanket in her hand.

Clare covered him with the blanket, and he felt wrapped in her kindness. "Da's down for a nap before he goes to the pub," she said. Clare tried to console him with a smile, clouded with sadness for him.

But his sister arrived too late. For even in the dimming of dusk, Seamus couldn't hide from his shame as the yellow circle he sat in gave testimony to his surrender.

"Shhh . . . shhh . . . you," she said. "Come. Let's get you warm and out of these clothes."

He rose with stiffness. "What about Da?"

Clare tucked her long black hair behind her ear, her crystal blue eyes soft and reassuring. "Grandma Ella says God watches over us when we're scared. Here, take my hand."

She took the lead while he shrank behind in terror and embarrassment. They managed to get in the house, and he changed his clothes and climbed safely into bed before their father rose that evening. But Seamus never forgot her strength and fearlessness in the storm.

And now here he was today. Bound. Helpless. Failing her and once again proving his father right. He would never forgive himself if she died.

He looked over again to Pierce and gave him a push with his foot. "Pierce. Pierce."

It took another nudge, but then his friend lifted his head and looked at Seamus with a stranger's eyes. "Is the Tailor dead?"

"It's Mack to be worried about." He turned to the man beside him. "Mack. Wake up."

Pierce chattered as he whispered, "Did you know what the Tailor did?"

"No. Not a bit. They put me down early."

"He stuck one of the crew with that tool of his. Right through the neck."

"It's no wonder we're in these." Seamus wormed his way over and prodded Mack with his boot. "Mack."

Just then he heard voices approaching, and in a few moments they were surrounded by several of the crew bearing pistols and clubs, headed up by the first mate and quartermaster.

"Tend to him." The first mate pointed toward Mack.

"Tending? Is that what this is here?" The quartermaster's reddened and scarred face twisted in disbelief. "We ought to be running 'em through."

"Step back, Sam," the first mate said. "You all. To the plank. Step lively, the captain is on his way."

The crew members snapped in response and unfastened the bindings, lifted the captives to their feet, and retied their hands behind their backs with rope. Then in a line they were led to an area of the ship where caskets were sent overboard. Mack had some injury to his elbow, but the commotion and reality of their situation brought a growing alertness to his grogginess.

What concerned Seamus most at this point was there were no passengers above deck. They must have put the ship on some type of lockdown, and there would be no jury or witnesses to their punishment. In all of his wildest childhood dreams, Seamus never imagined this would be how it all ended.

"Captain on deck!"

Seamus lifted his head to see Captain James Starkey approaching with anger in his step. To him, the captain had always seemed a caricature, a target of mockery, but in their present situation, his blue uniform with red sash, his polished medals, and the officer's hat spoke with the authority he had over their lives and deaths on the sea.

"Shall we walk 'em out, Captain?"

The quartermaster received a glare from the first mate, who then spoke with poise. "Captain, sir. Should we let them state their case?"

"As you wish." The captain fumbled with the hilt of his sheathed sword. "Speak."

The four prisoners were mute, and after a few moments, Seamus decided someone needed to respond. "Sir. We meant no harm. Our people are hungry, Captain. They're starving down below. My sister is dying."

The captain was unmoved. "Hungry? Aren't we all hungry?"

"Some less than others," the Tailor interjected.

The captain's eyes widened. He turned toward the quartermaster and nodded.

"With pleasure." The quartermaster grabbed a tight hold on the Tailor's wrists while a couple of the young sailors opened a gate to the side and pushed out and locked in the wooden plank.

The first mate stepped up to the captain. "Perhaps there is another way?"

Mack, who was alert with fear now, wept openly.

The Tailor was shoved onto the plank, and he stumbled briefly before regaining his balance. With his arms bound behind him and the stiff breezes whistling about, he seemed precariously aloft, but he turned to face his accusers with aplomb.

This caused even more of a surge in the captain's fragile composure and his complexion reddened. He pulled a long sword out from his scabbard and raised it.

For the first time, Seamus saw a breach in the Tailor's confidence and thought he might crack. But the arrogance returned, and a toothy smile formed, an expression of laughter in the face of his misery.

The man just didn't care anymore. He was embracing his fate as a prize.

The captain stepped up on the plank and pressed forward, sword at length and a maddening glint in his eyes. His cheek twitched.

The quartermaster and several of the crew barked cheers and whoops, but the first mate climbed behind the old man. "Captain. Please. I implore you."

The old sailor pressed the point of his sword on the Tailor's cheek and drew a thin stream of red. Brennan eased backward and glanced at the mere foot left on the plank.

"What say you now, you filthy Irish rogue, hah?" Spittle flew from the captain's mouth. "What say you now, you coward?"

The accused and the crew, they all gazed intently in silence except for the music of the sea winds, the dull lapping of waves against the hull, and the creaking of the ship.

The Tailor looked down to the cruel sea, now with his feet barely gripping the edge of the plank, and then he glared back at the captain. "I'd like to have some more of your whiskey, you miserable fraud."

The captain lunged forward and the Tailor arched his back to avoid the point of the weapon. And with two desperate efforts to regain his balance, Brennan fell backward and began to descend. As he did, the captain dropped his sword and it bounced off the platform, joining the flight of the Tailor as he plummeted into the outreaching dark arms of the sea.

Seamus peered over the edge of the ship, yearning to see the Tailor rise to the surface, but the whitecaps were furling and the ship was moving at a fair clip.

Stunned, the crew exchanged confused glances. The first mate pulled the captain in from the plank and to the deck.

"I only," the captain mumbled. "I only meant to frighten him."

The first mate assumed control. "Cook. Take the captain to his cabin and prepare some tea."

"I only meant to frighten him." The old sailor ambled away.

When he was out of earshot, the first mate motioned for his crew to gather the three remaining captives. Mack began to sob again, and fear pulsed through Seamus's veins.

"Whose man was that?" Greene said to the three of them, who now gave their rapt attention.

"He . . . has no family." Mack's voice wavered. "Just him alone."

"Will he be missed?"

It was an odd question, but Seamus felt encouraged by the direction this was heading.

Mack looked to his fellow prisoners. "No, sir. He kept to himself."

"Very well." The first mate looked to the sky for answers. "This leaves me with two choices. You can share that man's fate, or we can consider this matter settled."

"Fairly settled," Seamus said. He felt guilty for so easily abandoning the Tailor's protests, but the thought of seeing Clare again was the only thing driving him now.

"Indeed," echoed Pierce.

"You, sir?" The first mate looked to Mack.

"Oh yes." Mack nodded. "Quite so."

The quartermaster leaned in. "Shouldn't we at least give 'em a few stripes before letting 'em be?"

"Sam. The next in line for discipline is you, friend. Go back below."

He pursed his lips, then spat to the ground. But the quartermaster nodded and retreated.

"Gentlemen. The price for thievery is death on board this ship. Your friend drew blood. If your foolishness is not repeated, I see no reason to consider this incident further. Agreed?"

"Yes, sir," they replied in words or with a nod.

"Unbind them. Let them go. And give them rations to take with them."

"Sir?" One of the sailors seemed puzzled.

"There was courage in their deed. Bravery should be rewarded," the first mate said.

In a matter of minutes, the three wounded heroes descended the hatch to cheers and warm greetings, with food, water, and one less in their party.

There were few questions about the Tailor, and those that were asked received only vague, unsatisfying explanations.

No further thoughts of rebellion surfaced. The only fight left in the tattered army was waged against the ever-encroaching enemy of death.

# Chapter 17

# THE EAST RIVER

Clare opened her eyes to bedlam.

She hadn't seen much light for weeks, and now every lantern below was shining brightly with fresh oil. Her shipmates were scurrying about in a frenzy, pulling their straw mattresses off the shelving and dragging them down the aisle to the ladder and up through the hatch. Others carried the chamber pots, some carrying two, one in each hand.

Sitting up, Clare's head revolted and she paused to regain her balance.

Some women were on their knees around her with buckets of water, scrubbing the floors. Clare hadn't witnessed such a flurry of activity and excitement since their first day when the ship peeled away from the piers of Cork, drunk on hope and trepidation.

"Well, I'll be." One of the ladies rose from her labor, a dripping cloth held in her hand. Muriel, now a slender woman, was gazing in shock. "Sweet Jesus! She rose from the grave. Goodness, child."

"Get the boys," Muriel shouted out as some of the other women gathered around Clare in a flutter of awe and rejoicing.

Overwhelming her with sips of water and nibbles of food, they patted her down with cool cloths and forced her to lie down again.

In a few moments, Seamus and Pierce bullied their way through to Clare, and she was struck by the bliss expressed in their countenances.

"You're back," Seamus said. His face was splotched with patches of red and his skin was taut on his cheeks. He seemed to have aged several years.

He beamed through his gaunt apparition. "God of miracles. Would you believe I prayed? Your brother Seamus?"

"He did. I saw 'em meself," Pierce said. "Stranger sight ne'er seen. Hands clasped and knees bent. The whole picture."

"Here. Take some more of this." Muriel reached in with a spoon.

"You'll drown her with that." Seamus nudged the woman's arm away.

"What's happening?" Clare asked.

Seamus laughed. "Well. Mostly. You're alive."

"No," she said. "All of the scurrying?"

"We're just a ways out from New York," Pierce said.

"Can you believe it, Clare?" Seamus asked. "We made it. You made it. A few meals shy. But we're all here."

"What about all of this?" Clare pointed around her.

"By orders of the first mate," Muriel said sardonically. "There's some inspection coming in the harbor, and he says if we fail to pass, we don't dock. That was inspiring enough."

"I should be lending a hand." Clare started to rise.

"You do nothing of the sort," Pierce said as Seamus pressed her back down.

"Some fresh air would do her well." Muriel placed her hand to Clare's forehead. "The fever's all gone."

"You're the only one," Seamus said wistfully. "Dozens. Gone."

"Which is the only way the rations lasted." Pierce shrugged. "Fewer mouths, I'm afraid."

"Would you take me up?" Clare said. "I want to see the sky."

Seamus looked to Muriel for counsel.

"I do think it would do her well," the woman said. "Besides. If she appears ill, they may not let her pass."

That was enough for Clare to lift herself to her elbows again.

"Why don't you boys give her some privacy?" Muriel said. "We ladies will primp her and give her a fresh dress."

Clare put on Seamus's hat, was lifted to her feet and escorted ever so patiently by Muriel and another woman, who commented their surprise at how well she was able to stand on her legs.

Though dizzy, Clare was driven by the desire to reach fresh air, terrified by the thought she would be quarantined or delayed when they arrived to shore. After being imprisoned for so long, she was determined to will her way to freedom on land.

Tenacity wasn't sufficient, and despite her best efforts, she could only wobble and needed to rest every few steps to keep from fainting. Yet as she crawled plank by plank up the ladder, the idea of feeling the sun's rays, hearing the ocean's songs, and breathing in the cool air yielded more strength with each step.

At last, in victory, she surfaced from the womb of death, her eyes searing in the glorious sunlight, and she raised her slender arm as a shield.

"Clare!" Pierce ran over and lifted her up from the steward-ship of the ladies and carried her on his hip, and then Seamus was on her other side. They guided her to the ship's edge.

"You're just in time," her brother said.

She watched in amazement as the passengers were tossing mattresses, buckets, clothing, rags, and assorted belongings over the railing into the sea. The flotsam plunged into the ocean's billows and drifted rapidly out of view.

"Over there." Pierce pointed in the direction the lumbering vessel was headed.

Clare's eyes were still adjusting to the light, so it took a while, but finally a brown mass was rising from the horizon. "Is it?" she gasped.

"It 'tis," he said, his face gleaming. "We've made it, Clare. We've made it to America."

"Look, Pierce," Seamus said. "It's Lazarus herself, back from the dead." He lifted his hat from her head and rubbed her hair playfully. It was already a few inches in length.

"Lazarus is a man, you idiot." Pierce snorted. "Isn't that right, Clare?"

She wrestled the hat from Seamus and put it back on her head. "Are you asking whether Lazarus is a man or if my brother is an idiot?"

Their laughter was doused in relief and anticipation, and as the great city grew larger before them, conversation gave way to contemplation as their thoughts wandered to what might lay before them.

As they drew closer, they also saw a dark line thickening along the breadth of the sky.

Storm clouds roiling ahead.

# Chapter 18

# THE LANDING

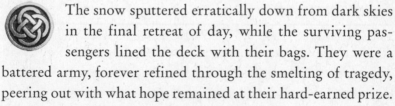 The snow sputtered erratically down from dark skies in the final retreat of day, while the surviving passengers lined the deck with their bags. They were a battered army, forever refined through the smelting of tragedy, peering out with what hope remained at their hard-earned prize.

They were all family now, nudging each other politely to procure a view. The exhilaration was palpable and growing, restrained only out of respect for those orphaned and widowed by the cruel hands of their bitter voyage. Witnessing a sight few imagined possible, they were awestruck as the *Sea Mist* drifted by Governors Island and headed into Hudson Bay.

The crippled ship was humbled to be in the same waters as the hordes of majestic vessels traversing in all directions, a rag-worn peasant among royalty, wealth, and enterprise. Decorated with colorful, boasting banners, ships of all sizes, some under the power of steam, weaved dangerously past each other, often-times resulting in exchanges of angry threats and insults from competing crews.

Clare's hands gripped the wooden rails as Seamus and Pierce stood on either side of her, protecting her space and holding her steady. One of the fever's victims had left behind a small handcart, and the other passengers granted it to Clare to use for transport once they came to shore. And several times, during the ship's slow approach to port, she had nested in it, covering herself in blankets.

But now, Clare's spirits soared as she marveled at the grandeur of Manhattan rising before her. As they neared the great snow-covered docks, the tiny moving dots on the shoreline became people alive with the bursting commerce of an upstart nation.

The inspections they all dreaded came and went without incident. Sharply clad bureaucrats arrived by an oared boat. After a few officious glances and cursory questions, papers were signed and then they left as quietly as they came.

Clare couldn't have been more relieved.

A steam tug edged the *Sea Mist* until it settled in alongside the wooden pier and into the awaiting arms and ropes of the dockworkers. The gangway was lowered, connecting the weary travelers to their new world.

The first-class passengers unloaded first, most seeming to be in good health and well fed, and a long stream of luggage trailed behind them. Finally, ropes lowered and steerage passengers broke ranks, no longer yielding to captain or crew, pouring onto the shoreline with an ardency tempered by their exhaustion and grief.

Clare was embarrassed to be wheeled in the cart as they angled down the plank as part of the motley caravan of immigrants, but she relented because she didn't want to slow the boys and hadn't the strength besides.

"The wind's picking up and snow's coming heavier," Pierce said.

Seamus pulled out another blanket and wrapped it around Clare. Her illness not only made her weaker but more susceptible to the cold.

The boys shouldered the two bags, which now were considerably lighter than when they boarded the *Sea Mist* more than two and half months ago.

A man with a snow-crusted plug hat stepped in their path. He had a fistful of currency. "Have you your dollars yet?"

"Our what?" Seamus said.

"Your dollars." The man gave a patronizing smirk. "Irish money is no good here."

"Of course we know that." Seamus motioned to Pierce, who extracted what was left from his leather purse and gave it to the stranger.

The man counted what was handed to him and tucked it in his shirt pocket. Then he glanced up as if calculating, before fanning through his dollars and giving several to Pierce as well as a few coins.

"Will you look at this?" Pierce said, proudly. "Yankee cash."

After a few steps in that direction, they were stopped by another man, this one a wiry fellow with black teeth. "You friends need lodging?"

"We're fine, thank you," Seamus said. "Friendly folk here, are they not?"

They were joined by Mack and Muriel, who had said some farewells.

"Are we ready to get going?" Mack said.

"We are that." Seamus nodded.

"Make certain you don't fall prey to the money changers," Mack said in a fatherly tone. "My cousin warned me they'll skin you as you get off the boats."

The boys were silent, and Clare didn't say anything either out of pity.

"Is she warm enough?" Muriel looked down at Clare. "Mack says it's a long walk to the Five Points."

Pierce loaded his pack. "The Five Points?"

"That's where me cousin lives." Mack put gloves on his hands. "The one you'll be staying with as our guests. The Five Points is where the Irish go. It will be like home, they say. Several from the ship are heading there together. Ah. They're moving now."

Not wanting to be left behind in the darkness of this strange land, Clare, Seamus, and Pierce joined the ragtag convoy of immigrants as they began their wide-eyed sojourn down the snowy, paved roads of the sprawling city of New York. Clare was awestruck by the brilliance of hundreds of gas lamps, massive works of architecture, and the richness of the citizenry and their modes of transportation, which filled the streets with horses, wagons, sleighs, and hordes of pedestrians.

As they cleared the way for the silk-dressed, top-hatted locals, Clare was keenly aware of the contrast of their own impoverishment, and few friendly faces greeted them as they passed.

It was strange as well to see so many people rushing by them with wrapped gifts and with arms full of vegetables, and breads, and carrying turkeys and chickens into their homes and apartments. There were also red ribbons strung on lampposts, wreaths hung on doors, and a spirit of festivity.

However, it wasn't until they came up to a well-bundled

group of carolers on a street corner, cheerfully singing in harmony, that it dawned on Clare. It was Christmas Eve.

This news gave them a lift in their step, but it didn't last for long as the streets began to empty as a result of the rising storm. They had no choice but to press on as the wind lashed at their reddened faces and boots sank deeper into snow as did the wheels of Clare's cart. Children faltered as did the elderly and infirmed and progress ground to a crawl, which only made it more intolerable.

"How much farther?" Seamus shouted above the tempest.

"Don't know for certain," Mack said. "We must be getting closer."

A man had overheard the question and he answered. "Less than a mile."

Even through the cover of snow, it was clear the neighborhoods were shifting, as the great homes and newly erected ornate buildings she first saw gave way to brokenness and dilapidation.

They turned a bend in the road and heard voices of mischief and saw a large gathering of men around a rusted barrel with wild flames ascending. Each of the scowlers were dressed alike in brick and beige plaid jackets with tall chestnut hats, many sporting mustaches. As they spotted the travelers approaching, the men nodded to one another and rose from their places, picked up irons, brickbats, and bottles and tossed in their hands what appeared to be stones.

"Keep steady," Mack said to the boys. Clare sat up.

"Shouldn't we turn around?" Muriel said.

"Just lads at play," Mack replied. "They'll mean us no harm."

The train of sojourners moved to the far side of the road with the adults positioning themselves between their children and the strangers, all the while trying to remain calm and unaffected as if not to stoke the tension further.

It was eerily quiet and Clare's entire body clenched as they drew closer to the men, who seemed to be feasting on the angst of their prey. One of the men stepped forward, a bearish fellow with black, bushy sideburns that nearly met at his square chin.

"Greetings, my good Hibernian friends." He took off his hat and bowed theatrically. "With the spirit of Christmas running through us, we'll offer you free passage through our property this evening."

His men responded with curses and jeers.

The leader held up his hand and they silenced. "We merely request . . . in a small gesture of your gratitude, that you leave the women behind."

Cheers erupted followed with heckles and gyrations.

The immigrants lowered their heads, flowing by as far along the opposite side of the road as possible, and a few hastened their steps.

"Where are you goin' so fast?" the man hollered. "That's it. Run, you grubby Micks. Here's your presents a day early."

Clare's body was jostled as Seamus wheeled the cart forward as they all were being pelted with objects. She heard bottles shattering against walls and the thud and screams when hurled items met their mark. The fleeing broke out to full panic as some of the immigrants slipped in the snow and others bent down to lift and carry the fallen away.

"Take her, Muriel," Seamus shouted, relinquishing the handles of the cart.

Clare looked back to see her brother joining several of the men who remained to confront their assailants. She lifted herself out of the cart.

"Seamus!" she screamed just as a bottle struck Pierce in the face and he collapsed to the ground. Two of the Irish lifted him and they all retreated back to the women and the children, being bombarded with objects as they ran.

One of those projectiles landed in a snowbank beside Clare, and a small boy scurried to pull it out. It was a potato.

"You just leave that there," said the boy's mother.

Clare unwrapped her scarf, filled it with snow, and placed it on Pierce's forehead, putting her arms around him.

"Keep moving!" Mack shouted, and they all hurried together, even Clare on foot, for a full block before sensing the danger was behind them.

"Welcome to the city of New York." Seamus eyed the damage.

"Don't worry yourself," Mack said. "Ireland is not far ahead. We're closing in on the Five Points."

As they traveled down the final streets leading to their destination, the weather lifted and just as suddenly the whole populace of this slouching neighborhood seemed to spill out from listing tenement buildings, seedy taverns, storefronts, and brooding alleys. Hordes of pigs and mean-spirited dogs comingled with street merchants, peddlers, and pickpockets.

The children of the community were dressed in rags and were unkempt and unsupervised. They played cheerfully in front of the increasing glut of brothels, which lined either side of the road. Prostitutes would take a break from enticing customers to pick up a stray ball or to fling a mound of snow.

The streets themselves became more deeply rutted and were mostly a mushy heap of soot, excrement, and rubbish with dingy blotches of brown blending with the white of snow.

Everything appeared more and more run-down. The buildings sagged with age and disrepair, windows and shutters hung by wires, broken doors flapped in the wind, and in many cases were merely frayed rags pulled across the door frame.

The travelers rounded a turn and then opened into a great clearing, a huge square with five traffic-laden streets emptying into a dissonance of poverty, vice, and flamboyance. It was a place that must have been ever more bustling at night than day.

"Welcome to our new home," Mack said loudly. "This here is the center of the Five Points."

They were too battered, too tired, and too underwhelmed by what they were witnessing to celebrate, but they did all pause to take in this milestone of their bitter journey.

If it was Ireland, then it was an Ireland Clare had never imagined, and perhaps never hoped to see.

Soon, the group who traveled from the docks, following warm embraces and tears, scattered to their own destinations and only the five of them remained. Clare, who had abandoned the cart and had been braving it on foot, was wearying and relieved when Mack led them to a three-story building. But it was rundown and bore an air of putrescence.

"Are you sure this is it?" Muriel asked with disappointment.

"I'm afraid so." Mack ascended the stairs to a shabby door just as a teenage boy came out and eyeballed them.

Clare couldn't hear the conversation, but soon the boy waved for them to follow him to the side of the building.

There he came upon a wooden hatch, with many footprints leading to and from it in the snow. He lifted it and a dim light revealed stairs leading down.

"There?" Mack said incredulously, as if suspecting some sort of chicanery.

The boy nodded.

Mack set his pack on the ground and turned to the others. "Wait here."

He descended cautiously, and within a few moments there was laughter and shouts of greeting heard below. Shortly, a man smoking a pipe stuck his head up and flashed his hands for them to enter.

"Come out of the cold, dear friends. We're so thrilled you made it safely. And just in time for Christmas, you are."

Muriel went first, and as she began to lift Mack's bag, the man took it from her and offered an arm in escort.

Pierce, Seamus, and Clare exchanged wary glances before reluctantly following behind. Clare had traveled as far as she could this night, and there was no spirit left in her to protest if she had wanted.

As she stepped down, the musty stench of mildew, urine, and smoke overcame her, and Clare feared she was the victim of another nightmare, fingers of death drawing her back down the steerage hull of the *Sea Mist*.

But there also was a most-welcomed warmth inside, and she spotted a crude stove at the other end of what appeared to be a dirt cave beneath the house. To avoid rubbing their heads on the ceiling, they had to crouch as they walked.

Spread throughout and covering most of the dirt floor were a couple dozen straw mattresses, many with sleeping occupants. There wasn't much room for their feet to navigate between the bodies lying around them, but just as the moth to the flame, they wove their way in the direction of the rustic furnace.

In the dim light, the faces that peered up as they passed were ghostly, bearing expressions of pain and poverty.

As Clare proceeded, the world about her began to spin and a wave of nausea and light-headedness came upon her. In her fragile condition, the activities and emotions of the day engulfed Clare with weariness.

Seamus assisted her in finding a patch of earth where she could lay down on her worn blanket. Here among strangers in the damp cellar of this foreign land, she heard troubling whispers just out of range of hearing.

Then Clare succumbed to the darkness.

# Chapter 19

# THE FIVE POINTS

Clare was uncertain how many days had passed.

She woke many times to the dampness, darkness, and groans of the others in the basement. Realizing where she was, Clare would cry herself back to sleep and dream of better days when she could feel her bare feet traipsing in the green grass of Branlow.

She wished she could sleep herself back into the arms of her family. Return to the farm. Clare regretted ever complaining about a single day she endured back home.

She had been well tended. Sometimes by Muriel, other times by Seamus, and even Pierce was there to give her sips of water, spoon her warm soup, and encourage her to walk around, even if only for a few steps each day.

But this morning, she sat up and discovered herself alone.

There was a thin line of light seeping through a crack in the wall, directly in line with her eyes, and strangely, it called to her. For the first time in a while, she felt renewed.

Clare had a sudden impulse to rise above the filth of this cave. She tightened her hat, brushed off her grimy clothes, and made her way out of the muggy grave.

As she climbed the staircase, her heart began to pound. A breeze whistled through the seams of the hatch. Pushing up against it, the door made a creaking sound and fanned open to a wall of cool, crisp air and a burst of light.

The snow she remembered was gone, and in its place was a bright sun and clear sky. Yet her bare feet couldn't avoid the muddy pools, so she lifted her dress to keep the hem from soiling any more than it already had.

At the front of the building, Clare stepped out of the mud onto a cobblestone road and reveled in the abundance of life. A couple of children, engaged in a game of chase, nearly ran her over.

One of them, a small brunette girl, stopped long enough to say, "Sorry, miss," before she continued her pursuit with even more vigor and laughter.

Just a ways ahead at an intersection, two boys were hawking competing newspapers in loud and squeaky voices. Horses pulled carts and carriages and men pushed handbarrows, some filled with rags or rubbish, and others with fruit, breads, and vegetables.

Clare realized for the first moment in quite some time that she was famished.

Across the street, the musical chants of a young girl sounded from behind a street stall filled with green, husky produce. She had smooth, coal black skin, and Clare was struck by her beauty and ebullience.

"Hot corn. Sweet corn. Sweet, sweet corn."

Clare was captivated by the thought of eating and rubbed her aching stomach. She hadn't realized she was staring down at the girl until the young lady's gaze locked with hers.

Clare turned away in embarrassment. How low had things come to be for her? When she glanced up again, the girl with teeth glistening against the ebony of her face was grinning at her. She held up an ear of corn and waved for Clare to come.

Clare just shook her head, her cheeks warming.

The girl abandoned her cart and bounced across the street with the corn, dodging a carriage on the way.

"This is for you, pretty lady," the girl said upon arrival. "Abigail's corn taste so good, the juices they slide down your chin."

"I'm so sorry," Clare said. "I don't have a single coin."

"Don't trouble yourself, miss. Abigail knows you needs to eats something."

A tuft of air brought the smell of the corn to Clare's nose, and she couldn't even feign resistance. She took it from the girl's hands.

"This is so kind of you," Clare said, eager to take a bite. "Thank you . . . Abigail."

"I needs be getting back. The thieves probably done robbed me bare." She turned and fluttered back to her stand, singing as she skipped. "Hot corn. Sweet corn. Sweet, sweet corn."

Clare bit into the bright, yellow cob and the sweet fluid burst into her mouth. She couldn't imagine anything tasting better. She gnawed away at the cob, biting through every kernel and then a second time, pulling whatever fragments of the corn remained until the cob was stripped of any hint of gold.

"News, ma'am?"

Clare turned to see a boy with ruddy cheeks peering up with a paper extended out to her.

"Just a penny," he said in a voice bridging between boy and man.

"No thank you, dear."

"Just a penny. Everyone has a penny."

"No. Not everyone."

"But this is worth a penny, ma'am. War news. The Mexicans are putting up a fight and Polk is calling for reinforcements. It says so right here. Word is the president is recruiting right here in New York. City corruption. A fire on Baxter Street. It's all right here. Just a penny."

"Had I a penny, it would certainly be yours."

"Suit yerself." With a tip of his hat, he scampered down the street, his voice fading as he got farther away. "War news! Right from the front lines."

Clare looked over to Abigail and was pleased to see she was serving paying customers. Glancing back toward the newsboy, she saw coming down the walkway a most welcome sight. Seamus and Pierce. And when they saw her, they started to run, holding their hats.

"Clare! What are you doing up?"

When he got to her, Seamus gave her a warm embrace. But then he pulled back.

"Do I smell that poorly?" she asked.

"'Fraid so. Nuttin' a good scouring couldn't fix."

"Are you sure you're fit?" Pierce said. "We were afraid you fell ill again."

"I'm done with all plagues," she said defiantly.

The boys' faces lit up. "Then let's go," Seamus said.

"Go where?"

"Should we tell her?" Pierce asked.

"We certainly should not. Not yet." Seamus's eyes glistened with mischief. "C'mon you. Let's get your belongings. We're out of this sinkhole. We have the most wonderful thing to share."

# Chapter 20

# A TWIST OF FORTUNE

In short order, they had in their arms all of their possessions, said farewell to their gloomy residence, and embraced the sunshine of new hope. Clare insisted they stop by Abigail's stand, where she ordered three ears of corn and paid the girl double what was due.

They waddled down the cobblestone road at Clare's pace, the boys refusing to give her any clues as to where they were heading. She distracted herself from itching curiosity by imbibing the unique character of the neighborhood.

She was amazed to see so many Irish faces staring back at her as they passed by, and she realized it was the people Mack was referring to when he described the Five Points as home away from home. Even under the brooding weight of difficult times, there still existed the underlying cheer and hope of her brethren, and it did bring her warmth to hear the familiar lyrical musicality of their conversations ringing out in the neighborhood.

But it also was a culture somehow blighted by their new environment. There were dungeon-like watering holes alternating almost every other storefront, many of them replete with drunken patrons despite it being the full light of day.

There were mothers with babies and the elderly and crippled begging on every corner. Dark individuals loitered in every cranny, with an unresolved yearning and turbulence in their eyes. Children, scantily clad, wandered in bare feet, picking up fragments of the black shards that had fallen from the coal wagons.

The decay of the buildings and the brokenness of her people struck Clare as odd and disappointing. She believed they were crossing the ocean to enter a city of great wealth, a land of opportunity, but instead, she found herself peering into the downtrodden face of poverty and foul corruption.

They hadn't traveled too many blocks when they came to a building, which in contrast to its destitute neighbors rose straight and tall with fresh green paint and bright gold lettering sporting the name McKinney's above the wooden door.

On the second level ladies with ornamented wigs and voluptuous, brightly colored silk dresses were leaning out windows, appearing bored and disinterested in the activity below.

"Is this where you're taking me?" Clare made no attempt to guard her displeasure.

Seamus laughed. "Don't worry, sister. It gets better."

They entered the wooden door of the first-level tavern, which was modestly appointed with oak tables and chairs, a large, blazing fireplace, and a bar with glass mirrors and shiny brass trim. The place wasn't crowded, but there were enough customers sprinkled about to give rise to a sedentary blending of chatter.

Stepping with the confidence of one who knew his way,

Seamus headed to the far corner of the room and tilted his hat upon drawing the stare of the barkeep cleaning glasses with a white towel. His eyes tracked them as they went past him and through an entranceway leading to stairs that were well lit with decorative oil lanterns mounted on the walls.

As they ascended, a couple of leggy women who were heading down ogled Seamus and Pierce with exaggerated interest.

"Are you boys coming to see us?" one said playfully.

"Maybe later, ladies," Seamus replied.

As they came up to the second floor, they passed by an entranceway with crimson light flaring from a lamp, where an older, serious woman was conversing with two of the shady women. Unable to stave her curiosity, Clare glanced at them as she passed and one of the women returned a scowl.

Clare raced to catch up with the boys who had already reached the third floor and were working their way down a hallway. They waited for her, and as Seamus lifted his hand to the brass knocker, Clare tugged firmly on his shirt. "Hold on for a moment, will you? You need to tell me what we're doing. No more secrets."

Seamus seemed irritated she wouldn't play along. "It has to do with the necklace you got from the keener."

Clare reached for her neck and realized the pendant was gone. She felt violated. "What have you done with it? You didn't sell it, did you?"

"It's not what we lost," Pierce said. "It's what we found."

"Our luck's turned, Clare Hanley." Seamus clapped the brass.

Soon, an iron slot of the door opened and a pair of tired eyes shifted back and forth before disappearing. The latch unhitched and the door sprang open, and in the frame was a rangy woman draped in a peach silk robe. Her eyelids were painted bright blue and her cheeks flashed red on thin and wrinkled skin. Clamped between her teeth at an angle was a cigarette in a long, slender holder, which she drew on seductively as her other hand braced on her hip.

"Well . . . well . . . well." She scanned Clare from toe to head in a way that made her shudder. Then the woman let out a loud, hacking laugh.

"So this is the princess, eh?" She took a slow drag from the cigarette, and the tip glowed red and then added to the ash that was hanging precariously. "Looks like you pulled her out of the sewer."

"Ah, she'll clean up just fine." Seamus turned back to Clare as if to urge her not to be offended.

"Oh, my sweet sunshine." The woman chortled again, which led to a cough causing the ash to fall off her cigarette. "Well . . . come in and let's see if we can scrub you back into a lady. Come, love. Let's see what ol' Tressa can do."

She shook her head as Clare passed by her into the entry room. "Whooo. Now I know what hell smells like. Boys, you take these buckets and fill them with water. There's a well in the back. And take those rank packs out of here before the entire place is spoiled. Heavens! Oh my! I'll light the coal and will start the water boiling."

Clare shot a glare at her brother. Seamus shrugged and then leaned over and kissed her on the forehead.

Tressa put her arms on her waist. "Are you two lads still here? Get on with you. If Paddy catches sight of her in this condition, he'll toss her to the street."

Seamus gave a nod to the woman and they carried out their bags in one hand and the pails in the other. In a moment the door was shut behind them, leaving Clare miserably alone with Tressa.

"Have a seat, girl. There by the fireplace." Tressa left the room and began to make loud noises in an adjoining room, which appeared from Clare's vantage point to be a kitchen.

Clare took a seat in an elegantly carved mahogany chair, upholstered with a rich, blue fabric. With the clamor of Tressa's labors in the background, Clare surveyed the parlor room. It wasn't large by any means, but the walls were covered with a floral pattern of delicate wallpaper. The ebony wood of the mantel framed a fireplace, and spewing tufts of dark, black smoke rose from the red glow of coal, something Clare had never seen burn. On the shelf above the fire rested a silver clock of fine craftsmanship and two brass candleholders, each bearing five half-melted candles.

Tucked within the room was also a reading table bearing a vase of newly bloomed tulips, a pedestal desk with papers and an inkwell, a sofa with legs shaped like lion paws, and a dark wood cabinet. It was a charming room, and despite the odd circumstances of her welcome, Clare embraced the hospitality.

Her moment of tranquility was short lived as Tressa reentered the room. "Paddy is going to be in a tether when he gets sight of you folks. Ragged as you are. Well. We'll fix that. Imagine my surprise when those two young 'uns burst into McKinney's this morn, tossing Patrick Feagles's name around as if they were important.

"Business with him? I saw those two fresh babies, wet off the boat, and had a mind to put them in their rightful place." She let out a laugh as she started to light up another cigarette. "You know Patrick Feagles?"

Tressa walked over to one of the shelves on the wall and pulled down a bottle of what appeared to be whiskey and two glasses.

"Oh, no thank you, ma'am," Clare managed to get out as Tressa began to pour the second tumbler.

"Suit yerself." The woman topped off her glass. She lifted it to her ruby-coated lips and sipped. "I didn't hear you. Did you say you know Patrick Feagles?"

The door opened and Seamus and Pierce came in carrying their buckets full of water, some sloshing onto the wood floor.

"Careful, lads. In the kitchen with those." She rolled her eyes. "Yes . . . those two roughies. Here to collect from Paddy?"

When they came out, she gave them another order. "All right. Now the two of you go downstairs and visit the ladies. Tell them you need the tub and that Tressa says so. And ask Darcy for one of her dresses." Tressa eyed Clare. "Yes. Darcy's will do fine. And boys, don't tarry with the girls. Much to do before Paddy arrives."

When the door shut, Tressa disappeared in the kitchen again and Clare guessed she was swapping out the water to boil, and the clanging of pots confirmed this. In a moment she reappeared.

"So yes," Tressa said. "Your brother and the redhead are about to get their heads bashed by my bartender's brickbat when they pull out a necklace they said they brought all the way from Ireland and were returning it to my Paddy.

"I recognized it right straight, I did. It was a gift he gave his sister when she visited a couple years ago. Sang in theatre. Strange woman, his sister. I didn't see much Feagles in her to be honest. But a beautiful voice. That's for sure."

"Madame O'Riley?"

Tressa gave her a mock startle. "So you do speak? Yes . . . her stage name was Madame O'Riley. But Paddy always called her Rose. Short for Rosaleen."

"So this is the home of Patrick Feagles? Madam O'Riley's brother?" It was clearing up for Clare.

"Yes, dear. *The* Patrick Feagles."

"I wonder what's keeping the boys?" Tressa rolled her eyes as if she knew the answer.

As if on cue, they heard a large clamor outside and Tressa opened to door to let Seamus and Pierce stumble in carrying a brass tub between them, moving carefully to navigate it around the corner of the hallway and in through the door frame. Tressa directed them to set it down in the middle of the parlor.

Tressa reached into the tub, pulled out a violet dress, and held it up, grimacing. "Well, there isn't much life left in this one, but it'll do for now. And it looks like Darcy parted with some undergarments as well."

Under Tressa's direction, the boys waddled a boiling pot of water from the kitchen and then another and both of these were poured into the tub. After the woman put in some salts and soaps, it looked powerfully enticing to Clare.

"All right. The two of you need to make yourself scarce. Give the girl some privacy. Why don't you go to market and fetch some vegetables and make a visit to the butcher for me. It's a night of celebration. Paddy Feagles is in for a rare surprise."

After grabbing her purse and pulling out some bills, Tressa shooed them out the door and then turned to Clare. "Don't stare at me. Get your scrubbing started. I'll be in the kitchen tending to the pot."

She disappeared into the kitchen and then Clare quickly undressed. She dipped her toe into the water. It was hot, but not unbearably so. She slid into the water and curled under the foamy suds.

Perhaps it would have been the most wonderful experience she had in the past three months, except that she was terrified the door would open. Still, even flooded with the anxiety of this moment and her uncertain hosts, the luxury of the bath settled in and she reveled in the thought of feeling clean, feeling whole . . . feeling Clare once again.

She had yet to settle since leaving her community back home. But how foolish she once was to grow weary of the monotony of her life at home. What she would give to be back in her stony hovel, nestled to sleep with her siblings. Despite the grumpiness of her father, he was the beast she knew.

But she must hurry as her time would be short in the bath. Clare wiped the dirt, sweat, and humanity from her face, arms, chest, and legs. With each stroke of the cloth across her grateful body, she felt more alive.

She dunked her face into the water and allowed her short hair to soak. Sensing the water getting warmer, Clare rose to see Tressa pouring more boiling water in the tub.

"Well, look what we found splashing in the water? There's really a woman underneath all of that filth." Tressa turned to go back to the kitchen but paused. "Those eyes are jewels, my dear. Pure sapphire. When we get sewn up, you'll be the charm of Manhattan. They'll come far and wide to you, dear."

Tressa placed the pot on the floor and wiped the sweat off of her forehead. In the process she smeared some of her makeup.

Eyeing Clare's heap of clothing on the ground, Tressa bent over, grunting as she did, and picked up the pile while pursing her lips as if she had swallowed a lemon whole. "My, oh my. What are we to do with these lovelies? Only one thing I can think of."

Clare watched in horror as the woman went to the fireplace, opened the screen, and tossed in her only clothing. Then as if to make sure the chore was complete Tressa pulled out the poker and stoked it until Clare's filthy garments were fully engulfed in flames.

"That's it for the water, so I'll best be getting the boys from downstairs so they can clean a few layers off themselves. You should be out in a few minutes so you can be ready when they come back. Here is a towel. Powder yerself in my room. There's a lamp lit for you."

"Ma'am?"

"There are no ma'ams here . . . just old Tressa."

Clare pointed to the woman's eyes.

"What's that?" Tressa appeared dumbfounded for a moment. She peered in the looking glass on the wall and laughed. "No need to give them a fright. Thank you, dear. If Paddy saw me like this, he'd up and leave."

She lit another cigarette and approached the tub. "Pretty girl, you are, young Clare." Tressa exhaled. "Pretty does well in this city."

In a moment, the door shut and Tressa was gone, leaving Clare alone to her thoughts.

She slunk back in the tub and closed her eyes, feeling more relaxed than she had in months. The serenity was precious. With reluctance she climbed out of tub and reached over for the towel, then she wrapped it around herself as water dripped onto the wood floorboards.

Clare walked to the mirror and stared into her own blue eyes. It was the first time she had seen her hair for a while. It was growing in nicely, but she still looked more like a boy than a woman. But she appeared strong . . . and yes, beautiful.

She imagined a man, handsome with a charming smile, putting his arm around her, gazing in adoration. Perhaps her long days of aloneness would soon be in her past.

Maybe the worst was over.

Voices approached and she scampered into the back room, all the while plagued by this question: *Who is Patrick Feagles?*

# Chapter 21

# PATRICK FEAGLES

 "Have you never seen such beauty?" Seamus peered over Clare's shoulder into the oven she had opened.

"Nor smelt it?" Pierce tried to nudge in as well.

"Back off, you two. I can't breathe." Clare tried to discern whether the beef shoulder was fully braised or not. This was Clare's first time using an oven and, in fact, she had never before cooked beef. The thought of ruining such an expensive meal terrified her.

"Do you think it's ready?" she said.

"How would I know?" Pierce said.

"Oh, if I could just cradle it in me arms." Seamus licked his lips.

Clare shut the oven door and the hinges squeaked. She tended to the vegetables boiling on the stove, a task she found more familiar and comforting.

"Where's the old lady?" Pierce asked.

"Shhh." She looked nervously toward the door to Tressa's bedroom. "She'll hear you. She asked if I would mind the kitchen while she was preparing herself for Mr. Feagles."

"We were taking our baths when she went in there," Seamus said. "With all of that fixing time, she ought to come out as the queen herself."

Clare noticed Pierce gazing at her. "What's with you?"

Seamus elbowed his friend. "Are you ogling me sister?"

Pierce snapped out of his trance. "No. No. It's just . . ." he started and blushed. "It's just you cleaned up well, Clare. 'Tis all."

Seamus patted Pierce on the head. "And you, my dear friend, smell lovely as well."

Pierce swatted the hand away.

"Do you think we could have a wee taste of the beast?" Seamus started to reach for the oven handle.

"You'll have no such thing." Clare slapped his hand. "I don't want either of you embarrassing me. And neither of you boys will get the first bite until you tell me how you came upon this place. Other than admitting to pinching my necklace, you haven't provided any explanations. How did you meet Tressa?"

"Firstly, I never pinched your necklace, my dear sister." Seamus reached into his pocket and held up the silver necklace, and the gem in the center of the braided clover sparkled even in the limited light.

As one would greet a lost friend, Clare took it from his hand and immediately put it around her neck, fumbling with the clasp. "But I thought you gave it to Tressa?"

"I only said I showed it to her. What a low opinion you hold of me at times." Seamus plucked an apple from the fruit bowl, buffed it against his shirt, and bit into it loudly. "Now for the story of how we're here, I'll start by saying it took quite some reckoning to bring us to this much-improved situation."

"'Twas a task indeed," Pierce chimed in.

"You see ol' Mack's cousin," Seamus continued, "the fella who offered us those brilliant accommodations in the basement."

Pierce raised his eyebrows. "Strange chap."

"Yes. Peculiar indeed. With you ailing and us near dry of funds, he put in our ear we should sell our belongings. Whatever could be spared. So I told him of the keener's gift."

"Yes. *My* necklace." Clare raised her hand to her bosom, where the pendant rested against her skin.

"Understood, dear sister. Yet I'm certain you'd agree it would serve us little if we were all starved."

"I suppose 'tis true." She sighed. "Still, I wasn't dead for asking."

Seamus raised his eyebrows. "Anyways. When I showed Mack's cousin the necklace for his appraisal, I could see greed flashing in his eyes, and I knew at once the keener gave us something dear. And I was morely convinced when this chap began to play his interest down."

"Out of pity for our condition," Pierce said in a mocking voice, "he'd give us a dollar to unburden us."

"Yes. That's what he said, more or less." Seamus nodded. "When he saw we weren't falling for it, he started pleading and begging, then hinting he would put us out to sleeping in the snow if we didn't see to him having it as his own. We told him we'd think on it."

Seamus took another bite of his apple. "So quick as we could, we started asking questions on the streets. It didn't take long to find the clover of the pendant was a symbol for the place called the Irish Gathering or Irish Fellowship . . ."

"The Irish Society," Pierce broke in.

"Yes. The Irish Society. It's a place for our people they said. We ventured to a building that had the same exact clover symbol on its door. Once there, folks told us we had something in our possession that rightly belonged to a certain Patrick Feagles."

"There's more," Pierce whispered.

"Well, there's that." Seamus lowered his voice as well. "The man we spoke to at the Irish Society seemed to believe this Mr. Feagles would be most grateful for the pendant's proper return. That is, if he didn't kill us for having it in the first place."

"He said that?" Clare gasped.

"Aye," her brother said. "But he was making more of it than there was, I am certain."

Clare was unconvinced and now more than a bit troubled. "And Tressa. How did you meet Tressa?"

Seamus offered a bite of the apple to Clare, but she shook her head. "We were told we'd find Mr. Feagles in the tavern below, it being called . . ."

"McKinney's," Pierce said. "When we got here and mentioned this Feagles's name, they pointed us to Tressa, who was sitting at one of the far tables."

"At first, she was ill pleased," Seamus said. "Until we showed her the necklace. One look at that and she was so sure Mr. Feagles would want to meet us she invited us to supper and even offered us her place to bed down."

"And here we are." Pierce spread his arms wide.

"So you know . . . nothing about this Patrick Feagles?"

Seamus shrugged.

Clare's anger began to rise. "And do you think it wise not to tell me this man might intend us harm? Had you not the good wits to share this story with me before you brought me here?"

"No," Seamus said with a patronizing smile. "He'll be so grateful to us for the return of his precious jewelry, he'll treat us generously."

"And how do you know that, Seamus?"

He glanced at Pierce and then turning back put a hand on her shoulder. "When we showed it to Tressa, she said it was a gift he gave his sister."

"Yes, I know. Tressa already told me Mr. Feagles was the keener's brother. And what of it?" Clare's head ached. She was preoccupied with wondering if they would be wise to flee the house while they still had the opportunity.

"Don't you see it?" Seamus said, in an incredulous tone. "For some reason the keener knew we would end up meeting up with her brother. It was a real gift she gave us. This Feagles is from back home. He's one of us."

Just then a door opened. Startled, they turned to see Tressa emerging from her room. Her face displayed an artistry of makeup, which despite being a bit heavily applied, succeeded in making the old woman appear more youthful. Clare could imagine a young Tressa would have drawn the eyes of many a suitor.

"Oh, how wonderful you're here." Clare worried that Tressa might have heard part of their conversation. "I . . . uh . . . I'm uncertain if the roast is cooked or not."

Tressa eyed them with suspicion. "Why are you muddling about? You all look as if you're standing before the gallows."

"We're just grateful, ma'am." Seamus smiled. "Pleased to be here."

"Say nothing of it, dear. Patrick would be angry with me if I treated poorly friends of his sister. He dotes on that woman fiercely and will be cheered by any news you have about her. Just about broke the man when Rose went back to Ireland."

Clare gave Seamus an accusatory glance. "I hope it won't dispirit Mr. Feagles once he knows we don't know her too well."

"He'll feast on the slightest detail. I told you he loves that woman. And speaking of feasting, that roast is done. Let's pull her out and prepare the settings. What time is it?" Tressa glanced at the clock, which showed it was nearly eight in the evening. "Oh my. Paddy ought to be home soon. Let's hurry ourselves so all will be ready."

Under Tressa's direction, Clare gathered the food onto serving china while the boys pulled a table from the wall and placed it where not too long ago the brass tub set. Whether driven by the anticipation of the meal or the man who was on his way, they hurried at their tasks, and in not more than a few minutes, they were gathered around the table, admiring the spread in awe and silence.

Before them, the meat sizzled atop a pool of gravy, as tiny rivulets of butter streamed down the curvatures of the corn on the cob. Beets, a brilliant purple and fresh from the market, brimmed to the edge of the dish, and further tempting their patience were the wheat aromas of oven-browned bread, which was still warm to the touch.

Clare and the boys gazed expectantly at the woman, hoping and even pleading with their eyes that the words of grace would free them from the cruel bondage of politeness. But no such words spilled from Tressa's lips. Instead, she spoke of everything else, intending apparently for not a single fork to be lifted until her Patrick Feagles came through the door.

Then at last, with Tressa seemingly exhausting every possible word, she released a deep sigh and there was silence, except for the steady ticking of the clock, which seemed to grow in intensity as disappointment crept deeper into her face.

"I'm sure he'll be here soon." Clare clasped her hands, which were sweaty.

"Maybe we should begin . . ." Tressa looked at the clock again.

"We should wait . . ." Clare said, but it was too late. Seamus and Pierce dug into the food like wolves over their prey. The chains were broken. Clare, who couldn't remember how long it had been since her last full dinner, had no more will to restrain them or herself. With each bite, strength returned to Clare, flowing through her body.

She barely noticed Tressa preserving a plate of food for Patrick, his chair ominously empty.

In a short while, it was all over. The last of the food was scraped from the serving platter, and after Seamus and Pierce used the bread to sop up whatever gravies remained on their plates, they leaned back in their chairs and exchanged sighs and groans of contentment.

Clare stared down with guilt at the food left on her plate. She abhorred the thought of wasting food, but her appetite was still fragile and she couldn't force another bite without gagging.

"Miss Tressa." Seamus patted his mouth with his napkin. "You've made our little venture to America already worth every effort. Had I known what awaited me here, I would have beaten the captain for speed."

"'Twas fine." Pierce smiled. "Fine indeed."

Tressa looked over to the plate of food she had set aside for Patrick and blushed. "I suppose his duties kept him. He's been at it hard lately. Patrick is a very important man."

"If you don't mind me asking," Pierce said, "what exactly does Mr. Feagles do?"

Before the question could be answered, a muffled sound came through the door. It was a man's voice, deep and drunken, echoing through the hallway outside and drawing closer.

"Jimmy, I'll crack your head. See if I don't come down there if I hear another word from ye."

The words and tone widened the eyes of those around the table, with the exception of Tressa who seemed to be oddly pleased with the approaching rancor. From Seamus's worried expression, he must have been recalculating the wisdom of his latest plan. But, there was nothing they could do but let it play out now.

"Don't worry," Tressa said. "He's mostly harmless when he's had a few."

They listened with heightened senses as the man's shouting shifted to a drunken song as heavy steps moved up the creaking wooden floorboards of the stairs.

> *Fair as a maiden, ever should be,*
> *The lies of a lady, looking at me,*
> *She brought down ships,*
> *And sails unfurled,*
> *Never seen beauty,*
> *Like Celia my girl.*

There was a fumbling at the door, the handle turned slowly, and the door cracked open enough to show the shadow of a man dressed in dark pants and a checkered waistcoat, with a gray cravat spilling lazily out from his neck. He took off his overcoat and hung it on the rack by the door after a couple of failed attempts. Without noticing them he leaned back out into the hallway and bellowed again as he took off his plug hat.

"Jimmy, I have a mind to come at you hard. Cheating me in my own place. I'll break ye with me bare hands. See if I won't."

Clare experienced both a terror . . . and a strange familiarity. There was something in the man's voice she recognized.

There wasn't time to dwell on this as Patrick Feagles slammed the door shut and placed his hat on a hook while mumbling to himself. Then he turned to face them and became alarmed at the sight of the strangers in his home rising to greet him. He squinted to try to see in the dim light and seemed both confused and angry in his stupor.

Just then as he leaned forward, his face became illuminated by the beams of light coming from the candles, like the moon would after bursting through a shroud of clouds. There, as Clare's mouth went agape in horror, the apparition of her past became eerily visible. Tall, broad shouldered, slumping forward with age and wear, teeth of amber hue, and leaning on a walking stick, Clare could see in this man the eyes of her father, now suddenly sad and frightened.

The sharp contours of his cheeks were undeniably of Hanley breeding and those bushy eyebrows and sideburns were ones so familiar and inviting to her during Clare's ephemeral youth.

For there standing before her, warmed as if risen from the bowels of the sea, was Patrick Feagles. No. Not him at all. Because clearly Patrick Feagles was a counterfeit. The man before her was Uncle Tomas, as alive to Clare now as the day she last saw him nearly four years ago.

# Chapter 22

# UNCLE TOMAS

Clare felt on the verge of fainting and fought back the scream rising from her toes, through her body, and surging to her face. But with much restraint she let out only a gasp, a soft release of surprise, and her uncle's eyes softened, relaxed.

Fear receded from his disposition, his confidence replenished, and he lit up with his customary charm. In an instant he was once again her uncle Tomas, the one who spoiled Clare and her sister Maggie and who was capable of provoking so much jealousy in her father.

Clare resented his arrogance returning so effortlessly. As a child she always admired her uncle's verve, his playful aloofness. But now, with his ruse dangling so precariously in their hands, his behavior seemed reckless and offensive. Yet as she glanced toward Seamus to measure his reaction, she didn't see a trace of disgust in her brother's face. Rather, he was smiling broadly, almost gloating, as one would who had an opponent mated in chess. Clare realized her brother was about to seize the opportunity to profit from this unusual circumstance.

"Mr. Feagles," Seamus said, plunging into the awkwardness. "It is indeed a pleasure to meet you at last."

Uncle Tomas was disarmed by Seamus's tone and he reeled backward. Then one of his eyebrows cocked, his head tilted, and Clare could sense he was on to Seamus and realized the ransom was set.

"Your sister," Seamus said without flinching. "She told us . . . so much about you. It's almost as if you're part of our family."

"Me sister?"

"Yes. We know her as Madame O'Riley."

"Of course," Uncle Tomas said warily. "You know Rose?"

"She gave us a pendant. Or should I say she gave it to my sister Clare as a gift for our American Wake."

Seamus nodded to Clare and she reluntantly unfastened the necklace.

Uncle Tomas reached out and took the necklace from Clare, and he brought the pendant close to his eyes. "I gave this to Rose," he said, his voice wavering. "Is Rose here with you?" He cheered with hope and handed the jewelry back to Clare.

"No," Seamus said. "She's back home. But she sent good tidings. We feared it would be a great imposition to come here uninvited, but your sister insisted we would . . ."

"Not in the least so," Uncle Tomas said. "Tressa, how thoughtful of you for welcoming these young people into our home."

Tressa's face beamed. "I knew you'd be tart if you found out I shooed them off."

"No. You did well, dear." Tomas leaned over and kissed Tressa on the cheek.

Clare tracked closely with how they interacted. Her stomach knotted with the thought of Aunt Meara back home, still grieving Uncle Tomas's supposed death. How tragic it would be for her to discover the fraud.

"There's dinner here for you," Tressa said. "The heat's gone, I'm afraid."

"Lovely, dear." Tomas lowered himself slowly into the chair and motioned to the others to join him at the table. "Would you fetch us some of the good rye I've been sparing? Just for times such as these."

Uncomfortably, they settled into their chairs around the table. When Tressa left the room and the clattering of glasses could be heard from the kitchen, Tomas leaned in toward the three of them and spoke in a hush.

"It would shatter poor Tressa's heart to hear more than she can bear. Trust me on this. Allow me to do my explaining in privacy and beyond Tressa's hearing." He turned to Seamus. "There will be much to gain for all of you. That I can promise. And when I speak my words, it will be well received. But know one thing with certainty for now. I am and must be Patrick Feagles."

Clare felt her stomach grinding. Filled with disgust and confusion, she wanted nothing more than to flee this man, this place. But where would she go? Looking deep through the eyes and into the soul of her uncle, she struggled to reconcile the anger she now felt toward him. Had she been so blind to his wickedness all through her childhood?

Oh. What she would give to restore her fond memories of him! Was it cowardice or grace to wish that she be driven toward forgiveness? Her mind sought out any possible justification of his behavior, but none could be found.

Worst of all, there was a much greater inquiry looming, one she dare not speak now. But Clare would soon demand an answer and this twisted her mind with anger, fear . . . and hope: If this was Uncle Tomas, living, breathing, and speaking before her, then where was her sister Margaret?

"So much to talk about." Uncle Tomas forced a chuckle as Tressa returned from the kitchen and placed the glasses down. "What news of back home?"

"Get to it, Patrick. He means to ask what have you to say of his sister," Tressa said above the sound of pouring. She filled each of their glasses to the brim with the amber liquid, with the exception of Clare, who politely waved her off.

Pierce picked up the bottle of whiskey and examined the label.

"What brought you to leave home?" Tomas's voice strained to be conversational.

"The plague." Pierce sipped slowly from his glass. "The taters."

"There's been talk of this." Tomas rubbed his chin. "And uh . . . where do you hail from?"

"Branlow." Seamus gave a wry grin.

"Is that right? Didn't know it reached County Roscommon."

"May I?" Pierce held up the bottle of whiskey.

"Of course, of course," Uncle Tomas said. "Have your fill." Seamus slid his glass toward Pierce.

"How badly has it hit?" Tomas asked.

"Bad. Enough to bring us here," responded Seamus coolly. "They'll need our support soon enough. It's why we're a bit hasty about finding work."

"Jobs?" Tomas grunted. He took a large bite of his food and spoke as he ate noisily. "It's not what they tell you, I'm afraid."

"About there being work in America?" Pierce said.

"Should I warm that for you?" Tressa reached out for Tomas's plate.

He shook his head without looking at her and pointed his fork at Pierce. "What did the charlatans tell you? So much work they'd be begging for your services before you had one foot landed on the docks?" He grimaced. "Anything to sell their precious passages. The ship owners are filling their pockets on the blood of the Irish. Aye. I'm afraid there's no work to be given. Only what is taken."

"That can't be." Pierce frowned.

"It 'tis." Tomas took a swig of whiskey and motioned to Pierce for the bottle. "But not yours to be concerned about. Rose did you a fine favor by bringing you here." He pointed a thumb toward himself. "Not many can help you, but I can. And I will."

"Paddy runs this town, he does," Tressa said, beaming.

Uncle Tomas seemed annoyed by her cloying manner. "That's making too much of it, but we'll get you landed proper. Food. A place to live." He glanced up from his plate and met Clare's gaze. "That is, if it suits you."

"If it's honest work, yes," Clare said.

"I'm not as particular as me sister," Seamus said. "Honesty is a fine enough principle, but I have a preference toward generosity when it comes to wages. It will spend the same back home whichever way it comes."

"There's only two kinds of earnings here in the Five Points," Uncle Tomas said. "That which comes easy and that which comes hard. It's as you please."

Seamus nodded. "Be a fair change of circumstances for anything easy to come our way."

"Easy would be just fine," Pierce said.

"Aye." Tomas toasted them with his glass. "Well then. The fates are favoring you now. Easy so happens to be me specialty."

"Have you not seen the blue eyes on this one?" Tressa nodded toward Clare.

Clare felt Uncle Tomas eyeing her as a woman for the first time and it unsettled her. She bowed her head reflexively.

"Tressa's right," Uncle Tomas said. "Beauty treads a gentler path. As it was back home. But even more so here. It will suit you well." Then he paused and looked at her awkwardly. "What happened to you here?" He pointed to his head.

"Her hair is coming back fine," Pierce said.

"Poor thing." Tressa shook her head. "Came to us in such disarray. We had to find her a dress."

"Is that so?" Uncle Tomas raised an eyebrow.

"We had some misfortune on the passage over," Seamus said, as if he felt responsible.

"Most do," Uncle Tomas said. "There's riches to be had making cargo of the Irish. More like piracy, it is. But enough of your recent misfortunes. Tomorrow is a new day for you all. Patrick Feagles is your man. A friend of Rose is a friend indeed." He pushed his plate toward the center of the table, yawned loudly, and stretched his arms.

"You need your rest, Paddy." Tressa took his plate away, with much of the food she saved for him still uneaten. "What a long day for you. And for these young ones as well. In the morning you can ramble further about jobs and no jobs and the plight of the people."

"They are staying with us, are they not?" Uncle Tomas said to Tressa.

"I invited them. Are you fine with this?"

"Quite." Uncle Tomas clasped his hands together. "We'll have you set up with your own flat tomorrow. It just happens there is a vacancy down the hallway."

"Is there?" Tressa asked.

"Yes." He chided her with his eyebrows. He smiled and turned toward them. "We're sending some tenants on their way. Never did care much for them and they attend poorly to their rent."

"That's kindly of you, but we wouldn't be able to afford that," Seamus said.

"I think you can." Tomas laughed. "Consider it the first payment of the work we'll find for you. For now, the floor in this room will have to serve you. Get on with it, Tressa dear. Grab some blankets for our guests and the boys might be willing to help with the table. Would you, lads?"

He was disarming them with his hospitality, and Clare hated herself for not protesting, but exhaustion found its grip on her will. After a few scurrying moments, the room was fashioned with blankets and throw pillows on the floor. Tomas stoked the fire, and the bright dance of airy embers was accompanied by a comforting gust of warm air. Then with a nod he retired to the bedroom to join Tressa and closed the door on its squeaky hinges.

Immediately Clare sought out Seamus's eyes, her heart burdened with troubling questions, but he responded with a finger pressed over his lips. "Tomorrow we'll get answers, Clare. You must sleep."

His callousness frustrated Clare, but she relented to the wisdom in what he was saying. She was angry, frustrated, frightened, and confused, but most of all she was spent.

Undressing to her slip in the darkness, she slid under the blankets and fisted them. Within a few moments, she was the only one still awake, abandoned to the snores and heavy breathing of her brother and Pierce.

Turning her head, her thoughts traced the mesmerizing dance of the flames in the coal fire, which was strangely in sync with the anxious pulsing of her heart.

She yearned to wake up to the Uncle Tomas of her youth with his warmth, laughter, and energy. The gifts, the adoration, and the way he lit up a room. This Patrick Feagles bore semblances of the man of her memory, but he was an imposter, dark and ruined. This she knew.

Was this what America did to an Irishman, and was this to be her fate as well? Into what strange country had she arrived? New York appeared rich and vibrant, yet it lacked the civility and character of the land on which she was raised.

And what of Margaret? Was Maggie alive? Would Clare get to see her again? Perhaps tomorrow?

The clock ticked fervently from above, and crackling arose from the hearth. Muffled voices of frivolity seeped through the floorboards—emanating from the rooms below.

Finally, Clare was able to console herself and surrender to the calming waves of sleep by meditating on the words of her brother: *"Tomorrow we'll get answers."*

# Chapter 23

# A Better Life

Clare awoke to the sounds and smells of sizzling rashers and eggs.

She opened her eyes slowly, surprised to see the sunlight already drenching the room with warmth. What time was it? Where was she? As she sat up, the drama of the night before returned painfully to her mind, creating a tightness to her stomach. The anxiety she felt awakened her senses.

Next to her Seamus slumbered, and Pierce was curled tightly in a blanket. Craning her head back, she saw the clock on the mantel read half past ten.

Clare took advantage of this time alone to put her dress on and then bent over her brother.

"Wake up, Seamus." She tugged on his quilted blanket. "It's nearly midday."

He mumbled protests about having been disturbed, but her words and the light must have saturated his thoughts and

Seamus rose. "Did we sleep that late?" Without waiting for an answer, he gave Pierce a sharp elbow.

"What's wrong?" the redhead said with a start. Then he rubbed his eyes and stretched his arms.

As the boys crept to their feet, Clare folded her blanket, laid it on the ground, and placed her pillow neatly on top. Despite the sun's strong influence, a chill passed through a crack in one of the windows, causing her to shudder. Clare crouched in front of the fire and rubbed her hands together, noticing how the coal glowed, crackled, and smelled differently from the turf used at home. She stood and found herself drawn toward the iron clanks of cookery and joined her hostess in the kitchen.

"Oh my." Tressa jerked, then slapped her hand to her chest. "You shouldn't creep up on an old woman, you know. But good morning to you, Miss Blue Eyes."

Clare smiled, but it seemed ingenious. Did this woman know about her uncle's past? But what if Tressa was just another unknowing victim of his fraudulent ways? How cruel it would be of Clare to add to Tressa's pain.

"How wondrous." Clare admired the bacon in the iron skillet as the last hints of bubbling pink turned brown before her eyes. Eggs gurgled in a separate frying pan, dancing on a pool of grease, their yolks perfectly domed with a sheen of yellow.

"Paddy instructed me to treat our guests royally." Tressa waved a spatula at Clare. "I must say, your arrival has moved the man to great cheer. 'Whatever the boys want. Whatever the lass desires.' Those were his very words to me this morning. Usually he's not much for welcoming visitors in his home. Grouchy about it, even. As he likes to say, 'Hospitality has the misfortune of causing folks to linger.'"

Tressa blurted out a laugh before glancing at Clare, then sobering. "Not that I'm opposed to your lingering at all. I'm a lonely woman, I am. Young ones like you brighten the day. It's just Patrick dotes on his privacy, what little he gets."

Tressa flipped the eggs clumsily, and she cursed as yellow rivulets escaped the transparent encasements of a yolk. Clare noticed a large eggshell in the pan, and as much as she wished to pluck it out of the pan herself, she decided not to even mention it for fear of being impolite.

"It's not that Paddy doesn't have friends. People love him, they do." Tressa looked up at the ceiling. "Rough. Too fond of drink. And a poor wagerer at that. But he'll make you smile and laugh. He's got his gentle side as well."

She coughed. "The smokes have it in for me." She turned to Clare. "You do like eggs and bacon?"

"Most definitely," Clare said without restraint before gathering her manners. "I mean, you shouldn't feed us. It was overly kind of you to let us bed here for the night."

"Bah." Tressa waved away her protest. "You wouldn't shame us by refusing our graces, would you?"

"Of course not, mam." Clare stared into the pan for a few moments before asking, "Will Mr. Feagles be joining us for breakie?"

"Oh no. Paddy is always out before sunrise. Matters not what time he goes down."

Clare tried to mask her disappointment but could tell she failed by Tressa's expression.

"Don't worry, dear. He'll be back before noon, which will be soon upon us. He told me as he was leaving this morn that he's got plenty to talk about with the three of you. As a matter of fact, he said to make sure you didn't leave before he got back. Grab those plates for me, would you?"

Clare nodded and retrieved a stack of dishes from a high black shelf braced against a wall covered with faux marble paper.

The china was white, encircled by a wreath of painted blue roses. One plate at a time, Tressa slapped on large portions of eggs and bacon.

As she did, Clare asked the question she had been afraid to ask. "And what exactly does Mr. Feagles do, may I ask?"

Tressa looked at her askance, and Clare worried she had crossed some line of propriety. Swallowing deeply as she held her breath, Clare was relieved to see the woman's momentary odd expression replaced with a warm smile.

"Oh, I suppose you wouldn't know," Tressa said. "Why you're newly on the island. Still with salt water in your hair and barnacles on your feet." She laughed heartedly and snorted before covering her mouth. "Why, everyone knows Patrick is a sporting man."

"A sporting man?"

"Oh, dear, you really are a fresh one, aren't you? Yes. A sporting man. Although, in truth, he's not much of a sporting man as fighting isn't his suit. It's more he caters to the sporting men and their ilk."

Clare shook her head. "I don't . . . I don't understand."

"Of course you wouldn't. Let's see. Well, most make a living by laboring on the streets or the docks or as a merchant or in the factories. But the sporting man doesn't believe in all this. He drinks, fights, gambles, frolics with the women, and then drinks again. In the Five Points you're High Society if you can live this kind of life."

"Sounds like proper living to me," Seamus said, entering the room.

"It is, if you can get it, young man," Tressa said. "Now these sporting men and all who wish they could be, need places for entertainment. You know, with the hard times comes a greater need for pleasure. A place to cool your heels and wet your mouth. Some ladies to soothe your nerves. And gambling. Oh, do they like their gambling. They'll wager on cards, the numbers game, man fights, dog fights, cock fights, and cockroach fights if they can."

"And Patrick provides these services?" Seamus asked.

"He does," Tressa said with some pride. "And a few more . . . that are probably not proper to mention. That would, of course, be Paddy and his partner."

"Seems a far distance from working a farm," Clare said.

Tressa grimaced. "Paddy? A farm? That's a fine notion." She laughed. "No. Can't vision that. But he's a fine businessman."

"You say he has a partner?" Seamus said.

Tressa's mood changed suddenly. "Well. Not so much a partner as the one man Paddy answers to. Although few know of him, and he's rarely seen. I've only seen him once or so meself. A rather strange man, but it's all worked well for Paddy. They have some type of arrangement that came to be not long after Patrick first arrived in the city. That was even before I met Paddy."

She handed the plates to them. "But enough of this talk. I've told you more than I probably should have. What blathering! Be kind and don't mention to Paddy I've been prating about his business. Come now. Let's eat. The food will taste better warm."

Clare had even more questions to ask than before, but guilt already plagued her for pressing the woman. They carried their breakfast out to the main room, where Clare was pleased to see Pierce had packed up their belongings and prepared the table in anticipation of the meal.

Within a few moments, they were seated and enjoying their breakfast, the only sound the clanking of the cutlery against the china.

As Clare ate her eggs and bacon, she felt almost giddy with the luxury of having two such meals back to back. But she kept her composure. She questioned whether it was proper to accept this hospitality at all until she understood the depths of her uncle's treachery.

She didn't dwell there for long. Instead, Clare surrendered to the sweet lure of indulgence.

After breakfast, Tressa took them down the hallway to an adjoining apartment, and with a rattle of iron, she chose a key from her ring and inserted it into the lock on the door. Before she could turn it, the oak-slatted door swung open.

Out sprung a man, tall and slender, with a pregnant woman trailing behind him. They were carrying bulging luggage and appeared to be harried and distraught.

"Ah, Mr. Bainsworth," said Tressa. "My apologies. I thought you had already cleared out."

The man, whose thin mustache appeared a bit crooked and hastily waxed, let out a deep sigh as he shifted the heavy bags to try to bear them more comfortably. "Well, as you know, our new arrangements were shared with us just this morning."

"You've been lovely tenants. You'll be missed." Tressa turned to the woman. "And you, dear. Take care of that little one."

"Come, Gladys." The man scowled as he allowed his wife to waddle before him and then they headed down the hall.

Tressa watched them disappear from the hallway into the stairwell. "Poor dears." She turned back toward Clare and the boys and tried to restore her smile. "I think you'll find this to your suiting." She entered as Clare looked back at the dejected couple and felt her guilt rise, but she couldn't think quick enough of what could be done.

With their packs and belongings slung over their shoulders, the three of them followed behind as Tressa moved about, opening shutters in the main room and the bedroom and lighting candles in the kitchen. The apartment had the same floor plan as that of Uncle Tomas, and though pedestrian in style it was completely furnished with tables, chairs, a bed, shelves bearing books, and pots hanging from the kitchen walls.

"This place has meaning for me," Tressa said as she opened some of the cupboards in the kitchen. "Oh, dear, we'll need to get some food in here."

She walked back into the main room, with the three of them following as chicks would a hen. Tressa bent over and picked up a wood bellow leaning against the hearth and pumped it a few times, causing flames and sparks to rise from reddened coals. "It's chilled in here, but it should warm up soon enough. We'll get some more coal."

Tressa headed toward the front door, then stopped, turned, and looked around reflectively, as if she was drawing memories from the walls themselves. "Paddy and I first met as neighbors. I was managing affairs downstairs and happily living alone where I am now. At least I believed so. He moved into this place. He didn't have many belongings at the time, and as you could see didn't have the greatest of tastes. But it didn't stop me from falling for him. He moved into my place and rented this out until, of course, a year or so later when he let his sister Rose live here until she went back to Ireland."

"Well. Enough of that," she said abruptly. "It's yours now. I'll head off to the market and work on filling your cupboards. I'm sorry they are so bare."

"This is quite lovely," Clare said. "But I fear it's too dear for us."

Tressa chortled. "You're a curious one, Blue Eyes. There is no rent for you, dear. Paddy has taken kindly to the three of you. Says he wants to keep you close to us, just as family."

"We couldn't—"

"It will help us get started." Seamus stepped forward, interrupting Clare. "We'll work our way to fixing our keep as soon as we can."

"Well, that shouldn't take long," Tressa said. "I believe Paddy's wanting to talk of that very subject with you today. He's got intentions for you two boys." She took off a key from her ring and handed it to Seamus. "Now, I'll be along. Off to the market for my new friends. Get yourself settled and your man should be by soon."

There was a screech that came through the floorboards, followed by the angry voices of several women entering in a discordant chorus of protest.

Tressa smiled warmly. "That's our girls down below. You'll hear a skirmish or two through the day. Must be another customer trying to skip his debt. It will all settle soon. Well, I must be going." She turned to go away but paused. "Paddy's looking toward your time together. Something about you young people has his spirits lifted."

With that, she departed. They listened as her steps on the floorboards faded away.

Seamus plopped down on a leather chair, then picked up a pipe sitting on the table beside him. He brushed the end on his sleeve and put it in his mouth. "Have you some matches? There is some smoking left in this."

Pierce picked up the wood bellow leaning against the hearth and fanned it, causing the coals to turn a bright and fiery red. He took a long matchstick from a tin box and lit it from the flames, and cupping his hands he walked it over to Seamus.

With a nod of appreciation, Seamus leaned in toward Pierce and drew in deeply on the pipe. The flame on the tip of the matchstick reached toward the bowl of tobacco and smoke rose from the orange glow.

"Can you believe this?" Seamus said. "See how our circumstances prospered in just one day?"

Pierce laid down on a sofa upholstered with a floral pattern with his arms perched behind his head and his feet propped on the armrest. "Do you think they'll let us stay?"

Clare wanted to say something to both boys, but her curiosity proved greater. She went into the kitchen and opened and shut cabinets, finding it bare of food but full of mismatched cutlery and dishes. Then she headed into the adjoining bedroom and sat on the bed to test out the mattress. Its springs creaked when she did, but it seemed comfortable and inviting. Looking toward the window, she saw dust dancing in the rays of light.

She stepped down from the bed and walked over to the black bureau nestled against the wall. Clare pulled out each of the four drawers, finding them empty with the exception of the lowest, which rattled with mouse droppings as she opened it.

"Disgusting," she whispered.

She began to shut the drawer, then stopped. She was being lazy. Clare pulled it out all of the way, having to jostle it at the end to fully free it from its frame. She carried the drawer over to the sunlight and cradled the drawer under her arm as she unlatched a rusty brass hook and pushed the window shutters outward.

The breeze came in fresh and cool, and Clare stuck her head outside and looked at the world of activity below. Carriages hoofed by, pedestrians sauntered, hurried, and squabbled.

Voices of children, merchants, and newsboys echoed through the dirty cobblestone roads.

Clare waited patiently for there to be a clearing in the walkway three stories below, and then she turned the drawer upside down and drummed on it. As she did this, Clare noticed something peculiar attached to the upper right bottom of the drawer. It was a small gold key, attached to the wood by a small pool of hardened candle wax.

*What could this be? Should I leave it?*

Clare tugged on it gently and it snapped out of the dry wax with ease. There it was now, in her hands. She had no way of putting it back. At this point, she'd have to give it to Tressa or Uncle Tomas and hope they believed she wasn't being meddlesome.

She bent down and returned the drawer to its place, then stood. She examined the key closely in her cupped hand, using the sunlight from the window. The key seemed too small to fit a door, yet it was sturdy and finely crafted. Its purpose must be to open a lock of some importance.

Clare went out to the main room to share her discovery with Seamus and Pierce, but instead felt angered when she saw the two of them sprawled out across the furniture. She slipped the key into her dress pocket and buttoned it.

"We can't stay here, you know."

Seamus released a slow exhale from his purloined pipe. "And why is that, dear sister?"

"Leave? Why's that?" Pierce said.

"Must I waste words on this?" Clare's pulse was starting to rise. "We're in this place owned by a charlatan, a fraud, the very one who happens to be our uncle, the brother of our father."

Seamus sat up. "What will we gain by exposin' him now?"

"Some character," she responded. "And what of Maggie? Don't you have a heart for your family?"

"Lower your voices," Pierce said. "We'll be heard."

"I'll speak my mind clearly. I won't be staying in this place. If it means I am on the streets by myself, so be it. I'll be better off than here with the two of you, pandering to my aunt's traitor."

Seamus stood and put his hands on Clare's shoulders. "Don't judge us so harshly. Yes. I want to hear all of the story. I want to find Margaret. But our uncle asked for us to hear him out. I suppose he is deserving of a little patience, and perhaps some grace. Even if he is all you fear he is, we have to sort through this properly."

"And how would that be?" She crossed her arms.

"We can't forget about our family. The ones back home. They're needing us to be successful. If we can make our way with our uncle's help, whether he's the villain you believe, we shouldn't be hasty to throw away our good fortune."

"We haven't had much of that," Pierce said.

Clare grunted and gritted her teeth, but the wisdom of what her brother said made sense.

"Let's hear him out," Seamus said. "And then we'll decide what's next. But let's keep our senses about us."

Their conference was interrupted by a firm knock on the door. Before they had much chance to exchange glances, the handle turned and bursting through the door came Uncle Tomas, with the verve Clare recognized from her youth.

Dandily dressed in dark brown pants, a taupe vest, and a black stovepipe hat, Uncle Tomas's smile spread broadly across his reddened face, displaying more teeth than should properly fit a mouth.

"How do you fancy your lodgings?" he said. "Come now. Gather yer boots, hats, and dresses. I have much to show you today. Found you work as well, I did. But we'll discuss all that later. Let's be gone. Time to see the city and pluck her fruits."

Clare tried to be angry, in loyalty to her aunt and as a guard against compromise. But, she found herself slipping into the grasps of her uncle's charm and this disgusted her. They gathered themselves and soon they were heading out with their merry guide.

As she followed behind, Clare fumbled with the key in her pocket.

## Chapter 24

# OF THE CITY

They walked through the crowded streets of the Five Points, and though Clare's emotions were churning with confusion and guilt, there was also a surging exhilaration.

Clare relented, fascinated and enraptured with the sights and activity of the village. The world rose around her in fresh vibrancy. As Clare and the boys struggled to keep up with her uncle's pace, something else soon became evident to her: The city was parting around the man.

"Hello, Mr. Feagles," said a man in a tattered jacket.

"Good day to you, sir," another bellowed from the doorway as they passed.

"Well to see you," said one of two women who passed carrying brightly colored parasols.

"Pleasure, sir," said a tall man with a scraggly beard as he bowed almost painfully.

In between these greetings there were those who would wave, lift a hat, smile warmly, and curtsy. Uncle Tomas would do his best to acknowledge each and every one of them with a nod, a wink, and at times a pithy greeting. He stopped a few to inquire about the health of their family or how their jobs were going. With a few he touched on politics or discussed whether the dark clouds on the horizon were going to make their way inland.

Clare watched with amazement, even though this all seemed more in character with the man she adored through her youth.

In between his interactions with the people of his neighborhood, he would share intimate details about those he had greeted, point out the most reputable merchants, and offered stories on the history and happenstances of the buildings. He would show them his favorite places for meals and libations.

Uncle Tomas stopped at nearly every food vendor they would pass, picking carefully through the offerings before tossing to the three of them the choicest of crisp apples, warm bread, buttered rolls, sweet pastries, and exotic fruit. So much so, they began to fill their pockets with the excess.

Her uncle didn't pay coin nor bill, and the merchants never offered a hint of protest. He floated through these streets scattered with rubbish, beggars, and thieves as if he landlorded the entire city, owning not only the buildings and the stores but the people themselves. With guilty delight she experienced a sense of entitlement and even a touch of royalty as she followed behind him.

When they paused at a tobacconist stand, Clare took the opportunity to drift off a slight distance as Uncle Tomas outfitted Pierce and Seamus with pipes. Clasping her hands behind her back, she meandered over to a merchant's window and gazed inside.

Through the glass she could see it was a women's clothier,

and although the shop was empty of patrons, it was full of a variety of colorful and well-crafted garments, each meticulously displayed. There before her eyes, posturing on a wooden mannequin, was a delicate yet tastefully subdued dress. It was woven from cotton fabric with broad vertical stripes alternating in light blue and off-white shades, with floral patterns along the seams. Draped over the shoulders was a hand-sewn lace scarf, which was secured with a gold and pearl brooch.

Clare looked back and saw the three men laughing as Tomas lit their pipes. When she turned to look at the dress again, she noticed her own reflection in the window and she stumbled backward. In contrast to the dresses in the store, hers was plain and ill fitting. She looked foolish with her brother's hat on her head, and when she lifted it, her hair was still much too short to her liking. Lowering her head, she wanted the image before her to go away.

"Do you fancy the dress?"

Clare felt a hand on her shoulder and turned to see her uncle's reddened face brimming with cheer. She shook her head.

"Come, I've sent the lads to the pub across the street, and they'll be busying themselves with a few pints. What say you and I do some shopping?"

She wanted to say no, but she found herself without a reason to explain why. Uncle Tomas opened the door and a bell hanging from the frame rattled. He waved her inside.

Clare glanced back at the tavern where Seamus and Pierce must have gone, and she was angered they were so easily drawn away from her. Nodding to her uncle, she entered the doorway and onto the uneven floorboards of the store.

Rising from a chair in the back of the room, as if from slumber, a rounded woman in a canary-hued silk dress greeted them in a loud voice laced with laughter.

"Well, strain me eyes. Patrick, where did you find this beauty? They get younger and prettier each . . ."

Uncle Tomas halted her abruptly. "Molly. This one is like kin to me. Family. Not long from home."

She paused and tilted her head at him. "Well, that doesn't make her a wee bit less enticing. Will you look at those eyes?" Molly cupped her hand under her double chin, and narrowing one eye, she surveyed Clare intently. "Hmmm . . . well. We'll need to get her out of those worn threads. Much to do here, I'll say."

Clare's uncle gave her a worried glance, as if to see if she was insulted, and then he turned back to the woman. "I'm not certain, but I believe the young lady favors the dress in the window."

"Certainly she does." Molly continued to analyze Clare, as a painter would stare down a canvas prior to pressing toward it with a moist brush. The woman twirled her finger in the air and, awkwardly, Clare gyrated in a full circle. This all made her uneasy, but there was also a sense of pampering that gave her a pleasant chill through her spine.

"Hmmm. Yes. Uh-huh." Molly contorted her face as she stared down at her subject, and then after several moments she clasped her hands together with resolution. "First, we must take care of something. Follow me."

With this Molly turned, revealing a rose colored bow, which was formed from the sash around the woman's bountiful waist.

Clare looked over to Uncle Tomas and couldn't help but spill out a girlish smile, and he raised an encouraging eyebrow in return. They followed Molly to the far corner of the store, where she was climbing a stool and then reaching up toward a row of wigs displayed on a row of hooks against the wall.

She pulled one down and started descending before pausing

and reaching for another. When she climbed down, she held one in each hand and looked back and forth repeatedly until she said succinctly, "It's this one here."

Clare questioned her uncle with her eyes.

"Go ahead," he said. "Try 'er on. Molly doesn't miss often."

"Missed have I once?" Molly grimaced. She held the wig out to Clare. "Here you are, precious. You'll love this one. I'm quite certain."

Reluctantly, Clare held her hand out and took the long, black hair from Molly. It was shorter than her hair was in Ireland, but it was nearly exact in color and style. She held it up for a few moments and then looked at Molly meekly.

"Oh, poor dear." The woman chuckled. "It won't bite you. Let me put it on for you. Come sit in this chair before the mirror."

Clare followed her directions and watched in the looking glass as Molly came from behind her and placed the wig over her head, adjusting it before pulling out a brush and tending to the stray hairs. "There you are dear. What do you think?"

It was as if Clare were looking at a lost friend, one she feared would never return. She had forgotten her beauty and, in fact, resolved herself to never seeing it again. But there before her was the woman who had beguiled the men in her village back in Branlow. Until now, until this very moment, she had treated her allure as a burden. It bothered her to draw the gaze of boys and men and have them babble in her presence.

Yet she was pleased with the face staring back at her. She welcomed it. Having been unnoticed, ignored for the past three months, she realized the gift she once had. Clare yearned to see the heads turn in her direction, men to pause and lift their hats. Was this wrong to feel this way?

"Are you okay, dear?"

Clare snapped out of her thoughts. "Yes. Yes, of course."

"Well?"

"It's lovely. I like it quite well."

Molly leaned in over Clare's shoulder and peered into the mirror. "Yes. That will suit you fine indeed."

Clare smiled and turned her head from side to side, thrilled at what she was seeing. "Ma'am?"

"Yes, dear?"

"Do you think I might try on that dress?"

## Chapter 25

# THE IRISH SOCIETY

 The wind swept up as Clare walked out of Molly's store, and had she not raised her hands to her new hat, it would have blown off her head. If the breeze had its way, it might have taken her new wig as well.

Glancing back into the glass of the storefront, pretending to be adjusting her hat, she admired her reflection, hardly remembering the frumpy woman who entered the shop less than an hour earlier. Off to her side, her uncle was grinning broadly, his arms full of boxes of other items he had purchased on her behalf. He had told her, "A lady needs more than one dress."

For a moment, the thought came upon her, *What have I done?* But she brushed it aside as quickly as it came. Not today. She was tired and felt entitled to one day of reprieve from poverty, oppression, and sickness. Clare felt new, clean, alive, and she liked the way it felt.

"Really, this is much too much," she said to Uncle Tomas as she turned.

"What good is hard work if it doesn't allow an old man to experience joy on occasion?"

Clare felt an impulse to hug him, but something inside held her back. They looked at each other awkwardly.

The cheer on his face faded to one of more seriousness, a touch of melancholy. "Clare, dear. I know you have questions of me. Concerns. Rightly so. Shall we talk?"

Clare peered into his eyes and saw sincerity. "I'd like that very much."

"Then come with me." He held his arm out to her and she received it. "I have a place I'd like to share with you. It means a great deal to me."

She began walking with him but then stopped. "What about Seamus and Pierce?"

Her uncle laughed as he looked toward the tavern across the street. "I believe the boys will be content. Don't you?"

"I suppose," she said, with a hint of disappointment. But then with all of the months of difficulty they endured, there shouldn't be anything wrong with Seamus and Pierce having a time of it.

They started moving again, stepping out of the way of a woman who passed them with a crying baby in each arm.

"Margaret?" Uncle Tomas watched her closely as he spoke her name.

"Yes," Clare said, her body tightening. "Tell me about Maggie."

He glanced up as if he was searching for the proper words. "You must first understand how much I loved your sister. Both of you girls. But if I'm speaking honestly to you, and I am, Maggie had a spirit in her as no other." He chuckled to himself.

"What happened? We heard your ship was lost."

"No. The ship made it here just fine. Just the usual hardships of voyage. It was when we arrived that the real troubles occurred."

Tomas shook his head. "Ahh, your sister Margaret, she was so full of life when we arrived here. She was dancing in the streets, breathing in this new place as if she was to take it all as her own. And she would of. Maggie would of. I'm quite sure of that."

An elderly woman wearing rags and with one eye missing from its socket came up to them as they walked. "Mister?"

Uncle Tomas dipped into his breast pocket, pulled out a few coins, and placed them in the woman's cup. He turned a corner on the road and gently tugged on Clare's arm. They stepped past a couple of pigs rummaging for food.

"But we struggled," Uncle Tomas said. "It was a hard life, it 'twas. We found a place in the Old Brewery building. We slept with the rats and the filth and with the dregs of the city. Some of us were just off a ship with no place to go, but many were thieves, murderers, and miscreants of society. If one ate, we all ate. But most of the time, none of us ate. We didn't have any fuel for the fire, and on snowy nights the only warmth we had would be from sleeping tightly together."

Uncle Tomas crossed the street with Clare on his arm, and they waited as a carriage passed by before dodging the mud holes in the street on the way to the other side.

"Good day, Patrick," said a man pushing a cart full of manure.

"Lovely day," Tomas said with a lift of his hat.

"It was Maggie's spirit that kept us all from giving up, I'm sure it was. She labored harder than all of us. While I'd try to scare up jobs at the harbor or in the streets, she did all she could. At one point she was even gathering hair from grates in the street for the wig makers." He looked up toward Clare's wig. "Yes. Imagine that."

The thought brought Clare shame, and she wished he wouldn't have shared that detail. "Your story is quite sad. I pray it ends happily."

"I'm afraid not, dear." He pointed her to a bench outside of a sundries store. When they sat, he placed the boxes down carefully and pulled out a pipe and lit it. As he exhaled, the cool air filled with smoke and mist.

A chill came over Clare and she shuddered.

"At one point, Maggie was even down to begging." He looked to Clare and nodded. "Yes, I'm afraid it's so. It made me ill to see her lower her pride to such a level." His voice began to waver. "I suppose I shouldn't have let her. We tried, we did. But she said it was a far better outcome than starving, and on this we could muster no argument.

"One night, when it was snowing heavy, which was good, actually, because it meant I could earn with a shovel. And earned I did. So much so I had bought us some corn meal and even a small piece of salt pork. Couldn't wait to share the news with Margaret, but when I got to where we were staying, she was not around. No one knew where she was.

"I grabbed a lantern and went into the throes of the storm. I walked every street, over and over again, until I could feel no toes in me boots. The snow grew angry and I couldn't even see me own hand even if I held it before me eyes.

"Who knows how long it was, but I finally saw Maggie." Uncle Tomas paused and gathered himself. "She had fallen to sleep in the snow on the side of the street. I could see the tracks where people had just circled around her as if she was rubbish. Her body was froze and stiff. Margaret was gone."

Clare put her arm around her uncle and pulled him into her.

"I'm sorry, Clare." He looked at her as a tear traveled down his wrinkled cheek. "Breaks me heart. I failed yer ma. I failed yer pa. I know he'd never forgive me, and I don't think that he should."

She gazed at the man who so closely resembled her father, and her emotions sparred with her sensibility. Her hopes to see Maggie again were dashed. It was as if her sister had died in her arms twice. How much cruelty could she bear? What kind of a God would allow so much hurt and pain?

"We didn't have enough to buy her a coffin," he continued. "I didn't want her body to end in the soil of this cursed land. I couldn't get her back to Ireland, but I could get her to sea. That very evenin', in the face of the storm, I carried her for miles to the shoreline o'er me shoulder, warmed by the flames of me anger. I pinched an oar boat off of the docks and gathered rocks and rope. I took Maggie out as far as I could row in the waves and dropped her body into the sea, with stones as weights.

"I came wee close to jumping in after Maggie and finishing it all. A shamed, broken man. It would have made the stories you heard truthful. But something kept me from that fate. A force drew me, powerfully, and I fought to keep me life. Having drifted out far, it took all of me being just to make it back to shore.

"That's when it all changed. No one knew who I was or cared if I sunk to the water's bottom. I decided I had enough of being Tomas Hanley, the poor Irish farmer. What had that gotten my father, your father? In that moment, I realized there were no thieves, no villains, just survivors. Shamed of who I was. That's when I became Patrick Feagles. It would be later when I would change my name to avert a scrap with the law. But that was the day it really happened."

Clare didn't know how to respond. She stared ahead blankly. On the street she saw two men scouring the road for fruit that had fallen from wagons. They carried it in baskets nearly as large as they were.

"What about Aunt Meara? Why didn't you ever write?"

He shifted. "Is that what she told you? I never wrote? I nearly wore these fingers to me bones writing that woman." His voice started to grow in intensity. "It was her idea for me to go to America. She told me she would come right behind me. As soon as I had enough for passage, she'd come out with me. I must have sent her twenty letters without one coming in return. Well, there was one received. She actually said, and I remember it to this day, word by word, 'If you don't have any earnings to include in the envelope, don't bother sending the letter.'"

"That's seems unlikely," Clare said with a huff. "She's heartbroken to this day."

"Believe what you will, child." Uncle Tomas's voice became harsh and he stood. "I'm not out to convince you."

Then, as if embarrassed by his expression of distemper, he softened his demeanor. "Come, Clare. Let us not cloud this day. These are difficult memories for me. Harder times. Forgive me and allow me." He lifted up the boxes and positioned them in one arm, then held out the other to Clare.

She stood, straightened out her dress, tightened the fit of the hat on her head, and then accepted his arm.

His smile returned to his face. "Right around the corner there is something I need to show you. It's the main purpose of our little walk together. I believe you'll be pleased."

Clare offered no resistance, although her mind was a flurry of emotion. She didn't know what to believe at this point.

Just a short way farther, they arrived at the corner of the street where an impressive building rose out among all others. It appeared newly remodeled and had the semblance of a bank, with its walls freshly painted in dark green and with gold trim framing the ledges and windows. Carefully crafted oversized cherry doors gave the storefront a sense of richness and exclusivity.

Above the entranceway was a large sign with the words "The Irish Society" and underneath in smaller print was written "International Headquarters. Five Points, New York. America. Established 1843." To the left of these words was the very symbol Clare first saw when the keener handed her the necklace, a clover of three leafs. Clare grasped for the pendant hanging around her neck.

Uncle Tomas grasped for the door handle, but it opened before he could reach it.

"Good day, Mr. Feagles." The man who greeted them was short of stature, and although sharply dressed in a long coat with tails, he seemed hardened by life, full of years and out of his class in these surroundings. "Let me take these boxes from you. And your coat as well, sir?"

"Thank you, James," Uncle Tomas said.

The inside of the building didn't match the appearance of its exterior, but still it was well kept with understated furnishings. There were tables against the walls, with several people seated writing on parchment with ink-quill pens. At the back of the room, a man sat behind a caged booth, and a short line of people were waiting to be served, in what fashion was unclear to Clare. Upon the walls hung gold-leaf framed portraits of men who she did not recognize but who posed in a way that made them seem important.

He smiled at her with yellowed teeth. "Go ahead. Sit yourself down, Clare, find a pen, and write home."

Things became clear as Clare realized the others at the table were composing letters. Without hesitation and feeling her heart rise on the news, she found herself a seat at the end of the table, next to a man in a dark wool coat who smelled of soured ale and whose eyebrows sprouted like gray weeds. He slid his chair to the side to allow her more room and then gave her a second look, this one accompanied by a lusty grin.

As she settled in her seat, her uncle squeezed her shoulder. "Write what you wish, Clare. And if you find it in your heart to spare mention of me for now, I'll be grateful to you."

Not knowing what to think of his request but overjoyed at the prospect of writing at last, she nodded and mutely smiled at him. But his attention was drawn toward the front of the room, and his face was etched with concern.

Clare turned to see the subject of his attention and locked gazes with a striking man, tall with blond hair and with circular wire-rimmed spectacles, which gave him an air of intelligence and refinement.

He was clothed with confidence and nobility, yet there was an underlying gentleness in his spirit Clare found powerfully alluring. The man bore a pure and gentle beauty.

Clare couldn't tell if he was staring back at her or toward her uncle, but she felt embarrassed enough to look down. She grabbed a blank parchment and drew a quill, gripping it firmly in her hand.

Unable to take her mind off of the stranger, she peered up briefly, yet often enough to see her uncle greet the man, then they went outside and spoke in animated fashion.

After a few nervous glimpses, Clare dipped her quill in the inkwell and lost herself in the fondest memories of those she had left behind.

Dearest family,

I write to you from a parish called Five Points, in the city of New York in the nation of America. Certainly on account of your prayers and God's favor, all three weary travelers—Seamus, Pierce, and myself—have safely arrived. Not to cause you concern and undue worry, but the travel across the sea was most difficult, and if not for the caring of my brother and Pierce, I surely would not have survived my fever.

After many months, and thousands of miles won by sea, we are now settling into our new lives. We have yet to secure full labors, but through good fortune appear to be on it soon. It is our earnest desire to share all of the harvest of our efforts we can spare. I pray it will come soon and steady, just like the rains I so miss from home. It seems, in fact, even things I once foolishly considered a burden in Branlow are now deeply longed for in my heart.

Most of all, we miss each and every one of you so dearly. I hope we can accomplish our great task soon and the land back there heals so we can be together, in laughter and, yes, I daresay . . . hard work. I miss the farm, the soil, and the green of the fields.

Davin and Ronan. Please mind your sister Cait. Such heavy burdens she carries now without me, more than you can imagine. I wish to hear stories of how you both were gentlemen to her and tended to your chores.

Ma, I pray you are feeling well, and Da, I appreciate you more each day we are parted.

I'll have much to share with each of you soon. You can expect many letters to follow as my adventure is yours as well. What great joy it would be to receive your correspondences, so don't delay so I know how to direct my prayers in your behalf.

Yours forever,
Clare

She blew gently on the letter to dry the ink, and as she held it up, she read it line by line. How dishonest it was of her to speak of prayer because in many ways, her faith was buried along with Grandma Ella years ago. Yet she allowed the words to remain because she saw it as a fresh and needed pledge.

"I miss you," she whispered.

"Are you speaking to me?" the old man with the large eyebrows said.

"No. I'm sorry." Clare was relieved to see her uncle entering the door. He paused and brushed his hair back, as if to clear his emotions, and then returned his hat to his head. Then the grin returned.

"Well? Is it ready?"

"It 'tis," Clare said. "What happens now?"

"The very best part of it all, girl."

She followed Tomas to the line formed at the cage, then lowered her head when she realized he was taking her to the front, despite glares shot at him when he passed.

The man behind the counter stepped to attention as Tomas approached, and a woman protested until she turned to see who it was. Thin to the bones with sunken cheeks, yet richly dressed in banker's clothing, the man fumbled with the curl of his waxed mustache. "Mr. Feagles, sir. How may I assist you?"

"Let me have the letter, Clare," Uncle Tomas said, and she handed it to him. He folded it without reading it. "Benjamin, post this to . . . are you ready to write this down? The Hanleys, Branlow, County Roscommon. On my credit, include a thirty pound note."

"Yes, sir, Mr. Feagles." The teller scribbled the information and then reached through the square opening in the brass bars of the cage to receive the folded parchment. "As the rest, sir?"

"Yes. That's right, Benjamin." Uncle Tomas turned to Clare and raised his eyebrows.

"Thirty pounds?" breathed Clare.

He seemed disappointed in her response. "We'll send more the next time around. You and your brother will be employed."

"No." Clare was flabbergasted. "I mean. That's truly generous . . . um . . . Mr. Feagles."

"Patrick."

"Yes. Patrick. That's our . . . that's our full passage paid." In Clare's mind she could imagine the surprised faces of her family as they opened the letter. "How long will it take to get there?"

"That's what this is all about. The Irish Society. We can't trust the thieving English with our money, so we charter our own ships. A little over three weeks by packet ship with good winds. Isn't that correct, Benjamin?"

"That's about right, sir. Twenty-five to thirty days."

Clare beamed and gave her uncle a hug.

He laughed heartily. "Let's go, Clare. We shouldn't keep these people behind us waiting."

She glanced behind her and saw the wrinkled brows of her audience. She was too happy to be bothered by their grumbling stares. She giggled and locked her arm in her uncle's. They were met by James, who handed them their boxes of Clare's clothing before opening the door for them with a bow.

Clare nodded at James with an air of royalty as she and Patrick Feagles exited the offices of the Irish Society.

# Chapter 26

# THE AMERICAN DREAM

The oak clock on the mantel reminded Clare she needed to hurry. She was drained, but exhilaration also fueled in her step, carrying her through the exhaustion. A life of toil was all she knew, and in some sense it made her feel alive and at home in New York.

Clare was doing well in this burgeoning metropolis. It had only been four weeks since she arrived in America, and already she had comfortable shelter and a wage-earning job.

Even more important, Clare had settled into a weekly ritual of posting letters to her family at the Irish Society each Sunday afternoon. It was her one day of Sabbath on an otherwise grueling seventy-hour workweek. But her laborious schedule was well worth the joy she experienced each time she slid her letter and surplus earnings to Benjamin in his cage.

In her correspondences she provided many of the intimate details of her journey in America; however, there was one she chose to omit. There was no mention of the man named Patrick Feagles.

It was the least she could do in gratitude for his patronage. Not only did he provide their apartment free of rent, but Tressa purchased all of their food and stocked their cupboards whenever they were away. This gave Clare the freedom to put almost every dollar she earned into those envelopes heading across the Atlantic. In some way, Clare allowed it to serve as slow penance for her uncle's sins.

Besides, the news of Patrick Feagles would only exacerbate Aunt Meara's grief. No. Clare wasn't fully convinced of her uncle's version of his marital discord, but she could see little profit in challenging the truth. It was best for all if Uncle Tomas remained in his watery grave.

Clare sealed the tomb by deciding to refer to him now only by his adopted name. She didn't know the sordid story behind his new identity and didn't feel the need to pry further into his past. On this side of the ocean, Patrick Feagles he would be.

Not only was Patrick providing for their daily necessities, but he had been good on his word about getting them work. Both Seamus and Pierce worked "in the business" as Patrick described it, and she didn't request any specifics on their duties, although she was convinced it would take them in an unfavorable direction.

Her brother had no such reservations. Seamus and Pierce were happily absorbed into the world of Patrick Feagles and shadowed the man as much as was tolerated. They would be out to the early hours of the day and sometimes not come home at all. Occasionally, she would see them at the card tables, in the taverns, or on the streets making transactions with nebulous characters.

Clare did worry about her brother, but it was time to loosen her grip of stewardship on Seamus. He was too old to coddle and it was time for him to reap or suffer from his own choices without her interference. Besides, he had tasted the freedom that came from being an immigrant in another country and no longer recognized her authority. For better or worse, Seamus was on his own.

As for Clare, she wanted nothing to do with her uncle's daily activities, and although she appreciated his generosity, her instinct pressed her to keep a distance. When Patrick had offered to assist in finding her a job, Clare accepted on the condition that she was only interested in "honest work."

"Honest work, eh?" He rubbed his chin and squinted as if he was thinking hard. "Not certain we have any of that here in the Five Points."

"Come on, Patrick, you know what I mean."

"All right. You want honest work. Then that's what we'll get for you."

Clare paused for a moment. "What have you in mind?"

"Your mother was quite handy with a needle, was she not?"

"She was."

"Did she learn you on any of it?"

"Some."

"Well, there you have it. I know a man who operates a seamstress factory. I'll see that you start tomorrow."

She laughed and then realized he was serious. "Just like that?"

Patrick flashed his yellowed teeth.

The next day, Patrick escorted Clare on the mile or so journey to the expansive four-story brick building of William & Howell Garment Manufacturers. As they entered the doorway, Clare was awestruck by the vastness of the factory. Machinery clattered as plumes of steam rose to the heights of the ceiling, and on endless rows of tables, mostly women were tasked with sewing and cutting fabric, while men tended to the equipment. It was unbearably hot inside, even in the cool of winter, yet Clare's senses were enlivened by the energy, voices, and diligence of those working the factory floors.

Patrick excused himself walking past a startled woman sitting at a front desk, and he headed to a side room, leaving Clare standing just inside the entranceway. The woman turned her glare toward Clare, who merely shrugged. It didn't take long until Patrick returned. He was accompanied by a nervous man wearing suspenders and sporting wire-rimmed spectacles who patted his moist forehead repeatedly with a handkerchief.

"Certainly, Mr. Feagles. We can find a station for the young lady. She does know the trade, Mr. Feagles?"

Patrick winked at Clare. "Why, of course, Mr. Howell. Her talents were well celebrated back in Ireland. It was a dear blow to her colleagues when they discovered she stowed away to America."

"I see," the man said, unpersuaded but apparently unwilling to challenge her uncle. "Follow me, young lady, and we'll get you your own station."

Clare's shifts began before sunrise and ended long after the darkness settled. Six days a week, with only fifteen minutes of breaks per shift. Her pay was a nickel per article of clothing, and as the floor stewards often reminded her, if she didn't hit her quota, there were many others begging to take her chair. Clare suspected the job would be hers until Patrick said otherwise, but she never pressed matters. Though thankful for her uncle's part in the matter, she was intent on keeping the job on her own merit.

Which was why, on this particular morning, Clare was so concerned about being late. She took one last look at the mirror and glanced at the clock. "Oh, dear."

As she went downstairs, she saw Patrick playing cards with Seamus, Pierce, and another man whose back was turned to her.

She considered trying to bolt quietly for the door due to her tardiness and her uncle's tendency toward long-windedness. But before she took two more steps, Patrick spotted her and beckoned her with a maudlin wave of drunkenness.

With no other recourse, she approached the table and as she did, the man sitting opposite her uncle turned and then stood and nodded to her in greeting. He was broad shouldered, with a square chin, draping sideburns, and deep brown eyes, which lit up faintly as he looked at her, like a candle peering from a dark cave.

She held out her hand to him in an awkward gesture of greeting, and he kissed it gently, surprising her and making her face rush with warmth.

Patrick eyed the two of them with a knowing smile. He lifted a bottle of amber liquor and went to pour it in a short glass, missing wildly before it filled. He held the glass to her in salute.

"Here's to the working woman." Then he lifted the glass to his lips, emptied it with one movement, then slammed it on the table.

Clare looked nervously at Seamus and then Pierce, who was glaring at the stranger.

"My dear Clare," Patrick said in a loud, slurring voice. "Is it time already for the good people to be laboring away? Have you no time for a game of chance?"

On the table were several empty bottles of, what appeared to be, whiskey, a pile of cards, and dollar bills scattered as if they were rubbish fluttering through the wind. Clare could only imagine how many shirts she would need to sew to make up for all of the money lying there in such slipshod fashion.

Pierce stood, leaned over, and gave her an awkward hug. "Off to work, are you?"

"Yes. And I mustn't be late."

"Mustn't you?" Patrick garbled. "Have you met John Barden? The great John Barden. The savior of the Irish civilization."

"I am new to his acquaintance." Clare wondered why she was blushing.

"Let us be strangers no more," John said in a deep voice without taking his eyes off of Clare.

"Do you know who John Barden is?" Patrick picked up his cards and reordered them.

"That is a champion fighter there before you," Seamus said to Clare and he rocked back in his chair with glazed eyes.

"Pleased to meet you, Mr. Barden," Clare said, trying to recapture her poise. "Now, I must be on my way. I surely will be late if I tarry further."

"Will we get to see you tonight?" John raised an eyebrow.

"Perhaps," Clare said in a flirtatious way so foreign to her. She turned and scurried for the door.

*What a terrific fool!*

Clare left the tavern into a wall of crisp air as the sun brought first light to the city. Her mind danced with both merriment and embarrassment and she replayed her encounter with John Barden as she ran almost the entire way to the factory.

Her efforts paid off, as she was one of several who entered through the large doors of William & Howell just prior to the hands of the large clock signaling it to be six o'clock in the morning.

Once inside she stood in line until reaching the desk where Diedre Turrell logged her in the attendance rolls with her large-plumed quill. "A bit tight, Miss Hanley, wouldn't you say?" The woman, whose hair was as tightly wrapped in a bun as possible, barely looked up from her book. "Next time. Fifteen minutes early or that will be half a day's wages."

"What?" breathed Clare, whose mind was drifting. "Yes. Of course. It won't happen again."

Clare scampered to her desk and barely sat down before the morning bell rang loudly, signifying the start of day.

In one movement, the entire room was alive with rattling machinery.

"Good morning, Miss Clare," Magdalene Beglan said cheerfully. She was a master seamstress with more than thirty years of experience and was tasked with teaching Clare the intricacies of the craft. Although her knuckles were gnarled like a tree's knot, she was still able to outproduce most of those on the floor.

Magdalene's rounded and cheerful face was squeezed into a bonnet that covered much of her gray hair. She had a kind disposition and was patient with Clare, whose skill level required it. However, under her mentor's gentle tutelage, Clare's development in the craft was admirably swift. But that didn't protect her from the whispered gossip that blossomed across the factory floor.

The constant prattle among the women kept the job's tedium at bay, and Clare's preferential treatment was a subject of intrigue. One of the more scandalous versions of the rumors stipulated that Clare was a mistress of Patrick Feagles. She learned there was no defense against the wildfires of the tongue and was left to suffer the indignity of ogling and laughter.

Magdalene did her best to shield Clare from the roguery, but the woman who sat on the other side of her workstation offered no such relief. In fact, Sara Atwood, a short woman with protruding eyeballs and frazzled blonde hair, tormented Clare with inquiries concerning Patrick Feagles. He was a man, apparently, Sara found to be most fascinating.

And today would be no different.

"So what was your Mr. Feagles up to this morning?" Sara asked with a churlish grin.

Clare sighed and sought relief from Magdalene and then turned back to Sara. "If you have such a keen interest in Mr. Feagles's character, you might question him directly."

"No," Sara said. "I much prefer asking you. It's safer. After all, he's a man of some mystery, wouldn't you say? And what was it exactly he had hanging over Mr. Howell to get someone as green as you a job like this? Something thick I'd say."

"Sara Atwood, have you no decency!" Magdalene snapped.

"Just being friendly with the girl." Sara held up the shirt she was sewing. "Will you look at that?" One of the sleeves was askance.

"Fine work there." Magdalene shook her head. "If you used your eyes more than your lips, you wouldn't be making so many mistakes. If the foreman sees that, he'll take your chair."

Sara looked to the left several stations down where a sturdy man with a forward lean at his shoulders walked with an air of authority, his arms clasped behind his back.

"Carl?" Sara snickered. "He wouldn't have a mean thought about me."

"He'd have plenty if he bothered looking at your needle-work," Magdalene said.

"Ouch." Clare shook her hand in response to the pain of the needle piercing her index finger. A bubble of blood formed on her fingertip.

"Be careful, child. You're working with white fabric. Make sure you bandage it."

Clare nodded at Magdalene. Looking at her hand, she could see the evidence of her learning miscues. They were scabbed and calloused and appeared to have aged many years in just her first few weeks on the job.

"What have you learned about your cousin?" Sara asked. "Has he arrived at a decision about . . . you know?"

"I'm afraid so." Magdalene sighed.

"Is he really going to go?" Sara's eyes opened wide. "What does your sister think of all of this?"

"She's devastated, she is." Magdalene met Clare's eyes as she glanced up from her task of wrapping the bandage around her finger. "They are mustering a new army regiment here to join the war."

"The war?"

Sara giggled. "The war. Yes, the war. Dearest Clare haven't you seen the posters all over the Five Points?"

Clare's face heated. "Yes. Of course." She had seen the recruiting signs on her way to and from the shop but hadn't paid much attention to what they said.

"I don't know why we're down in Mexico in the first place," Magdalene said with a huff.

"It's Mr. Polk." Sara folded the shirt she had repaired and stacked it with the others piled on the corner of her table. "I think he's quite handsome . . . in a presidential way, of course."

"Well, your man ought to get his own people to do his fighting," Magdalene said. "I've heard it said more than half the army are Irish lads. With work so scarce, the boys will carry a rifle rather than go home penniless. And what a price for their families to pay. Oh, dear."

"'Tis a shame, I'll give you that," Sara said. "But I must say, they do look smart in their uniforms, don't they?"

"It must pay well, I suppose."

"Not much, Clare," Magdalene said. "Considering the risk. The boys will do it because they get food and tents to sleep in so they can send their full wages home."

"Speaking of a battle," Sara said, "have you heard of John Barden?"

"You know what I think about boxing." Magdalene snorted. "Grown men bludgeoning each other as greater fools watch. What has society become?"

"What was that name?" Clare asked.

"I said John Barden," Sara responded, scrutinizing Clare. "Do you know of the man?"

Blood rushed to her face again, and she instantly regretted her question. "I may have heard of him."

"Did you see her face?" Sara smiled perversely. "I never seen it shining so."

"Leave the girl be." Magdalene waved her off.

"I will not. Our Clare not only likes him, she's a bit smitten."

"You're m-making too much of it," Clare stammered. "He's a friend of Patrick's, that's all."

"Of course he is. That's how you know him. But that isn't explaining the roses in your cheeks."

"He's a strapping man, that one." Magdalene smiled. "There's no shame in fancying him."

"I never said I fancied him." She raised her eyebrows at the old woman. "And I thought you were on my side."

"Well, his face is pretty for now. But not much for long."

"Really, Sara," Magdalene said. "You are tiring."

"What? Clare knows."

"And what is it I know? I barely know the man."

"Really. You haven't heard?"

"Are you ladies enjoying yourselves today?" The foreman had snuck up on them, with his arms folded across his chest above his large belly, and Carl rocked back and forth on his heels with an air of authority. "I expect more from you, Magdalene."

"Yes, Mr. Wallace."

"We was just talking about John Barden," Sara said. "Clare here is a dear friend."

"Is that so?" Carl said, with genuine interest expressed in a face pockmarked and ruddy in complexion.

"To be honest—"

"Don't listen to her," Sara interrupted Clare. "She's bashful about her love interests."

"What says old John about the fight?" Carl asked. "That Billy Tunnel must have him cowering. I'm surprised he hasn't left town."

"That shows what you know about anything," Sara said. "John is not afraid of nothing. He'll send ol' Billy back home, and he can take you with him."

Carl seemed to savor Sara's spunk. "Is that right? Well, I'm sure you'll be willing to put up your earnings on a proper wager."

"I just might." Sara lifted her nose but with a voice that wasn't as convincing.

"We'll get back to our work, Carl," Magdalene said. "I'll keep the ladies on it."

He nodded. "That would be a rightly notion. Mr. Howell has been disappointed with our quotas." He leaned forward and whispered, "We're supposed to let three go today, just to send a message."

"Well, I will assure you," Magdalene said, "we won't give you further reason for it to be one of us."

Carl fingered through the stack of shirts on Clare's table, and as he looked at her, she lowered her eyes and started to weave her needle again. From the periphery she could see him tuck his arms behind his back and start walking away.

That was all she needed to hear. Despite Sara's incessant blathering, Clare kept silent for the remainder of the day. But that wouldn't keep her mind from being filled with unfettered musing. Try as she might, she couldn't escape the brooding eyes of John Barden.

# Chapter 27

# THE ESCORT

When the final bell rang that evening, Clare was relieved she still had a job. Not that she really believed it was possible for her to be fired. But a pall had come across the factory floor as the news of the dismissals brought palpable tension throughout the building.

The darkness of the evening was upon them, and in the sparse gas lighting hanging from poles in the street, a flurry of white drifting snow was visible, although it had yet to collect on the ground.

Amidst the exodus of tired seamstresses into the flow of the streets, Clare locked arms with Magdalene and Sara. They had a couple of blocks in common before they scattered in separate directions, and it was their ritual to sojourn together. Even Sara's rattling was preferable to the eerie sounds of Clare's shadowy Five Points commute.

The first time she had taken the journey home by herself, Clare was stricken with fear. Most of the streets she traveled were well populated with men who glared as she passed, drunks, prostitutes, beggars, as well as groves of stragglers from labor ending.

She felt comforted in these crowds, as malcontented were many of the faces she passed. What chilled her to the core were those patches in her journey where there was an uneasy quiet, and she was alone except for those whose presence could be felt, but not seen, peering out from alleyways and dark crevices.

This was why she cherished having companionship for at least the beginning of her nightly trek home.

"Is misery the snow and wind," Sara said.

"Yes, it's biting." Magdalene wrapped her dark wool jacket tightly around her. "I hope it eases or we'll be trudging through it in the morning. What about you, Clare, poor dear?"

"Oh, I'm fine," she said, although the bright red coat Patrick had bought her offered more style than warmth.

Sara tugged on the two of them and they stopped in the middle of the road as they were crossing the street. "Is that . . . ?"

"Why it certainly is!" Magdalene said in a startled whisper.

Clare traced the direction of Sara's finger and saw standing on the corner, leaning against the gaslight with his arms crossed, none other than John Barden. When he saw he was recognized, John stood alert and tipped his high black hat, which was brimmed with snow.

What business could he have in ill weather at this time of night? Surely John couldn't be waiting for her? Clare glanced to her left and right on the chance there was someone else beside her who could be drawing his gaze.

"I suppose there is more to the story," Sara cackled.

"Come, Sara. Let's not be two old meddlesome ladies."

"There's only one old lady here, Magdalene. But go, go." Sara pushed Clare in his direction.

Clare tried to resist but stumbled forward. She had a terrible thought that her wig might be askew, but a quick survey with her hands seemed to confirm it was properly placed. *How presumptuous. What if he isn't even here to meet me?* There was no other choice now, as her two friends had abandoned her with trailing laughter.

Clare tried to recover her dignity and approached him with a trimmed gait. "Are you following me?" She tried her best to sound bothered by the notion.

He appeared amused. He stepped into the brightness of the lamp, and a glint of charm peered through the rough granite of his face. "If I say no, you'd be disappointed. Wouldn't you?" He spoke in a slow, deep, and measured voice.

"Not short on confidence, are you?"

"Lacking confidence is a liability in my profession." He smiled smugly. "Here." He unwrapped his coal black wool scarf from his neck and then put it around hers with a gentleness unusual for such a large man.

It made her uneasy for this relative stranger to be doing this for her, yet it was comforting as well. She tightened the scarf, which smelled of a masculine blend of tobacco smoke and sweat and was flecked with snow.

"Shall we?" He held out his arm.

Clare took his arm and then struggled to keep up with his lengthy steps as they moved forward. She glanced behind her to see Magdalene and Sara giggling and waving at her. She grimaced.

"And what exactly is your profession?" she asked as her free hand felt again to see if her wig was aligned.

"That would depend on who's asking, I suppose. To my employer, I serve as what you might call a peacemaker."

"A peacemaker?" she said with sarcasm.

"Yes. When I'm around, people seem to quiet their spirits."

"I thought you were a prizefighter."

He raised an eyebrow and smiled with mischief. "Now, Miss Hanley. Sport fighting is not legal in the city. Do I seem like someone who would venture outside of the law?"

"Then do you work for my uncle?" As soon as the words spilled from her lips, she tensed.

"Your uncle?" He frowned.

"Not my uncle." Clare stumbled. "I don't know what I was saying. I meant Patrick Feagles."

John met her eyes with a knowing glance, which made her wonder if he knew she wasn't telling the truth.

"Patrick? No. He is not my employer." He laughed. "I work for the man Patrick works for."

Clare was puzzled and now curious. "Patrick. Mr. Feagles. He works for another?"

"We all work for someone."

A strange chill swept through her body, and Clare stopped and glanced back toward an alleyway they had passed.

"What is it?"

At first Clare didn't answer. She just stared into the darkness, hoping for an answer, but fearful of discerning a shape. "It's . . . it's nothing."

"Did you see something?" His face showed concern for her, but there was a confidence as well that reminded Clare of how little she had to fear.

"Come." She pulled him forward to continue on their way back home. She waited several steps before she glanced back over her shoulder. Tonight wasn't the first time. All this week she had the strangest sensation she was being followed. Could it be a jealous Pierce? No. He made clear his affection for her and had been clinging of late, but certainly Pierce was above this type of behavior.

"These streets aren't safe for you to be walking alone at night. I think I'll escort you from here on out."

Clare started to protest, but then she relented. "That would be lovely. I would like that."

They progressed with few words and Clare felt comfortable in the silence. Occasionally she would glance over and admire his stature, his sense of strength.

As they approached their neighborhood, there were loud voices ahead. Men and women were shouting. No. Not shouting, but chanting.

"Oh no."

"What?" Clare could see up in the distance the shadowy figures of a few dozen people in front of her building, holding torches and gesturing with their hands at the rooms above.

"It's the do-gooders," John said. "They take issue with Patrick's . . . ladies."

"What are they going to do?"

John laughed. "They might hurl a Bible. Just a cloister of rich, old crabby ladies too bored with their husbands to stay at home."

"Set the captives free, set the captives free," the group chanted loudly and not perfectly in step. A few offered their own refrains, such as "Come to Jesus," or "Repent of your sins." Others hummed melodies.

As Clare came closer she could see it was indeed mostly older women, many wearing fur jackets and fanciful hats. Some had their eyes closed as they fervently issued their petitions, pointed fingers, and held open hands in the air at the windows of the second floor of Patrick Feagles's building.

A couple of the prostitutes peered down at the gathering below, and Clare glanced up just in time to see one of them hurl an object at the group. The sound of glass shattering didn't seem to phase the gathering.

"Come." John began to walk her toward the front of the tavern.

As he did, a man stepped in front of Clare, startling her. It was the tall, blond man with rounded spectacles she had seen outside of the Irish Society.

"Here, take this." The man handed Clare a small printed booklet.

She took it from his gloved hand, mesmerized by the compassion in his face.

"Out of her way." John gave the man a shove.

"John Barden," said the tall man. "You know better than to stir trouble with me."

Clare was amazed at the sense of calm in his eyes. Her father and the other men in her life were never ones to back down from a challenge. But they always did so with anger and bluster. The quiet confidence in the stranger's posture was unlike any she had seen and she found it alluring.

The prizefighter pressed his chest against the man. "It won't be stirring I'll be doing."

"Tell me what your boss will say when he makes the headline tomorrow morning."

"You have nothing on us, Royce. Never will."

A couple of the women who were singing came up to them. "What's happening, Andrew? Shall we summon the police?"

John Barden stepped back. "Won't be necessary, ladies. We were just conversing about politics."

The man they called Andrew held out a tract to John. "There's news in here for you."

John nodded to Clare and they turned toward the tavern. She joined him but looked over her shoulder at the blond man and tried to resolve her curiosity in his striking demeanor. What was it about this man? Certainly, he was handsome. But there was something more profound. Something that aired a sweet fragrance hidden deep in her past.

When John opened the door to the tavern, the music of her homeland emanated from inside, and she spotted a fiddler and a wooden flute player accompanying a man leading the crowded tavern in song.

There was such a noticeable contrast to the earnest chanting outside and drunken frivolity inside that Clare found herself unsettled.

"Can you believe that?" John said, almost at a shout so he could be heard.

"What?" Clare's thoughts drifted to the ladies who reminded her of Grandma Ella and the man who handed her the pamphlet that she had placed in her coat pocket.

"They thought you were a whore."

"A what?" What could she have possibly done to conjure this image in their minds? Was it the way she was dressed? Her appearance? Clare's joy drained and queasiness crawled through her skin and into her gut.

"Clare!"

She looked up to see Seamus flagging her as he worked his way through the crowd. John's words were boring into her conscious, yet Clare found relief in seeing her brother. The busyness of her life and her brother's odd hours had made it difficult for the two of them to connect, even though they lived in the same home.

Seamus, wearing his tweed wool cap, which covered some of his curly black hair, took a calloused look at the fighter but gave him a nod of respect. "John."

Then he grabbed Clare by the shoulders and wove his charm, his blue eyes sparkling. "Can you spare a moment with us, sister?"

She didn't answer, but Seamus didn't wait for a reply. He took her by the hand and walked her through the dancing, drinking, and laughing toward Patrick's table in the far corner. Clare glanced back and was comforted to see John was following as well.

As they approached, Patrick stood and greeted them warmly. "There's the man we were discussing just now." He turned toward a squat, balding man who was seated beside him. "This is John Barden."

The man who looked decidedly overdressed for the tavern stood with gracefulness and flair and held out his hand. "That would be the great John Barden." He spoke with a drawl, one that Clare had never heard before.

"Have a seat, John, and join us for a wee pour." Patrick flagged one of the barmaids who arrived shortly with a bottle of Irish whiskey.

"There is something I've got to tell you," Seamus spoke as quietly as he could in Clare's ear.

She nodded but found herself distracted by the presence of this new stranger. John dragged a chair from the neighboring table for Clare before retrieving one for himself.

"This is Reginald Sanders," Patrick said. "He's managing affairs for Billy Tunnel. They've both come all the way up from Atlanta, Georgia."

"Mr. Tunnel sends his regards," Reginald said. "He's anticipating a fine challenge based on all he's heard about you, Mr. Barden."

"Is that so?" John's gaze met Patrick's. "I hope there weren't exaggerations."

"Not so, Mr. Barden." Reginald reached into the chest pocket of his vest and pulled out a piece of paper, which he unfolded carefully. "This is our Atlanta newspaper. This here is on the front page from just last week. It's talking about Mr. Tunnel's visit to New York, and I think you'll see some flattering words about his opponent." He slid the paper over toward John, who gave it only a casual glance.

"Everything is in place for this Saturday," Patrick said. "We've made the proper arrangements with the authorities."

Clare looked into the eyes of John Barden and struggled to read his dark brown eyes. There was a strength, an air of pride, but melancholy as well. She sensed he was trying to cover up the fact that he didn't want to fight.

As Patrick and the man from Georgia continued to discuss the details of the fight with John, Clare felt a tap on her knee and turned to see Seamus trying to get her attention discreetly.

"This is for you." Seamus's eyes directed her to look beneath the table where he was handing her an envelope. He put his hand over hers, as if to signal for her to keep it safe.

"What is this?" she said quietly, turning to confirm that their conversation was being ignored.

"It's everything I lost. And then some."

She opened the envelope a crack and could see it was filled with American bills. Clare closed it quickly and pushed it back toward him.

"Take it," he said. "Save it for someday important."

"Where did you . . . ?"

"We're doing good work for Patrick. There will be much more where this came from."

"I'm not sure I want to know . . ."

"You don't need to," Seamus said. "Send it home. Maybe you can include a note saying your brother isn't the failure they thought he was."

His eyes watered and Clare could smell his breath well enough to know he was full of drink. She didn't approve of any of this, but her brother was desperate for a victory and she had no will to deny him of it now. She tucked the envelope in the pocket of her dress.

"There you are." Seamus waved to someone in a crowd.

Clare turned to see who it was and saw a young woman with large brown curls and bright red lips, who was dancing to sounds of the music. She blew a taunting kiss at Seamus and began to gyrate and spin as she grinned mischievously and curled a finger, beckoning him to join her.

At the other end of the room, Clare caught sight of Pierce coming through the main door and then scampering to the stairs leading up to their room.

A flash of anger caused her to rise and scurry after him.

Clare burst through the door, where an alarmed Pierce spun around from where he was stoking the fire.

"What is it? Are you all right?"

"You would know, Pierce Brady, wouldn't you now?"

The redhead stood erect and furrowed his brows. "What are you speaking of?"

"Why are you following me, Pierce?"

"I'm not . . ."

"Don't lie to me, I know that you were."

"Back down, Clare. You're mistaken." Pierce said this with such conviction, it forced Clare off her rampage.

"That *was* you, wasn't it?"

Pierce took her hands, guided her to an upholstered chair, then dragged the oak rocker next to her and sat down. "What's troubling you, Clare? Speak your mind. It's just me."

She took a deep breath and let it out slowly. "I'm not sure. I was coming home from the shop and John Barden was with me . . ."

"He was?" Pierce's tone betrayed his disappointment.

"Well, listen. John was being a gentleman in escorting me home, and I'm gracious for it because I had a creeping feeling the whole time there was someone lurking behind. Please, Pierce. I'll forgive you if you tell me the truth. Was it you? I need to know."

"I already answered you," he snapped at her. But then his face softened, and he sought out her eyes. "There's something you ought to learn about John Barden."

"I'm not interested in any gossip."

"It's not. It's the plain truth."

Clare paused, uncertain she wanted to hear what he had to say. She saw in Pierce what seemed to be a jealous spirit, but she nodded.

"It's your uncle. He's in a bad way."

"What do you mean by that?"

"There's a man he works for. A business partner of sort. He's got it out for your uncle. From what I've been hearing, he's wanted to take Patrick out for a long time."

"Where did you hear this?" asked Clare. It seemed nonsensical to her.

"It's all true, I'm afraid. Much of it we heard from your own uncle's lips, you know. When he drinks, there's few secrets. He's taken a liking to your brother and me."

Clare tried to read through the veil of what Pierce was sharing. "What does John Barden have to do with any of this?"

"He's a fighter, he is. And not just for prize. He works as a strongman."

"For this business partner who has no name?" This was all too much for Clare to absorb. She wanted it all to be a lie.

"According to your uncle, few know he exists. Your uncle serves as this man's voice, his face, his interaction with the world. He operates from the shadows. It's part of their arrangement." Pierce shook his head in response to Clare's dubious glare. "I know I'm sounding batty. It's strange for me and it's coming from my own mouth, but you must believe me. Seamus and I . . ."

"What about Seamus?"

"We've seen things. We've done things." Pierce glanced down at his lap.

"What kind of things?"

He looked at her. "Things you mustn't know. But believe this, Clare. We're in it deep. Deep as can be."

Clare reached into her pocket and pulled out the envelope her brother gave her. She pulled out a stack of dollar bills and slammed them on the table beside them. "Is this what this is about?"

Pierce appeared startled. "He gave that to you?"

"Answer me."

He stood and paced back and forth a few times, stroking his fingers through his hair. Then resolutely he kneeled down beside her. "Seamus and I have a plan. Here." He pulled a folded piece of parchment from the front pocket of his herringbone wool trousers, opened it carefully, and handed it to her.

"What is this?" Clare saw the poster and her heart caved. It had been ripped from a nail and was worn from weather, but the words framed around a large ink-drawn eagle screamed to her in large letters.

**"To Arms! To Arms! 500 Men for the United States Army! To the patriotic citizens who are willing to fight for their country."**

Clare had read enough. "What is this?" Her voice cracked.

Pierce took it back from her, folded it neatly, and tucked it in his pants. "We're short on choices, Clare. Now listen. This is a good plan."

"What do the two of you know about fighting? The American army? As strangers in this country? What good will you do your family buried in the soil?"

"It's not like that. The war's a hoax. They tell us there is little chance we'll see a single bullet fly. The Yanks are walking right through the enemy, and the talk is they'll be surrendered before we hit port. At the worst, it will be six months and we'll be back for you and we'll all go home together."

*Go home.* The words rattled in Clare's mind. Did she even want to go home? Yes, she missed her family, but she was getting accustomed to her new life and it invigorated her to be able to send her letters and support. The idea of crossing the ocean on a death ship again seemed distant and unwelcome.

"When?" she asked.

"After the fight. There's more to tell, but I can't right now." Pierce reached for her hand and pressed it gently between his. "You mustn't speak of any of this. Not even to your brother. He swore me not to tell you, but I felt you needed to know. And you can't . . . listen closely . . . you can't breathe a word of this to John Barden."

Clare watched Pierce's eyes as he mentioned the name, and they flickered with the flames of disdain. "What have you against John?"

Pierced paused and bit his fingertips. "If I tell you more, it may not be safe for you."

"Now you *must*, Pierce."

He curled his lip and nodded. Finally, he spoke in a soft voice. "Your uncle has something in his possession that has kept him alive. I don't know what it 'tis. He wouldn't tell us, but he said it would ruin this business partner of his if it ever comes to light."

"But what does this have to do with John?"

"I believe he's trying to use you to find out about your uncle."

Clare had heard enough. She stood and he did as well, stepping back out of her way. It wasn't that she didn't trust Pierce, it was all too much to bear. "I'm tired."

He walked toward the door and lifted his jacket off of the rack.

"Where are you going?" Clare asked, suddenly not wanting to be alone.

He turned slowly. "I should join them downstairs. We're supposed to be planning for the fight Saturday."

"All right," she said, disappointed.

"Clare. I can trust you on this, can't I? All of it?"

"Yes."

Pierce put on his coat and stood there awkwardly. "You do know why I told you all of this?"

Clare looked at the man who not too long ago was a boy. She could see the longing and the pain in his eyes. "Yes, I do."

He nodded with sadness, turned, and the door closed behind him.

Clare felt terribly alone and frightened. There was so much going through her mind now, but her tiredness gave way to the pounding in her chest.

She took the candelabra from the mantel and lit the candles in the fireplace. She walked to the table, gathered the scattered dollars, and tucked them back into the envelope with her free hand and carried it to the bedroom. She set the candelabra on the small table by the bedpost, then lifted the mattress where she had hidden a leather pouch. In it were her earnings for the week, and she put in the money Seamus had given her as well.

Tomorrow she would visit the Irish Society and it would all go home.

As she returned the pouch to its hiding place, something fell out and hit the floor. *Clink.* Dragging her hand along the dusty floor she came upon a small object. It was the key she had found hidden under the third drawer of the cabinet.

She recalled Pierce's story. Did the key have anything to do with what her uncle was hiding? Clare put it back in the pouch and tucked it under the mattress again.

It was hard to fathom how much their lives were unraveling. This wasn't anything they could have dreamed. She went to the window, opened the latch, and pushed out the shutter doors to a frosty breeze. Clare looked below, hoping to see the strangers who were chanting and singing hymns.

But they were gone.

Just the wind, and the sounds of the tavern below. Disheartened, she closed the shutters, sat on the bed, and took out the pamphlet the blond man had given her. She held it to the light. On the front it said, "Have Ye Peace?"

Clare laughed in response. She was as far away from peace in her soul than she had ever been. The thought of peacefulness relit a fire in her heart she feared had died. She missed Grandma Ella, and tender thoughts of their times together swept across her with a dash of euphoria. Her grandmother lived as hard a life a person should ever endure, but she always bore an inner contentment and beauty Clare found herself craving.

She opened the first page and read the words:

> *"And there arose a great storm of wind, and the waves beat into the ship, so that it was now full.*
>
> *And he was in the hinder part of the ship, asleep on a pillow: and they awake him, and say unto him, Master, carest thou not that we perish?*
>
> *And he arose, and rebuked the wind, and said unto the sea, Peace, be still. And the wind ceased, and there was a great calm.*
>
> *And he said unto them, Why are ye so fearful? how is it that ye have no faith?"*

"How is it that you have no faith?" she whispered.

Clare reread the verses over and over. They spoke to her with healing and reassurance as if she had discovered a lost friend in her presence. She cried herself to sleep.

Chapter 28

# John Barden

 It was Friday night and Clare needed to hurry as John would not be able to stay up late. Tomorrow was the big fight.

Seamus stepped into the room. "I didn't mean to disturb your preening. Just grabbing a scarf and me hat. Pierce and I are going to have a late night."

"Is it for the fight?"

"It 'tis. We're gathering wagers. As much as we can. Ol' Patrick is hoping to cash out on this one."

"He is? Is he betting on this Billy Tunnel?" She couldn't keep the disbelief from her voice.

"Billy?" Seamus laughed in that way he did when he was up to something. "No. He's putting everything on your man. So are we, as a matter of truth."

She was pleased to hear this. "So John is quite a fighter, isn't he? And to think all of the things people are saying about Billy

Tunnel and how he's going to hurt John badly." She scoffed. "I see you've got good sense about you. You believe in him as well."

Seamus cocked his head at her. "Clare, dear sister. It's not about faith in your man. It's purely self-serving."

"What do you mean by that, Seamus?"

He wrapped a red plaid scarf around his neck and put on his hat.

"What's going on?" she asked.

Seamus flashed an air of arrogance. "It's best you don't know."

She grabbed his scarf and pulled him to her. "Young, Mr. Hanley, do not forget who you are speaking to. This is the same face who was cleaning your bottom when you were crawling on all fours. Now speak to me before I beat it out of you."

Calmly, he unfolded her fingers and removed her hand from the scarf. "Take a close look at me. Does this look like the same lad who left Ireland?"

There was an intensity in his voice that made Clare step back. He had changed, and replacing the puckish smile of her Seamus was the glare of a man who was courting the shadows of darkness. It chilled her to the core.

"I know of your intentions," she said sternly.

"What?"

"Your plans. Our friend told me."

"What did he tell you?" Seamus said, his anger rising.

"Calm yourself. I know about your enlistment. I know about the trouble you're in. What I don't know is the nature of it all. Those details he left out."

"He wasn't to burden you with all of this," Seamus said. "He'll get a piece of me for this."

"A burden? I'm your older sister. I'm responsible for you. What am I to tell your family?"

"You can tell them the boy's a man, and he'll do just fine."

"What sort of bother are you in?"

"It's nothing to concern you." His eyes softened. "Really, Clare. I won't lie to you. We've got ourselves in a mix and there are those who have issues with us. But it's all going to resolve itself tomorrow."

"The fight?"

"That's right." He nodded.

"And how would that be?"

Seamus hesitated. He raised his hat and settled it back on his head. "Your man is going to win tomorrow. But it won't be because he's the better fighter."

"What is that supposed to mean?" Her brows tightened.

"Patrick has . . . he's made arrangements."

"Does John Barden know this?"

Seamus's face was enraged. "He doesn't and he must not. You can't tell him. He has to think he earned it fairly or we'll lose everything. People would empty our blood on the streets. They'll cut us, do you understand?"

Clare was used to cleaning up her brother's messes his entire life, but this was beyond her mending. "Does this have to do with our uncle's business partner?"

"Yes. You've heard about him as well? 'Tis true. They have dealings between them that go back a ways and that we know nothing about. Other than Patrick wants out in a big way and the agreement in this fight will settle all debts. Once and for all."

"So I don't understand," Clare said. "What has this to do with you? Why do you have to leave for the war?"

"No one knows about this, Clare. Not our uncle. Just Pierce, me, and now you. And that's the way it must stay. Our uncle's debt will be square, but not ours. We'll have some earnings from the fight to give to you, and some for our pockets, but our time is short here."

Her heart leapt to her throat. "What have you done?"

Before her question could be answered, there was a loud rapping on the door.

"He's here." Clare went to answer the door. She felt a tug on her arm.

"You can't say anything," Seamus said. "Nothing at all. It would cause us great harm. All of us."

"I understand." Clare walked to the door and let John Barden in.

They wove through the well-wishers on the way out of the tavern. John's celebrity was rising one day ahead of the big event, and he pulled Clare through the growing crowd with an eagerness to be outdoors and away from the madness. The questions were peppered at him as they passed.

"How ya feeling, John?" said a man with a sunburned face.

"Well enough."

"What do you think about Billy?" asked another. "Can you duck his left?"

"Those are my intentions."

"Don't you shame us, John Barden," piped in a woman serving beer.

"Aiming not to, ma'am."

With that they had made it to the doors and they spilled into the paved roadway, and they galloped for a distance with Clare giggling. Tonight, there were no evangelicals picketing the walkway and she felt a tug of disappointment. It surprised her that her thoughts carried to the face of the blond man.

There she was again, musing about a man who believed her to be of ill repute. At least if she was to believe John. In her mind she replayed the brief encounter with the stranger, his strength and grace, the momentary embrace of their eyes—or was that her imagination? No. There didn't seem to be disdain or even pity in his warm nature. But why else would he have handed her the pamphlet if he wasn't convinced she required rescuing?

Could an able-bodied, stouthearted man, the one to share a lifetime, truly be gentle and kind? It seemed an unlikely pairing of qualities in her estimation. Her father certainly did not believe this possible. He once told her a husband's sole responsibility and the measure of his worth was provision of food and shelter, not good cheer.

But she had to stop thinking of this Andrew person. She should be focused on the one standing beside her. "Tell me, John Barden. Are you getting a little anxious about all of this?" Clare asked as they slowed to a stroll.

"I will once the day arrives, but tomorrow is a long way off." He turned to see her expression.

"Where are you taking me?"

A horse pulling a carriage trotted by, its hooves clacking on the surface of the pavers. Three young boys ran by them, entertaining themselves with some sort of evening devilry. Clare couldn't help but think of her two brothers back in Branlow.

"There is something I want to share with you," he responded.

After an uneasy pause, Clare asked, "Am I not to inquire?"

"I love the Five Points. The newspapers don't speak kindly of her. They see the beggars, the poor, the beaten, the homeless, the drunks, thieves, and whores. But I see a place full of good people, short on blessings, but full of hope and courage. I see a place groaning for its chance to prosper. Only to be kicked down when it tries to rise to its feet. Sounds like the Irish, don't it?"

Clare leaned in closer to John. "Beautifully stated. Fine poetry coming from a fighting man."

"Well. No man can fight without having something to believe."

"So when you fight, you fight for the Five Points?"

He laughed. "The Five Points can fight for herself. I fight to earn."

"Noble."

He shrugged.

"So . . . how did you come to meet Patrick Feagles?" She scrutinized his reaction.

He turned to face her as if understanding some deeper meaning in the question and then looked away. "I think you know who I work for."

"I do? And who would that be?"

"Listen," he said. "I know your brother and his friend don't take kindly to me. Ours is a business relationship."

Clare gasped inwardly, fearing she had crossed a line.

"I'd prefer"—John stroked her cheek—"if you and I can be about anything but business."

"That would be fine," she whispered, warming to the touch of his hardened hand.

He stopped as they came before a tenement building. "We're here."

Sitting on the stone stairway leading to the oak doors of the entranceway was an old man caressing a bottle. Curled up tightly beside him, as if to draw warmth, was a small girl only a few years of age. A bony dog looked up and growled. Both eyed

John and Clare with suspicion as the two of them walked up and entered the tall, squeaking doors.

It was almost total darkness inside, and they waited for a moment for their eyes to adjust. Clare felt her senses rising to the surface.

Then she felt the tug of John's hand leading her. He leaned over and spoke softly in her ear. "We're going upstairs. Mind your step."

Her hand was enveloped in his large hand as he drew her upward.

"Are you all right?"

"I'm fine," she lied. What madness could have overcome her to put so much trust in a man of whom she knew so little?

After a few flights of stairs, they came to a halt. Clare heard the tap of his knuckles on a door. She had questions for him, but the words didn't arrive. Instead she could only hear her own breathing and the frantic pacing of her heart.

In a few moments, the door opened a crack, and a woman peered out at them with a lantern held before her gaze. She was disheveled with mismatched clothing, a dirty face, and oily brown hair splayed wildly from her scalp. Yet Clare could discern an underlying winsomeness in the woman, whose sharp, even features shone through her filth.

"Well, if it isn't the viper himself," said the woman in a voice that was gentle and tired.

"Let us in, Tara," John said.

"Did you bring money?"

"I have."

The woman stepped back from the door and opened it to allow them entrance. As John came in, he drew Clare in behind him, who wished she was anywhere but here.

"What have you brought here?" Tara glowered at Clare. "Another one of your whores?"

John's voice modulated to one Clare had not yet heard, and he pointed an angry finger at her. "Woman. Do not test my anger."

"How do you like his temper?" she asked Clare. "Have you felt it yet?"

"Where is she?" John asked with firmness.

"Sleeping. Don't you wake her."

"I'll be quiet."

"Where's my money first?"

John stood close to her. "You'll get your money when I say you do. Look at you, drunk and filthy." He reached over to a small round table and picked up a near-empty bottle. "What's this, my dear?" He went over to the fireplace and poured it onto the flames, which hissed and reached up greedily in response.

"What are you doing, John?" she shrieked. "That was all I had left."

He held the bottle up, and through the flicker of the flames, anger could be seen in his expression. "This isn't what I give you the money for."

The protest in Tara's voice fled and she shrank back. "I just had a wee sip, John. I promise. I'll give it up for you. I promise. I will." She stepped forward to reach for him, but he shrugged off her advance.

"Come, Clare."

She followed sheepishly behind him as he grabbed a candle from the mantelpiece.

"If you wake her, I'll put this bottle to your temple," Tara said from behind them.

Ignoring her, John entered the small adjoining room, which through the dim light could be seen to be sparsely appointed.

Merely a drooping wardrobe and an enfeebled bed. Worrying that Tara would follow behind and crack her over the skull with a bottle, Clare hurried behind him into the room.

In the bed was a girl, of age four or five, with brown hair, peacefully embracing the soft arms of slumber. Her chest gently rising and falling with the tides of her sleep. John bent down slowly and kissed her with a tenderness that belied his stature and air. As he caressed the girl's hair with adoration, Clare was moved by what she witnessed. She never experienced such affection from her father.

*Is this the great fighter?* Strangely drawn to his vulnerability, Clare was struck by the sight of the hardened features of his face brushing against the soft cheek of the child.

He turned to Clare and spoke softly. "This is what I fight for." John kissed the child again on her forehead. Then he pulled the blanket up to her neck and left the room with Clare on his heels.

John pulled out a wallet from his jacket and extracted some bills, which he handed to Tara.

"Four dollars? Is this all?"

"There will be more. After tomorrow."

Tara's expression changed to one of concern. "You take care of yourself."

"I will. Don't waste your worry on me."

He nodded to Clare, and not knowing what to say or do, she followed John in silence through the darkness.

When they came outside the building, the old man, his daughter, and the forlorn dog were nowhere to be seen. A soft, cool mist was in the air and Clare tucked her hands into her coat. John's arm came around her shoulder. She shuddered and he withdrew it.

John looked away into the night. "What's bothering you? Speak freely."

"Why?" she said to him.

"Why did I bring you there?"

She nodded.

He lowered his head as they walked. "There is no one else in my life I can trust."

"But we've just met."

"That's true," he said. "It's pathetic, isn't it? The great John Barden."

Clare wanted so much to care for him. She felt pulled into his emotional injury.

"I've tried to love Tara. For my daughter."

"That's exactly what you should do," Clare said.

They walked in silence for a block or two as Clare fought back her tears. Again, she felt a strange sensation that someone was following her, but this time didn't say anything about it or even glance behind her.

Up ahead she could see the lights of the tavern approaching. John held her arm and they stopped. Could he see the glistening in her eyes?

"Listen, Tara and I aren't married. If something should happen to me . . . tomorrow, I fear the worst for my daughter. I'll have earnings coming to me. Would you see that they get to her?"

Clare felt numb inside, but her maternal instincts rose. "Yes, John. Of course I will. But don't speak that way. Maybe you shouldn't fight—"

John put his finger to his lips to hush her. "I have risks much greater than the fight." The sadness in his eyes returned. "It's your brother you should be concerned for."

Her face flushed with anger.

"He's in danger," John said.

Clare tried to read his face in the dim light of the gas lamps. "Why?"

"My employer is interested in acquiring something in Patrick's possession. The man I work for . . . is a determined man. There is a rumor out there that your brother knows where this particular item is."

"What is it?"

"Clare." John peered deep into her core. "If you care for him, you need to get your brother as far away from this as possible. He's a mere child thinking he's a man."

"I don't believe this at all." Worrying she would start crying, Clare began to cross the street.

"Clare," John shouted. "Will I see you there tomorrow?"

She didn't answer. Instead Clare darted through the doors of the tavern, past the blurred faces of revelry spewing cruel laughter that mocked her flailing emotions. Up the stairs she went, her emotions beginning to bleed. She covered her face as she went by two women loitering on the second floor. Finally, inside her flat, she closed the door behind her and let it all burst out.

Numb, she meandered into her room and drifted to the window where she opened the shutters. She longed for the hymns she heard the other night, the songs of the evangelists. Something told her they held an answer from her youth she had long forgotten, buried in the wasteland of her distracted life. There was an aching in her soul and she yearned to rest in a peaceful embrace. Clare desperately wanted the heavy burdens lifted from her shoulders.

Yet instead, in the evening below her window, there were only the relentless echoes of drunken pleasure.

A man wheeled a cart of dung, or night soil as they euphemistically referred to it, slowly down the road and closing behind him was a single horse carriage with a dangling lantern. When it passed, Clare noticed movement against the shadowy walls of the tailor's store across the way.

Squinting, she tried to discern the shape and stared at it for a while until at last the figure moved into the light of a gas lamp. It was the face of an elderly woman she had never seen before, wearing a once-ornate hat and a shabby coat.

And she was looking directly at Clare.

Clare panicked and pulled her head back, just for a moment, but long enough. When she craned her neck out again and panned the dark, rough-hewn street in all directions, she was dismayed.

Her pursuer was nowhere to be seen.

## Chapter 29

# THE FIGHT

 "Shall I pull the clock off the wall for you, dear? That might keep you from staring at it so." Magdalene's countenance shined warmly as her gnarled fingers needled the fabric.

"Am I looking at it that much?" Clare asked sheepishly.

"Why don't you just go to the fight?" Sara folded some trousers on her table.

"I'm not interested in it, that's all." Clare didn't even sound convincing to herself.

They worked in awkward quiet for a spell and then Sara spoke up. "What happened between you and the prizefighter?"

"Sara," Magdalene huffed. "Where are your manners?"

"I'm just asking what you're thinking." Sara mocked a scowl at the older woman.

Another few uncomfortable minutes passed, and this time Magdalene broke the silence. "It's obvious your mind is elsewhere. Why don't you go early?"

"I told you, I don't want to." Clare pulled out a pair of shears and mashed out a pattern. "Besides. I couldn't get out of shift anyway."

"With Carl?" Sara laughed. She whistled and waved to their foreman who was at another row, scribbling in his work journal.

"Sara!" Clare put her head down. "Don't you even think about it."

"Nonsense," said the blonde. Sara had caught the attention of the potbellied man and he was strolling toward them. She turned to Clare. "What will it be? Sickness? Tragedy?"

"Tell him the truth, Clare," Magdalene said calmly.

"What is it, Sara?" Carl slouched up against the back of her workstation.

"Clare needs to leave, that's all."

His gaze drifted off of Sara and onto Clare.

"Well, tell him," Sara prodded.

"She's taken a liking to John Barden," Magdalene said.

"She has?" Carl stood up and took a few steps toward Clare's desk. "I've taken a liking to the man myself. Five dollars' worth. And why should I care about Clare?"

"You should care . . ." Magdalene started. "You should care because he's never lost with Clare at his side."

Carl's eyebrow raised. "Is that true?"

Clare shot Magdalene a sharp glance.

"True as day," Sara said.

"She won't take credit for it," Magdalene said, "but with my money on John Barden myself, I'm not wanting to test superstition."

He raised his head in doubt.

"Well, you old bramber." Magdalene planted her hands on her hips. "It's enough you want to throw my paltry wages to the wind. How much did you put out on the fight?"

"Enough." He knotted his forehead and pivoted his head in both directions. "All right then. Go that way. It's not as if we'll miss your productivity."

Clare froze.

"Well, girl?" Magdalene waved her hand at Clare. "Get you gone. If you don't go now, you'll miss it all."

"For your own good," Carl said, "you better be sure about your man."

Clare gave Magdalene a hug and then slid out the side door into the night.

By the time Clare arrived at the gaping entranceway to the Old Brewery building, she was short of breath and sweaty from her scampering. The crowd had amassed to the point where it seemed hopeless she would be able to nudge her way to the front.

"Wonderful evening for a prizefight, wouldn't you say?"

Clare turned and was flabbergasted to see the man who had dwelled in her idle musings since she first met gazes with him. It was the blond man who had handed her the tract. Up close, there was no disappointment in his appearance. He seemed taller, more handsome, and even kinder than she had imagined.

"Yes, lovely day." What? Couldn't she think of something more dignified to say?

"Of course, it's interesting to be covering the story of a fight that doesn't really exist, that is, if you ask the alderman or the constables."

"Story?"

"Oh yes. I'm Andrew Royce, with the *New York Daily*." He held out his hand and she gave him hers and he gripped it.

"I thought you were—"

"Yes. I'm that too. Did you read—?"

"Several times." There was a shout and Clare saw there was movement in the crowd. What awful timing for this encounter. "I probably . . . should go."

"I understand. But if you could spare just a moment. I've wanted to speak to you, for some time."

"You have?" Clare fumbled with her wig.

"You're close to Patrick Feagles, am I right? Would you mind a question or two?"

Clare felt duped. To think he had genuine interest in her! "I would mind and I really must go."

She watched his face drain. "Right. Terribly sorry about delaying you. None of that matters. Perhaps we could talk about that tract some day?"

"Perhaps." Clare's emotions churned. "And another thing."

"Yes, what's that?"

"I'm not a prostitute." With that, she stomped away and blended into the crowd.

Clare climbed up on an oak barrel and craned her head around to find a view through the crowd. There, in a small clearing in the center of the vast room, the two fighters danced anxiously in their last preparations for the bout. Her uncle leaned over and spoke into John's ear.

For Clare, it seemed imprudent for her to see him in the flesh, but even from this distance she could clearly see the sharp definition of his body, which was contoured and firm.

As he shuffled his legs and threw punches in the air, John appeared nervous, almost frightened. Clare watched him under the rabid attention of the hundreds of onlookers and her emotions surprised her. Rather than experiencing a heightened reverence toward him in the brightness of his celebrity, she felt pity for the man.

Something about last night unsettled her spirits. Although his devotion to his daughter was touching, her heart pained for Tara. As broken as the woman was, there was still hope in her eyes and Clare wanted no part in blowing out the dull, flickering flame. She didn't want to pass judgment on John, but the thought of a deeper relationship between them seemed instinctually wrong.

Opposite John was a man who must be Billy Tunnel. He was not what she had expected. He wasn't particularly well built, was a bit stooped, and had pale skin, shimmering wet in the light. But he shadowboxed with fluidness and poise.

The audience was rabid with shouts and cheers and the expansive room seemed on edge to break out in fights all through the crowds. A chill from the cool air combined with the morbid enthusiasm for violence in the air and made her ill.

Just outside of the ring, she spotted first Seamus and then Pierce, holding out fists full of currency, taking in final wagers from those who bellowed at them with arms waving wildly.

Clare climbed down and burrowed her way through the interlaced bodies before her. Her efforts were met with curses and shoves. She pressed through it, and though she found her romantic interest in the fighter waning, she still worried about John's safety. She felt weak for caring for the man but could not resist the seduction of the moment.

Despite her frantic appeal as the time grew short, few were yielding as she progressed. Several pushed her back, while others grinned at her greedily as she went by, groping and clawing. She almost turned back in the face of the fury, but she persevered through the indignity.

As she approached, a bell sounded to gather the attention of the assembly. Seamus noticed her approaching and shouted out, "Let the lady through. Clear the way."

It did little to coax cooperation from those in her way, but it did encourage Clare to push more forcefully, and at last she broke through close enough to catch the attention of John Barden. He seemed equally surprised and pleased, but in his presence of mind merely winked to acknowledge her.

"Make room for her, or I'll pummel you."

Clare spun to see Patrick Feagles with a cigar in his mouth reaching out to her, and she accepted his hand.

"Didn't expect you here," he shouted, barely audible above the clamor.

"Neither did I."

The bell sounded and the two warriors began the clash.

John was resolute as he marched toward his opponent, and with a confident step Billy lurched forward and the place erupted in fury, one raging beast with a thousand flailing arms. Clare felt the weight of the frenzy pressing in on her, and she thought she might get crushed.

"Get 'em, John," rose one voice above the audience.

"Enough dancing," came another.

"Give him something, Billy."

The battle had just begun, but even to her inexperienced eye, Clare could see the inequity. John Barden was sturdy and relentless. But Billy Tunnel glided with an eloquence that was captivating. He dodged, ducked, shifted, and faded with ease to each and every one of John's angry swings. And then, seeing an opening, Billy would strike with a precise combination. Stomach, cheek, stomach. Jaw, waist, arm.

"Have you been drinking, Johnny?" was just one of many

taunts hurled toward the outclassed fighter, and they grew in cruelty and frequency.

Seamus and Pierce wrestled their way to where Clare and Patrick were standing at ringside, and both were displaying strains of concern.

"What's the matter with him?" Seamus said to Patrick.

"Don't worry." Patrick handed each of them a cigar after lighting them from his own. "We've got to entertain them first."

Clare watched as John became more frustrated and his swings grew wilder. It seemed certain no one had told him the fight was fixed. Billy mesmerized him with a flair of mockery, like a bullfighter waving a cape before impaling the bull. This only inflamed the Irishman further.

Soon a trickle of blood streamed from the corner of John's mouth. Staggering back after a blow by his opponent, John glanced briefly at Clare, and in that flash of a moment, her heart sank with the shame and fear expressed in his eyes. She felt helpless.

Billy's taunting dance gave way to a seriousness, and sensing an opening he began to pound more furiously. Already winded and abused, John clung to the Southerner in desperation as the crowd booed.

"Can't they stop it?" Clare asked Patrick, whose confidence had begun to wane.

"Stop it? It hasn't started." He pulled out his cigar and cupped his mouth with his hand. "Let's go, lads!"

Discontent in the audience grew. The insults were hurled by those who wagered their earnings on John, and even those who favored Billy seemed disappointed by the lack of suspense.

Clare glared from face to face to try to answer the vitriol being fired at John, but she was invisible to them and was jostled as they compacted toward the ring. She could only think of one thing to do in the midst of the maelstrom. "Please, God, protect him."

She must have uttered it loudly because it drew a response from Patrick. "He better start fighting, or he will need God's protection."

Somehow through the beating, John gathered his courage and remained determined. Whether through his resolve or through Billy's lapse of focus, an errant fist met its mark and for the first time, fate shifted in the fight. The Southerner stumbled back and tripped and nearly lost his feet.

John lunged and began to throw whatever last efforts of his arsenal remained. Out of a dozen punches, only two hit, but with enough vehemence it riveted through the room and the audience responded.

Patrick elbowed Seamus. "I told you, lad. Here it is now. C'mon, Johnny."

Billy staggered and John placed his arm on the fighter's neck and swung with his free arm. Clare felt sick as she found herself urging John to finish him off, but she just wanted it to be over. Bottles were thrown and shattered on the floor.

In an expression of pure agility, Billy slipped out of John's grip and danced back as first a gasp of surprise and then exultation came from the gathering. His brow was split, and crimson flowed freely. He wiped it with the back of his hand and examined it, and anger rose in his demeanor.

As John pressed inside, Billy responded with a flurry of blows, executed with skill and force. The Irishman stumbled backward and his knees wobbled.

"No. No. No." Patrick threw his cigar to the floor and he spun and raised an arm to someone in the back of the room.

John regained his balance, yet Clare could now see his face

was bloodied, eyes puffed and his lip swollen. He was dazed yet leaned forward into the fight.

Without hesitation, Billy threw a combination of swings and the third one, an uppercut, sent John backward to the floor in a defenseless flop, his head bouncing violently on the hard floor.

Almost simultaneously, dozens of whistles sounded and Clare looked back to see scores of policemen flowing into the crowd from the main entrance with batons raised and rage in their eyes.

"What's all this?" she shouted to Patrick.

"Insurance."

A few scuffles broke out, but most of the onlookers streamed out of whatever doors they could find. Even Billy Tunnel was being whisked away by his manager.

In the cover of the mayhem, Clare fought her way to John and slid down beside the fallen warrior. His eyes were open and staring vacantly at the ceiling.

"Is he gone?" Seamus asked.

"Is there a doctor?" Clare said.

"If there was, they are running away from the law," her brother responded. "We've got to get him out." Seamus barked at a couple of men standing near. "You there. Give us a lift. Quickly."

They lifted up the battered fighter and carried him between them.

"I know a way," said one of the men. "Follow me."

Seamus glanced back at Patrick and Pierce who were being hounded by gamblers seeking their payout.

"The fight was ended, without resolution," Patrick hollered, but he hardly quelled the venom.

"I've got to stay back," Seamus shouted.

"Be careful," Clare said to her brother.

The men were dragging John Barden away and Clare scampered out after them.

## Chapter 30

# THE FALLEN

*When is the doctor going to arrive?*

Clare found herself alone with John and regretful she had allowed the men who carried him to her bedroom to abandon them. They promised they would fetch a physician, but now she suspected help was never summoned.

She was terrified to leave John's side for even a moment but was weighing this fear against the dire need to muster assistance.

But who would come? And who could she trust not to give away John's location? Surely the police would be searching for him as well as the hundreds who had lost money on the Irishman.

Clare was comforted by the rising and falling of his chest, but could see little life in the bludgeoned face of the fighter. Dipping a rag into a tin bowl of water, she stroked away the blood and sweat from his disfigured face. It was hard to imagine this was the same man who, only an hour before, stood before her as if he were carved from granite.

The front door snapped open in the other room and Clare was overjoyed. But this emotion subsided as she heard Pierce's loud and drunken voice.

"There's a stink in the house," he slurred.

"Mind your temper," Seamus pleaded.

"It's been minded long enough." Pierce stumbled into the bedroom.

Clare stood to face them as they entered the candle-lit room, her instinct of protection rising. "Keep him out of here, Seamus."

Seamus playfully put his arm around the redhead, but it was swatted away.

"Hands off me, Seamus. I need a word with the great fighter. Mr. John Barden."

"Pierce, I'm warning you."

"Just a few words, I'll have, love." Pierce pushed his way past her.

"Seamus!"

Pierce turned and waved his arms downward. "Don't worry. I'll speak kindly to him." He glared at Clare. "I know what he means to you."

Clare looked to Seamus with concern, but he nodded to calm her.

"What a fine display it was tonight." Pierce leaned over John.

"Please, Pierce," Clare pleaded. "Leave him be. He's nearly dead."

"Yes, but not nearly dead enough. Ha! The great John Barden. The defender of Irish pride. Champion of the Five Points. Look at you now."

"That's enough there," Seamus said. "Come with me."

"Come with you." Pierce spat on the floor. "We lost it all. Everything we earned since we got here. We leave with nothing."

It was an awkward thought to come to Clare, but she felt relief that Seamus had given her his money the other day. She had it posted with a letter today at the Irish Society.

Clare noticed John was starting to stir. "Step back from him." She could almost see the life filling back in his eyes, which were buried deep inside his swollen face.

"John, can you hear me?"

"Can you hear me?" Pierce said, trying to hold his ground. "Thought you would die from shame." He pulled a knife out from his pocket and with a snap it glistened before John's face. "See here. Maybe I should just finish the job for you."

Anger crept into John's bloated expression, and he started to prop himself up in the bed.

"Pierce! Put that down." Clare couldn't believe what she was seeing. "Do something, Seamus."

John painfully started to lift his torso up with his arms. But just as he did, Pierce shoved him back down.

Seamus grabbed Pierce's arms from behind, pinned them, and pulled him away from John. As he did, John rose from the bed and swung his legs to the floor. With a sudden lurch he was upon Pierce, his hand digging into the redhead's neck and shoving him against the wall, and the knife fell to the ground.

Clare was stunned by John's manic assault, and after a moment of indecision, she tugged on his muscled forearm. When this found no reprieve, she started to lash at him with her fists.

"Stop! Please, John."

Seamus had reversed his role and was now trying to pry away John's death grip on Pierce, whose face burst into redness.

The boy's eyeballs protruded grotesquely and he flopped helplessly.

Despite the violence committed on him by Pierce's would-be rescuers, the intensity of John's dark pursuit was unyielding and seemed to be urged on further as his victim gasped toward final submission.

"You're going to kill him, John," Clare shrieked. "Enough!"

She could do no more as the lanterns of Pierce's life dimmed, and his body wearied of the battle.

"No!" she shouted.

Then Seamus somehow got leverage on the big man and yanked him back from Pierce. But he tripped in the process and then John was upon him, punching him, and then his arms gripped Seamus's neck in a fit.

"John, no!" Clare was appalled by the hunger for vengeance in the fighter. How could she even have fallen for such a violent man? "Stop!"

Just as the word escaped her mouth, Clare heard a hideous animal cry from John Barden. He staggered up to his feet and put his hand to his abdomen, looking down in disbelief. He raised his palm toward the glow of candlelight, and the moist crimson glistened. With murderous intent, he glared at Pierce, but only for a moment.

John succumbed to his debilitating wound and collapsed to the floor, crawling in serpentine agony. A dull, steady groan emanated from his quivering lips.

Numb, Clare looked to Pierce, where she saw the slender, wet knife slip from his grip, plunging to the floor where it echoed in a metallic dance.

"What . . . have you done?" Clare began to sob and felt her knees buckling.

With a rasp in his throat, Pierce began to slowly unfurl his crumpled body along the wall, and Clare dropped to her knees beside him, grateful he was yet living.

"Go get Patrick," she said to a dazed Seamus.

Her brother nodded mutely and then stepped over John's body and exited the bedroom.

Before long, Tressa filled the room with her matronly presence with Seamus trailing her in silence.

"Oh, my poor dear boy." She bent down to John's blood-splattered body writhing on the ground. "Help me lift him to the bed."

With Seamus bearing the weight, they lumbered John's body onto the bed and somewhere between the floor and the bed, the fighter lost consciousness.

There was a pounding on the front door and they exchanged disquieted expressions.

"Patrick wouldn't have knocked," Tressa said. "Leave it be. It might be the girls hearing the commotion from downstairs, or it could be someone meddling. Cops maybe."

"They know we're in here. I'm going to find out for myself," Seamus said.

When her brother left the room, Clare held her breath and she listened for trouble. The door clicked open, there was an exchange of voices, and Seamus returned with a gray-haired man, whose blue suspenders barely held up a large pair of trousers. The man waddled toward the bed with a black leather case in tote.

"More light," he said as he rolled up his sleeves. "Boil me some water."

They backed up in submission to his authority and sense of urgency.

"I'll gather some lanterns from my house," Tressa said. "But Doc. You haven't been tipping it heavy tonight, have you?"

"Nothing more than usual," he said nonchalantly and began working on his patient.

After they brought all that was requested, the portly physician didn't want them loitering about, and they cleared the room. Once in the living area, Seamus brought the fireplace to full frame.

Not much later, they heard the front door handle rattle, and following a curse and before they could answer it, a key sounded in the lock and it sprung open. Patrick Feagles stood before them wearing a snow-speckled coat and wool cap.

"Is it true? John Barden got pricked?"

"I'm afraid it 'tis." Tressa nodded to the bedroom door.

Patrick's face reddened and he entered the bedroom, with the others hovering near the door, hoping to catch an update on John's condition.

"In the name of Mary!" Patrick exclaimed. "Is he going to die, Doc?"

"It's likely." The physician continued to work the wound.

"Do whatever you must. His death will be mine as well."

They scattered before he reemerged and when Patrick did, his eyes were lit with fury.

"Who did this to him?" Patrick closed the bedroom door behind him. "I want to know now and you can save the lies."

"It was an accident," Pierce said.

"An accident? Did he just happen to fall on a blade?"

"He went mad on us on account of losing the fight. He tried to choke me." Pierce pointed to the striations on his neck.

"You should have let him, you imbecile," Patrick spat out. "Have you forgotten who this man belongs to? He'll kill me, he will. All of us."

"Don't speak that way," Tressa said.

Patrick took his hat off and ran his fingers through his thinning hair, looking like a cornered and wounded animal. "Could there ever be a more terrible night?"

"How did John lose?" Seamus asked, with a tinge of revulsion. "I thought Billy . . . I thought it was all arranged and by you."

Patrick drifted over to the studded leather chair and slid down into it. "I did. It was."

"Well . . . apparently," Seamus said, "no one remembered to tell Billy."

"You? What had you to lose? A week's earnings or two? What would you know about loss? No. This was well hatched by a skilled adversary, one I've been losing to for years. The fix was on us, boys. But worse than that, he'll think we took our vengeance out on his man John Barden. We're good as dead."

"You two need to get out of here," said Tressa.

"She's right." Patrick nodded.

"We're not leaving without Clare," Pierce said.

"You will if you care for her." Patrick glared at him. "If she's seen with you now, she'll share your fate."

Clare stepped forward. "We're not separating. We'll go together or not at all."

"That's foolish talk, sister," Seamus said. "He's right. We need to go our ways until this settles down. But what about Clare?"

Patrick rolled his hat in his hands. "Tressa knows where she'll be safe. Don't you, dear?"

The woman looked to Patrick with questioning in her eyes. "Over there?"

"Yes," he said with resolve. "It's time. It's the only way now."

"Where are you taking her?" Pierce asked.

"It's preferable you don't know in case you get caught," Patrick said. "She'll be well taken care of. Much better than she is now."

Clare's uncle stood. "Now get going, lads. Find yourself a dark cave and don't show your heads for quite a while."

Outside, police whistles could be heard.

"Somebody must have heard the screaming," Tressa said.

Patrick walked over to the window and peeked out, being careful not to be seen. "There's a door behind the bar. You know about it. Just don't leave by the front door. I think they are coming in. Godspeed to you boys."

Tressa gave each of them a hug and Clare did as well, though her head was spinning with indecision.

"Be good to yourself, Clare." Seamus kissed her on the cheek.

"Wait for us," Pierce said. "We'll be back soon enough."

With this they opened the door and they were gone, their footsteps echoing down the hallway. Clare shuddered as a thought came upon her that she might never see them again. *Should I run after them? Is it a mistake to let them leave me behind?*

"Go, Tressa."

"Are you sure about this, Paddy?" The woman's face was etched with sadness.

He took off his wool coat and put it on Clare. "'Tis no way, I fear. Perhaps he'll consider this settled and finally put an end to it all."

Tressa started to cry. "I'm sorry, dear," she said to Clare. "We must go."

The whistles sounded outside again and shouts were heard. Patrick craned his neck toward the window. "They must of caught wind of the boys and are in chase. I don't know why they aren't up here yet. Go, woman. Be gone."

Clare felt the urge to say good-bye to John, but she couldn't deny the urgency. And when Tressa grabbed her arm and pulled her toward the door, Clare didn't resist.

Into the shield of the darkness they fled.

# Chapter 31

# Into His Arms

"Are you all right, dear?"

Clare, who was rocking in a chair by the window in a corner of this musty room, covered her eyes and sobbed softly to herself. She was anything but all right. Was John Barden dead by now? Was her brother safe?

After a few moments, she gathered herself and wiped her tears with a handkerchief embroidered with initials she didn't recognize. "I'm sorry . . . a . . . Miss Winters. Yes. I'm fine. I just need some rest, that's all."

Sitting across from her with a cup of tea in her hands was a slender woman in her late thirties who wore a bright blue, tightly trimmed dress, with brown hair swirled and steeped precariously high upon her head. "I know, love. You must be exhausted. Completely. But you have your visitor coming. We can't keep him waiting. It's all been arranged by Patrick."

Clare glanced outside the window again, drawn toward the candles glowing in the night.

"They've been there for hours," Miss Winters said.

"Who are they?"

The woman drew the cup to her lips and sipped slowly and audibly before clanking it back to its china saucer. "Oh, we see them about once a week. They are mostly harmless, saying they are here for the ladies. But in the end they hurt the girls because they can't earn if their patrons are fearful to show. Our customers don't care to be noticed by the people they share a church pew with on Sundays. Might even be one of their wives.

"Jurists, bankers, merchants, men of high reputation, pillars of the community—they all come to us here in the Five Points to escape the boredom. It's quite simple. We take care of their most basic needs, so they come back."

"You make it sound so civil," Clare said.

"Is it not so? Look at them out there, waving their Good Books and dripping with self-righteousness while they deny themselves their innermost thoughts and passions. It's a dishonest way to live, I think. From my eyes, that is."

The reverberation of voices beginning to blend in harmonies emanated from the candle bearers. It was a hymn Clare didn't recognize, but she found it comforting nonetheless. It seemed her chaotic life had drifted so far away from the songs they sang, and she found herself longing to join in those sweet, soothing melodies.

"Why am I here?" Clare asked.

"Did not Tressa tell you? I thought she had explained it all."

"She seemed as if she had more to say, but merely told me I would be meeting with someone who could help us. In our situation."

"Then she did tell you all you need to know." Miss Winters

reached over to a teapot and poured more of the pekoe fluid into her cup. "Can I?" She motioned to the empty cup closest to Clare.

Clare shook her head and looked back out the window. "How can this man be of assistance?" It was hard to see much beyond the flicker of the candles in the moonless dark outside, and she had yet to see the face she was seeking. Even when Tressa had walked her by the evangelists to enter this building, he was not to be seen.

"I'm not free to share more than you were told," Miss Winters said. "I just encourage you to relax and allow what is to be to be. Some would consider it an honor."

Was that Andrew? There was a tall and slender figure walking among the elderly women outside. But did she want to see him? After all, he was just interested in her to get to Patrick.

There was a tap on the door that startled Miss Winters. "There. That's him." She stood, straightened her dress, and patted her hair.

"You look lovely, dear," she said to Clare. "Quite lovely."

As the woman opened the door, Clare felt her pulse rising and wanted desperately to flee, but there was nowhere to go. She couldn't bear to watch who was coming through the door.

"Clare. This is Mr. O'Riley."

Clare stood and turned to face the stranger. Small in stature, dressed sharply in a well-tailored jacket, he peered at her with darting hazel eyes, overgrown gray brows, and an aquiline nose.

"Yes. She is precious indeed. And reminds me so of someone I once knew well." He held out a hand to her, and when Clare reluctantly held hers out, he grasped it tightly with both hands. "That will be all, Miss Winters," he said without taking his eyes from Clare.

Clare pleaded without words for the woman not to leave her alone, but Miss Winters merely gave her a nod of encouragement. "Yes, Mr. O'Riley. Can I get you anything else?"

He shrugged with irritation and then Miss Winters slipped out of the room. The sound of the door snapping shut sealed Clare's abandonment. Only minutes earlier she was at the outreaches of fatigue, but now terror awakened her senses.

"Please, child. Have a seat there. We have much to discuss. I've been anticipating our acquaintance for some time, you should know. I know you better than you might think."

Clare froze and glanced at the doorway.

"Oh, dear," he said, a half smile curling on his lips. "There is nothing to be afraid of. Please." He pointed her in the direction of two chairs in front of the fireplace.

She tucked back her dress and sat down, her body completely stiff with fright.

Mr. O'Riley went over to the door with a noticeable limp and pulled across the slide latch. He pulled his arms out of his jacket, as if it pained him to do so, and placed it on a hook on the back of the door. Rubbing his hands together he shimmied to the fireplace and pulled some long matches out from a box.

Eyeing the door again, Clare wondered what it was that was holding her back. Fear? Morbid curiosity? Concern for her brother?

He blew onto the small flame and the dry coal lit easily and spread. "There it is. That should do it." On the mantel he pulled down a glass carafe and two glasses and he began to fill both. "Imported from Dublin. Have you been?"

"I have not yet been."

"Roscommon, right?" He handed her a glass, and she took it with no intention of drinking. "Branlow?"

"How did you . . . ?" She felt her senses crawling with displeasure.

"Oh, Clare. I told you." He set the whiskey bottle on the table between them. Then he pulled his chair close to hers and sank down, groaning as his joints bent. "Don't ever age. It's my greatest regret."

In the background, Clare could faintly hear the chorus of a hymn being sung. It was too low for her to discern any words, but she found it reassuring.

"I understand you've been acquainted with my daughter?"

Clare shrugged and her finger circled the rim of the glass.

He cocked his head sideways. "No. Don't you remember?" He leaned in close to Clare and reached one of his wrinkled hands toward her chest, causing her to snap back.

Mr. O'Riley cackled, with the death throttle of a longtime smoker. "Oh, child. Be still." Extending his hand at her again, she trembled as he reached for the chain around her neck and pulled out the pendant from her dress and cupped it in his hand.

Then it registered. Madame O'Riley. "She's your . . . ?"

"Yes, she is." He laid the pendant back on her chest and then slouched back in his chair. "With the same surname still. Never married, although we had our fair share of suitors, including your uncle, a Mr. Tomas Hanley. And your father as well. Liam."

"What about my father?"

"If it makes you feel better, your father knew my Rose years before he married your mother. You see, I knew your grandfather and your grandmother . . . the Englishwoman. They would come to market in Roscommon, looking for dairy cows, and they would always bring the two boys, Liam and Tomas. Those two fought all of the time. The two boys, that is. And when they saw my Rose. Well . . ."

"I don't believe you," Clare said.

"It was innocent, child. They were two young boys, barely men. My Rose didn't think much of your father. Thought him too serious. But she did fall for your uncle. She said he reminded her of me."

"Why are you telling me this?" Clare found herself repulsed by the very sight of this man.

He lifted the glass to his mouth and sipped the whiskey as he stared into the glowing embers of the fire.

Then Clare heard the voices again from outside. Lofting. Sweet.

> *"What wondrous love is this, O my soul, O my soul!"*
> *"What wondrous love is this, O my soul, O my soul!"*

"That's probably why I never cared for the man." He laughed again. "But that didn't keep him away from my Rose. They were off again and on again. Even while he was married to your aunt, I'm afraid. Meara. Right?"

"Why must you tell me this?" Clare's eyes filled with tears.

"There's an ending to this. Hang with me, Clare. It's an interesting story." He sipped his drink. "I learned early on your uncle had a rare talent I simply didn't possess in my business ventures. He's very good when it comes to people. They love him. Find him amusing. So I put my feelings aside and offered him work. We prospered. When I arrived here in this land of prosperity, I sent back home for him. He said he would only come if I would give him my Rose. So now you learn something about me."

"You traded your own daughter?"

"Such a crass way of thinking about it. It was a good business decision. But, yes, that's how it began. Until I got leverage on him. In fact, over and over again. Turns out he's a poor gambler. And here we are now. Paying his marker."

"What do you mean?" The words stuck together as she spoke.

He put his hand on her knee. "You are even more beautiful than Margaret."

"What?" Clare's throat was dry and her body stiffened.

"Those eyes. Such perfect blue."

"What did you say about Maggie?"

"Before we do this, my dear, I have one more question, and please be careful how you answer this. Your uncle has something I need to get. Do you know where it is?"

"I don't know what you're talking about. What about Maggie?"

"Come now. I shouldn't have upset you. Have a drink."

She started to get up, but he pulled her down. "It doesn't have to be this way."

"Let go of me." She tried to shove him, but he had surprising strength.

"This is no way for my new bride to behave, now is it?"

"What?" Clare felt disgust at being so close to him.

"Oh, my. Didn't your uncle tell you about the arrangements?"

"Unhand me." So this is where it would end? This was her punishment for seeking the man of her dreams? Oh! What joy to be alone for life rather than spend one day betrothed to this vile creature.

His hand reached for her neck, and he leaned in close and stroked her cheek with the back of his hand. "So soft, so precious."

Clare reached out for the glass on the table between them and in one motion, with all of her force, she struck him on the side of his temple and he stumbled backward.

Without pause she leapt to her feet and turned for the door. He reached for her, catching her hair, and as he pulled the wig, it flew off her head.

In an instant she was at the door, fumbling with the latch, and just when it loosened and she pulled the door open, he was upon her again and slammed it shut. With one fluid motion, Clare spun and kicked him in his lame leg and he crumpled to the floor.

In the full speed of panic, she went out the door and hurtled herself through the hallway, running past a startled woman who had just turned the corner. She pressed to the doorway, fumbled with the handle, and flung it open to the outside world and into the coolness of the night.

The flickering faces of the women holding candles turned to gasps and shrieks as Clare ran into the mass, flailing her arms and crying. The lights were spinning around her and she felt her legs beginning to sink.

As if time were frozen, she saw arms reaching up to her, cradling her fall, and bringing her close to his body. She fought back, but he held onto her tightly.

"You're fine now. Shhh. You're fine."

Confused and losing her balance, she melted her resistance. "He's coming."

"No," said the voice, warm and gentle. "You're safe now."

She looked up and saw the round spectacles of the tall figure who had lived in her imagination. Andrew.

Several kindly old faces leaned around him and peered down with compassion. The chatter of concerned, whispered voices grew as someone put a coat over her, another wrapped a scarf and she heard things like "Poor dear," and "What could have happened?"

But in the chilling darkness, as the world faded around her, she felt him lifting her, and sinking into his strength, Clare could only see one face.

And she surrendered.

Into his arms.

## Chapter 32

# THE DAWN

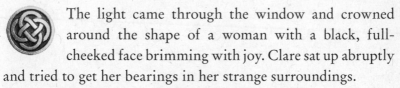 The light came through the window and crowned around the shape of a woman with a black, full-cheeked face brimming with joy. Clare sat up abruptly and tried to get her bearings in her strange surroundings.

"Are you waking, miss? Well fine day 'tis. Thought you was to sleep all's the day. But here you is now, looking at Cassie. Oh, happy day. We've been on our knees for you, girl."

"Where am I?" Clare looked around the inside of what was the most beautiful room she had ever seen.

"Oh, sweet sunshine. Wait till the master hears this." With her arms waving in the air, the curvy woman scampered from Clare's sight, although her words echoed all the way down the hall.

Clare shivered with the delight of comfort. Her body was literally sunk into a feather bed with silk sheets and quilted comforters. She had never experienced such pampering, although her back did ache with the pain of oversleeping.

The room abounded with wealth—mahogany cabinetry, cherry furniture, richly patterned papered walls, and gold trimming and garnishes throughout. A brass mantelpiece framed a large wood-burning fireplace, which snapped with vibrancy. A fire in a bedroom! What extravagance.

But most glorious of all was a floor-to-ceiling bookshelf that spanned an entire wall, with more leather-bound tomes than she had ever seen in one place.

She heard conversation approaching and Clare panicked, not knowing if she should get out of bed or crawl deep under the covers. Making up her mind, she rounded her feet only to find how far it was to the carpeted floor. She was dressed in a silk sleeping gown and reached for a robe hanging from a brass rack standing beside the bed.

"Oooh. I afraid she's making to run. Lordy, Lordy, child. What are you doing up from bed?"

Clare panicked and jumped back in the bed and tucked herself under the covers.

"That's better, little one. All right, Mr. Royce. You can come in now as she's proper and not being all foolish as she was."

Clare's eyes shifted to the doorway, where her blond man knocked on the door frame and took his felt cap off in respect.

"Mr. Andrew has been worrying like a cat to kittens, he has. Asking me every other minute. 'Is she up?' Praise Lord Almighty. He's done me mad with questioning. Ain't that right, Mr. Andrew?"

"May I?" he asked. When Clare nodded, he grabbed a chair and dragged it to the side of the bed where he sat down and smiling, looked at her through his glasses with tender, green eyes. His blond hair was well groomed, parted from the side, and carefully combed.

All of the sudden, Clare remembered she was without her wig, and feeling exposed, her hand went to her hair.

"Cassie," Andrew said in a rich, gentle voice, that of an Englishman. "Would you mind seeing if Miss Holmes would prepare our guest something to eat? I'm sure she's quite famished."

"Who else gonna get it? If it was up to you, she'd just perish before our eyes. What would you like, sweet child? Miss Holmes can cook up anything."

"Why don't you start with some biscuits, eggs, and some hot tea, Cassie?" Andrew turned to Clare. "Of course, if that suits our guest?"

Clare tried to hold back a nervous smile. She sat up against the headboard, keeping the blankets pulled up to her neck. "That suits her fine."

"Excellent." He nodded to Cassie, who lifted her chin and scuttled out of the room, talking to herself. "I think you'll feel rejuvenated with some warm food in your stomach. You've been sleeping for a long time."

"I hope I haven't been an inconvenience," Clare said. "I should probably get going."

"Oh." He frowned. "And where would that be?"

Clare tried to think of an answer and shrugged her shoulders.

"We're hoping you would stay here with us," Andrew said. "Just until you find a place to go."

"And where am I?"

"You are in the home of Mr. Charles Royce." He paused for a moment expectant of a response. He chuckled. "You do not know who Charles is, do you?"

"No sir."

His face dimpled as he smiled. "Charles is my father. My father is the publisher of the *New York Daily*. Many would say he's a very powerful man in this city."

"What's the *New York Daily*?" she said sheepishly.

Andrew laughed. "I wouldn't suggest asking that question in front of my father. He's a bit proud of his accomplishments."

"A newspaper. Ah yes. I remember now."

"Have you read it?"

"I do like to write. Does that count for something?"

"A writer? And by what name does this distinguished author pen her works?"

"I said I like to write. Not that I am an author. And it's Clare. Clare Hanley."

Cassie burst into the room with a tray in her hand and with words spilling out of her mouth. "Now if I'm gettin' in the way of your conversing, Cassie will just be as quiet as can be. Nothin' from these lips. Just ears. Sometimes Cassie uses just those. No ma'am. No sir. Maybe my shoes will squeak or these bones will creak, I won't say a thing."

"Where's the eggs?" Andrew asked. "Just tea and biscuits here."

"You can ask that question to your own mother, Mrs. Royce herself. She's telling Miss Holmes, 'Don't be filling the girl up when we'll be supping soon enough.'" Cassie raised a plate of biscuits to Clare. "Mrs. Royce is wanting to meet you, miss."

"Yes. I'm quite sure she does," Andrew said with more than a hint of cynicism. "It will be a great pleasure for Clare to meet my parents, wouldn't you say, Cassie?"

"Now there you go, Mr. Andrew. Talking 'bout your mammy and pappy, forgettin' they fed you and give you trousers and this house. Shame, shame, boy. Cassie ain't raise you well."

"Well if Clare is to meet my mother and father, she'll need her strength. I'll leave you ladies to the subject of pampering. Cassie, would you assist Miss Hanley with the preparation of a warm bath and in finding some fresh clothes?"

Overwhelmed with gratitude, Clare could find nothing to say. She watched him leave before turning to see Cassie with her hands on her hips, looking at her with consternation.

"He dotes on you finely, and you shouldn't be encouraging it none. The missus will have none of it and you'll be back on the street. Aww. She's a good enough woman, been kind to me, but serious in wanting an upright Christian woman for her son. Nobody could be blaming the woman for that. Now could they?"

"Not at all." Clare held back the joy she felt inside. There was something so authentic about Cassie she wanted to give her a hug. But she feared raising the woman's temper.

Cassie dangled a finger in Clare's direction. "Now, you drink up all that hot tea to warm yourself good and eat those biscuits. Cassie's gonna water the tub and we'll get you prettied up for your dinner with the master and missus. Oooh. I got sup to make and just about all my chores. No rest for Miss Cassie."

The chatter faded as the housemaid left the room, leaving Clare behind at last to enjoy the quiet and peacefulness of her room. She bounced playfully in the feather bed and wrapped the white laced blankets tightly around her and giggled. Clare sat up and sipped on her tea and devoured her biscuits.

And then, those books! She pulled down dozens and ran her fingers over the covers, each smelling of fresh bonded leather. Oh, if she had days to spend in this room alone.

But a stray remembrance of the previous evening interrupted her revelry. The image of Mr. O'Riley's face made her queasy. And what of John Barden? She had lost any romantic notions for the man, but she didn't want him to die.

Then there was her brother Seamus. Poor Seamus.

Of course, she wasn't entirely sure of this Andrew. What type of motives would he have for bringing her to his home? Was this all about Patrick Feagles?

All of the sudden, Clare felt the urge to flee. Yet there was something powerful, something deeply rooted in her conscience that was encouraging her to stay.

# Chapter 33

# THE DINNER

The echoes of brightly polished silverware clattering on imported French china was all that could be heard in the absence of conversation. Clare's finely upholstered chair tucked into a mahogany table bearing a mirrored sheen, covered with intricately hand-sewn runners and place mats, illuminated by candles lifted by golden holders. In well-crafted silver bowls and platters was the most spectacular spread of food she had ever seen.

A turkey, which had been roasted to a perfect brown, surrendered to the blade in carefully sliced piles of juicy white and dark meat. Corn, not served on a cob, but stripped and piled high with fresh creamery butter lay beside mashed potatoes, which were served with gravy and accompanied by warm, fluffy rolls.

Clare sipped water cooled with chips of ice from a crystal glass so intricately designed she feared breaking it. As she set it down carefully, her eyes rose up across the table to see Andrew gazing at her in amusement, acknowledging the tension at the table.

At one end of the long table was seated the matriarch, Mrs. Royce, who with a long neck perched between a painfully slender body and a sharp, angled face, drew circles in her plate of food with her fork when she wasn't looking up to scowl at their guest.

Opposite her was a perfectly rotund man, who more than made up for a lack of breadth with an extensive width. As if unwilling to embrace his shape, he wore a fine silk suit, gray with a large red tie, which was easily two sizes too small, and Clare worried that at any moment buttons from his jacket would break loose and shoot across the dinner table.

His gray hair extended broadly from the sides of his head, and only a few long strands remained atop his barren pate but were proudly groomed and displayed nonetheless. His unusually reddened cheeks softened his demeanor as did a broad toothy smile, which appeared frequently and without much prompting.

His desire this evening seemed only to keep the conversation pleasant, just as his wife appeared equally committed to draw the air out of the room. Mrs. Royce had a spirit of disenchantment Clare found disarming.

Andrew, on the other hand, although apologetic by his gestures, seemed entertained and, much to Clare's horror, quite willing to prick the tigress.

"So, Mother. You might be pleased to know that Clare is a writer of some skill."

Clare disapproved with her brows.

"Is this true?" Mrs. Royce shifted in her seat. "I'm surprised a woman of your . . . profession would choose to ignore those talents."

"Well . . . I . . ." Clare tried to decipher those comments.

"Perhaps she could teach you something about writing, hmmm?" Charles held up a turkey leg in his fist in emphasis before biting into it.

"My father believes I lack discipline in the craft of his choosing."

"Andrew is a fine journalist," Charles said with his cheeks protruding with food. "He'll make an exceptional publisher. If we can spare him from his unfortunate distractions."

"My parents don't approve of my ministries in the Five Points."

"That's not the case, Andrew," his mother said, raising her nose. "We've always supported the work of the church. It's just there are some tasks that should not be borne by a man of your . . . stature. We can help people most if we keep a certain distance. Just for proper perspective, that is."

Andrew glanced toward Clare with a look seeking forgiveness.

Mrs. Royce patted her napkin against her lips and raised her chin. "There is nothing wrong with a mother not wanting her only son to gather . . . strays."

As if on cue, Cassie emerged through the doorway and started to pile up empty plates. "It sounds like we might be readying for dessert. Oooh my. Miss Holmes be preparing rhubarb pie. I can taste it myself. Not that I dipped my fork in it, but then again someone's gots to make certain it's cooked through."

Andrew grinned at Clare and shrugged. "Cassie believes the cure to any ailment is a full stomach. She nearly fed me to death as a child."

"Poor child you is. The missus and master spoiling you with kindness and you don't thank them for nothin'. Ain't that right, missus?"

Mrs. Royce rolled her eyes and pushed her plate from her. "Can you bring in our tea, Cassie? And quietly if at all possible as we were enjoying our conversation."

"Yes, missus. Enjoying? That's strange word to describe it. Not that I was hearing nothin'. But you carry on. I'm a gonna quietly clear this table and tell Miss Holmes we's ready for rhubarb."

"So, Miss, uh . . . ?" Mr. Royce said.

"Hanley, sir. Clare Hanley. Just Clare is fine."

Charles leaned back in his chair and clasped his hands. "So, Miss Hanley. What do you think of the news from back home?"

Cassie had returned from the kitchen again and removed some more plates, including Clare's. "What news is that?" Clare asked.

"The crops. They've failed again this spring."

"In Ireland?" He had her attention. It would be one thing to have a season of the rot, but if the farms struggled again it would starve her people.

"Terrible development. Terrible indeed. Especially with so much of the land committed to potato."

"Was yours a potato farm, Clare?" asked Andrew.

Clare nodded at him, still digesting the news.

"Perhaps, son . . ." Charles put his finger to his chin and tapped. "What do you think of having Clare here help you with a story on the plight of her people? The perspective from one so recently arrived would be intriguing."

"That would be delightful." Andrew smiled. "What do you think, Clare?"

Cassie came in with a platter of tea and put it in the center of the table. She nearly toppled it as she was watching to see how Clare would respond.

"Good graces, Cassie!" Mrs. Royce said. "Do watch what you're doing."

"We've been hoping to get better circulation in the Points," Charles said. "Maybe getting more of an Irish angle on our stories is what we're missing."

Andrew's demeanor brightened. "Say yes, Clare, won't you? It would bring wind to my sails. Take some of the drudgery out of the business."

"The Irish perspective," Mrs. Royce scoffed. "Shall you write feature stories about drunks and brothels? The inside, untold stories?"

"Mother!" Andrew's gaze darted to Clare. "Sometimes you are intolerable."

"I've never written for a newspaper," Clare said.

"Neither has my son hardly," Charles said. "Maybe this will give him some focus. Whatever it takes, I'm willing to try."

Cassie came in with a pie, ruby red peering through a cross-hatched crust. She started to slice it and pass it out on plates.

Mrs. Royce appeared discomforted. "Perhaps we should just attend to Miss Hanley's recovery so she can return to her people."

Charles hardly looked at his plate as his fork shoveled in the pie. "You should visit the dock tomorrow. Talk to those coming from the ships. The stories have grown cruel. You've crossed recently, Miss Hanley?"

Clare nodded, beginning to feel overrun.

"Ha!" Mrs. Royce waved off the slice of pie when Cassie tried to hand it to her. "You're sending your son to the docks?"

Charles began to grow irritated. "I didn't ask him to go swim in the harbor. Is it your intention to humiliate our son in front of his guest?"

"Don't be bothered by it one bit, son." Cassie poured tea into Clare's cup. "No shame in that. On account of him nearly drowning as a boy, anybody's gonna fear the water some."

Clare couldn't shake the news of the crop failure. It infused uncertainty in her mind. Although she had been sending support and letters from the Irish Society faithfully every week, she had yet to receive a letter in return. Perhaps she could hear some news from some of the immigrants arriving by ship.

"Could you take me there, Andrew?" she asked, startling the others.

"Andrew, please," his mother said, softening her tone. "Don't embarrass yourself, son. When's the last time you were at the shoreline?"

"Poor boy," Cassie said. "Wouldn't even take baths. We needs to wash him while he was sleeping."

"Now I'm embarrassed," Andrew said, "and I'll need to remind you all that I'm still present in the room. I prefer if I'm a target of scandal and gossip, you'll have the decency to do it behind my back."

Clare laughed and then quickly covered her mouth and pretended she was coughing.

He looked at her with warm, sweet eyes. "And I believe our greenhorn journalist would benefit from a full evening's rest."

As he wiped his mouth and then rose from the table, they all did as well.

"Shall we declare a toast?" Charles lifted his glass.

"We most certainly must." Andrew lifted his as well.

"To the Irish," Charles said. "May their land heal and their people prosper."

"Hear, hear," echoed Andrew.

"And to our young Miss Hanley," Charles continued. "May

her words be true, bearing pain to the enemies of justice and freedom to the oppressed."

As the glasses clinked, Clare smiled at Andrew's kindness.

She was a fraud to have anything to do with writing at a newspaper. But in that moment, she determined to try with all of her will.

Clare didn't know why it mattered so, but she didn't want to disappoint Andrew Royce.

## Chapter 34

# NEW YORK DAILY

A couple of days had passed before Andrew granted Clare a visit to the *New York Daily*. He insisted she get her rest before going back outside, and she was too exhausted and emotionally wounded to fight his recommendation. Although she spent much of these days worrying about her brother and thought of searching for him. But where would she go and would her efforts to find him only lead his pursuers to his hideaway?

So when Andrew and Clare finally approached the building that housed the *New York Daily*, excitement was welling inside her. For a farm girl who loved books, the idea of being within the walls of a place where history was written and shared everyday was beyond fathom.

A massive stone structure, it was on what Andrew described as Newspaper Row. Once inside, although functionally plain, Clare was impressed with the grandeur of activity.

The mixture of shouts and conversations blended with the clanking of machinery. There was a buzz about them in the main floor of the facility, and people flashed by her in a frenzy.

"Is there something wrong?" she asked, leaning into his sturdy frame.

"Yes," he answered smugly. "They are on deadline."

"Deadline?"

"The paper goes out every day, with or without our story. If a story isn't ready, in most cases that means it will die on the floor and you'll have an irate editor."

Clare's eyes widened. They had spent the entire day interviewing Irish passengers as they came staggering off the ships. Few even had the energy to talk, and it saddened her to realize her horrifying experience crossing the ocean was commonplace. The news back home was dismal as well. The Black Death had spread and few territories had been spared.

The thought of her family suffering from such hardship without her being there to comfort them was unbearable, but she needed to know more. What about Branlow? How bad was it there?

Clare had hoped to stay longer to track down someone closer to home, but Andrew did seem affected by being close to the water, and she relented when he asked her to leave.

"Don't worry. Our story isn't due until tomorrow. One of the benefits of being the owner's son." He pointed in the direction of the presses. "Shall we give the lady a tour?"

"I would thoroughly enjoy that." Clare put her hand to the hat Cassie had found for her. Although she still felt naked without her wig, the bonnet provided some level of comfort and her hair had grown quickly, now several inches in length.

As they approached the churning presses, Clare embraced the joyful awe of a child, watching the paper rolls being cranked through the moving type. Several men worked the machine, applying oil, feeding in paper, and dragging the stacks away to be folded. Clare had grown accustomed to hearing the newsboys call out the headlines from the street corners, but seeing how it was wrought was fascinating.

"This room over there." Andrew waved at one of the men who had looked up. "That is where they sell the ads. Quite uninteresting if you ask me. But there is something over there."

They burrowed through the crowd and stopped to peer over the shoulders of the artists drawing various images and caricatures in ink on canvas.

Finally, they climbed up a winding wooden staircase that led to the second floor, which was more of an oversized loft.

"This is where the writers and editors roost, those enlightened souls who exploit and corrupt the freedom of the press."

"You speak of it so favorably," Clare said. "I think this is all wonderful. Perhaps Cassie is right and you are spoiled."

"Who is this pretty one?" said a woman perched on a stool tucked under a clerk's desk. She was dipping a pen into a well of ink.

"This is Clare. Our new writer."

"Is that so?" The woman had a face so plain she almost looked like a man. "She doesn't look the part."

"Is my father in?"

"He's with the mayor."

There were muffled shouts coming through a closed door behind the woman.

Andrew turned to Clare. "It may surprise you, but not everyone appreciates our stories. Come, let me show you our desk."

"You might as well give it to her," the woman said wryly, "seeing as you aren't fit to use it yourself."

"One thing you'll learn," Andrew said to Clare but loud enough for the other woman's benefit, "is that the fumes from the ink turn good people into crabby ogres."

Clare's face warmed. "Andrew!" she said as he whisked her away. "Perhaps Cassie is right. You might be terribly spoiled and impertinent as well."

"That's the spirit, Clare, but save your eloquent cynicism for print. That's the gold we mine." He stopped at a nearby table. "Wait a moment. I haven't seen yesterday's paper yet." He pulled up a newspaper, and after he opened it, her eyes widened with the headline: MEXICO CALLS NEW YORK'S FINEST.

"What is that story about?" she said.

He turned the paper. "The ship sailed yesterday with the New York regiment."

"Did they list names?"

"That's inside." He fumbled through the pages and then opened it up. "It's right here."

He laid it on the table and her fingers slid through the alphabetical listing, and there it was, beautiful to her eyes, the name "Seamus Hanley." And again she looked and there was "Pierce Brady."

"Thank You, Lord!" she said loudly. "They're off to war."

He seemed puzzled. "You must really not like somebody."

"Oh." She gave a half smile. "It's rather complicated. My brother and his friend. Let's just say they needed to leave town in a hurry."

"That does sound complicated. Intriguing as well. I'll pry it from you later. In the meanwhile, here it is." He swept his hand to point to the small desk in the corner of the room. "Have a seat."

She looked to see if anyone was watching. Convinced she was unnoticed, Clare seated herself and he pushed her in her chair under the desk as she beamed. The thought of people actually getting to write for their means of wages was invigorating.

"What a perfect fit you are Clare Hanley. As if you were meant to write of the heavens."

"You haven't even seen a word from me yet."

"It's unnecessary. My instincts are without blemish." He pulled out the papers where they had drawn their notes and laid them on the desk before her. "Besides, if you can write my stories for me, I can do what God has called me to do."

"God calls people?"

Andrew's face brightened. "Why yes, of course He does. He calls each of us to serve Him in our own distinct ways."

"You believe that?"

"I do. The problem is so few people are willing to listen to what He has to say."

"I suppose He just speaks to you."

He smiled at her. "He's got a calling for you, Clare Hanley, of that I'm certain. And He's got a calling for me."

"Really?" She still wasn't sure whether or not he was speaking in jest. What divine purpose could she have? It reminded her of conversations Grandma Ella would share with her in their walks down village roads. "And what would your calling be, Andrew?"

He spun her chair around to face him and knelt beside her, locking gazes with deep sincerity. "Let me show you."

As the horse clapped against the street pavers, Clare peered out from the window of the carriage, her emotions surging. The buildings of the Five Points were rising around her and the memories of her last night here lapped up like flames.

Andrew, who was sitting beside her in the leather-studded seat, held on to her hand. "Was this a mistake in bringing you back here so soon?"

She turned and her nerves melted with the compassion in his eyes, peering at her through the round frames of his spectacles. "I'll be fine." She managed to smile.

The light of day was subsiding and the evening shuffling of laborers returning from work were being greeted by street merchants and peddlers. Having witnessed the grandeur of the neighborhood where the Royce home was located, the Five Points appeared more poverty stricken and dirty to her than ever.

So many times she had seen the carriages driving by with their wealthy passengers glaring at the occupants outside, and now she was on the inside looking out. What a strange turn of fate it was for her, and one in which she didn't feel entirely comfortable.

"Driver ho!" Andrew shouted, and the carriage soon came to a halt. Shortly, the door opened and a hand reached up to Clare, and as she stepped to the ground, her boots sank into the mud of the streets. A pig nearly ran her over as it grunted past.

Andrew gave the driver some coins, who nodded in gratitude, climbed the perch, and with the sound of a whip was off and heading away through the traffic. Was she back in a place where she more suitably belonged?

He held her hand and she felt safer. Andrew drew her off of the street and away from the clattering of passing carts, wagons, and carriages. They worked their way up through the flow of pedestrians and turned into an alleyway alongside a dilapidated three-story stone building.

"We need to go in through the back entrance," he said, excitement in his voice.

Clare felt unease as she feared seeing someone she knew,

someone she had met through Patrick Feagles's world. Although only a couple of days had passed, she felt as an intruder in his neighborhood.

Up ahead there was a group of men gathered in a half circle, shouting and clamoring about as they focused on something on the ground before them.

"Just keep your eyes down and we'll pass them quietly," Andrew said in her ear.

They were mostly unnoticed as they approached, but one man with a grizzled beard looked up and glared at Clare hungrily. He tilted up a bottle of drink and nodded at her as she went by him.

Clare pressed closer to Andrew and they walked past the men without incident. As she glanced back, she could see through a gap in the group that there were two roosters facing off, held back by their owners as the men shouted out wagers and flashed bills.

In a moment, the cocks screamed in battle and shouts lifted. Clare increased her pace to a trot.

"Right here," Andrew said as he turned the corner and they came to stairs leading to the rear entranceway of the building. Glass was on the floor where windows had been busted out, and they crunched as they ground it with their boots.

Andrew halted abruptly and Clare realized there was a small shape visible in the encroaching darkness.

Letting go of Clare's hand, Andrew knelt beside the child sitting on the first step.

The boy was no more than eight years of age, with knotted curly hair and a deep black face, skinny to the point of illness.

"What's your name little man?" Andrew said.

The boy, whose hands were tucked in the sleeves of his jacket, glared back with distrust. Finally, he said, "Saturday."

"Saturday?"

"Yes. My mammy done born me on Saturday."

"I see." Andrew smiled. "And where is your mammy?"

The boy shrugged.

Andrew reached into his pocket and pulled out some money. "Would you do me the kindness of seeing she gets this? It's been owed to her and I'm grateful for your service."

Saturday pulled one of his hands from his jacket and took the coins, examining them in the remaining light.

"Oh. And these have been heavy in my pocket." Andrew pulled a biscuit from his pocket. "Would you be able to eat this for me, Saturday?"

The boy nodded and put it to his mouth.

Andrew nodded to Clare and they mounted the short steps leading up to the door. He pulled out a small tool and began to jimmy the lock. Shortly, a click sounded and the latch was freed.

"What are you doing?" Clare whispered, relieved to see that the boy had left.

Andrew didn't answer but instead opened the heavy door and he disappeared inside, leaving her alone.

"Andrew?"

"Come inside and close the door behind you."

Upon entering the building, the smell of mildew and decay overwhelmed her, and Clare was tempted to exit. It was complete darkness inside and she heard some scratching noises, followed by the flash of sulfur, and she could see Andrew holding a match to a lantern.

"I had this stashed away in a safe place."

"Why are we here?" Clare asked. "What would the landlord say?"

"Oh, he's thrilled with us being here. He's hoping I'll buy it from him."

"Why didn't he just give you a key?"

"I'm in negotiations," Andrew said. "I can't let on my enthusiasm, now can I? The windows are boarded up from the main street, so they can't see our light."

Clare heard a scuttling about on the floor and she backed up.

"Those are just the rats," Andrew said nonchalantly. "I've already informed them their lodging arrangements are temporary."

She saw the lantern moving toward the front of the building and Clare lurched forward and grabbed onto his arm. "I'd like to go now."

"But I haven't shown you anything yet," he said with disappointment.

"All right then. Start showing."

"How can I give you the tour if you're so dour?"

"No. Please go ahead," Clare said. "I'm anxiously awaiting the tour."

He turned up the flame of the lantern and the light filled the room fairly well. The building was completely empty of furnishings, although it was clear it had been inhabited for a long time in its past.

Andrew cleared his throat. "This is the first floor," he said, now speaking as if he were addressing a small audience. "In the far corner, will be the kitchen, where soup will be prepared and bread will be baked."

Andrew held the light closer to her face as if he was reading her reaction. She gathered an expression of pleasant surprise and hoped it look genuine. It must have worked, as his voice grew in ardor. Clare worried she might have inadvertently delayed the moment when she might have been able to escape this mausoleum.

"On the first floor, we would put in benches and tables, where every night, anyone with hunger could find respite from the cold. A sanctuary from the cruelties of this life. No one would be turned away, and each would know their comfort would be provided by the grace of God and by no man or woman.

"And up here. Come up the steps."

Clare lifted the hems of her dress with one hand and held onto his hand with the other. She could barely see the wooden steps below her feet, but she could clearly sense their instability. With each step, she worried the stairway would give and they would plunge to the ground. But Andrew pressed forward.

"And here on the second floor, this is the floor of second chances. We'll teach them how to darn, how to seam, how to tailor, how to write. You see. The women. They can earn twenty dollars a week in the parlor houses. We have to provide them with a way to support their children. It's why they do what they do.

"We can't give them hope without a way out. What do you think? Won't it be marvelous?"

"How will this all be paid for?" Clare asked.

"We're still working through those details. Our Tract Fellowship ladies believe they can raise it. I'm afraid we won't get a penny from my father as he prefers to write about depravity as opposed to actually solving it. And my mother? You know how she feels about my work.

"Onto the third floor. But mind your step. The stairs are unstable."

Clare yearned to leave but didn't want to muzzle his zeal. Step-by-step she climbed and was greatly relieved when her feet touched the surface of the third floor.

"Here we'll have lodging. They always need a place to go when they make the change. Only for a short time, as we'll fill up quickly. But long enough for them to have a respite."

Andrew traveled across the room until he came to some

shutters on the wall. He unlatched the handle and opened the windows and fresh air came in, which Clare saw as life itself.

She leaned out and could discern through the darkness of a moonless night the shapes and figures of the main street below.

"The light," she said. "They'll see the light."

"Yes." Andrew held the lantern out to the Five Points. "That's exactly what I want them to see."

There, in the midst of the mildew and the rat dung, Clare felt a sense of empowerment and contentment as she had never experienced before. As the evening activity sprung to life in the city, she looked down below at the sprawling populous neither with fear nor awe. Instead, her heart ached for a generation of the lost and restless.

In Andrew, she could see such peace and honesty in his countenance she found herself inexorably drawn to his being. He turned to see her gazing upon him, and even in the dim light she could see him blush.

"Andrew?"

"Yes?"

"Do you believe, as your mother does, that I was a prostitute before you met me?"

Andrew let out a deep breath slowly and seemed to struggle with his answer. "Would it bother you tremendously if I told you it didn't matter?"

"It would," she responded immediately.

"Then I don't."

Clare saw in the sincerity of his answer that not only did he believe her, but that it really *didn't* matter to him either way. *What a curious fellow!*

His eyes softened with tears, and she reached out and touched his face.

He put his arm around Clare and drew her in, and she gazed out, far beyond the city horizon, to a place she never dreamed possible.

# Chapter 35

# THE SHORES OF VERACRUZ

VERACRUZ, MEXICO
*March 1847*

 Above the chilled air of the evening arose the clandestine sounds of oars digging into the water, the grunts of men straining against the tides, and the lapping of waves against the sides of the longboats.

It seemed surreal to Seamus that having never fired a weapon in his life, he sat in his United States military blues, thick cotton trousers, a greatcoat, and cloth forage cap gripping a rifle he was issued yet barely knew how to clean. What little training he and Pierce earned occurred aboard the majestic brig that sailed them through the Atlantic, around Straits of Florida, and over the Gulf of Mexico. They hadn't even touched soil when they were told they would be transported from their ship to one of these long, narrow surfboats that would be used in an assault of their enemy.

As to their enemy? The Mexicans? Seamus could not garnish a full explanation as to why the Americans were at war at all. All he knew was that this recruitment wafted him out of the danger in Manhattan and would provide him with wages, whether he discharged his weapon or not. And for his part, he would be perfectly content never to hear the sound of gunpowder.

Pierce, on the other hand, seemed intoxicated by the aroma of battle. He wasn't in need of a cause. Sometime shortly after putting on his cotton trousers, waistcoat, and sash, he had subscribed to the feverish hunger of many of the men on the ship.

His friend sat across from Seamus in the bench of the boat, gripping his rifle and nodding his head in a rhythmic manner.

"Do you know what you're to do?" said the slender sergeant to his right.

"No, sir, I don't," Seamus said.

"Well enough, lad," the sergeant said in a voice lower than the rowing. "We'll be landing shortly. You're to disembark, keeping your rifle above your head, high like this as you go to beach. Keep it out of the water or you'll spoil the powder, and you'll have them laughing at you as they run a bayonet through your heart. Keep your head down as the bullets will ride in like wind and bring tears to your mama."

"Yes sir, Sergeant O'Malley."

As they approached the harbor of Veracruz just before sunset, the target of their desire was beauteous to behold. Mastheads dotted the coastline before a shorefront that lead up in a sharp ascent to a castle-like fortress. It seemed both frightening in its impenetrability and too opulent to destroy.

Seamus's heart pounded as they came closer to shore in the

shield of darkness. They were among forty or so other surfboats, with an arsenal of great wooden ships creeping in behind
them. They were approaching with power and stealth.

The sergeant pulled out a telescope, extracted it to full
length, and panned their approach.

"What do you see?" Pierce asked.

"It's hard to tell much without light." The sergeant folded
the telescope back with a snap. "Steady. Steady. Another thirty
yards and we'll be in it, boys. Steady."

"Why aren't we being hit?" Pierce said.

"Can't say." The sergeant sat up, fastened his haversack
tightly, and lifted his rifle. His movement was mimicked
by those in the boat who weren't rowing, and several clicks
sounded as the men tested the bolts of their chambers.

"'Tis strange we haven't been shelled," he continued, "but
it's coming. We'll be in the hailstorm soon."

With a thud, the longboat came to a halt in the sandbar and
they jolted forward. A flurry of curses came from the sergeant's
mouth as he climbed out of the surfboat and the other soldiers
spilled over with such recklessness the vessel took on water.

Like a swarm of locusts emerging from the dark shadows,
men spilled out from the dozens of ships, and in the full weight
of fear they churned through the waves with their rifles held
above their heads, some falling and tumbling into the waters.

"Stay close," Pierce shouted to Seamus as they ran blindly
into what they expected to be a torrent of fury.

Seamus could feel the gasping of his breath as he had
exhausted nearly all of his air in the frenzy of the landing.

*To the dunes. To the dunes.*

He knew a relatively safe position could be assumed if they
could make it to the sand hills that lay ahead. They seemed miles
away as Seamus ran toward them when he heard the first crack

of lightning in the sky and the evening skies lit up with brilliant flashes.

Seamus felt naked in the light and tumbled into the sand, then began to crawl on all fours.

"Get up!" Pierce pulled him from the shoulder of his coat. Seamus lumbered to his feet, and as he did felt something ripping into his back and he fell again. He promptly realized it was one of his compatriots who had rammed him from behind.

Up again he sprinted ahead, trying to make Pierce's profile out from among the rushing infantrymen.

Another burst in the air above and Seamus screamed, his head vibrating with terror. Just ahead were the dunes and already they were getting claimed by those ahead of him. They had all scattered from their ranks, and for the moment it was everyone for themselves to find an oasis of safety.

Again, a splash of light and this time it helped him identify Pierce shouting and waving toward him.

Another thirty steps and he would be there. Now Seamus could hear the whistling of crossfire like the flapping of angry wings.

*Please, God. Have mercy.*

Back to his hands and knees, he pounded away at the sand, churning it behind him.

Ten yards more.

An explosion. Bright colors.

He was grabbed by Pierce and pulled into a small mound of sand, and Seamus dug himself deeply into it as if content to bury himself entirely in its firm arms. His mouth filled with sand.

Pierce pulled him out by the lapels of his coat and shook him violently. "Have you ever had such a thrill?" His eyes lit with madness.

"I can think of a few better." Seamus spit the sand out of his mouth.

There were still many figures approaching from the shadows, and it gave Seamus comfort to see the forces at hand. He also discovered that most of the firing he had heard was coming from cannons of the American ships at sea.

A soldier crouching in his run came toward them and landed at their dune. When he got closer, Seamus was pleased to see it was the sergeant.

"This is strange they are laying down," he said to the men. "I don't know if they are cowards, plain stupid, or if they are outflanking us. Be on guard. Our orders now are to settle in and let the cannons wear them down a bit."

"Yes, Sergeant," Seamus said, still wiping the grit from his teeth.

"Shouldn't we make a run?" Pierce asked. "While we have them in our sights?"

The sergeant took off his cap and wiped off the sweat from his forehead. "It's not my job to keep you alive, Private Brady." He placed his hat back on and adjusted it. "Just to make sure you don't die an idiot."

The sergeant addressed the rest of the men. "Keep your sights sharp for a while, but if we don't get countered, we'll tent up here." With that he left and disappeared into the darkness.

"What was that about?" Seamus punched Pierce in his arm.

"What? I thought we were here to fight?"

"You'll do well to listen to the sergeant, every word," said Private Sean Wheelan, a squat man with a pug nose and an eye that drifted.

"Is that so?" Pierce said.

"He's pulled many a lad from the fire, that one." Wheelan was wiping sand from his rifle with a rag. "It's a keen blessing he didn't sign up with the other side."

"What do you mean by that?" Seamus asked.

"San Patricio's Army. He was one of the first recruits."

Seamus and Pierce shook their heads.

"Really? You Micks haven't heard of Saint Patrick's Battalion? San Patricios as the natives call them. Our own people. The Irish. Fighting for the Mexicans. The sergeant was there at the Rio Grande before the first shot was fired in this war. The Yanks on one side of the river and the Mexicans on the other, just staring each other down. Taunting and parading, but none with the gumption to shoot. Well, the Mexicans learned how many Irish boys were wearing the American uniforms and sent pamphlets across the river, pushing the Catholic cause and promising to pay double wages."

"The sergeant crossed the river?" Pierce sipped from his canteen.

The whistle of approaching artillery came in, and they covered up as it exploded close enough to hear but too far to cause them damage.

"They are honing in," Seamus said nervously.

"Ah, we're safe here in the dunes," Pierce said. "The only way we'll be hit is by our own ships. So you're telling me the sergeant is a traitor?"

"A traitor to what?" Wheelan said. "He's here for the same reason as all of us poor saps. It's not about what we do here; it's about what we send home. Don't matter if it's dollars or pesos."

"But the sergeant is here with us," Seamus said.

"'Tis. Is true. He went out with a few dozen others and swam the river. Persuaded by Major John Reilly, the San Patricios leader himself. But as the sergeant tells it, he was stricken with remorse before he reached the other shoreline. He turned and came back."

"That's a fine thing he did," Seamus said. "I kind of fancy the fellow."

"Ah, we all do." Wheelan nodded. "Yet it didn't stop him from getting saddled. Never mind he came clean. They nearly shot him for it, and it's why after all his heroics, he's still a sergeant and probably always will be. They can't clear the rank for him, but they give him the tasks of a captain. Maybe he should have kept swimming."

Pierce patted his rifle. "Are we going to get to shoot this thing?"

"Suffering!" Seamus started scratching his hands. He felt stinging in his legs, then his back, and it spread to several parts of his body.

Wheelan laughed. "It's just the sand fleas, boy. You'll worry more about the fleas, the scorpions, Yellow Fever, the blasted heat, and Mexican bandits than you'll do about any army."

"I feel them too." Pierce stood, scratching at his legs. Shots fired and they whipped past his head.

"Down, you fool." Wheelan pulled Pierce to the ground.

Pierce fought back. "I'm going to let them have it."

But before he could stand, a mighty racket was sounded, and from the water the cannons of several dozen ships unleashed their arsenal into the belly of the Mexican fortress.

With each blast, Seamus cringed and dug himself deeper into the back of the dune. He wanted it to stop, as his head rung and his flesh tightened.

Yet, it didn't cease. And in a few hours, they took shifts trying unsuccessfully to sleep.

The war raged on for several days, but this time it was the late winter storms creating the fury. The northers had swept down into Veracruz, and relentless winds whipped up the sands to the point where the entrenched soldiers could hardly see their own feet. Swarms of heavy rains would come and go, drenching the encampment and making impossible the plans to bring the heavy artillery ashore.

The return fire from the fortress had caused the ships to retreat out of cannon reach, which meant they would wait until the weather cleared before carrying on the assault. For Seamus it all added up to the most miserable cold he had ever experienced.

"Do you think they'll allow us a fire yet?" Seamus said.

Wheelan chipped away at the stick he was whittling. "Nothing like telling the Mexicans exactly where to shoot their load."

"I'd rather take a cannonball in the mug than bear this weather much further."

"It's the boredom that's killing me," Pierce said. "We haven't moved in four days."

"Soon enough you'll be begging your maker for more boredom." Wheelan sat up alertly. "Here comes the sergeant."

"Gentlemen." The sergeant was chewing tobacco and spat out into the night. "Private Wheelan. They are sending some engineers on a scout mission. The captain's requested you come along."

"Captain Lee?"

"That's the one," the sergeant said. "In all his glory."

"'Tis a good thing," Wheelan said. "To stretch these legs."

"Requesting permission to go as well," Pierce said.

Sergeant O'Malley began to shake his head but seemed to change his mind. "If the private here is willing to nurse you, then you can."

"Him as well, sir?" Pierce pointed to Seamus, who was less than thrilled about the recommendation.

"It's up to Private Wheelan."

"We'll stick tight, Sergeant," Private Wheelan said.

"Let's get on it," the sergeant said.

Before Seamus could muster a protest, they were weaving their way through the muddy dunes where they met up with several others, including a tall man named Captain Lee. He must have sensed their greenness because he eyed both Pierce and Seamus with derision.

Sergeant O'Malley spoke up. "Captain, they're new volunteers but they'll serve well. They wanted patrol duty."

Captain Lee, with his prominent sideburns, raised his chin and turned toward the enemy lines, just as another torrent of rain swept upon them. He spoke with a smooth, slow voice, which revealed his Southern heritage. "We can't get the ships in close enough, and the general wants the enemy to submit by firepower, thereby holding down our casualties. That means we're going to need to set up a battery emplacement as soon as the skies clear." He looked up despondently. "If they ever do."

"What do you need us for, Captain?" the sergeant asked, having to shout above the tempest.

"It will take us a while to build the emplacement, which means it'll be necessary to find the right location. We're going to make an excursion to those city walls up there and see if we can find the soft spot in their defenses."

The Southerner spoke at a steady volume and they found themselves leaning in to hear his directions as the rain pelted. "Now, gentlemen, I don't consider it necessary to inform you of how delicate this foray is, but I will provide you with this chance again to remove yourself from this duty."

Seamus wanted above all to have the courage to step forward. To retreat without concern of anything but his safety, but he found himself mesmerized by the captain's air of confidence. He wanted no part of the danger, but he didn't want to be left out either.

"Well enough," the captain said. "Let's proceed. Leave your packs here as we won't be spending any more time where we're going than necessary. We'll have little use of gunpowder in this sleet, so secure your bayonets and let's pray to the Almighty they won't be needed."

The soldiers who had not yet done so snapped their bayonets into place, and they fell in line behind the captain. There were a dozen among them, and Pierce, Seamus, and the sergeant ended up at the rear.

Then like specters sifting up through the hills, they began their slow ascent as the winds howled around them, making their steps silent to the world. As they crossed the last of the sand dunes, they went down to their knees and crawled on their stomachs.

Seamus's ears had never felt so alive and he could hear every noise in the air, and each one made his blood rise in a growing crescendo. He didn't know why he found himself thinking about Clare, and he wondered how his sister was doing alone in the city. Many weeks had passed since he had fled Manhattan, and this was the first time he questioned his abandonment of her.

He needed to leave the city, but should he have taken her with them? Certainly, there were other options besides enlisting in the army. But now, of course, it was too late. Just another instance of Seamus making a poor decision and having it affect others. He even started to think of his brothers and sister back home.

*God. If I make it out of here, I promise to take better care of my family. You'll see that I will.*

They came up to a short stone wall, and just as they arrived they heard voices approaching. The captain signaled for them to freeze, and they all tucked up tightly and silently against the wall.

Seamus was grateful for the pounding torrent because it cloaked the screams of his heart in his chest. Through the beating of the water against the stones and the jarring gusts, the strange words of their enemy grew louder, and it was clear there were many passing on the other side of the wall. They must have wandered upon some major crossway outside the city walls.

They were marching at a steady pace, boots pulsating. The clamor of stilted conversation. The barking of a senior officer. *"¡Rápidamente, muchachos!"*

Growing louder. Hundreds.

He stopped breathing.

Without raising his head, Seamus glanced at Pierce beside him in the dim light of a partial moon and saw his friend's body quivering, his face struck with terror. Seamus worried Pierce would shake his cover.

Seamus placed his hand on Pierce's calf and gripped it to strengthen his resolve, and it seemed to work.

Although it was just a few minutes in total, it seemed an hour before the soldiers passed, and leaning up, Seamus saw the captain peering over the wall. When he guessed it was safe, Seamus did as well, creeping up. He caught the last winding marchers disappearing from sight in the distance.

The captain motioned for them to proceed and Seamus tapped Pierce to get to his feet. In a few moments the men leapt over the stone wall and ran for a patch of trees across the way.

Once in the cover of the trees, protected from the rain and from the eyes of the enemy, Seamus regained his calm. The worst was over. At least for now.

The captain gathered them together. "Just a ways through these woods will be the walls of the fortification. We'll be able to use one of these here trees to scale the encasement. Then we'll gather our reconnaissance. I need a few men stationed here by the edge of these trees to make sure we aren't flanked. Sergeant, you and two of your men."

"Yes sir. Privates Hanley and Brady."

Seamus felt relief to see the captain and the others vanish into the trees without him. He was more than happy with his assignment.

"All right you grubs," said the sergeant. "Let's spread out here and keep out of sight." He grabbed Seamus by his coat. "Remember, Captain Lee is an important man in this army and a particular favorite of the general. Which means his life matters a whole lot more than yours, Private. Are we clear?"

"Yes, Sergeant."

They put about thirty yards between them with Pierce to the left and Seamus in the middle. Sitting under the cover of the trees, Seamus couldn't imagine what danger there would be at this point, but O'Malley's warning rang in his ear, so he kept his focus and held his rifle firmly.

Once again the rain came down in force, and with his emotions tempered, Seamus now realized how brutally cold it was outside. The temperature itself was frigid, but what made it so painful was that his cotton uniform was completely soaked. He set his rifle up against a tree and wrapped his arms tightly around himself as his teeth began to clatter.

What he wouldn't give to be sitting in front of his turf

fireplace back in Branlow. He had complained about the cold back home, but after tonight he would never again.

Seamus looked over to where the sergeant was hiding, and he couldn't make him out in the darkness at all. When he glanced toward Pierce's position, his friend was clear to see. He wanted to shout out to him to cover up better, but right then he heard the sounds of soldiers approaching.

Seamus grabbed his rifle and flopped prone on the ground. Coming down the pathway before the short wall was a sentry unit of a couple dozen Mexican troops. Rather than marching as the other battalion, they were clearly on patrol and with weapons in hand. Had they been alerted to their position?

Glancing over at Pierce, he was relieved to see his friend was out of view now, which meant he heard the troops as well.

Closer they came. Stepping like cats on a fence, they surveyed the stone wall closely and then peered ominously into the woods. Two soldiers stepped in and Seamus put his head down.

The crunching of leaves and twigs under boots grew as they approached and then paused.

"*Nadie,*" said one of the men.

"*Entonces, vamos,*" said another.

The stepping sounded again, but it was fading. Seamus lifted his head to see the Mexicans moving down the pathway in the direction of Pierce. Once again, a few peeled off into the woods, skulking and prodding with their weapons. But then they cleared out and headed down the trail.

Seamus let out a deep sigh. He imagined the captain and the men would be back soon, and this unfortunate adventure would be concluded.

But then, one of the Mexicans was peeling from his group and tracing back to the woods by Pierce.

Lifting up to a crouch, Seamus decided to head toward his friend. Stepping ever so carefully through the foliage, again grateful for the blanketing fervor of the rain.

As he got closer, he couldn't see Pierce, but a soldier set down his weapon and fumbled with his pants. He began to urinate probably only about ten feet from where Pierce must have been hiding. When finished, he buckled up and then turned to leave and then froze in attention.

All of the sudden, the soldier grabbed his rifle, ran over in Pierce's direction, and pointed the bayonet. "*Se levanta,*" he barked and Pierce stood and surrendered his rifle to the ground.

"*Digame. ¿Que esta haciendo?*"

Seamus circled around the man slowly, terrified by the choices facing him.

The Mexican poked Pierce in the chest with his bayonet, causing him to stumble backward and fall. He raised his hands in defense.

The soldier leaned over Pierce and then turned as if he was going to shout to his companions, but Seamus was upon him and drove the tip of his blade into the back of the man, causing him to gasp with an awful sound that was engulfed in the watery deluge. The Mexican fell to the ground, removing himself from Seamus's blade.

Pierce covered his face with his hands and sobbed uncontrollably.

"Get up, Pierce. The captain's coming."

The sergeant joined them and examined the corpse of the Mexican. "He's dead."

With a rustling of branches, the captain and the other men gathered around the dead solider as one of them lifted Pierce to his feet and handed his rifle to him.

"Captain Lee," Seamus said firmly with a newfound

confidence that even surprised him, "there are a dozen other soldiers who will be looking for this man in a few moments. We must go."

The captain met the eyes of Seamus and gazed deeply as if into the bottom of his soul. "What's your name, Soldier?"

"Private Seamus Hanley . . . sir."

He nodded at Seamus and then waved the others to join him as he left the woods into the clearing, and they slipped over the wall and down to their encampment.

As they streamed back to camp, Seamus kept thinking of the nod he received from the captain, and it filled him with pride and lifted every step. All his life, he never once experienced that kind of affirmation from his father.

Making sure no one saw him, Seamus sobbed quietly as the rain came down.

Chapter 36

# JALAPA

The impenetrable fortress of Veracruz was brought to its knees by the heavy artillery relentlessly launched into the heart of the city. The soldiers said it was reasonably bloodless with the surrender more a result of attrition and destruction than hand-to-hand battle. This, of course, was not the case for Seamus, who was haunted by the image and sounds of his bayonet sliding into the flesh of the man he killed.

Also remaining strong in his mind were the conflicting images of defeat, a stream of dispirited Mexican soldiers stacking their muskets, their wives and children at their sides emptying from their homeland in tears and sadness. As an Irishman, belonging to a people long oppressed by English dominance, it was difficult for him to be on this side of victory.

With the threat of the "vomito," or Yellow Fever, season approaching, the generals were anxious to clear out the area, and the American soldiers were equally excited to leave this land of sweltering heat and ravenous mosquitoes. The wind of victory at their backs, they marched up north to face Santa Anna's army.

Now, with several weeks of a treacherous journey through unforgiving lands behind them, they arrived at Plan del Rio, where they were set to gather forces and prepare for the impending assault.

The thrill of their prior battle wins fading, the restlessness about what lay ahead swept through the American camp, sprawled with tents, horses, artillery, and thousands of troops.

For Seamus, his memories of Veracruz were bittersweet. His killing caused him nightmares, but his exploits also spread throughout camp, and he had earned favor with Sergeant O'Malley and, more important, Captain Lee.

This strained his relationship with Pierce, who struggled to reframe how the stories were told. When his fellow soldiers mocked him for being on his knees and begging for his life, he insisted he had been knocked to the ground. Seamus supported his friend's version, though it didn't seem to diminish Pierce's jealous ranting.

So when Seamus was summoned to be part of a special mission with Captain Lee, he didn't bother mentioning it to Pierce. Instead Seamus grabbed his haversack, a day's rations, his rifle, and slipped out in the early morning.

This time, there were only four of them: Sergeant O'Malley, Captain Lee, and a lieutenant Seamus had never met before. The ground was black, jagged, and dotted with cacti, chaparral, and mesquite.

Seamus's sense of worth had grown through his recent experiences and even more so now as he stood with the others listening to the directions from the charismatic captain.

Captain Lee removed his gloves, unfolded a map, and rolled it out across a tall boulder. "Over there at the crest of this butte may lie as many as six thousand enemy troops, of which at least some we are certain to encounter during our patrol today. This territory has been deemed impassable by our leadership, including our own General Scott, but I believe otherwise. It will be our assignment to prove this point by identifying a clear path. If we are successful in doing so, it would provide the U.S. Army with a considerable means of surprise."

Sergeant O'Malley tightened a strap on Seamus's pack.

"Of course," continued the captain with his measured drawl, "if one of us is discovered through the course of this assignment, this advantage would be nullified. We must avoid capture or even being noticed at all costs."

The captain folded the map back together and placed it in his pocket, then snapped the button tight. "Many lives will depend on this success. Am I understood?"

"Yes sir," Seamus said in chorus with the others.

Without further discourse, they began to climb up the hardened terrain over rocky ledges, sharp crags, and across ice-slick surfaces. Seamus couldn't imagine how they'd make it through themselves, let alone an army. But it was clear by the goatlike ascent of the captain he was determined to find a way.

Spreading out in a wide canvas behind the captain, they each struggled to keep pace with their leader's inhumane progress. After a few hours Seamus had lost view of the other two trailing men and to his eyes, Captain Lee was as small as a jackrabbit up ahead in the distance. Panic started to set in as Seamus knew he had lost his bearing with the geography blending together, and his only hope was to keep the captain in his sights.

The chase continued for a couple more hours, with Seamus fearing even to take a break for water. He had lost contact on several occasions, only to be relieved to spot the captain's hat bobbing above a bush or boulder.

Suddenly, the officer came to a stop and dove behind a large fallen tree. Seamus slipped behind a bush himself and felt helpless as three Mexican soldiers came into view within yards of where the captain was hiding. In amazement, he watched as they came up to the log, sat down, and unpacked their lunches.

There was a noise behind Seamus and realizing he was completely exposed from the flank, he lost his nerve and hurtled down an embankment toward a grove of trees. Once in the shade of cover, he looked back to see who was behind him as his chest rose and fell, desperate for air.

Another noise. Twigs cracking. He wasn't alone.

There was nothing ahead except for short manzanita bushes, and with no other direction to go, there was only one choice.

He ran with all abandon.

Blindly. Tripping. Back to his feet. Forward again. Arms flailing.

It was hard to know for how long. It was difficult to know the distance. But when Seamus finally stopped, one thing was certain: He was completely lost.

Panning around, he strained to identify something that would provide a clue. There were some mountain peaks off in the distance, but he couldn't recall which direction they were in reference to his camp. Was it to the east or west of that range? Or was it south?

Seamus sat down on a boulder, then pulled out dry tack from his pack and ate it as he sipped from his canteen. On the ground by his boots, two scorpions scuttled by and he raised his legs until they passed.

As he glanced up at the mountain peaks again, he noticed the sun was sliding down behind them. He figured he had only thirty minutes of daylight remaining. He'd have to press on.

Seamus stood and swung his pack around his shoulder.

When he bent down to reach for his rifle, he heard a clicking noise and turned slowly to see three Mexicans pointing pistols at him.

For soldiers, they wore peculiar uniforms. They were like robes, all white, with a leather sash, and they had straw-woven, broad-rimmed hats on their heads. Their faces were dark skinned, with bushy mustaches and browned teeth.

"*Buenos dias, amigo,*" said the gray-haired one with a clouded eye. He nodded to another who responded by retrieving Seamus's rifle and patting him down for weapons.

"*¿Habla Español, no?*"

Seamus shook his head.

"*¿Perdido, sí?*" He spoke slowly. "Choo lost?"

"Are you Mexican army?" Seamus asked.

"*¿Soldados?*" The Mexican laughed. "*Sí.* You could say so, my friend."

At the same time a dull thud was heard, pain streaked through Seamus's head and then everything went black.

When his eyes opened again, the world was upside down and moving violently.

Strapped across a burro, with his head on one side, his feet on the other, and his hands tied behind his back, Seamus awoke to throbbing pain in his head.

He craned his neck up as far as he could and saw he was being led into a place that seemed pulled from an artist's painting. It was a mountain village, framed by spectacular snow-topped granite peaks, towering green forests, and dabbed throughout was a brilliant bloom of spring wildflowers.

As they traveled farther, with the strangers obviously uncon-
cerned for Seamus's indignity and discomfort, the road became
cobbled and earthen-shaded mercantile buildings sprung up on
either side.

From his limited vantage point and lack of mobility, Seamus
could only see one of his ambushers who was leading the
burro with a rope. But he heard the voices of other men as they
exchanged pleasantries and greetings with the residents they
were passing.

After being taunted by boys playing in the street who
rapped at Seamus's ankles with slender rods, they finally arrived
at their destination and the animal was tied to a post. Seamus
was loosened and lifted to his feet. The blood rushed to his head
so quickly he stumbled.

"*Esta aqui, amigo,*" said the tallest, with a broad smile.

Two of them gripped his arms from either side, and they
walked past a couple of armed soldiers who nodded at them
as they entered through the shuttered doors of an adobe brick
building.

Seamus recognized the smell of liquor and beer as soon as he
entered the room, which had all the appearances and sounds of a
tavern. There were a couple dozen men scattered throughout the
place—relaxing at tables, sipping glasses, with some engaging
in what appeared to be a serious game of cards. Some Mexican
*señoritas* were serving drinks and consorting with the guests,
who, for the most part, were dressed in the uniforms of United
States soldiers.

Seamus could tell by their faces and voices that many, if
not all, were of Irish heritage. In the corner sitting on a crate,
a Mexican man with an eye patch strummed a guitar as he
warbled a sad, Spanish melody.

One of the captors cut the rope from his hands, while the

other two seemed to be in stern negotiations with a Mexican officer, presumably haggling over the ransom.

As Seamus rubbed his sore wrists, a woman with dark skin, brown eyes, and a large mole on her cheek approached with a seductive sway. "They bring handsome boy. You seat. I see you thirsty."

She took his hand and sat him in a chair at a table where a grizzled American soldier appeared to be waiting for him. The man uncorked a bottle and filled up two shot glasses, sliding one over to Seamus.

"Welcome to Paradise." The soldier held up his glass in a toast.

"What is this?" Seamus picked up his glass and gave it a wary sniff.

"Tequila. Made from the cactus you see all around. It's got a pleasant kick to it I think you'll find to your liking."

"Why am I here?" Seamus asked.

"First. My apologies for the *bandidos*. They haven't quite got the hospitality part down. It's not what Major Reilly had in mind at all. But for a few pesos, they're rather capable at rounding up rabbit soldiers."

"I didn't defect," Seamus said defiantly.

"Of course you didn't, lad. None of us in this room have. We just had bigger plans than dying for the Yanks." He pursed his lips, gave a whistle, and held up his hand. "Gabriela. Could you bring our soldier here something to eat?"

Seamus emptied the shot glass in one snap and winced. It tasted different but went down just like whiskey.

The man lifted the clear bottle and refilled it without asking. "What's your name, son?"

He thought for a moment about refusing to answer. "Seamus."

Gabriela put a plate on the table. There was some meat, which appeared to be pork, and some round flat pieces of bread.

"Tortillas," the soldier said.

"No for you, *Señor* Doyle." She slapped playfully at the man's hand as he reached to the plate to grab one.

"I think Gabriella likes you," Doyle said. "Go ahead. Eat your food."

"*¿Como se llama?*" Gabriella asked Doyle.

"His name is Seamus," Doyle said. "Yes. She likes you."

Gabriela circled behind Seamus and her fingers dragged through his hair. When she hit the lump on his head, he flinched.

"Oh, you head hurt bad? I make better for you. I come back." She left and Seamus couldn't help but watch her as she shifted away.

"Yes." Doyle nodded. "Gabriella always makes it better."

Seamus leaned forward across the table. "How do I get out of here?"

Doyle chuckled. He pushed the plate of food in front of Seamus. "Eat, boy. You're going to need this."

Wanting at first to throw the plate on the ground, Seamus looked down and the smells got to him. He put a piece of the meat in his mouth and chewed, and then grabbed one of the tortillas and shoveled it in as well. He figured it must have been because he was so hungry, but it tasted as good as anything he had eaten, and it fixed the aching in his stomach.

A roll of laughter came from a table at the far end of the room, where several American soldiers looked on as one of the señoritas danced voluptuously on a chair.

Gabriela returned and set a bowl of water on the table and dipped a hand cloth into it. Seamus observed as she wrung it out, allowing the excess water to drip before placing the warm cloth on the bump at the back of his head.

"The San Patricios," Doyle said. "You've heard of them, eh?"

"I have." Seamus dragged the last tortilla across the plate to sop up what juices remained.

"It's the Irish army of the Mexican Republic. They're Catholic people, you know? The Mexicans."

"So I've heard." Seamus leaned back in his chair as Gabriella rubbed his shoulders.

"They pay better," Doyle said, "a better cause. Here we're Irish kings rather than maggots in America. Mark my words, son. You'll be thanking those bandidos the rest of your life."

The doors burst open and in came a brawny boy with long, flowing red hair, a sunburned face, and wearing a Mexican uniform. In his hand, hanging from an iron pole was a green flag with a gold harp. "*Erin go bragh,* laddies," he shouted. "The battle's coming to us."

There was a mix of cheers and groans in response, and the Irish soldier vanished from the room as quickly as he arrived.

Seamus sipped from his glass and accepted a cigar from Doyle, who had lit it for him.

"My boy no fight." Gabriela wrapped her arms around Seamus and kissed him on the cheek.

The Mexican guitarist began to play loudly and sang to some woman of his distant memory. Seamus couldn't understand a single word, but it spoke to him nonetheless.

Some of those in the tavern broke out in a jig, spun, whistled, and swung each other from arm to arm.

Seamus realized Ireland was in every town.

## Chapter 37

# The Drawings

Clare examined herself in the looking glass as her hair was being brushed by her roommate, Daphnc. She was a middle-aged, single woman who was raised in the Carolinas before spiriting to Manhattan to become an actress. But as fate would have it, she discovered her true calling to be penning theater reviews and became famous for it in her position with the *New York Daily*.

It was Andrew's idea for Clare to move out of his home as soon as she was well, since his intentions for her had been declared. Her departure was met with cheers by Mrs. Royce, who made no secret of her disappointment in her son's affections toward Clare.

On the other hand, Clare's surprising talents in journalism brought the gushing favor of Mr. Royce, which only exacerbated his wife's disquietude. In some ways, Clare's passion and ability in contributing to the newspaper freed Andrew of the burden of performing well for his father. Clare, in many ways, became the surrogate of Mr. Royce's succession plans.

And as things turned out, Daphne—of good cheer, strength of character, full of verve, and with unswerving loyalty—became both a dear friend and mentor to Clare. They walked the short two blocks to work together every day even in this sweltering month of July. They shared deep secrets and served as unfailing advocates and shields for one another in a patriarchal and often hostile work environment.

"You look charming, my dear." Daphne hugged Clare around her shoulders. She stroked Clare's hair, which was now shoulder length. "Me with my tired, gray-speckled, drooping locks. I would sacrifice everything for just one day with this beautiful hair."

Clare laughed. "There wasn't a hair to be counted on this head just ten months ago. Seems like years ago."

"I'll say it has returned in full glory. And this dress is simply divine."

"Do you really think so?" Clare adjusted the shoulders and admired the embroidered neckline garnitures of the fuchsia evening gown. She barely agreed to Andrew's spoiling her with this gift. And only because he insisted it would honor him at his milestone event. Clare turned her head side to side and pursed her lips. "You wouldn't tell me otherwise anyway? What a sweet liar you are."

Daphne gave Clare a nudge. "Believe me, I'm working hard to find a flaw. Something, anything, to quench my jealousy."

"I just want everything to be perfect for Andrew tonight," Clare said.

"Of course, my love. But I'd say there's something to celebrate in this as well." Daphne picked up the newspaper sitting on the cabinet. She read from it in dramatic fashion, *"The Terrifying and Fragile Victory of the Slave Underground.* By our own Clare Hanley. On the front page, no less."

"Oh, please do stop it!" Clare waved her hand in the mirror.

"'Accompanying the relentless pursuit of that elusive prize of freedom is the ever-present hounds of oppression bearing down upon them: the unquenchable bloodthirst of the vengeful slave owner. Sensing the moist muzzles and warm breath of their pursuers at every bend, every turn, there is no lasting reprieve. So while free of their shackles, they remain imprisoned by the cruelty of their trepidation.'" Daphne fanned herself as if she was to faint.

"Enough, dear sister." Clare watched her cheeks color of rose. "You're intolerable."

"You deserve it and more. You're changing lives, Clare. You know that, don't you?" Daphne's expression changed. "So, have you any news from back home yet?"

Clare grimaced. "Unchanged, I'm afraid. Every week I go to the Irish Society to send my letters, and every week they shake their heads. I don't know why they haven't written back. It does concern me greatly."

"Any news about your sister . . . what was her name, dear?"

"Margaret." The very mention of the name made Clare sad. "Andrew has been researching records for me, but we've come up empty. There's no sign she ever made it here, after all."

Clare stood up from her chair. She felt stiff and uncomfortable with all of the layers of clothing. "Do women *really* wear this?"

"They do. The ladies, that is."

"I'll be glad when the evening is over and I can climb out of all of this. How does one even fit out the door?" Clare gave a half spin in front of the mirror.

Daphne handed Clare her gloves.

Three short knocks came from the door, and Clare nearly jumped. "Be honest. Do I look foolish? Please tell me the truth or I'll never forgive you for the remainder of my life."

"Well in that case. Hmmm. There's much at stake here, give me time." Daphne smiled and kissed Clare on the cheek. "Now let's not keep him waiting." She walked over to the brass handle and opened the door to Andrew, dressed in full tails and top hat. When he saw Clare, he removed his hat and pressed it to his chest.

"Who is this princess that stands before me? And what have you done with my handmaid Clare?"

"Your princess will be selling this dress tomorrow," said Clare. "How many meals—?"

Before she could finish her sentence he leaned over and kissed her to silence.

"Willful waste makes woeful want," she whispered with a smile.

"I know," he said. "Your grandmother is absolutely correct. But she is not coming tonight."

Andrew insisted Clare keep away from the building during its renovation in order to allow the transformation to be a surprise. Even with her travels through the Five Points in her role as a journalist, she had been purposeful about honoring his request. So as their carriage slowed to a full stop and with the full advantage of the summer light, she was awestruck by what towered before her.

There, in the place of that abandoned breeding ground of vermin, was a sublimely handsome building, with fresh paint, ornate shutters, and new glass windows. Proudly displayed was a large sign with a blue background, which read in raised gold lettering: The House of Refuge.

"Why Andrew . . . my goodness, Andrew."

He glowed as he helped Clare out of the carriage, and then they joined a long line of dignitaries waiting to gain entrance. Through the windows she could see many had already been welcomed inside. As Clare gaped at the conversion before her, a stately woman in a flamboyant pink hat waved them to the front of the line by the doorway.

"Make way for the architect of this grand vision," she said with authority. "This is our dear Mr. Andrew Royce." She led the polite applause. "To save the decrepit souls of the Five Points."

Andrew tried to show his appreciation of the comments, but Clare could tell he was miserable with the attention. He mouthed the words, "I'm sorry."

Clare giggled. She enjoyed seeing him shrink under the platitudes, which in her mind were well earned. He had labored for months, raising the funds, formulating the plans, and directing the work crew.

They entered the building, which was eloquently decorated with azure ribbons swooping from the rafters, dozens of intricately designed wreaths hanging on the walls, and the entire area lit with hundreds of candles. The chamber music of Bach performed by a string quartet of somber musicians rose above the clatter of high-society pretense and gossip of guests who sipped from crystal champagne flutes.

As Andrew and Clare entered, handsomely attired attendees turned and expressed delight in seeing them, opening a pathway as if they were royalty.

Though the night belonged to Andrew, he never swayed in his attention to Clare, proudly presenting her with a "This is my inspiration," or "She endured each challenge at my side," or "Who faithfully supported such foolish notions."

Clare on her part would counter with genuine humility. "I can claim no part in any of this."

Although the intention of the event was to provide a tour of the new building to their guests followed by a brief speech, the attendance had overwhelmed these plans. Instead, with barely room to move, Andrew did his best to try to personally thank each and every person who had come.

And it was these crowded conditions that made it possible for Clare to be caught completely by surprise when she felt a tap on her shoulder.

"Will you look what my little Clare has done," she heard in a voice both familiar and frightening.

Patrick Feagles.

Both he and Tressa were dressed in a way that showed their strains to fit in this evening but which betrayed they were well above their class.

Clare stood stunned.

Andrew turned and put his arm around her protectively.

"Andrew, this is . . ." Clare began.

"Yes, I know. Patrick Feagles."

Patrick held out a hand, but Andrew didn't reciprocate.

"Well . . . I see." Patrick withdrew his hand. He tried to wear a smile. "This is good. Good thing you're doing here. Just wanted you to know we were proud of you, Clare. And you, sir, as well."

Clare bit her lip but didn't speak. Not in protest, but because she could hardly breathe. It wasn't easy for her to avoid such a prominent figure in the Five Points, but she had managed to evade him for months.

"Did you hear of John Barden?"

"No," Clare said, lying.

"He made it through. You know. From his . . . run-in with a knife."

"The fighter?" Andrew asked.

"The one indeed. Well. Anyways. He left town a few weeks back. But not before wanting me to thank you for providing for his daughter. You know. The money and all."

Clare nodded.

"Patrick," Tressa said, wearing a clash of colors as if the paint had been spilled on the canvas. "They have many guests to greet. Let's leave them be."

"All right, then. We'll do just that." He tipped his green plug hat. "Congratulations to you. The both of yous."

Clare wondered why she felt sympathy for them, but as the couple turned, she fought the desire to reach out and call them back. In some ways, it was unthinkable to ever speak to them again after their part in virtually selling her off to Mr. O'Riley. She shuddered at the memory of that evening. Yet, there was something pitiful about her uncle and Tressa that eased her toward forgiveness. But before she could consider it further, they disappeared into the crowd.

"Oh no," Andrew said. "No. No. No."

Clare looked at Andrew, following his gaze to a commotion out front of the building. He pressed his way through the gathering with firmness and many apologies, and Clare trailed in his wake.

Outside, a few of the stewards were trying to shoo away what was a growing gathering of ragamuffin onlookers, pressing their faces against the front windows to catch a glimpse of the revelry inside.

"What exactly is going on here?" he asked his men with restrained anger.

"Why, Mr. Royce," answered one of them. "We are trying to explain to these people that tonight is not for them."

Andrew let out a deep sigh. "I must correct you, sir, but tonight is precisely for them." He turned toward the downtrodden. "Come. All of you inside. Out of the cold. There's food and drink. It's a time of celebration and we want you to be part."

"But sir," the steward protested, but there was no stopping the procession now, and they entered to shrieks and horror of the guests inside.

Andrew was clearly amused by the whole idea, and Clare started to laugh, covering her mouth as soon as she did.

Sensing there was someone behind her, Clare turned and was startled to see before her the very same elderly woman who had been following her months ago. She was dressed in the blue hat and worn black coat she had on when Clare first saw her in the lamplight.

"Are you all right?" Andrew asked her.

"Do you recognize her?" Clare said with a nod toward the woman.

"Yes, of course. It's Greta. She lives in the streets mostly. Perfectly harmless although a bit batty, I'm afraid. Why? What is it, Clare?"

"I think she's been following me. I need to know why."

Glancing both ways before crossing the street, Clare approached the woman, who appeared alarmed and turned to leave.

"Wait! Please don't go. I just have a question. Please, Greta."

Upon hearing her name, the old woman stopped her retreat and stepped back into the light revealing a face impressed with the tracks of a difficult life.

"Thank you," Clare said. "Please tell me. I must know. Have you been following me?"

Greta's gaze darted nervously between Andrew and Clare.

"It's all right, Greta." Andrew smiled. "You can trust her. There is nothing to fear."

The woman slowly extended her hand to Clare's face and touched her on the cheek with coarse fingers.

Clare glanced at Andrew, and he assured her with a nod.

Then Greta reached into her coat and pulled out some folded papers, frayed and yellowed. Meticulously opening each of them up, it was clear they were treasured by the woman. Then she found the one she was seeking and handed it to Clare.

Clare took the paper and when she saw what was on it her mouth dropped. It was a delicate charcoal drawing of herself, yet it was a depiction of what she looked like when she was five years younger. What was most astonishing to Clare was she recognized the artist's hand.

"Where did you get this?" she blurted out.

"What's the matter, Clare?" Andrew put his hand on her back.

"Answer me, woman!"

Greta's eyes flared and she staggered backward.

"Clare! You're frightening her." Andrew put his palm on Greta's shoulder. "She didn't mean that. She won't harm you. I promise." He pointed to the other papers in the woman's clasp. "May I see those?"

Instinctively, Greta pulled them toward her protectively. She was near hyperventilation, but exhaled a few times and then gave them to Clare.

Clare sifted through them. One was a drawing of Davin. The next Ronan. Then Caitlin. Each of them five years younger.

"What is it, Clare?"

"These are Margaret's drawings. Maggie. My sister. This is how she remembered us when she left. No one else could have done this."

"Maggie's *my* friend," the woman burst out. "Give them back."

"Greta," Andrew asked. "Where did you get these?"

She glared at them in suspicion. "Maggie said I could have them." Then she spoke as if in confession. "Until I found you."

"Where's Maggie?" Clare's heartbeat rose. "Where is my sister? Do you know where she is?"

Greta seemed confused by the question and replied as if the answer was obvious. "At the island, dear."

"The island?" Clare mumbled back, and Andrew didn't look pleased with Greta's response. "What is it, Andrew?"

"Blackwell's Island. That's where Greta was before being released."

"The prison?" Clare struggled to find meaning in all of this.

"There's a penitentiary on the island. But there is an insane asylum as well."

"Is this right?" Clare asked Greta. "Is Maggie alive?"

"Of course, dear." Greta tapped at the drawing of Clare. "She told me you would come. And to give you this."

Her head twisted with myriad emotions. Maggie alive? Could this be possible? It would seem so. But what about the lie her uncle told her? What else did he know?

Clare spun around. Maybe her uncle hadn't left yet. But Andrew interceded, pulling her in and holding her close to him. "I'm going to kill the man!" she said, and pounded her fists against Andrew.

But Andrew held firm. "Shhh. There. There. It's going to be fine, Clare. Shhh." He stroked her hair and she unclenched her body and surrendered in tears.

"We'll go tomorrow," he whispered in her ear. "First we'll learn the truth."

Clare surrendered to his strength and drew comfort from

Andrew. She never imagined someone would care for her this deeply.

He rocked her gently and as Clare opened her eyes, she realized in horror that many of the party's guests had been watching them from the windows. They were pointing and gesturing with the drunken fascination of meddlers and gossips.

Some of the city's most influential citizens just witnessed her tirade with Andrew, including his parents. Clare was mortified by the knowledge she had sabotaged his special evening.

"Andrew?" She was submerged in embarrassment and remorse.

"Shhh, I know, Clare. None of that matters to me." He put his hands on her cold cheeks and smiled at her with eyes glistening with joy. "Tomorrow. We're going to get your sister."

## Chapter 38

# BLACKWELL'S ISLAND

"Are you certain I should leave you here in this condition?" Daphne's brow furrowed.

"Most certain." Clare continued to pace back and forth across the creaking wooden floor of their apartment, as a cup of a tea in a saucer rattled in her hands. Despite not returning from the celebration until late in the evening, she hadn't slept at all last night. "Go, go." She waved Daphne to the door. "You'll be late on account of me, and without the advantage of courting the publisher's only son."

Daphne wrapped a scarf around her neck, glanced in the hanging mirror, and straightened her hat before opening the door. "Shouldn't I come with you?"

"Leave!"

Her roommate exited and Daphne ascended the staircase leading from their doorway to the busy street above.

Clare glanced at the clock on the wall. What was keeping Andrew? Even with his father's connections, he feared it would be difficult to get clearance to Blackwell's Island, and now she fretted he might have failed.

She couldn't fathom delaying her reunion with her sister even one more day. After all of these years believing she was lost, and now to be only hours away from seeing Maggie's ebullient smile?

Yet Clare was plagued as well by the thought Maggie may have suffered her mother's fate. Why would she be in an asylum? Of all people she knew, Margaret was the most carefree and unaffected by the worries of the world. It made no sense at all.

Hearing a stir outside, she felt the weight of her worries subsiding. Andrew must be back. But a glance through the window only increased her unease.

It was a man with worn blue pants, rolled up to his thighs. He was laboring down the stairway, with one leg nothing more than a peg of wood.

Clare panicked. Should she pretend she wasn't home?

A firm rap came on the door and she froze, certain at any moment the hobbled stranger would peer through the window, only to discover her cowering inside.

"Clare. It's me. I know you're in there."

She recognized the voice and was dumbfounded as she went to unlatch the door to open it for the visitor.

There before her, in a battle-borne United States Army uniform, and with his hat in his hand, was her friend from back home. Yet he was difficult to recognize as he had aged many years though having only been gone for months.

"Pierce?" Clare put her hand to her mouth at the sight of him.

"Aren't you going to ask me in? Do I frighten you so?"

She clasped him tightly, trying to draw out his pain, and began to cry.

"Pity is an ugly welcome."

Clare stepped back and brushed a tear from her eye, trying to recover some joy in reuniting with her friend. "It's wonderful to see you. Can I . . . get you some tea?"

Pierce hobbled in and scrutinized the room before settling into an oak chair, groaning as his body lowered into it. "I'm not here for long, Clare. My ride is waiting outside."

"But where are you going? You just arrived."

He glared at her with cold, empty eyes. "Boston. One of my mates said his father could offer me a job. Fit for a cripple, I suppose. Not that it matters to you."

"Of course it does. Why are you speaking like this? I want you to tell me everything." She pulled a chair beside him and placed her saucer and cup on the table between them.

Pierce avoided her eyes. "Don't you want to know?"

Clare paused. "Yes. Yes, I do. How did it happen?"

"The Battle of Cerro Gordo. A thousand heroes and I end up taking a musket shot to my foot while tending horses. Swelling set in and they decided a leg wasn't worth a life."

"I'm so sorry, Pierce."

"You're doing well enough," he said with contempt.

She squirmed in her chair. "I'm so grateful you found me. It's so good—"

"To think." He scoffed. "To think I actually came to ask you to come with me."

"Come with . . . ?"

"Fool that I am, huh?"

Clare shook her head. "I can't, Pierce."

"You can't?" His voice rose.

"I don't want to. I'm happy here." From the edge of her view she saw someone descending the stairs. It was Andrew. She let him in.

"I would be ashamed to admit to you who I had to promise political grace to, but here are the clearance papers," Andrew said. Pierce's presence caught him off guard. "Clare, I'm sorry. I wasn't aware you had a guest." His gaze appealed to Clare for an explanation.

"You aren't leaving already?" Clare said with genuine disappointment as Pierce struggled to get up, waving off her offer to assist him.

"I can see it's time." He limped toward the door, buttoning his jacket.

"Pierce?"

He looked at her dispassionately. "Oh yes. Your brother?"

"Please."

Pierce studied Andrew with distaste. "I'll spare you the details. The news is not what you'd want to hear, I'm afraid."

"Is he . . . ?"

"He may be alive, or he may have already been hung."

"What do you mean by this?" Clare's legs grew weak.

Apparently moved by her emotion, Pierce's voice lost its edge. "There is no other way to say it, Clare. Your brother turned traitor."

"What?" Clare collapsed back into the chair.

"He fought for the enemy."

Even with Seamus's history of failure, this seemed too much to fathom. "I don't believe what you are saying. That's not my brother you speak of."

"San Patricios?" Andrew asked. "Irish defectors recruited by the Mexicans."

Pierce seemed impressed. "Yes. How did you know?"

"We work for a newspaper." Andrew bent down beside Clare and wrapped his arm around her.

"I don't understand," Clare said, her anger growing. "How did you let him do this?"

"Clare," Andrew said softly. "Don't."

Pierce put his hat on. "Yes. Well. You know your brother, Clare. Maybe it was a mistake to tell you. You could have believed he died a hero." He started to go out the door and turned back. "I don't believe I'll see you again."

She didn't see him go, and lost herself in her tears.

Andrew just held her in his arms for the longest time in silence. Finally, he whispered in her ear. "There is nothing you can do about your brother. But you can with Maggie."

As they headed down the creaking boards of the pier, the seagulls waited until the last moment before scattering away and then circling in behind them. Ahead of them was a line of people waiting to embark the paddle-steam ferry, whose engine grinded as black smoke rose, though still moored.

"Is it happening to you already?" Clare asked of Andrew. His face was blanched and clammy.

"I'll be fine." He took off his glasses and wiped the profuse sweat beading on his forehead.

"I don't expect you to do this."

"You're not going alone."

They took their place in the back of the line as passengers handed their paperwork to one of the boat's crew. With each step forward, Andrew's agitation noticeably increased.

"What's with him?" said the man when it was their turn to board.

"Just a bit of a dizzy spell." Clare grabbed the papers from Andrew's grasp and handed them to the steward, who seemingly read every line.

"Reporters? The *New York Daily*, eh?" He returned their credentials and nodded for them to move forward.

As they ventured across the plank to the steamship, Clare felt the full weight of Andrew on her shoulder.

"Please don't do this," she pleaded.

"Don't ask me again," Andrew snapped.

"Over there is a bench inside where you won't have to see the water." They were only a few steps away, but when they arrived, he nearly collapsed onto the wooden seating.

The woman next to them drew her children close into her arms. "He doesn't look right," she said with disgust.

Clare scowled at the woman and put her arm around Andrew and stroked his face as the ship lurched and began its short journey across Hudson Bay.

Being in the steamship brought back memories of her passage across the Atlantic and the depth of illness she suffered. Yet was there ever a day on her trip as difficult as this one was with Andrew? She felt incapable of placating his hysteria and could only hope the trip would end soon. As it turned out, Blackwell's Island was the last stop on an elongated loop the steamship was navigating, and by the time they arrived at the boat landing, Andrew's nerves had completely frayed. Fortunately, there was a doctor aboard, who tended to him during the last stretch of the trip.

Finally, the boat drifted into the landing and the nightmare drew near its conclusion as the rope tethered them to shore. The doctor received permission to leave before anyone else, and they bore Andrew away from the dock, each to one side of him, as he dragged along. Clare was already dreading the return trip to Manhattan.

For Clare, the day was overwhelming. Today's news about her brother. The anxiety regarding Maggie's state of mind. And now having to deal with Andrew's condition. What more could she bear?

As it turned out, the doctor was also en route to the asylum and generously offered to share his carriage, an offer they promptly accepted.

Now, away from the water's edge, Andrew's recovery was swift, although he remained mired in embarrassment. The doctor, who was an Englishman as well, tried to downplay Andrew's reaction by suggesting hydrophobia, as he described it, was a common malady.

"There's only one proven way to overcome it, I'm afraid. The simple act of bravery you performed today. That's what's needed. It's a fear to be faced."

"I wouldn't use the word *brave* in describing what just happened," Andrew said. "Hopefully, Doctor, you don't have plans to commit me."

The doctor smiled as if in courtesy but became somber. "You've never been to Blackwell's asylum, have you?"

They shook their heads, and glancing out the windows of the black cab, Clare could see the vast, gray walls of the buildings approaching.

"It is a despicable place, if I'm being honest. Devoid of all humanity. As physicians we do our best to treat our patients with care. But we're mostly overrun. I apologize for my lack of manners. You are here in the capacity of reporters? Isn't that what you told me?"

"The *Daily*," Andrew said.

"In that case, I hope you have the courage to write what you witness." He pulled out a silver pocket watch as the horses were drawn to a halt. "Quite late, I'm afraid. Good day to the two of you, and sir, I wish you better returns."

The physician's dire description was corroborated the moment they entered through the sweeping doors of the fortification. The stench of feces, urine, and vomit emanated from every pore of the building.

Having passed by the hallways of the woman's wing, Clare had already heard and seen enough slivers of horror to have drained herself completely of whatever enthusiasm she had to see Maggie. In its place now was unfiltered dread.

Never in full sight of visitors, but caught in glimpses around bends and far ends of hallways, they saw pale, thin arms reaching out of cells, patients restrained in hideous buckled jackets, and the haunting sounds of clanging chains, moaning, frightful laughter, and emotional agony.

In Clare's mind one clear thought was paramount: She would not leave this place without her sister.

After many false turns, they were finally directed to a processing chamber, where an ogrelike woman behind an imposing wooden counter greeted them with the callous disinterest of someone who loathed their position.

They were ignored as she scratched away on paperwork. After a while, Andrew cleared his throat. When that didn't work, he tapped on a bell that caused her to raise her head with some clear irritation.

"We're trying to find a patient."

"And you are?"

"I'm Andrew Royce from the *New York Daily* and this is . . . Clare."

"And on what authority?"

Clare handed Andrew their paperwork and he placed it before the woman, who pulled out spectacles attached to a chain and perched them on her nose.

After a few moments, the woman looked up from the papers. "What name?"

"Margaret Hanley." Clare stepped forward.

The woman dragged over a large leather-bound book, opened it, and thumbed through pages. "Hanley, you say?"

Clare's anxiety rose with each page turned, and she watched with intensity as the women's finger slid down the list of names.

"No, I'm afraid not." The woman closed the book and shrugged.

"What do you mean you can't find her?" Clare said. "She has to be in there." However, fear crept into Clare. Maybe they had it all wrong. Perhaps Greta met Maggie somewhere else.

"What about your uncle's name?" Andrew said to her. "Could it be under that?"

"Yes," Clare said, her hope flooding back. "Try in the name of Margaret or Maggie Feagles."

The clerk gave her a wry expression. Then grudgingly she opened the tome, and sifted through the pages. "I'm afraid. She's not here. No one here by any of the names you mentioned."

Clare's lips began to quiver and she fought to hold back the tears.

"Are you certain?" Andrew asked. "It's quite important."

"Yes. I am sorry for you." The clerk's tone had softened. "But there is nothing else I can do." Then she raised an eyebrow in suspicion. "I thought you were here for the newspaper? Is this someone you knew personally?"

"Thank you," Clare said, defeated.

Andrew pulled her into him and put his head close to hers and then turned to leave.

"Wait." Clare thought of something insidious and in some ways hoped she wasn't right. "Excuse me, miss. Can you look up one last name for me, please? The name is Margaret O'Riley."

The book opened again, pages were turned, and Clare scrutinized the clerk's every slight facial expression.

*Please, God. Let me see Margaret. Let me see her once again.*

The woman paused and pursed her lips in surprise. "Well, there is a Margaret O'Riley, after all." But then her countenance fell. She looked up to Clare with an expression of charity. "Perhaps this is not the same woman."

"Tell me," Clare said. "What does it say?"

"We get quite a few O'Rileys in here, as you can imagine."

"What is it?"

"It's all right, Clare," Andrew said.

"It's not all right. Tell me what it says."

The woman glanced to Andrew and then back to Clare. "The record shows a Margaret O'Riley being admitted on January 17th of 1845. Over two years ago. Checked in by her husband, a Mr. Gorman O'Riley, based on his claims she tried to kill him with an ax. This was witnessed by a Mr. Patrick Feagles."

"I want to see her. Now." Clare felt her blood rushing to her head.

The clerk kept reading, her lips moving as she did. Then she closed the book, this time for the last time. "I'm afraid that won't be possible." She removed her spectacles. "It says she was inconsolable in confinement and refused to eat. I'm sorry. But she died six weeks later."

Clare sank into Andrew's arms. There was profound grief in her pain. She had believed with all her heart she would see Maggie today.

Almost immediately, the hope of expectation was replaced by something deep and onerous, bubbling to the surface of her being. Black . . . black.

It was approaching.

## Chapter 39

# The Chamber

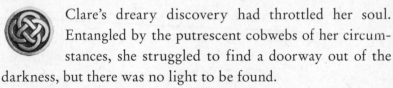 Clare's dreary discovery had throttled her soul. Entangled by the putrescent cobwebs of her circumstances, she struggled to find a doorway out of the darkness, but there was no light to be found.

This journey down the chasm of melancholy shifted direction after a few days and veered through a landscape more sinister in nature. She drifted through murky waters to the banks of another emotion, depraved and tenebrous, tentacles that slowly reached into the forgotten caverns of despair.

There, billows of anger sifted in through the haze and in the distance a building drumbeat summoned a beast of murderous intentions: hatred, unforgiveness, and the sweltering shadows of revenge.

Depravity streamed through her veins. She yearned to rage wildly against her oppressor. To feel the blade of revenge to penetrating flesh.

Despite all efforts of encouragement from Daphne and Andrew, Clare curled in bed, knotted in grief, motionless and without purpose, begging to be left alone in her misery.

Most revolting to her was Andrew's desire to pray over her, to read her Scripture, and to speak of God's promises. Clare wanted only to spit out the very thought of a benevolent God existing in this corrupt world. She knew what He was now. He had played her the fool and abandoned her for the last time. He was no different than her father and now she would trust no one.

Through the fog of her depression, Clare had some aware-ness that Andrew was intending to preserve her life before the bottom fell out of her dreams. He was keeping her byline in print, conducting interviews, and writing her stories by day, working at the newly launched mission at night, and sharing the duties of caring for her with Daphne and even Cassie at times, insisting that she never be left alone.

Through the blurred vision of the world outside, all filtered through her misery, Clare could vaguely discern that Andrew was wearying under the burden of this task. Perhaps it was her concern for him, or maybe it was the silent cries of her remain-ing family back home that helped her to pierce through her veil of gloom. Regardless of the source, after a few weeks, the winds began to blow away the haze, and the burden of waking up less-ened with each day.

It was a particularly bright morning when Clare felt inclined to rise from bed, slide out the drawer of her oak wardrobe, and pull out Maggie's drawings, something Clare thought she would never again have the courage to do.

The sight of Davin, Ronan, and Caitlin sketched by Maggie's hand caused her to choke with emotions, but the sight of her brothers and sister caused her to smile as well.

Then she noticed something.

"Oh, you're up, Clare," said Daphne as she came out from her room with her shoes in her hands. She saw the drawings and put her arm around Clare's shoulder. "I'm sorry, dear. I didn't know."

"No, I'm fine." Clare arranged the drawings side by side. "Do you see something odd about these?"

Daphne shrugged. "I just think they are beautiful."

"The background. They are all the same. They each have the same trees. The same gate. And look at this structure." Clare tapped her finger on each of them.

"I don't . . . ?"

"My sister was trying to tell us something. She must have believed one of us would come after her to America, but she didn't know which one of us it would be. So she drew all of us and asked Greta, who must have been about to be released, to deliver some kind of message."

"Well," Daphne scratched her head, "let me think. That does look familiar, now that you are pointing it out."

"Think, Daphne. Where is this?"

"Those trees. They could be anywhere. But that structure. It looks like . . ." Daphne stopped as if she didn't want to say anything.

"Go ahead," Clare said with ardency.

"Well. It looks like one of those . . . what do you call them . . . you know, those little stone buildings you would see at a graveyard?"

"The key!" Clare went to the cabinet and pulled down the gold key she had found in the apartment.

"What's that?" Daphne seemed perplexed.

"I know what the key is for now."

It was the third cemetery they had visited, but they knew instantly as the carriage pulled up and rolled them to a stop that they had arrived at the precise location. Maggie's drawings didn't have detail. There were no gravestones, no shrubbery, no flowers, nor any of the surrounding buildings. But she had charcoaled in by memory an almost perfectly drawn perspective of a thin grove of trees at the far end of the yard, which framed the precise mausoleum depicted on the paper.

As they dismounted the cabin, Andrew handed a few coins to the driver.

"Should I wait for you, sir?" said the tall man who was bent at the waist as if he had been leaning over a team of horses all of his life.

"That won't be necessary."

It pained Clare to wait for Andrew, as she was anxious to unearth what had been so important for her sister to share. At the same time, Clare was hesitant to discover more dark secrets. There remained a fragility in her soul, one which had her at the precipice of her inner strength.

Passersby crossed before the iron gates of the cemetery with disinterest, going about their daily business. Though the gates were closed, the latch was open and they fumbled with it, before a man with a rake in his hand assisted them from the inside.

"Need to keep the swine out," he said. "All types." He greeted them with a warm countenance and with the respect due those in grief.

They nodded and, trying to be circumspect, walked toward the mausoleum with their heads down and holding hands.

"This is your first visit here, is it not?"

Andrew turned and spoke in a measured voice. "Yes. As a matter fact, she's visiting relations for the first time."

The man tilted his head. "Then how do you know where you're going?"

Andrew took the drawing of Davin from Clare and showed the image to the man.

"Ah yes. The Hanley vault. Mr. Feagles is here often to pay his regards."

"This is Clare Hanley," Andrew said. "From back home. I think the lady would appreciate some privacy."

"Oh yes, of course." The man put his gloves back on. "Get's a bit lonely here on the job. Not much conversation . . . as you can imagine. If you need of anything, just let me know." He returned to his raking, but Clare sensed they were being watched from behind.

They came up to the stone structure, which was bruised and cracked by weather and time. Vines grew like veins all around it and were barren of leaves. A few worn stairs led down to a splintered and faded wooden door with large, rusted hinges. Engraved above the door was a stone placard which read:

**The Hanleys**
*Branlow, Co. Roscommon, Ireland*
**Tomas Hanley 1798–1842**
**Margaret Ames Hanley 1817–1845**

"Are you sure you want to go through with this?" Andrew asked.

Clare pulled the key from her pocket and handed it to him. "No more lies." Clare covered her mouth and nose with her scarf.

Andrew inserted the key and giving it a twist, the lock responded with a firm click. He pulled on the door handle, and though jammed, it freed itself following a few determined tugs, sighing with the pains of age as bent beams of light penetrated the interior.

"Wait here," he said firmly.

He slipped in and following a few anxious minutes, he stuck his head out. "Come inside, love."

Her knees wobbled and the faintness of having not eaten well for a couple of weeks made her flush, and Clare stepped gingerly.

Andrew shut the door behind them, and it made her uneasy as it snapped to a close, sealing them from the outside.

Oil lamps, which Andrew must have lit, hung from either side of the cramped stone chamber draped with cobwebs. Oddly, instead of caskets or even urns, there was a wood table in the center, and pressed up to it was a solitary chair.

A tallow candle was propped in a wooden holder, and Andrew lit the wick with one of the tall matches that lay scattered beside it. On the table there were a few papers, an inkwell, and a quill pen.

"What is this?" Clare said.

"It appears to be a place your uncle comes to work. A secret office."

She fumbled through the papers and they seemed insignificant—some notes, a letter that had barely been started. "This can't be it."

"It appears so. Maybe he realized the key was missing."

"But it must have been a spare," said Clare. It looked like it hadn't been moved for years. "There must be something else."

"All right then." Andrew took down the oil lanterns and handed one to her. "Let's look for a hidden chamber. But we must hurry. Every minute we remain will draw the curiosity of our friend outside. He may have already sent for your uncle."

Clare hovered the lamp close to the floor, searching for any clues in the patterns of the dust, her fingers probing to discover some sort of loose stone. Andrew ran his palms along the walls, seeking out anything that appeared odd.

Yet after scrambling for several minutes, they came up empty, their hands blackened as their tension was rising. Disappointment flooded through Clare. She never should have let herself hope that they would find something. She pulled out the chair and sank into it, watching Andrew as he continued to probe and poke.

"It's no use." She let out a heavy sigh. "I'm not sure what I expected we would find."

Andrew's face was chalked with dust and grime. She could tell he was desperate to give her some sort of victory, and he looked at her with eyes of apology. Then his countenance shifted abruptly. "Stand up."

"I'm finished," Clare said. "I can't do this anymore."

"No. Off the chair."

Confused, she got up and he swept the chair from her and set it against the wall. He stepped on it, pausing as the wobbly legs of the chair caused him to stumble. Bracing his hand against the wall, he raised the amber glowing lamp above him, as the wick danced shadows in his glasses.

"There's a ledge here," he said. "And it appears to go all around. It's difficult to see." With his tall frame bent slightly to keep from hitting his head on the ceiling, he slid his hand around as far as he could reach, and then moved the chair and continued the process.

After repeating this a few times, he suddenly froze and looked down at Clare with joy in his eyes. "I've got something."

Stepping down carefully from the wobbly chair, he had a small wooden chest in his free hand. He set it on the table and slid the candle close to it while Clare hovered over it, now holding both lamps.

The chest was of modest proportions, with a pale wood frame with cracked corners and leather straps fastened with a tarnished buckle. A lock with a slender keyhole kept its contents sealed from them.

Before Clare could ask about a key, Andrew put his coaled hands in his pocket and pulled out some slender tools. "I haven't yet taught you all of the tricks of a journalist."

He slipped a pick and small angled rod through the aperture of the lock, and in a few moments it clicked. He paused to make sure she was ready and then expectantly lifted the lid.

To Clare's disappointment, it was a cracked leather book.

Andrew pulled it out and the words *Irish Society* were imprinted on the cover. He untied the leather string that bound it, and as he lifted the cover, she could see lines and handwritten numbers on the pages within.

"What is it?" she asked.

"It's a ledger. Financial records. Labeled as the Irish Society. It dates back from almost four years ago." He thumbed the pages with interest.

"What else is in there?" Clare said with impatience.

Andrew reached in, pulled out a stack of envelopes, handed them to her, and returned to his close examination of the book.

Clare gathered the envelopes, and as she began to arrange them, her breathing stopped. Her mouth opened with dread as she recognized the handwriting and the address they were being sent. "Oh no. Oh no, no, no."

"What is it, Clare?"

She tore open the envelopes one at a time and withdrew the

letters she had so meticulously and lovingly penned for her family back home.

"Clare?"

"These are . . . my letters. They are all here. They were never sent."

"Your letters? How is that possible?"

"Almost every week, I went into that building and gave them my letters for home. And all of my earnings. Every last bit of it."

The impact of what she was saying came over his face, and deep empathy flowed from his eyes. "I'm sorry, Clare."

She ran her hands through her hair and glanced to the ceiling as she started to gag with emotion. "The remittances. Did they go home?"

Andrew reached into the chest and pulled out the bills, bound together with receipts.

"These are the slips," Clare said. "These are the fees I paid. He must have . . . he must have intercepted them from the Irish Society."

Clare felt betrayed, but more than this, she was profoundly angry with herself. "Of course. He wouldn't have allowed any of those letters to go home. It would have exposed him as a fraud and made its way back to New York. But what horrible evil would keep him from at least sending the money on its own?"

Andrew tapped on the book. "This is what I'm seeing in the book. Your uncle has been skimming from the Irish Society all along. There are records here that show his involvement from the beginning of it being formed. It's him and a . . . Mr. Gorman O'Riley. Isn't this the same surname as Maggie . . . ?" He caught himself before he went further.

The very mention of the name made Clare nauseous. "It's what he wanted all along," she said, almost inaudibly. "The ledger. That's what my uncle had on the man. He was threatening to take them both down."

"We need to go." Andrew folded the book and retied the string. "There's money in the chest as well, but we should leave it. Just take what you're owed. Bring your letters and I'll carry the ledger."

Clare was numb with the knowledge of the damage inflicted on her family. She had heard the reports of continued blight in Ireland and had witnessed the incoming flow of starving expatriates of Ireland.

But she had been in denial, confident that her weekly provision would keep her family immune from the effects of the famine. Her whole purpose in life was taking care of them. Those she cared for so dearly. And she had failed. Miserably.

"He murdered them. My uncle destroyed them all. What a desperate fool I am. How could I?"

"Clare," Andrew said sternly as he extinguished the light. "We must go."

He pulled her by the arm, as her mind was plagued with the tragedy of her discovery. They exited and Andrew locked the doors behind them. Continuing, they went up the steps and marched across the graveyard to the gates.

The caretaker waved to them as they left, apparently unaware of their life-threatening mischief.

Clare was disappointed. She had hoped the man had alerted her uncle and that Tomas himself would be waiting at the gate for them with vengeance in his eyes. In all of her life, she was never more prepared for a confrontation. Clare wanted to rip out the man's deluding smirk, his manipulative heart, and whatever fragment of pleasure remained in his loathsome marrow.

Instead, Andrew flagged a cab and Clare gazed mutely

out the window as they passed through the streets of the Five Points, as humanity unfurled before her jaded eyes.

After a while, she turned to Andrew. "I need to go home."

"Yes. I know." He grabbed her hand and caressed it in his, and then his fingers gently swept clear the hair hanging in front of her swollen, moist face. "And I'm coming with you."

She began her protest, but he interrupted her.

"But first," he said with conviction, "there is something we must do."

# Chapter 40

# AUTUMN WINDS

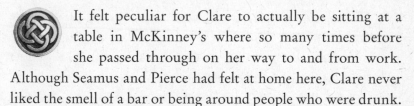It felt peculiar for Clare to actually be sitting at a table in McKinney's where so many times before she passed through on her way to and from work. Although Seamus and Pierce had felt at home here, Clare never liked the smell of a bar or being around people who were drunk.

Life had covered much ground since she first was introduced to Tressa and entered in Patrick Feagles's twisted world. It made her ill to think of how badly she fell to his ruse.

"They should be down soon," Andrew said. "It's not too late for you to leave."

"Oh no," Clare said. "This is exactly where I want to be."

The bartender was mopping the floor, taking advantage of the morning hour when the bar was typically most clear of patrons. "Sure you folks don't need a nip of something?" he asked, while cleaning under the table next to them.

Suddenly, shouts rang out and pounding noises could be heard coming down the stairs.

"You're going to break me arm, you filthy swine."

Clare and Andrew rose, watching in pleasure as they saw Uncle Tomas emerging from the frame of the stairwell, struggling against the firm grasp of two constables.

Tressa was trailing behind in near hysteria. "Be careful! You're hurting him!"

A measured smile of contentment came over Clare when her uncle caught sight of her, and his rebellion faded to confusion.

"Have a seat here, Mr. Hanley." Andrew pulled out a chair at the table. "You're welcome to join us." He motioned for Tressa to a chair. He nodded toward the two constables who moved back a step but kept close and vigilant.

"What is all of this about?" Uncle Tomas said. "Clare. Are you behind this?"

"This is merely a courtesy visit," Andrew said. "We wanted to provide you with some news before your fellow Irish citizens of the Five Points get their chance." He pulled out a gold pocket watch. "In just a few minutes, by my estimation. Which is why we'll be short."

Clare slapped a copy of the morning's *New York Daily* on the table and spun it square so her uncle could see it clearly. She reveled at the way his eyes traced to the headline in horror and as the arrogance drained from every pore of his being as he read the copy. His shoulders fell and his fingers dug frantically through his hair, his eyes darting back and forth. He was a cornered animal, sifting through his mind for any possible method of escape.

"It's lies," Tressa said. "After all we did for you, Clare. How could you betray us?"

"Shut up, Tressa." Uncle Tomas held out his hands in surrender to be bound. "I suppose you'll be arresting me."

"Oh no," Andrew said. "That would require more kindness than you deserve. We think it's much better that you're free . . . among your people when they learn the truth."

"You can't do that," Uncle Tomas said, his voice cracking. "I insist you bring me in."

"Gentlemen," Andrew said to the constables. "I believe you'll need to continue with your investigation. Certainly there are many more details that need to be assessed with such a complicated case."

Andrew nodded to Clare, put his hat on his head, and together they rose from the table.

Clare needed to flee before hatred gave way to any sign of pity. But she had one more question. There was something that didn't make sense to her.

"So, Uncle," she said, venom in her tone. "How exactly did you get Margaret to agree to it all? Marrying that miserable old creature for your gain? She was so strong."

He leaned back in the chair and crossed his arms. Uncle Tomas appeared old, broken, and pathetic in Clare's eyes. "Your sister wanted the world. Every drop she could taste. I found a way where her glass would be filled. Overflowing. I loved Maggie. But the tragedy was she would do anything for me."

"Love? You'll never know love."

Clare turned to Tressa, who was heaving with sobs. "There's a better place inside of you. I hope you'll find it."

Andrew put his arm around Clare and they walked out of the tavern, pausing before they climbed up into their awaiting cab. There was a stirring in the air and they glanced toward the intersection at the end of the street.

"It's happening already," Clare said to Andrew, surprised she felt no guilt.

There was finality in hearing their headline trumpeted by the newsboys, and they watched as people turned in their steps, grabbing for their own copy, with anger in their faces.

Clare looked back through the window of the tavern and saw her uncle pouring himself a drink.

* * *

The carriage was parked in front of The House of Refuge, which had long lines out front leading into the soup kitchen. The cab driver stroked the head of one of his horses as Andrew and Clare made their final arrangements.

"The packet ship leaves this evening," Andrew said in a hurried manner. "Which means time is very short if we're going to be on it when it leaves. It's a cargo ship, mostly, but also the fastest in the fleet. We use the service every week to carry the *Daily* to Dublin and London, one of their best customers, you might say. So I was able to make arrangements for the two of us. It's no longer safe for you here, Clare."

"Andrew." She put her hands on his cheeks. "Sweet Andrew. You know you won't be able to come with me."

"Everything will work out, Clare. All of it. But there isn't much time."

"Andrew," she said again. "You can't make the trip. Why you shouldn't have even gone to Blackwell's Island."

He shook his head, his eyes glistening. "This is different, Clare. I have no choice. The fear of losing you is the only fear I have." He kissed her on the forehead.

"Oh." He reached into his vest, pulled out a small leather portfolio, and unwrapped the tie. "This is for you." He opened it enough for her to see there were a stack of bills, all of them English pounds.

"Why are you giving me this now?" she said with apprehension. "Why don't you bring it with you?"

"Just take it." He tied it up and then pressed her hands around it. "I promise you, I'll be there. You'll be on board first and you can get our places settled. The driver has all of the directions. He's a man I know and trust. Daphne is packing your clothes and she's preparing travel food. You're to stop there and proceed immediately to the harbor. You'll be safe as soon as you board."

They embraced for the longest time, and it was painful for her to let go. She pulled her head back. He had removed his glasses and she peered into his warm, green eyes. She saw her own reflection, a woman deeply in love. She straightened his hair with her fingers and wondered what life would be without him.

"We must go," he whispered.

Then Andrew turned and hurried toward the door of the mission. But before he could go inside, a woman flagged him down. She leaned heavily on a cane with one hand while struggling to hoist a toddler on her hip with the other. Andrew kneeled down, put his hand tenderly on the woman's shoulder, and listened to her needs.

Through the windows Clare could see all levels of The House of Refuge filled with the vibrant activity of his vision. From a window on the second floor, two small children pressed their faces and hands against the window and looked down at her.

Clare's stomach knotted with the thought of allowing Andrew to abandon his dream.

As she leaned over the edge of the ship's well-polished wooden banister, the breeze lifted Clare's hair, which now was well below her shoulders. The ship steward, who had assisted her in porting her bags on deck, had boasted she was aboard an American-made clipper ship.

"It'll get us to Dublin in less than four weeks," the steward said as he gawked at the majestic sails and masts of the great ship.

Compared to her first voyage, this vessel would get to Ireland in short order, but Clare still feared she was too late. She couldn't know if Seamus had managed to send money home, but one thing was certain: Not a penny she sent had made it to them.

It pained Clare to imagine in what condition she might find them if her family's crop had failed in the spring, as she heard was the case with most farms on the west side of the tragedy-struck island.

Her anxiety only compounded as she had seen the hideously sunken faces and diseased bodies of her countrymen as they streamed in haunting processions off the ships unloading in the busy Hudson Bay Harbor.

But even these profound worries were eclipsed by the sinking dread she endured as the sun slipped beneath the horizon. The ship was due to pull away from the great city at any moment, and her angst soared as she witnessed the crews unhitching the massive ropes from the pier.

With the light diminishing, her eyes strained to recognize in the crowd the face she so longed to see again. She imagined with desperation that any moment, there would be a noise sounded, an arm raised, and he would come running at the last possible moment, and together they would share the rest of their lives.

She saw Andrew in every man, in every moment, and in every shadow. After the ship unmoored, there was a sudden pitch, and the tugboat's steam engine engaged its gears.

Clare knew it was ludicrous to expect him to be aboard with her. He had already demonstrated his love for her and the boundaries of heroism in accompanying her to Blackwell's Island, and she feared he nearly died in the effort.

Besides, Andrew belonged in the city, and the city needed him. This was his ministry. Manhattan was the place of his destiny.

Yet all of this sound reasoning, which she repeated over and over again, couldn't salve the cavernous wound of her heart.

She loved Andrew beyond everything else. Even more so now as the reality of a life apart from him became so tangible. Grandma Ella said she had prayed everyday for a man of his character to arrive in her granddaughter's life. Now Clare would pray for herself.

*Please, God. I've never wanted anything more in this world. Bring him to me now. Do this and I will forgive You for all else.*

The tug now had the ship firmly in its talons, and Clare felt her life slipping away as the people below erupted in cheers and waved to ones who were departing.

She couldn't bear to watch the joyful exchanges of greetings around her, and she felt painfully alone.

Across in the distance, Clare spied a figure leaning against a tree, staring directly at her as the ship pulled from the harbor. And though only visible as a hint of a shadow, she knew it was Andrew.

"Good-bye," she whispered, and then retired to her room.

# Chapter 41

# BRANDED

It was at the Battle of Churubusco where Seamus learned he was a fine soldier.

Hoisted atop a castle-like convent in a village not far from Mexico City, he and nearly a hundred of his fellow San Patricios rained heavy artillery fire on the advancing American troops.

For a brief time, there was some belief in the members of this brave Irish battalion of the Mexican Army that they would be successful in further delaying the inevitability of defeat. Short on ammunition, on the brink of starvation, and fighting for a military that was hopelessly overmatched, they were keeping the enemy at bay.

But as the unleashing of incoming American weaponry found its range and began pummeling the fortress with fiery explosions, it became clearer that survival would only exist in the form of surrender.

Seamus was one of the last soldiers to put his weapon down. That was unusual considering he still lacked a purpose for fighting.

Having seen the flesh of his new comrades, boys from home, torn, pierced, and left to burn, he had become hardened to the agonies of battle.

Yet as he gazed out through the rusted bars of his stony prison, toward the vast courtyard in the distance, he was unprepared for the horror of hanging. Orders were sounded, the mules were whipped on their flanks, and bodies fell violently and necks were broken. All that was left was the final sickening dance of the fallen Irish soldiers.

Seamus heard the familiar rattling of the keys at his door. It was his time now. With five empty cots in the cell, his fortunes had run dry.

Entering the room was an American in a black suit with a white collar, bearing a worn leather book in his hand. Seamus figured this would be his last rites. It wasn't the hangman, but the harbinger of what was to come.

Seamus returned his gaze back on his fellow San Patricios dangling from the ropes outside. "Are you here to comfort me?" he said wryly.

"There is only One who can comfort you now, son," said the man who appeared too hard spent to be a minister. "I'd prefer to hang you and leave you be."

Seamus spun around. "What?"

"I lost many of my closest friends with you filthy Irish defectors."

"You're my priest?"

"Just a messenger," he said. "A pastor without followers is just a man moving his lips." The man took off his black-brimmed hat and sat on the edge of one of the beds. He pointed for Seamus to sit down across from him.

Seamus was struck by the frankness of his guest, perhaps even amused. With a fragment of shrapnel still lodged in his leg, he sat down gingerly.

"Why'd you do it, son? Why did you fight for the enemy?"

"If I knew that answer . . ." Seamus replied and then he let out a short laugh. "All of my life, I've been losing. Perhaps it's a good ending. My calling. Isn't that what you call it?"

"That's what they tell us," the pastor replied. His eyes softened. "We spend most of our life doing things for the wrong reasons. Sometimes they can still get us to the right place."

Seamus put his hands up in the air. "So here am I."

The minister studied Seamus closely and grinned. "I was hoping I wouldn't like you."

"C'mon, minister. Get in on it, will you? Read me some of that book and how everything will be all right."

The pastor tapped on the front of his Bible. "This book? It tells me I'm not to waste pearls on swine."

Seamus stood. "Perfect. Just perfect. The last breaths of this miserable life and I can't even get a decent good riddance."

"Sit down."

Reluctantly, Seamus did as he was ordered.

The pastor clenched Seamus's hand with force. "I've seen you. Lads just like you on every battlefield. Running away. Lost as lost can be. You're short on time, son. This is how it will end, and it won't finish well."

"What do you know about my life?" said Seamus.

"Life is a fierce wind. What we hold on to is all that matters. I can see you haven't been clinging onto anything."

"Freedom," Seamus said. "I'm free." He panned the cell he was in and laughed at the irony of what was just said.

The minister was unmoved by Seamus's flippancy. "Freedom is only valuable if you use it to make a good choice."

"What choice would that be?"

"Hmmm. I can see you won't be asking me to pray for you. But how 'bout I pray for someone more deserving of prayer?"

Seamus thought of Clare and bowed his head in shame, unshed tears stinging his eyes.

The pastor put his hand on his shoulder. "Come, son. Who is it, and I'll pray for them. Right here."

"My sister," Seamus said ashamed of his tears. "You see my father always said I was worthless. I spent my life proving him right. But my sister. She saw something in me I was never able to find."

"What's her name?"

"Clare."

"All right then, friend. We'll pray for Clare."

"Sir?" Seamus tried to mask his tears.

"Yes, my son?" The gentleness in the man's eyes was a flower in the weeds of his scarred and wrinkled face.

"Could we say a prayer for me as well?"

Seamus had bled himself out of screams.

He was among those of the Saint Patrick's Battalion whose lack of devotion to the cause was determined worthy of a reprieve. Instead of suffering the noose, he would be given an alternative punishment.

Having lost count somewhere beyond the tenth stroke of the

mule skinner's skilled whip, Seamus was unaware of how many remained of the fifty prescribed. The lusty cheers from the onlooking crowd had already devolved into hushed murmurs. The sight of flesh hanging from the backs of those receiving their penance had dulled the spirit of celebration.

Seamus figured this was God's cynical response to his prayer.

In some ways he embraced the pain and humiliation as a way to be granted forgiveness for all of his life's mistakes. But this didn't keep him from begging for unconsciousness, a wish which was finally granted.

He didn't know how much time had passed until he drifted aware again, cruelly recovering his circumstances as ugly, twisted faces gaped at him with freakish curiosity.

"Spare that one," said a woman with a gravelly voice. "He's much too pretty."

The laughter that followed blended into the cruel sounds of wicked merriment and lust of vengeance. As Seamus struggled to keep the nausea from rising in his throat, he turned his head to see a thick-armed, bearded soldier working the reddish coals of a smoldering fire.

Seamus snapped in an effort to free himself, but there was no slack in the ropes and the pain of the gaping wounds neutered his will to escape.

The soldier lifted an iron brand from the fire and, with a cigar hanging from the corner of his mouth, raised the bright red glowing tip close so Seamus could see it was the letter *D*. The blacksmith nodded to a soldier behind who then pushed Seamus's forehead against the back of the tree so he couldn't move.

Blowing smoke out of his cigar, the blacksmith inched the firebrand toward Seamus's cheek. As the iron reached its mark, the searing pain exceeded any of that caused by the muleskinner's craft, and the sickening smell of burning flesh filled his nostrils.

Then Seamus drifted away.

On the outskirts of El Paso del Norte, Seamus arrived on foot to a crossroad and rested on a boulder overseeing a panoramic of whistling and dusty terrain—barren, except for cacti, and speckled with sparse desert shrubbery.

His beard of three weeks had filled in well, growing over the bloody scabs where he had picked away the mark of a defector with the tip of his blunt knife.

He couldn't know for certain, but he suspected the minister had arranged his release from the decrepit prison; yet Seamus hadn't an opportunity to thank the man and wasn't sure he would if given the chance.

All he owned was in a pack he found discarded by death or desertion by some American soldier in a ditch by the side of the road north of Durango. When he retrieved his meager belongings after being released, he was stunned to see his last payroll was intact, though with the collapse of Mexican currency, it would be barely enough to get him past the border.

He pulled out a piece of jerky, which he was told was made from a fallen horse, and a chunk of goat cheese, which he pared with his knife. Having abandoned any evidence of his service in the Mexican Army, he wore the simple clothes of the villagers, which he bought with the proceeds from a short, fortunate run of cards.

It was an unusually hot day in late autumn, and it caused

him to lift his hat and wipe away the sweat under his bandana. He amused himself by watching the antics of a lizard scurrying by his feet.

The road that forked ahead was in poor condition, and for a while he had it to himself as he pondered in which direction he would proceed. He made plans only as far as El Paso and never believed he'd arrive.

He was enjoying this brief moment of solitude when in the distance a cloud of dust appeared, and soon he could see it was a wagonload of American soldiers approaching at a solid clip and he clenched.

As the cart came closer, the driver pulled on the reins and slowed to a halt. There were two soldiers in front, and another eight or so riding in the back, passing around jugs of some libation, each taking heavy swigs.

"Where to, stranger?" sounded the driver, who was bald and sporting a scar from his eye to his cheek.

Seamus looked over the soldiers and spat out pieces of grizzle from his jerky on the ground. "Haven't decided."

"Where you from?"

"New York."

"Sounds like you're from farther than New York, lad." The man slapped at a fly on his hairless head. "You can come on board with us, if you'd like. We're heading toward New Orleans. You can catch a riverboat to make most of your way home."

"Thank you kindly," Seamus said. "But I'm still taking in the sights of this beautiful country."

The passenger up front with bushy gray sideburns leaned over. "You don't want to go that way, soldier. That's toward the West. Through the mountains. In the snow. Indians. Ain't nobody certain what's out there."

"There's more of these wagons behind us," said the bald driver. "You can catch the next one." He gave the reins a snap and guided the train to the right. The men in the back of the wagon held up their bottles and tipped their hats in a lusty salute as they headed out.

Seamus lifted his pack and watched the wagon until it faded from view far in the distance. Then he reached down and scooped up a fistful of dust, and flinging it in the air, he observed which direction it flew.

Now with new resolve, Seamus took the pathway to the left and ventured out into the Great American West.

## Chapter 42

# DUBLIN HARBOR

Clare had never been to Dublin, and had it been an earlier and more naive time in her life's journey, she would have been overwhelmed with the grandeur of its maritime commerce. But after departing from the port of New York and traveling on one of the fastest transport ships in the world's fleet, she was becoming accustomed to city life.

Still, the emotion of returning home to the land and people she loved carried Clare to a tearful reunion. And as the clipper slipped into the bustling harbor, she embraced the approaching island of her heritage as a lost friend.

Her return journey across the Atlantic had only heightened her trepidation. The stories of the plight of Ireland ran deep and dire as told by the crew and passengers who had witnessed it firsthand. The descriptions of rampant famine and the deaths of tens of thousands were like none she had heard in the newsroom of the *New York Daily*.

Which is why as the ship crept toward mooring, the activity on the docks was stunning and nothing like she expected. Rather than seeing a lifeless harbor of a population on the brink, there instead was a vibrant flurry of commerce.

Being driven into the open arms of loading ships were herds of cattle, sheep, and pigs as well as wagonloads of wheat, barley, and oats.

"Strange sight to behold," said an older man of affluence, wearing a white jacket and pants, leaning his considerable weight on a gold-tipped cane.

"Yes," Clare said weakly, trying not to encourage further encroachment. Through the course of crossing, she already had her fill of Mr. Galloway, a Londoner who was an Irish lace trader on a mission to tell everyone there was still good business to be had in Ireland.

"Where is it going?" Clare asked, surrendering to politeness.

"Mostly across the Irish Sea to the Motherland. Some perhaps to France. Proof that your people can be productive."

"But I thought there was famine."

"Oh," he said. "That you'll see plenty of to the west."

"Then why are they sending the food away?" she said. "I don't understand."

"Where are you heading?" he asked, abruptly changing the subject of conversation.

"Branlow. County Roscommon."

"Pretty country. Although, in the heart of devastation, I'm sad to say. How are you getting home?"

Clare wasn't sure she wanted to answer the question. "I've only thought the trip out this far, to be honest."

"You don't say! Well, here's an idea. I have chartered a cargo carriage to County Mayo. I'll have plenty of room, and having a lady aboard will take the edge off the boredom."

"I wouldn't want to burden you," Clare said, warming up to the prudence of accepting his offer.

"Nonsense." He tapped the tip of his cane on the deck of the ship. "It's practically on my way. Why, we can both provision in the city and be on our way."

"Oh. I won't have anything to purchase in town."

He tilted his head. "You haven't been home for a while, have you? The supplies are terribly scarce where you're heading. You'll want to get as much food here in Dublin as you can. I have a spare crate you can use."

"That is most kind of you." After all she'd been through, could she trust another man? She tried to think of other options, but this was the immediate way for her to get back home. And now, the draw of her family was far greater than any of her own personal fears.

"In fact." He leaned in as if he was sharing a trade secret. "Whatever you buy here will get you ten times the rate out west."

Clare was reminded the largest pain may be the weight of conversation, a stiff price to pay for her ride, but she would just have to endure. Once the great ship settled to final rest, her heart surged in anticipation and trepidation of what lay ahead.

⬡

The spacious carriage was pulled by two sturdy geldings, strong enough to handle the heavy load of luggage, crates of produce, tradable supplies, and raw materials for the production of lace. Clare had heeded Mr. Galloway's advice and spent nearly all of her money on bags of oats, wheat, and Indian corn. She also couldn't resist the temptation to splurge on some gifts of clothing and sweets for her family.

The cabin of the carriage was plush with an exquisitely upholstered velvet interior. Clare sat across from Mr. Galloway, who had a basket of apples on either side of his seat. She thought it strange, but didn't bother asking why for it would lead to some endless dissertation.

After leaving Dublin, which was overrun with beggars, the crippled, and the infirmed, the rain came hard and they traveled against an influx of Irish driving livestock and pulling wagons loaded with produce and grains. The farmland on the outskirts of this historic city also appeared to be bountiful and teemed with laborers.

But with each mile they drove deeper inland, the shadowy hand of contagion began to show its might. The stream of impoverished stragglers increased alongside the road, and Mr. Galloway responded in a way that was difficult to determine whether it was more charity or sport.

Snapping back the fabric window of the carriage, he would stretch his hands and head out and fling apples at those he passed, drawing delight from both his accuracy and the scrambling of those who responded to his volleys.

Clare declined his offer to join in and instead grew mortified by the scenes of tragedy unfurling before her eyes.

Clare cried softly to herself as she watched the horrific tapestry of starvation. A nation hobbled, thread born and tattered; empty stares, bones protruding from skin pocked with sores; and the limping, listless shuffle of hopelessness. Babies clinging onto their mothers shriveled breasts; children naked, filthy, and starved. Many either sleeping or dead on the sides of the road.

As they passed, hands were held out, families screamed for help; some youth tapping their remaining strength in a futile effort to chase down the carriage.

Mr. Galloway insisted it was unsafe to stop and would

pound on the wall if his driver slowed too much when the roads thickened with the famished.

He spoke incessantly through it all and seemed disappointed with Clare's lack of participation in conversations about his solutions to the "Irish problem."

Mercifully, he succumbed to the incessant swaying of their wagon and fell asleep with loud snores.

Clare stared into the abyss of her people's burden and desperation, and when she could bear no more, she drew her curtains shut.

Two excruciating days had passed in the journey, with Mr. Galloway generously covering the cost for Clare's room at the inn where they stayed overnight. She tried to repay him with as much dialogue as she could bear, but as they entered the boundaries of County Roscommon, the undeniable confirmation that her parish would not be spared from the devastation consumed her with grief and guilt.

*How did I ever fall prey to my uncle's deception? Why didn't I pay more attention to the rumors of tragedy back home? Why isn't this story being told?*

They were only about twenty miles away from her home when they heard shouts and desperate pleas, and looking ahead she saw a large gathering of men encircling a house, like wolves surrounding their prey. As they approached she could see people being dragged out from inside. On the thatched roof of the mud house, two men had climbed up and were tying a rope to a center beam.

"What's happening?" Clare asked.

"Hmmm? Oh. They're tumbling a house."

"What do you mean?" Clare asked as they rolled past the confrontation and she continued to watch as it trailed behind out of view.

"It's a much more profitable use of land. With the potato failing, the landlords are clearing farms for ranching. Cattle is good business." He chuckled. "Of course, there is the unfortunate issue of getting the people off the land."

"What are those men doing on the roof?"

"The house wreckers? It's actually providing good jobs. They hitch to the center beam just so. Give it a good pull." He made a popping noise with his mouth. "There she goes."

Other than providing directions, Clare remained silent for the remainder of the journey. All around her was desolation, devoid of people or activity, as Branlow appeared to have been abandoned.

The roads became more difficult, slowing the progress of the carriage as it jarred and bounced the last mile. Finally, they rolled up to the gateway leading to the Hanley farm.

Clare was relieved to see her home still standing, although as she stepped down from the carriage, only the winds greeted her, and the eerie stillness chilled her spine and buckled her knees.

*Am I too late?*

She trembled as she moved forward, each step heavy with foreboding. The land was green and beaded from fresh rain, but there was no evidence of a crop emerging in the field. Hearing orders barked behind her, she glanced back and was pleased Mr. Galloway was busy directing the driver on which baggage to unload.

She was alone.

There was no smoke coming from the chimney, nor the smell of peat burning. The front door of the house creaked as it bowed with each gust. No laundry was hung to dry, and the once ever-present baying and cooing of the neighbor's livestock was noticeably absent.

Clare pulled on the rusted handle, and when this was insufficient, she gave it a firm tug and it freed itself from the warping frame. As the door yielded, the foulness of illness and death surged to her nostrils.

In horror, she saw the house had been stripped of all belongings, and perched against the barren wall were the ghastly shapes of two emaciated children, intertwined in what must have been their final embrace for warmth.

"No!" Clare screamed, putting her hand to her sobbing mouth, and collapsed on the filthy floor, convulsing with unquenchable pangs of grief.

"No. No. No!" The accompanying guttural sounds were garbled, and she pounded her fists in the grime of the floor, oblivious to the bloodying of her knuckles.

Behind, she felt the presence of Mr. Galloway and the driver, and they struggled to console her, but she fought their efforts to pull her to her feet.

Clare wanted to lash out and began to swing wildly behind her, but then something caused her to cease the tantrum and freeze. It was then she noticed before her, peering out from the two conjoined corpses—two pairs of eyes watching her.

Chapter 43

# THE FIELDS

 As much as she abhorred Mr. Galloway, she was grateful for his presence when she discovered Caitlin and Davin were still alive.

While she rubbed her sister's and brother's arms and then legs to bring them warmth, the Englishman and his driver split several of the wooden crates and started a fire as rain began to pound against the roof. They also carried in all of Clare's belongings, and he even parted with a couple of blankets and a stew pot, both of which, he opined, could have brought a bounty of lace.

But following these gestures of reluctant kindness, Mr. Galloway informed her his pressing business required that he depart before the rutted roads got any muddier and more difficult to navigate.

Before leaving he dusted off as much as possible of the black soot on his clothes. Then he offered some last advice. "Make sure you don't feed them solids for at least a week. Only broth. You'd kill them with a full meal in their condition. They look stronger than most and should be fine."

"I owe you much," she said before he left, giving him an awkward hug.

He nodded and panned the room with pity in his eyes. "To better days, young lady. May God have mercy on you and your people and forgive us all for our sins."

He left, just as the rain picked up to a torrent, so much so Clare never heard the carriage leaving. Yes. God did have mercy on her. She thought nothing was more important to her now than the breaths of her two precious siblings.

"Thank You," she whispered. Clare was filled with an inexplicable sense of joy and contentment. If this was what her life was to be, she would make the most of it, and a good life it would be. She would pour her life into these children, and each day would be a blessing compared to the horror of being without them.

Clare held tightly to the spindly bodies of her brother and sister for a long time, unwilling to release her grasp for fear they would drift away forever. Eventually, she would need to start nursing them if they would have a chance of surviving.

Fumbling through her luggage, Clare pulled out her dresses, which now embarrassed her to think of how much they cost. She fashioned a makeshift mattress, placing Caitlin and Davin gently on top and then covering them with blankets.

Running her fingers through her sister's stringy hair, a tear dropped from her eyes to Caitlin's sunken cheek and Clare wiped it away. She caressed Davin's face and kissed him on the forehead, which was covered with sores.

"I'll never leave you again. This I promise you."

Then Clare scrambled to her feet and her instincts took over, stoking the fire, washing their faces, squeezing water from a cloth into their mouths, and nurturing them with every ounce of her being.

Clare was convinced she would never sleep again until they were back with her, but the exhaustion of travel, the drain of emotion, and lack of rest finally overwhelmed her at some point in the night. When her eyes opened, the fire was out and the morning sun could be seen leaking through the cracks in the doorway and windows.

Hearing a dull moaning coming from Caitlin, Clare crawled around Davin and peered longingly into her sister's eyes, which were open but vacant.

She mumbled something incoherent.

"What? Cait. It's Clare." She pulled her sister's hand out from under the blanket and rubbed it.

A smile crept over Caitlin's pale, skeletal face.

"Father," Caitlin breathed. "Is that you?"

"It's me, Cait. Clare."

"Father. I knew you'd come back from the field."

After restarting the fire and trying unsuccessfully to feed her sister and brother some broth, Clare agonized over the thought of leaving them, especially since she already knew what she would find. Despite his shortcomings, her father would have never left his children alone to die.

Once she made the decision to go outside, it didn't take Clare long to find Da's body.

His gnarled, stiff form was at the far end of the field, not visible from the road for those who passed by. In his hands was a burlap sack, and inside it were tuber sprouts, with a line of them freshly planted leading up to where he had succumbed to his lifetime battle.

"You know your old man as well as anyone." Father Quinn stood next to Clare and looked over the freshly turned dirt at the corner of their field. "When it was clear to the others to leave for the workhouses and live closer to the soup kitchens, he was one of those who refused."

Clare could hardly recognize the priest, who seemed to have aged ten years since she last saw him, his hair graying and body gaunt.

"I'm so sorry, Clare. Liam swore he would send the children away to live with their aunt. I never thought he would lie about such a thing."

"It's not your fault." She held his hand.

He didn't seem to agree with her. "Your father was notified of eviction a few weeks ago. I thought he left." Father Quinn looked around at the neighboring farmers. "I'm surprised the wreckers haven't been through this neighborhood yet. It could be any day now, I'm afraid."

"Where has everyone gone?" Clare asked.

"Dead for the most part. The fortunate few made it out alive." Father Quinn shook his head. "I should have known. Liam kept rambling on about the Flight of the Earls."

"Oh." Clare smiled. "That story." Her da wasn't much on Irish history, since there weren't many victories to boast. But he did talk about the Earls. Hundreds of years before they had fostered a rebellion against their enemies, the English. But, finally, under cloak of darkness, they disappeared from Ireland, with rumors being they would return accompanied by a mighty foreign army.

That day never came. Her father always thought the tragedy was that they ever left. That they abandoned their land. There was nothing that mattered more to Liam than the land Clare was standing upon.

"No. My father would never leave this farm."

"You know," Father Quinn said cautiously, "he had a family plot in the cemetery. Why . . . ?"

"This was his church," she said.

They stood silently for a while, as the wind whistled in the background.

"What about you, Clare?"

"I'm going to stay here. We'll make a go of it unless they drag us out. Even then, it won't be without a fight. My father had made a good start to the planting. As soon as Cait and Davin are about, we'll carry on." She looked around the farm. "Yes. It's nice to be home again."

Father Quinn put his hat on his head, obviously displeased with her answer, but he must have remembered her well enough to know there was no bother pressing the subject further.

"All right, Clare. Well. You're several good miles from neighbors now, of those who remain. I don't come in this area much anymore. We've all been stretched, you know. But I'll check on you when I can."

"I know you will." She smiled at him.

"It's good to see you, Clare," Father Quinn said. "If only it was in brighter circumstances."

Even though she asked God for permission, the first chair was the most difficult.

Clare had carried it out of her neighbor's house three times, only to pause in the front of their yard before turning around and returning it to where she found it. She felt like a fox with a hen in her mouth. For Clare, stealing was stealing, even if her neighbors were never coming back.

Finally, she grabbed the chair, and then another, and brought both of them to her home, glancing over her shoulder as a thief would the entire way. When she got it into her house, she closed the door behind her and latched it, as if someone was in dark pursuit.

Then she sat down in one of them and, looking at her siblings, all her guilt melted away. This was the start of her new mission.

Within a few days, she had visited most of the vacant houses around her and now had scavenged a fine collection of tables, cabinetry, pots, shovels, a winnow, mattresses, shelving, and even a large stack of turf, which now burning in the fire, gave her home a familiar smell.

It was the table she coveted the most but saved for last because it was heavy, and she had far to travel. But after finding a wheelbarrow, the subject of her true affection became claimable. She finally wheeled the table down the road, and after unloading it carefully and dragging it through the front door, she looked up and gasped.

There propped in a chair was Caitlin, pale and pasty, but up and alert. When she saw Clare, she struggled to her feet.

Clare interceded just in time and grabbed her sister before she fell. Now in her grasps, Clare began to bawl.

"Caitlin. Oh, my dear Cait."

"Look, Davin." Caitlin's voice warbled. "It's Clare."

Sitting up against the wall was her brother Davin. The couple of weeks of broth had already begun to round out his face.

"Davin!" Clare carried Caitlin over to him and the three embraced without words for many minutes.

"Does Da know you're home?" Caitlin asked, finally breaking the silence.

"I have so much to share with you." Clare could see the weariness in their eyes. "But first, you need to rest for me some more."

Disappointment creased their faces, but they hadn't the will to fight, and soon their eyes were closed again. Clare tucked in beside them under the blankets.

It wasn't until the evening hour that they started to stir again, but this time, the two seemed even more alert and full of energy. While Clare heated the soup, they both stood and seated themselves in chairs around the table.

Clare set bowls and a spoon down for the three of them and filled each bowl with a steaming ladle full of turnip and carrot soup. She sat down, tucked in her chair, and then, lifting her spoon, nodded at them and began slurping her soup. She glanced up to see them staring at her aghast.

"What?" Clare said. "Are you not hungry? Do you not like it?"

Davin crooked his head at her in confusion. "Why, we haven't said our graces."

Clare laughed. "I am so terribly sorry. Davin, would you do us all the kind favor of offering our petition?"

Her young, curly-haired brother sealed his eyes and lowered his head in full sincerity.

"Dear God. We thank You for this our daily bread. And for answering our every night prayer that You would bring Clare home to us." He glanced up and smiled at Clare. "And here she is. Just as You promised. Although we still are praying some man will take her. I think she's pretty enough for it."

Clare expected an "Amen," but he wasn't finished.

"And we thank You for Ma being with Kevan again. And Ro too. But don't let them play all of the games without me, 'cause Cait just plays with dolls. Keep Seamus from trouble. And Da. I hope he gets his taters back. Amen."

Davin opened his eyes wide and saw Clare sobbing. "Did I forget something?"

"Oh no," Clare said. "That's perhaps the loveliest of prayers. You've reminded me how to do it, that's all."

That night, Clare shared her gifts with them, and each she allowed one small sweet.

They spoke for hours about many things, although much Clare decided not to share until later.

When they went to sleep, Clare took a walk in the cool Irish air, and her thoughts drifted to Seamus. She felt deep empathy for him as she more clearly understood his pain, his yearning to be significant in his father's eyes. All the while, her father was only leading them to a lonely death in the field of earthly desires.

Just as she did, Seamus was trying to draw from a well that would never be deep enough to satisfy.

Clare pondered Davin's prayer. Was there to be a man in her life after all? Would Nanna Ella's prayers for a godly husband ever come to be answered? She wished it would have been Andrew, but as her heart was now healing, she was feeling less dependent on that dream.

Perhaps she had found what God called her to be. A mother to the motherless.

Two weeks had passed before Father Quinn visited again as promised, and this time he paid only a short visit, with the purpose of bringing her some bad news.

"The word is the landlord is coming any day soon, and there'll only be a short notice."

"Well, he can come today," Clare crossed her arms across her chest and raised her chin, "and he will face the full wrath of a woman."

Father Quinn seemed amused but unconvinced. "These are hard times, Clare. You'll need to be practical for the benefit of the children."

"I think I'm done running. My father had a few things right." The words seemed foreign to Clare, but she embraced them as her own. "This is our land. Our people."

"Hmmm. Did you know that your father received a letter from Seamus?"

"What?"

"Yes, he did. A letter posted from Mexico that I delivered myself. It must have had money in it, because all of the sudden your father was buying provisions. And given the choice to buy food for his family, he spent just about all of it on those tuber roots. Despite two seasons of failure."

The words stunned Clare for a moment. "I hear what you say, Quinn. But this seems to be our best chance. This is what Hanleys do."

He gazed at her with sadness and sighed. "Suit yourself, Clare. But there's one last thing. The tinkers have been spotted in the area. Not too close to here, but you must be on guard. You worry me something awful being all alone out here."

"We'll be fine," she said.

Clare watched the young priest walk away. The wind howled around her, and for the first time since she came back, she felt afraid and alone. Trying to shake it off, she picked up a hoe and headed out to the fields to continue her father's work.

A raven's foreboding caw captured Clare's attention, and glancing up, she saw a dark cluster of clouds heading their way.

Later in the evening, long after her siblings had fallen asleep, Clare found herself alone, staring into the fire. Outside the rain and wind punished their stone hovel, and steady drips flowed from the roof to buckets and bowls scattered along the floor.

Clare rocked gently in the chair she had acquired just the other day. It reminded her of Grandmother Ella, as did the Bible which lay in her lap.

But as the drips plopped, the fire crackled, and her chair creaked with each sway, Clare realized how lost she had been. The anger inside, the disappointments in her life; they had all conspired to push her away from this book.

Inside, there was a question that ripped at her soul.

She sat there for the longest time before she could find the strength to ask God the question buried deep within her heart.

*Do You remember me?*

As soon as she asked, an instinct, a vibration, or some inner voice alerted her that something was amiss. Her pulse surged and she saw Caitlin had experienced it as well, as her younger sister awoke and sat up stiffly in her mattress, looking to her with alarm.

She signaled to Caitlin with a finger over her mouth to be still, and with her senses raging, Clare tried to discern anything above the hammering of the rain outside. Nothing. Nothing.

Then. *Rap. Rap. Rap.*

In a panic, Clare went to the door, and as quietly as she could, she slid the wooden bar into the latch. Then she scrambled to the hearth. After pulling a poker off of its hook, she positioned herself between her siblings and the door and squatted down to stay out of the window's viewpoint.

*Knock. Knock. Knock. Knock.*

A man's voice muted by the walls and downpour sounded as if he was shouting to another in the distance.

Davin was now up and was clinging to Clare's leg and whimpering softly. Caitlin pulled her brother tightly to her.

"Are they here to take the house?" Caitlin whispered.

"No." Clare wished it was the house wreckers. "It wouldn't be them. Not at this time in the night." But Clare was all too well aware of who it was.

She grasped the iron rod in her hand. Whoever it was would be walking into a real donnybrook. Clare was tired of being run over and was determined to defend her siblings to her last breath.

Clare was ready to take a final stand.

Another shout echoed but this was more distant and trailing.

"Are they leaving?" Caitlin said.

"Let's find out." Clare unwrapped her brother's grip from her calf. Then she crept to the window and slid the curtain back ever so cautiously, fearing at any moment she would be face-to-face with her enemy.

She eased her head up to see outside.

Slowly.

Finally able to look out, she saw a man preparing to step into the passenger seat of a wagon, which had a canopy protecting them from the rain.

The full moon brought enough glow through the drenching rain that she hoped she would see who it was, but the stranger's back was to her. Then in a flash, the man turned as if to look at her house one last time and then mounted his seat, and the wagon lunged forward.

"No!" she screamed. "Wait!" Her feet bare, she ripped open the door and tugged at her hems and skittered through the mud in mad and unbridled pursuit.

"Andrew! Andrew!"

But the wagon, which had several lanterns on either side, had already gotten a good start down the road. Clare picked up her pace, ignoring the splintering pain caused by the rocks in the dirt digging into her soles.

The ruggedness of the road worked to her favor as the cart labored to make it down the road. But it was one of these same divots that caught Clare's foot, twisting her ankle and causing her to tumble into the rain-splattered mud.

Now on her knees, the torrent from the angry clouds coming down on her and pain thrashing through her body, she screamed again. "Andrew!"

The wagon stopped. And shortly thereafter, a shadow hurtled toward her through the showers. She struggled to her feet.

"Clare!"

"Andrew!"

They cradled each other with all their strength, and Andrew lifted and spun Clare in one fluid movement, laughing full throated in joy. Then they wept together and sobbed with the music of love in each other's ears.

Pulling back, she touched his cheeks and stroked his hair, making certain he wasn't some moonlit apparition. But it was her Andrew, real and alive and looking deep into her eyes with longing and passion.

Slowly, he drew her close and kissed her as the water drenched their clothes, hair, and lips. Clare swayed to the sweet symphony of the rain.

# Chapter 44

# Sowing and Reaping

As the wagon driver Andrew had hired snored in the corner of the room, covering himself with his jacket and using a sack of grain for a pillow, the four of them cuddled around the emblazoned peat fire. Clare clung to Andrew tightly and rested her head on his shoulder, wanting this moment to last forever.

Davin hid behind Caitlin and giggled, and his sister elbowed him.

"What is it, young sir?" Andrew said, his face full of joy.

"Go ahead, Davin," Cait said. "Tell him what you told me."

He shook his curly locks with bashfulness, but then spurted out, "You're the one."

"I'm the one?" Andrew seemed baffled.

"Yes." Davin laughed, as if it needed no more explanation. "You're the one I prayed for. So my sister wouldn't be alone."

"Davin," Clare said with a tilt of her head.

The boy's face turned serious. "How did God get you here so quick?"

"Oh," Andrew said with a groan. "I can promise you there is nothing quick about crossing the ocean in that horrible ship. I'm sorry to tell you that your sister Clare has grown fond of a complete coward."

Clare fisted Andrew on the arm. "Stop that, you." She turned to Davin. "This is a very brave man, I'll tell you. He rescues me all of the time."

"This is true." Andrew smiled. "As long as it doesn't take place anywhere in the vicinity of large, dark, breeding pools of tumultuous, nausea-inducing, dreadful salty, fishy water."

"So," Clare started, "was that you watching my ship leave the harbor?"

"Guilty, I'm afraid. It was me cowering in the shadows. In fact, if not for the benefit of Irish ingenuity, I wouldn't have made it on the next ship the following day. Although that one day cost me one month. It was a much slower ship."

"Irish ingenuity?"

"Actually, it was a bottle of Irish courage. First time I ever drank a drop and hopefully it will be the very last. Being afraid is not a good thing when you're spending most of your time bent over the rail of a ship."

"Clare says drinking is the devil's spit," Davin said.

"And she, my little friend, is entirely correct. He spit all over me, and me on him. Several times."

"He's funny." Davin giggled.

"And handsome," Caitlin said with a puckish grin.

"And hungry." Andrew rubbed his stomach.

"Of course." Clare sprang to her feet. "How impolite of me."

"I agree," he said to Davin and Caitlin. "Maybe she doesn't want to share her food. What do you think?"

"Clare always shares," Caitlin said sternly.

"Then it's a good thing, I suppose, I brought a whole wagon of food to share with you all. Although, at least it started off being full. I met quite a few friends on the road."

"I'm surprised there's a bit left at all." Clare hung a cauldron of water above the fire for the oats she was preparing.

"Clare?"

She noticed a shifting in Andrew's tone which worried her. "Yes?"

He stood up and squared before her. "I brought something else with me as well."

"Oh? And what would that be?"

"I have passages back home. For all of us. And a few extra it seems."

Clare froze. "We are home, Andrew. It's not much, I know. But we aren't going anywhere."

"I know, Clare. I can understand your love and concern for your people. Your land. With all they are going through. But someone needs to tell this story. Maybe that's what God has been preparing you for all along."

"I suppose it could be so." She would have never imagined such a grandiose purpose to her life. "How does one really know?"

He smiled warmly and held her hand. "Just ask Him."

"My grandmother spoke to God all of the time. They said she was crazy."

Andrew looked deep into her eyes and then raised an eyebrow. "I believe you're crazy now as well, aren't you?"

Clare laughed. "Perhaps. How could you tell?"

"That's the best news of all for me. Headline. Top of page."

He was so beautiful to her now, handsome and nurturing, a genuine gift. Then something stirred inside her and she leaned back and stared into the fire.

"So, you're going to leave us, aren't you?"

He put his arms around Clare and kissed her on the ear.

"Where you are, Clare Hanley, is where I'll always be."

"There have been some . . . *concerns* regarding your present situation," Father Quinn said uncomfortably, nodding toward Andrew, who was chasing after Davin in the field.

"Stay out of the field, you fools!" Clare sighed deeply.

She turned to Father Quinn as she shook her head. "What are you talking about? Speak plainly."

"I'm trying to, Clare. Now just . . . just calm yourself." He cleared his throat. "There have been some in the town who worry about . . . you know, things that may have the appearance, at least, of some impropriety."

"Goodness, Quinn. Are you talking about yourself?" Clare put her hands on her waist.

"Well . . . perhaps. You know how I feel about you. How I've always felt about you."

"In that case, you can put your mind to ease, because that man over there is the perfect gentleman." She gave a double-look and saw Andrew wrestling in the soil with Davin and laughed.

Father Quinn rubbed his chin. "All right. Maybe I'm just a wee bit jealous."

"That's the man I know." Clare hugged the priest. "I always will care for you, Quinn." She pulled her arms back from him and then straightened out his collar.

He swatted away her hand. "You're always fussing with it."

"Hello, Father." Andrew dusted the dirt off of his clothing. Davin was clinging to his arm with both hands.

"Andrew. This is Father Quinn. Not only is he our priest, but he apparently is part mother as well."

"So . . . has this"—Andrew pointed to himself and Clare—"been a topic of gossip?"

"Andrew," Clare said wryly.

"Well . . . uh. Yes. Perhaps. But Clare set me straight."

"I think it's scandalous," Andrew said capriciously. "And I believe you're just the man to fix this."

"Are you asking me to . . . ?" Father Quinn looked puzzled.

"Yes. Precisely. I'm saying we'd like to have you marry us. Right here on the land of her fathers."

"I'm afraid I can't do that. Unless you're thinking about conversion."

Andrew put his arm on the priest's shoulder. "Father. Man of God. There are people dying all around us. Are there not greater concerns in times like these?"

"You have a point there, I suppose." Father Quinn nodded. "I don't have much time."

"Then let's get on with it," Andrew said.

"Are you forgetting something?" Clare raised an eyebrow, bemused by the spectacle.

"What?" Andrew said, beaming in the moment.

"There's this tradition where the man actually finds out if the woman is even interested."

"Oh." Andrew grinned. "She's interested."

Davin went hollering toward the house to find Caitlin. "Clare's got her man. Caitlin. Caitlin! There's going to be a wedding."

It took only about thirty minutes for them all to be gathered in the field in their finest clothing, before the setting sun, with Father Quinn speaking as best from memory as he could.

Finally, he gave them a blessing and finished with the sign of the cross. "May God always embrace you tenderly in His arms."

Then Andrew turned and faced Clare. He kissed her gently, their first time as man and wife.

After meticulously stacking the sacks of foodstuffs that Andrew had brought in the corner of the room, Clare stepped back to do a full inventory of all they had.

Doing a rough calculation, she determined there was enough there to feed the family for about two months. If they rationed tightly, they might be able to stretch it to three.

Then again, this was assuming Andrew would be able to resist the temptation to feed the rest of the community. He already gave three sacks of wheat, Indian corn, and oats to Father Quinn to take with him and distribute "under the Lord's leading."

Andrew didn't seem concerned, but Clare worried enough for the two of them. What it meant was that this crop they were planting would need to be fully harvestable or they were leading themselves down a deadly road.

Somehow, though, even these concerns didn't trouble her deeply. Even without having much at all for food and possessions, her life seemed so full and complete. The world of loneliness she left behind appeared so distant and foreign, a faded painting on the wall.

Fretting wouldn't be productive, so she went outside to join her family at their chores.

"How long has it been since you hung laundry?" Clare said to Caitlin, who was pressing clothes against a washboard in a copper bucket filled with soap.

"I've kind of missed it," Cait said. "It's a fine thing to have clothes to wash."

Off in the distance Davin was at the neighbor's scavenging turf logs and adding them to the wheelbarrow.

Heading to the main field behind the house, Clare smiled as she saw Andrew without his shirt, his body glistening. He had his back to Clare and was wrestling the field with a rake.

Yet it only took a few more steps for her to see what he was doing, causing her to freeze in her steps. Then with her hands to her ears she let out a terrific scream.

Andrew spun around in fright, holding his rake like a weapon.

"What is it?" Caitlin said in a panic, running up to her from behind.

Clare stepped over to the stump, slumped down, and covered her face with her hands. The stump was from the same tree she used to swing from as a small child.

Then Clare started to laugh. Harder. To the point of tears. Her stomach convulsed with joy as she struggled to even breathe. When she looked up, her face drenched in tears, she saw three faces looking at her as if she was completely mad.

Davin, who had run from the neighbor's, pointed over to the field where Andrew had been working. "What are you doing?"

Caitlin let out a squeaking giggle.

"What?" Andrew looked behind him at the field.

"You just raked out everything we planted for the past week," Clare said, recovering from her bout of laughter.

Andrew looked back. "Oh. Well . . . I wanted to make it all smooth."

"Come here." Clare stood and beckoned Andrew with a curl of her finger.

Defeated, Andrew threw down his rake and trudged over to her.

"I love you." Clare brushed back his hair with her fingers. "And I want you to know something."

"Oh yeah? What's that?"

"Where you are, Andrew Royce, is where I'll always be." She kissed him on the cheek and then turned toward Caitlin and Davin.

"My dear sister and brother."

They didn't answer but looked at her with expectation.

"How would you two feel about seeking your fortunes in America?"

Davin's eyes brightened. "Really? Really, Clare?"

"But . . ." Caitlin appeared disturbed, ". . . what about the family farm? We can't just leave it, can we?"

Clare pulled her younger sister to her. "My dear. The dirt will be here whenever you wish to return."

"Well," Andrew said, "just as I was developing my agricultural talents. I suppose I need to hire a wagon in town. What say you, Davin?"

"Can I ride in the front?"

"All the way to New York." Andrew took Davin's hand and they started walking away.

"But I thought we needed to take a ship."

"I get sick on ships . . ." Andrew grimaced. "This time we're following the wagon trail."

Clare sat back on the stump and Caitlin joined her. They were silent for a few minutes as they stared across the field toward the grave of their father in the distance.

"I'm so proud of you, Cait," Clare said.

"But . . . I lost everyone. Ma. Da. Ronin. Only Davin."

Caitlin started to cry and Clare was reminded again of the weight she left behind.

"It's not ours to bear, Cait." Clare stroked her sister's hair as she looked far as her eyes could reach. "It's been a hard lesson for me. We just need to be grateful. That's all."

"Do you think Da would be mad with us leaving?" Cait said.

Clare thought about it for a moment. "Probably."

Giving Cait a gentle squeeze, Clare stood. "Pack up, my dear. We're going home."

# Chapter 45

# TO DISTANT SHORES

Clare hadn't forgotten her promise to Pence.

They made an effort to track him down in the city of Cork. Some said he had died, others said he was imprisoned, and a few others believed he had managed to cast away on a ship to faraway lands.

When they finally arrived to the ship, the last-call bells were ringing and the crew was making final preparations. On this passage, there was no steerage space, no crudely converted cargo hull with inhumane conditions.

Although the quarters were tight as could be expected in a transatlantic voyage, Andrew had first-class accommodations for their trip, and Clare and he even had their own room. Though cramped and not as speedy a vessel as the American clipper Clare had taken to Dublin, it would be a much different experience than her first voyage.

Still, as she stood on the deck, pointing out the functionality of the topsail, bowsprit, buntline, scuttlebutt, outrigger, and

413

many other nautical terms to a wide-eyed Davin, Clare felt the surge of expectation as the ship headed out of harbor and into the dark, open mass of sea.

It reminded her of Seamus, and this recollection carried with it a moment of tenderness. So full of promise. Such a precious, gentle, troubled soul. Clare prayed he would be open to God's leading.

She glanced over to Andrew, who was sitting out of view of the water, struggling with nausea but doing well all things considered.

Down the deck a way, a fiddler began to slide his bow across his instrument and, after a few tuning strokes, played the Irish songs of old.

Caitlin and Davin sauntered over to listen and watch as the passengers were drawn to dancing.

Clare went over to Andrew, sat down, and held his hand in hers. "How are you doing?"

"I was just thinking," he said.

"About?"

"Look at your people. Unspeakable tragedy. Suffering. Devastation. And yet, they have a spirit above it all. This story needs to be told. And you're the one to do it."

"Yes," she smiled. "I know."

They sat together for a long time, listening to the creaking of the masts, the flapping of the sails, the lapping of the water against the sideboards, the cries of the birds, and the sweet sounds of uncharted hope.

Then from far in the distance, as if hovering over the sea, Clare discerned an ethereal sound ascending. Or was it the wind? It reminded her ever so clearly of when Grandma Ella would hum a song of reverence. Her nanna struggled to sing fully in key, but it never mattered. The pure adoration in her heart always perfected her music to tones of beauty and grace.

Clare's memories of the beloved woman gushed and overwhelmed her with a deep empathy for the pain and suffering endured. Had Clare ever been told these stories of grief, betrayal, and disappointment, or was she hearing them for the first time? They were hardships well beyond any Clare herself had faced.

"Nanna?"

There was no answer but Clare's thoughts were swept back to that agonizing evening when she cared for Grandma Ella as the woman lay on her deathbed.

Words were shared that night that Clare never understood. Until now.

"Clare. Clare."

"Yes, Nanna." She gently wiped a cool, wet cloth against the woman's wrinkled and clammy forehead.

"My dear, dear Clare."

"Shhhh. Please, Nanna."

"It's you! You, sweet Clare." She struggled to rise from the bed as if she had heard something she was compelled to share. "You're my reason."

At the time, Clare dismissed these last few utterances as merely the ramblings of a dying woman. But now they resonated with truth and poignancy. Grandma Ella's entire journey was to breathe hope into Clare. And for generations to follow.

Into the breeze and with abandonment Clare celebrated with her grandmother, and they wept as one, with immeasurable fondness.

"What's wrong?"

She turned to Andrew, who looked at her with confusion and concern.

Clare laughed and rested her head softly against his tall shoulder.

"There's nothing wrong," Clare whispered. "Far from it. It's just she's been waiting for this moment all of her life."

# DISCUSSION QUESTIONS

1. What did you enjoy most about *Flight of the Earls*? Which were your favorite characters? Why?

2. Was there a character in particular you most closely identified with throughout the story? How so?

3. What did you see as the central themes in the novel?

4. Describe the relationship you have or had with your father (or father figure in your life). What did you most appreciate? What would you have wished to be different?

5. How has your relationship with your father influenced your life for better or worse? Have you fully expressed your gratitude or, if needed, granted forgiveness?

6. Do you have a relationship with God the Father? How would you describe it?

7. Have there ever been times in your life when you've felt as if you've been forgotten by God? If so, are you still in that place today? Why?

8. Grandma Ella plays an important role in *Flight of the Earls*. How would you explain it?

9. Do you have a Grandma Ella in your life? Who is it and how has he or she influenced your spiritual growth? Have you played this role in the lives of others? If so, share some examples.

10. Proverbs 12:20 reads: "Deceit is in the heart of those who devise evil, but those who plan peace have joy" (NIV). Uncle Tomas certainly had deceit in his heart. How do you deal with the difficult people in your life?

11. Proverbs 16:9 says: "The heart of man plans this way, but the Lord establishes his steps" (NIV). Do you feel as if you're allowing God to lead the way?

12. When times are tough is your core reaction to blame God or to trust Him? What do you feel makes you react that way?

13. Jeremiah 29:11 states: "'For I know the plans I have for you,' declares the LORD, 'plans for wholeness and not for evil, to give you a future and a hope'" (NIV). Do you believe God has plans for you? If so, what do you believe them to be? What is your life purpose, and do you feel it's more God's idea or yours?

14. David offered these words of wisdom in 1 Chronicles 28:9: "And you, Solomon my son, know the God of your father

and serve him with a whole heart and with a willing mind, for the Lord searches all hearts and understands every plan and thought" (NIV). Are you serving God the Father with a whole heart and willing mind through all circumstances? What steps could you take to grow closer to Him?

# ACKNOWLEDGMENTS

One of the most daunting tasks in writing a novel is composing the acknowledgments, because invariably there aren't enough pages to thank everyone deserving of a proper tip o' the hat and click o' the heels.

My deepest gratitude goes to my Lord and Savior Jesus Christ from whom I receive every breath and every gift in my life.

What a gift I have in my beloved wife Debbie, who has endured much to allow this author to pursue wild adventure on the sea of writing dreams. If not for her love, prayer, encouragement, patience, and great sacrifice the ship would have undoubtedly ended up timbers against the rocks.

So too with my beautiful daughters Kaleigh, Mackenzie, and Adeline, who were my daily inspiration for this book and who graciously shared their Dad time with writing deadlines. Make no mistake, this novel was a complete family effort.

For Sheila, my mother and critique partner, for instilling in me the love of books and analyzing mine line-by-line. For my two sisters, Cathy and Jacqueline who lovingly abided with growing up with the weird kind of brother who ends up a writer. And for Philip, my father, for forging perseverance into my character and to Larry Smith for his overflowing support.

Gratitude goes out to my spiritual mentors Jim Johnson and Allen Batts who challenged me at every bend and then helped to piece Humpty together when he so often fell off the wall. And for my Friday Morning Men's Bible Study and Wednesday Evening Couples Group, whose faithful members never stopped praying for me, even when my writing schedule pulled me away from fellowship.

Huge adoration for my agent, Janet Kobobel Grant of Books & Such Literary Agency, whose wisdom, fierce representation and kind heart makes her both a great friend and as good as they get.

For Julie Gwinn, whose vision, creativity, and early belief in this debut novelist made all of this possible. And to the rest of the gifted team at B&H Publishing Group including cover artist extraordinaire Diana Lawrence, Kim Stanford who carefully wove together these pages, and Patrick Bonner who worked tirelessly to connect the novel to its readers.

A deep bow to my award-winning editor, Julee Schwarzburg, who with such a delightful personality infused encouragement, brilliance and artistry into the project.

To my many wordsmith friends such as Karen Barnett, Connie Brzowski, Lauraine Snelling, Kay Strom, Brandilyn Collins, Randy Ingermanson, Tricia Goyer, and Stephanie Grace Whitson who have selflessly put their projects aside to provide feedback on mine. And those of my Author Insider tribe, and friends on Facebook and Twitter who cheered me on and shared the novel around the world.

Thanks as well to my dedicated staff at Global Studio, who put their expertise and affection in the effort to publicize the author and this book. You all are dear to me.

Great appreciation goes out to Rachel Williams and Dave Talbott for putting together such an anointed event as the Mount Hermon Christian Writers Conference, where I was mentored, educated, and inspired and found both my agent and publisher.

Every author of historical fiction stands on the shoulders of dedicated scholars. There were so many brilliant history books I leaned on for the research of this book, chief among them being: *Paddy's Lament* by Thomas Gallagher, *Gotham* by Edwin G. Burrows & Mike Wallace, *The Great Irish Potato Famine* by James S. Donnelly Jr., *Shamrock and Sword* by Robert Ryal Miller, *The Story of the Mexican War* by Robert Selph Henry, *Five Points* by Tyler Anbinder and *The Gangs of New York* by Herbert Asbury.

And finally . . . much love to my readers, who provide purpose and pleasure in every word I write.

# DOWNLOAD THE FIRST CHAPTER

*the next exciting book in the 'Heirs of Ireland' series.*

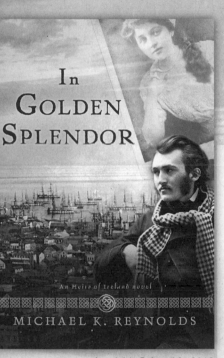

In
# GOLDEN
# SPLENDOR

An Heirs of Ireland novel

MICHAEL K. REYNOLDS

Available July 15th, 2013

Irish immigrant Seamus Hanley is a lost soul, haunted by his past as a U.S. Army deserter and living alone in the wilderness of the Rocky Mountains in 1849. But after witnessing a deadly stage coach crash, he finds purpose in the scattered wreckage—a letter with a picture of a beautiful and captivating woman named Ashlyn living in San Francisco at the height of the Gold Rush. Moved by her written plea for help, he abandons all and sets out on an epic journey across the wild and picturesque American frontier.

Scan the QR code with your smartphone to download the first chapter of *In Golden Splendor.*